Homefront Heroines

Print ISBN 978-1-64352-254-8

eBook Editions:
Adobe Digital Edition (.epub) 978-1-64352-256-2
Kindle and MobiPocket Edition (.prc) 978-1-64352-255-5

Published by Barbour Books, an imprint of Barbour Publishing, Inc., 1810 Barbour Drive, Uhrichsville, Ohio 44683, www.barbourbooks.com

Our mission is to inspire the world with the life-changing message of the Bible.

ecpa Member of the
Evangelical Christian
Publishers Association

Printed in Canada.

Homefront Heroines

4 Historical Stories

Johnnie Alexander
Amanda Barratt
Lauralee Bliss
Rita Gerlach

BARBOUR BOOKS
An Imprint of Barbour Publishing, Inc.

Moonlight Serenade

by Rita Gerlach

Dedication

*To my mother, Rose, and my dad, Larry, in heaven, whose romance
began when they worked at the Navy Yard in Washington, D.C.,
and continued with the hope of fair winds and calm seas
as Daddy served on the USS Vulcan in WWII.*

*To my son, Michael, serving in the United States Navy, following
in his grandfather's footsteps with honor, courage, and commitment.
And to those like them who took the oath, especially the men
who bravely fought in WWII, and to the women who
stepped into their shoes to serve on the home front.*

Chapter 1

Hope Valley, Pennsylvania
Monday, an hour before midnight
December 7, 1941

Snow fell that infamous night. America was at war with Japan and Germany, and the world had changed in one instant. Kate St. Clare lay in bed, her hands clutched across her chest. Her heart pounded and quivered. She prayed, her eyes fixed on the shadows that moved across the ceiling.

In the next room she could hear Papa snoring. Nothing much ever seemed to worry him. He'd rise in the morning. Dress in his blue jean overalls and work shirt, boots, and his Tom Mix hat. He'd have coffee and pancakes and head out to the barn without saying much about what they had learned the day before. Mother would move about the kitchen, and Kate's two sisters would be in a hurry to get out the door for school.

They lived in a place of serenity not far from Gettysburg, deep in forests and fields. Meadows white in spring with Queen Anne's lace. Knee-deep in snow in winter, where the shape of the mountains mimicked the gentle waves of the sea.

Kate lay there thinking her routine would not be any different from any other day. She'd scoot out of bed at sunrise, put on her denims and riding boots, and head out to care for the horses. She'd fork fresh hay into the stalls, pour feed into troughs and fresh water into buckets. Then she'd let the horses out into the pen and muck out the stable. She loved every minute of it, didn't mind calluses on her palms or bits of straw in her hair.

If she could, Kate would bunk in the stable to be near the horses. Instead, she shared a room with her younger sisters. Jan and Jean were twins. Then there was the baby of the family, tawny curly-top four-year-old Amber. All were asleep curled against each other with their bow mouths breathing in and out the fresh air of the country.

Sighing, Kate rolled out of the covers and pulled on her boots. She looked at the girls as they slept, peaceful, tucked up in a double bed. The twins were unexpected at a time when her parents thought God would not bless them with another child. Mother always said miracles and surprises arrive together, and ten years after Kate, the twins were born, followed later by Amber.

Kate brushed a curl off Jean's forehead and laid an extra quilt over the girls. Amber stirred and Kate hushed her. She then slipped out of the room and tiptoed down the hallway. Her parents' bedroom door stood ajar, and Kate peered inside. Mother was kneeling at the bedside with a blue silk scarf over her braided hair.

Their church held no tradition concerning wearing veils or head coverings. Yet whenever Mother felt the call to prayer, she'd go into her room, kneel, and place a scarf on her head. No commandment demanded it, but it gave her a sense of closeness to her Savior.

"Mother?" Kate whispered. "Are you all right?"

Mother pushed back the scarf and got up from the floor. She crossed the darkened room over to Kate. "Don't worry about me.

Go back to bed."

"I can't sleep."

"Neither can I, dear. I've been praying for my boys and Frank all night."

"I can't stop thinking about them." Kate struggled to hold back tears.

"We won't know anything for a while. I'm sure they're safe and we'll hear something soon."

"I hope you're right, Mother. They're so young." Tears fell down her cheeks. "What if. . .oh Mother."

"We have to be brave, Kate, and pray."

Kate balled her fists. "I can't help hearing the president's speech over and over again. Why didn't he do something to prevent this from happening?"

"And I can see you're angry."

Kate looked into Mother's green eyes. "At Japan, I am. How could they have done such a horrible thing? All those sailors—"

"Remember what Mr. Roosevelt said about fear."

Kate frowned. "He put it elegantly, but we are afraid. How can we not be?"

Grief creased Mother's brow. "It's something we must bear. It won't be easy. I'm afraid this war is going to go on for a long time."

They linked arms and walked down the hallway. Kate stopped at the top of the staircase. "Do you think Frank loves me?"

"He wouldn't have asked you to marry him if he didn't."

"I'm not so sure."

"Go back to bed and get your sleep. We've got a lot to do in the morning."

"You need sleep too. I can't get over how Papa is snoring away through all of this."

"Don't think he hasn't been affected. Before he fell asleep, he pulled me next to him and held me tight. He does that when he's afraid."

Kate looked down the stairs to the front door. The harsh wind rattled it. "I'm going out to the barn to check on the horses. They should have stable blankets on them."

"Your father wouldn't let them go without."

"I want to be sure. Sometimes Penny pulls hers off. I won't be long. Caring for the horses calms me down."

"But the snow will be up to your knees, and I don't want you falling sick."

Kate shook her head. Mother still worried about her and treated her like one of her little sisters. The stairs creaked as she made her way down to the first floor. When she reached the bottom, she snatched her coat off the hall tree and slipped it on. She grabbed a knit hat from off the table, pulled it over her ears, and tucked her hair into it.

Mother started down a few steps. "I'll make you a cup of hot cocoa."

"I won't need it." Kate pulled on her wool gloves. "By the time I get back, I'll head straight to bed. That's where you should be. Papa will get restless if he wakes up and you aren't beside him."

Mother gave Kate a sad smile. "Boys have bears to cuddle when they're small and wives to hold when they grow tall."

With anxiety coursing through her, Kate put her hand on the door handle. "Don't be long, Kate," Mother told her. "I'll lie awake listening for your footsteps."

"I'll kiss you good night when I come back inside."

She lit the brass lantern kept on a side table, pulled back the latch to the front door, and stepped out into the wintry night. Snow fell thick and the wind blew it into peaks against the walls of the barn. Tugging at her hat, she trudged across the yard. The lantern light spread over the snow and quivered in the wind. Reaching the barn, she kicked back the drifts built up against the doors and managed to pull the left side open and step inside. Her mare rallied from the floor of hay, looked out from her stall, and snorted.

"I knew it." Kate huffed and hung the lantern on a post. "What do I have to do to keep you from taking off your blanket, Penny? Don't you feel the cold?"

The mare shook her glossy mane and flicked her ears. Kate threw the blanket over the mare's back and pulled a cord through a loop underneath. Penny turned her head and nibbled at the blanket's edge.

Kate ran her hand down Penny's nose, back up again to her ears. "You're being a naughty girl. Don't you want to be warm?" The mare made a low guttural sound, and Kate put her arms around Penny's neck.

"What am I going to do? What if Frank never comes back?" she whispered into the darkness amid golden lantern light that passed over the stable wall. "God, please don't let bad news darken our doorstep."

Chapter 2

Monday, December 28, 1942

A biting wind drove down from the mountains, pushing stormy clouds across a wintry blue sky. For an hour Kate rode her mare over the grazing fields belonging to her parents' farm. She turned Penny to the right at a crest and looked down the slopes toward the stream that cut through the land like a silver ribbon. She carried an ache in her heart, bitter she had lost her brother Brian, sorrowful Pearl Harbor had stolen her life with Frank. Could she pick up the pieces and move on?

As she held the leather reins, she considered the idea of answering the ads she had seen from the U.S. Employment Service. She had no doubt Mother and Papa would be proud of her if she did, and they'd get along without her for the duration. Raised on a horse farm, she could do anything she set her mind to. She worked with her hands. She shoed horses. Mended everything from fences to barn stalls. She knew how to use tools, from the simplest hammer to a soldering iron.

Her mare pawed the earth and snorted. Kate watched Papa step out of the barn, push back his hat, and hug his coat tighter to himself. His hair had turned gray over the last few months, his face weathered because he spent much time in the sun. Papa was the one man she looked up to above all others. He stood a head taller than her, lean and robustly built. His dark brown eyes were sensitive for a rugged face. But his gait had changed since the loss of his son. Slower, more methodic, as if he'd aged decades.

Mother came out onto the porch, lifted her hand above her eyes, and looked in Kate's direction. That glorious auburn hair had also become streaked with gray, and her frame had grown thin, her eyes forlorn.

Jan and Jean carried kindling into the house. Their chatter resonated up the hillside. They were too young to understand the gravity of the days they lived in. The family shielded them from the gruesome news coming out of Europe and the cruel hardships that captured Americans and Allies were going through in the Pacific.

Kate nudged Penny with a touch of her knees, and the horse stepped down from the crest and galloped toward home. Kate slid off the saddle when she reached the front of the barn and led the mare into the shadowy stalls.

"Have a good ride?" Papa stood in the light of the barn door.

"I know Penny did. I need to brush her down." She reached for the brushes, special ones Papa had given her.

"The wind has whipped up. Looks like we're going to have snow. Make sure the horses are settled. They get skittish when there's a strong wind."

"I will, Papa." Kate set Penny's saddle over a rail and began brushing down her coat. A low, throaty murmur told Kate the mare was content. "I've been thinking. I want to help with the war effort. I want to honor Brian and Frank, and I think it would make Brad proud of me."

His eyes softened. "I see. What do you have in mind, Katy-did?" He always called her by that pet name when she came to him for advice about a decision she needed to make. It gave Kate a sense of security that Papa would be there for her no matter the circumstances.

"Applying with the U.S. Employment Service," she said.

"All it takes is a decision. Take action, and walk out on it. Prayer is always good in any decision making." He put his arm over her shoulders and gave her a squeeze.

Kate warmed and smiled up at him. His counsel was never harsh. Firmness had no need to be.

"I hope I'm not bothering God," she told him. "I've been asking Him every day for guidance."

"I have no doubt He hears you, sweetheart." He picked up a bucket of oats. "It's hard to believe they've been gone a year. So many families grieving this month. Thank the Lord we don't have to sorrow as those with no hope."

Kate set down the brushes and ran her hand down Penny's nose. She closed the stall gate and walked out into the sunshine with Papa.

"Have you ever been worried about making a decision?"

"Many times."

"How did you overcome those feelings?"

He smiled and pinched her chin. "I was afraid to ask your mother to marry me. I knew I had to. I couldn't live without her."

"You had a *knowing*?"

"That's one way of looking at it. Once you step out in faith, the fear no longer has a hold on you."

"I'm not afraid, Papa. I'm in a kind of 'wait and see' moment."

"I've had those too, Katydid. Now, let's go in for some lunch.

Your mother has made meat loaf sandwiches."

Kate smiled. "My favorite." She leaned up, kissed Papa's cheek, and walked beside him toward the house. She paused at the foot of the steps and set her hand on his. "Thank you, Papa."

"For what?" he asked. "Sandwiches? I had nothing to do with that."

"No, for talking to me. I believe I have the wisest papa in the county."

Papa shook his head as a ruddy color came into his humble face. Kate placed her arm through his, and they went inside.

The following day Kate headed down the steps of the redbrick church that had been their refuge for the past two generations. She walked beside Mother and looked up at the bare trees. Sunlight twinkled through them and alighted on the squirrel nests lodged in their crooks.

Since her conversation with Papa, the parable of the good Samaritan had occupied her mind. *Help them, Kate. Be one of the millions of women willing to pick up the pieces.*

Since Pearl Harbor, folks still greeted her and her parents with a kind word of sympathy for their losses. Other families faced the dreaded news they had lost a son in Europe or in the Pacific. Some were missing in action or prisoners of war. The women's circle met weekly to make socks and scarves for the troops and wrap bandages for the Red Cross. The old women reminisced over their younger years doing the same tasks in 1917. She'd been attending with Mother. Still, it was not enough. Kate wanted to do more.

"You're daydreaming, Kate." Mother heaved Amber up on her hip.

"I like to think when we walk here. The trees are lovely even in

December. I'm glad gasoline is being rationed. That way we walk more, take in the beautiful things around us."

"And you've a lot to think about, don't you? It seems we women always do."

Kate pointed ahead. "Look at the girls. They're going to get their shoes and clothes dirty." She hurried to her sisters, who had raced ahead and were playing in a heap of rotting leaves and melting snow. After a scolding and a good brushing down, she brought them back to Mother.

"You used to do the same, remember?" Mother said.

"I know, but never in good clothes. Jan and Jean have put more holes and tears in their clothes than I ever did. They need to be more careful."

Mother nodded in agreement. "Jan. Jean. I've told you not to be so rough with your clothes. Cloth has been rationed. I couldn't get my hands on a good bit of cotton or wool if I tried. You won't be getting anything new until the war is over."

The girls looked up at their mother through tears. "No crying," Kate said. "We all have to make sacrifices."

They neared the country store at the end of the road. "Kate, would you see if Mrs. Mullins has a can of cinnamon spice? I've run out, and your Papa is craving an apple pie." Amber had fallen asleep on Mother's shoulder. "I need to get the girls home."

"I can take Amber for you, Mother. It isn't often you get the chance to chat with another woman without the little ones around."

"She loves you, Kate, but you know she'll cry. She's attached to me cuddling her like this."

Kate pushed back Amber's curls. "I'll need the ration book."

"It's in my purse." Mother turned for Kate to pull it out. "I hope she has butter and coffee. Get some peppermint sticks for the girls if she has any."

"I'll be sure to get what I can."

She picked up sleeping Amber's little hand and pressed it to her lips. Then she walked over the stepping-stones that led up to the store. Rusty hinges squeaked as she went inside. The brass bell above the door tinkled, and Mrs. Mullins popped up from behind a counter. "Mornin', Kate."

"Good morning, Mrs. Mullins." Kate smiled at the elderly men who gathered in the store daily. They sat around the potbellied stove in rickety rocking chairs, smoking pipes. They were veterans of the last war and Civil War old-timers who loved to tell their tales of heroism.

"Good morning, gentlemen."

They tipped their hats. "Any word from Brad, Kate?" one asked.

"Not yet, Mr. Barnes. But we hope to get a letter soon."

"Pacific, is he?"

"Yes, sir. On the *Nevada*."

Mr. Mullins, the owner of the establishment, drew a pipe from between his teeth. "That ole girl suffered during the Pearl Harbor attack. It's a wonder the St. Clares didn't lose both sons, praise God."

Kate looked down at the ration book in her hand. She swallowed the lump forming in her throat.

"Well, Kate. We're all praying the war ends soon and the boys come home," Mr. Mullins went on to say. "If Brad made it this far, he's sure to make it back."

"Bless the Lord he comes home all in one piece." Ninety-five-year-old Mr. Cooper spoke up. "I served in Grant's army and lost my leg at Gettysburg. I can tell you, war is perdition on earth." He struck his hand on the arm of the rocker. "The boys are going to need healing when they return." His voice cracked, and his eyes turned to a place faraway. Kate pressed her brows at what he had said.

"The wounded, is that what you mean, Mr. Cooper?"

Mr. Cooper shook his head and pointed at his sunken temple. "I mean here, missy. For some those images never go away." He shook his gray head, and his tattered Union soldier cap tipped forward. "Gettysburg will be with me until the day I die."

A surge of compassion raced through Kate. Her father was young when he signed up for the First World War. Some nights he would wake in a sweat. Mother's soothing touch and the softness of her voice calmed him.

"I'll never be able to imagine what you experienced, Mr. Cooper, or my papa. I hope life since then has been a happier one."

"It's been milk and honey, Kate, with some vinegar."

She smiled. "The town will hold a parade and a picnic in the square when the boys come home. Some home cooking, family, and friends will be the balm in Gilead."

"We're all lookin' forward to that," said Mr. Mullins.

Mr. Cooper slapped his knee. "Don't forget a barn dance with fiddle playin', Kate."

Kate ran her hand along the counter. "We won't. I'll save the two-step for you."

A cackle rose from Mr. Cooper's lips. "That'll be dandy."

"Where's your mother, Kate?" Mrs. Mullins asked.

"She's taking the girls home. We've just come from the women's circle at the church." Kate picked up a jar of relish and set it back down.

Mrs. Mullins positioned it on the counter. "What do the ladies do besides knit? Gossip?"

"Any gossip was uninteresting, Mrs. Mullins. Mother and I did not participate. In fact, I didn't even knit."

"Hmm. What occupied your time then?"

"V-Mail to Brad. I've never gotten the knack of knitting."

"Neither have I." Mrs. Mullins shrugged. "I guess I'm too busy with the store. I do admire the women making socks for our boys. Gives them a touch of home."

Kate slid the ration book across the counter. "What can we get? Mother asked for cinnamon."

"I've got two cans. But let me see about the rest." Mrs. Mullins looked over her shelves and pulled down some items.

Meanwhile Kate looked around the store. A few years earlier there had been bolts of bright calico fabrics, blocks of butter, and chocolate bars. Now many of the shelves were bare.

"Fortunate for you, your farm has chickens, Kate," Mrs. Mullins said as she placed a pound box of sugar in a bag. "You must have eggs galore, and milk from your old Guernsey."

Kate smiled. "We are blessed, Mrs. Mullins. I'll never tire of eggs, and Sally gives the sweetest milk."

"And you have a Victory garden too? Did it do well?"

"We had enough to share with neighbors."

"Did you plant any root vegetables this fall?"

"A few, like carrots. Papa made a cold frame for greens and herbs."

"So talented a man, your father."

"Yes, I'm proud of Papa's ingenuity." She buttoned her coat. "Well, Mother wants to make pies this afternoon. So I should get going."

Mrs. Mullins leaned over the counter. "I can't imagine what it must be like for those living in big cities. Surely they can't plant Victory gardens like we can." She shook her head. "So unchristian of people not to share, wouldn't you say? Just this morning I noticed. . ."

Kate said nothing as Mrs. Mullins droned on. As much as she enjoyed conversation, it was well known that the lady proprietor of the general store would gossip her customers' ears off. Kate could not judge those who had a lot of mouths to feed and were unable to share. After all, that was one of the reasons Mother and Papa planted a Victory garden in the spring. Kate found it fascinating and wonderful to see seeds sprout from the rich Pennsylvania soil, reach for the sun, and grow into fruitful plants. The tomatoes turning deep red, the cucumbers succulent.

She pointed to the shelf behind Mrs. Mullins. "You forgot the cinnamon."

When Mrs. Mullins turned to fetch the can, the postman came in. He set a few letters on the counter, tipped his hat, and hurried out.

"Oh, a letter from my cousin Marilee. She lives in Gettysburg, you know. Childless, poor dear. She got married last year. Imagine that. A woman of sixty-two finally getting married. He has children from his first marriage. I guess she's happy." Mrs. Mullins sounded like a hen clucking out in the yard. As she spoke, the red-combed rooster that meandered around the pen crowed. It didn't interrupt Mrs. Mullins one bit.

Mrs. Mullins folded the top of the bag down and handed the ration book back.

Kate looked at it. "You forgot the stamps."

"Oh, sorry." Mrs. Mullins pulled out the stamps from a drawer under the counter. "Mr. Mullins and I were not blessed with children either. My sister was, God rest her soul. Her son, my nephew, stayed with us a few weeks each summer when he was in his teens. Did you ever meet Ronny?" She lifted her head. "He's in the Navy."

Kate held her breath a second and looked down at the counter. Ronny Jordan's face came back to her. He chased her one summer when she was fifteen, won her over, and then broke her heart. She'd fallen hard for the sandy-haired, brown-eyed boy who looked manlier than the others did. As his aunt continued singing his praises, Kate remained silent but felt an ache in her heart. She knew from the reputation Mrs. Mullins had of spreading gossip throughout town, it would be best to say nothing more.

"I'm sure you couldn't have missed knowing Ronny." Mrs. Mullins leaned her elbows on the counter. "I think he had eyes for you."

Kate shook her head. "I'm sure he didn't, Mrs. Mullins."

"I'm sure he did."

"He might have been one of those boys who liked to pull my hair in church."

Mrs. Mullins straightened up. "If my Ronny did that, he most likely was trying to get your attention. Still, it was cheeky of him. I would've had Mr. Mullins march him right over to your house and have him apologize."

"I suppose we will never know for sure, unless *your Ronny* admits it. It was a long time ago for any of us to remember."

A somber expression fell over Mrs. Mullins's face. "How are your parents?" Thank goodness, the subject changed. "So sad about Brian."

"I doubt she and Papa will ever get over it." Kate picked up her bag.

"I'm not sure where Ronny is." Mrs. Mullins shifted through a few flyers near the register while Kate moved to the door. "Wait a minute, Kate. You might be interested in reading these. We're well into this conflict, but women are still needed to do the work our boys left behind."

Kate took one of the flyers and placed it inside the bag. "Thank you, Mrs. Mullins. I've already inquired about that."

Mrs. Mullins smiled. "That's the Kate I know. I bet you could take apart an auto engine and put it back together again if you had to."

Kate smiled. "I never have. Doubt I ever will."

"Can you weld? I don't mean big stuff, just little things."

"Papa taught me how to use a torch, and I know how to solder. I've had to fix the tractor."

"You see that poster over on the wall? They call her Rosie the Riveter."

Kate winked. "Keep that poster, Mrs. Mullins. One day it will be history."

Some of the elderly gentlemen were snoozing in their chairs. Kate bid Mrs. Mullins a good day and walked out. She hurried down the steps into the sunshine with a sigh of relief and started home. The hedgerows alongside the road were dusty, and weeds were withered and brown as the dirt. She plucked a dry thistle and twirled it between her fingers. *Ronny Jordan.* He had to be in his late twenties by now—or close to it. Ten years later they wouldn't recognize each other. He definitely wouldn't remember Kate, or so she imagined. These days she wore stockings to church instead of bobby socks.

As she entered the yard, the chickens made a ruckus and scattered. Jan and Jean were playing on the swing tied to a limb on the maple tree. Rex, the family dog, leaped up at her as she crossed over to the steps and went inside. Come summer, Mother would open all the windows and sheer white curtains would flutter in the breeze. But today they were shut tight against winter. At least the weather had been fair for several weeks. It made comings and goings easier, and she was able to ride Penny.

Mother called to her from the kitchen. "A letter came for you, Kate. I left it on the table in the living room."

Kate set down the bag and hurried to the table. *Washington, D.C.* The return address caused a thrill to race over her. She tore open the flap and took out the papers tucked inside the envelope. A quick note of instruction and then an application if she was interested in acquiring work through the War Department to aid the effort. She scanned the list of jobs. Welders. Riveters. Mechanics. She slipped the papers back into the envelope, put it in her pocket, and headed for the kitchen.

Mother wiped her hands across her striped apron. She handed another to Kate made of checkerboard flour sacks that felt coarse to the touch. Mother smiled. "Did you get the cinnamon?"

"A large can of it." Kate pulled it out of the bag. "And all this too. But it uses our rations for the month."

"Think you can help me? You have a knack for how much spice to use. You never overdo it or underdo it like I do."

Using a teaspoon, Kate opened the lid on the McCormick's can and sighed. "I'll never be able to bake like you, Mother."

Mother frowned. "That isn't true. You won a blue ribbon for your peach pie at the county fair two years in a row."

"I learned that recipe from you. I'll give you all the credit."

"What's wrong? Something troubling you?"

Kate plunged a wooden spoon into the bowl and stirred the cinnamon into the apple slices. "I'm fine, Mother. You know how I get restless. That's all it is."

"You don't have to tell me if you don't want to, Kate. I saw the return address and can't help but wonder why you're getting mail from the National Service Office."

"It's a list of jobs for women to help with the war effort."

"I know what I'd do if I were you." Mother rolled out the pie dough.

Kate looked at her. "What? What would you do?"

"I'd fill out the application and send it back. See what happens."

Kate put her arms around Mother. "That's my intention, Mother."

"You're twenty-five, Kate." Mother turned back to her pie dough. "If it weren't for this awful war, you'd have been married for a few years by now and in a house of your own. . .possibly with a couple babies."

Stirring the apples with more force, Kate said, "I'm grieved to have lost Frank, but I've wondered if I would've gone through with marrying him. He didn't act like a man in love."

"Some people have difficulty expressing what's in their hearts."

Papa walked through the back door in his denim overalls. He set his hat on the doorknob, paused, and slapped his knee. "Is that what I think it is. . .apple pie?"

"It's not baked yet, Papa." Kate smiled as she poured the fruit into the pie dish.

He kissed her cheek. "Kate, my girl. The man that snags you will count his blessings."

"For my cooking, Papa? I hope that's not all."

"Why, sure. After all, the way to a man's heart is through his stomach. Ain't that right, Mother?"

Mother smacked him on the shoulder. "You should know."

Papa picked up a slice of apple before Mother laid the crust over the top. "Doc Freeman just left. Says he can't figure out why Penny isn't carrying a foal. She's healthy and strong, and our stallion is fine. I suppose it's timing. You know what they say. Timing is everything."

Mother wiped her hands across her apron. "Penny will be fine."

Kate set the pie in the oven. "I had hoped she'd carry a foal by now. You'll write to me when it happens, won't you? I have a good feeling I'll be doing war work soon."

"Of course we will, Kate." Mother sighed. "You know, your Papa and I are proud of you."

Kate smiled. She picked up a leftover slice of apple and popped it in her mouth. She thought on what Papa said, that timing was everything. She felt sure that soon time would rush her forward at an exhilarating pace. She had to trust the path the Lord laid out for her, that He would lead her to do what she was able to do at the perfect moment.

Chapter 3

Washington, D.C.
July 1943

*I*t didn't take long for Kate to miss home. She set her head against the window of the bus, closed her eyes, and pictured her family. Papa would be piling hay in the field to feed the horses. Mother would be hanging out sheets, and the girls would be playing with their dolls in the shade of the maple tree.

Her thoughts were interrupted when someone nudged her on the shoulder. "Miss, we're here. You don't want to miss your stop."

Kate sat up in the seat. "Thanks. I dozed off." She opened her purse and checked her hair in the mirror of her compact. Good enough for a country girl with auburn curls.

The elderly lady beside her craned her neck and looked to the front of the bus. "It's all right. I dozed off too. It's easily done at my age, so I can't blame the heat." She wore a blue flat straw hat with pink artificial flowers, and although the temperature was through the roof, she had a sweater draped over her shoulders.

"I can," Kate said. "It's so hot. I could use a cold drink. Couldn't you?" She ran her handkerchief over her neck and forehead. Good thing she had decided to wear a lightweight summer dress and cotton undergarments; otherwise she'd be soaked.

Stockings were scarce and expensive. The only pair she owned she'd tucked into her suitcase. She doubted she would wear them except for Sundays once she found a church to attend. They were a luxury, and acquiring silk ones was next to impossible. Before the war, stockings were for dates, dances, and parties. But her work would keep her too busy for social occasions now. Still, she could dream of wearing silk, how it felt on her legs, how cool in summer.

The old lady tugged at her sweater. "I always feel chilly. That's what you get for growing old. You will too someday."

Kate gave her a little smile. "I know. But I'll fight it every step of the way."

In awe of the size of Washington, Kate glanced out the bus windows. Cars and yellow taxicabs zipped through the busy streets. People stood on corners waiting to cross when the lights changed. A few servicemen lingered outside a bistro that had red gingham curtains in the windows. Kate's stomach growled. She had nothing left of the sandwiches and apples Mother had packed for her.

Brakes squealed and exhaust wafted through the open windows. The ride in a hot Trailways bus had been grueling. It was, after all, July, one of the hottest months in the year. The close quarters caused the inside of the cabin to grow more pungent with each mile. Men smoked. Perfume and cologne mingled. Add perspiration to the mix, and the air smelled like a high school locker room.

As the bus made it around a curve and drove into the terminal,

Kate drew in the scent of lilac that passed through her window. She smiled. Home. She missed the lilac trees that grew in the yard next to the azaleas.

The bus slowed to a crawl and stopped. The old woman wished Kate good luck, rose from her seat, and stepped out into the aisle. The driver yanked the door handle, and the door folded open. People hurried from their seats and sidestepped past Kate. They lugged suitcases and bumped into the seats. Kate waited. No reason to move until the aisle cleared. She'd just be caught up in the pushy crowd.

The driver stood, shoved back his cap, and looked at her.

"Hey, get up, miss."

"I'm sorry. I'm always the last to leave."

"Yea, you and a dozen other people. Time to get off."

"What's the hurry?" Kate whispered, annoyed at how rudely he spoke to her.

He squinted. "The sooner this bus clears the sooner I can go home."

"Oh, let her be. She ain't hurtin' anyone." A stocky man in a brown pinstriped shirt poked his finger at the driver. "No one wants to stay on your sticky old bus."

The driver twisted his mouth, folded his arms, and sat back in his green vinyl seat. The man who'd rebuked him looked at Kate and gave her a thumbs-up. Kate grabbed her pocketbook. She looped it over her arm and moved out into the aisle. Hauling her suitcase from the overhead bin, she groaned. She had stuffed it with as many clothes as she could squeeze into it, along with Margaret Mitchell's *Gone with the Wind* and John Steinbeck's *The Grapes of Wrath*. Mother had given the books to her before she left home, and Kate promised she would absorb every page.

Most precious of all, tucked under a pink cashmere sweater

lay her grandmother's wedding Bible. Kate kept it wrapped in rice paper to protect the white silk faille cover and lace applique overlay. Within the pages, Katherine O'Brien had marked favorite verses and placed a flower or two that had turned dry and lost their vivid colors.

"Those novels will teach you a lot about good storytelling, dear," Mother had told her. "But Grandma's Bible will teach you wisdom."

Kate remembered her grandmother sitting in a rocking chair beside the living room hearth with her Bible open on her lap when Kate was a small child. To have it passed on to her was a precious gift.

She'd grown up away from big cities, big-city lights, and big-city noise. The horse farm her parents owned had molded her character. She could train the feistiest of horses using the calming method her papa had taught her. She doubted she'd see anyone but a policeman on horseback in Washington. She had read about Rock Creek Stables, but it seemed a place where wealthy riders boarded their mounts.

A sailor, dressed in his whites and shouldering a canvas seabag, made his way up the aisle. He smiled at her, and she smiled back. He only meant to be friendly to a pretty girl before sailing off to fight in a war that both strengthened and burdened the heart. She pictured him standing firm on a deck that rocked in the North Sea. Or seated behind a machine gun turret as Japanese Zeroes dove toward him. He looked about eighteen. She said a quick prayer that God would keep him safe and bring him home to his loved ones.

She pressed her fingers together to feel her engagement ring. It had been almost two years since she lost Frank. Some of the girls back home who had lost boyfriends in the war had taken off their rings after they got news their men were shot down over the Pacific or killed on the battlefield in Europe. She just hadn't been able to bring herself to do it yet.

"Thanks," she said quietly.

"For what, miss? You need some help with that suitcase or something?"

"Thanks for serving."

"Got a girl at home, sailor?" The blond in the seat in front of Kate drew a piece of gum out of her painted red mouth and gave him a saucy look.

"Yes, ma'am. I'm heading there now. I've got a wife and a kid waiting for me." He moved on and the blond shrugged.

Blondie looked at Kate. "You got a sailor or a soldier?"

Kate looked away. "I had a sailor."

"Pearl Harbor?"

Kate's eyes softened. "He was on the *Arizona*. Lost my brother there too."

"I'm sorry. Must be hard."

Kate nodded. "Very, but I'm better now."

"Got kids?"

"Frank and I weren't married yet."

Kate wished they had married and had a child. A child would have been a comfort to her. Frank had wanted kids too. He grew up an only child, and his parents were both gone by the time he reached eighteen. Before going into the service, he worked at the Esso station in town and lived in the upstairs apartment. As time went on, he showed up at the farm more and more, and stayed for dinner. Soon Kate found herself believing she had fallen in love.

She pushed away her thoughts and scooted into the aisle. The blond went ahead of her and looked back at Kate over her shoulder.

"Hey, what's your name anyway? Where're you from?"

"Kate St. Clare. Pennsylvania."

"My name's Carolanne Price. Pleased to make your acquaintance."

Kate smiled, surprised that a city girl could be so friendly.

"So you're here for work? Plenty of it in D.C. with the men gone to war. Have you got something lined up? I could talk to my boss if you want."

"You'd do that for me. . .a perfect stranger?"

Carolanne shook her head. "Honey, we're in the same boat, sisters, kind of. Nowadays we have to look out for each other. It's one way of helping our boys over there."

"I agree. That's why I came. I want to do something to help the war effort. You don't have to bother talking to your boss though. I put in for a job at the Yard."

"Is that so? Well, maybe we'll be in the same shop."

"I'll be a light welder," said Kate.

Carolanne's brows arched. "You don't say? That's what I do. Be ready for a taskmaster for a supervisor. Those guys are too old to serve, and they resent women stepping into the guys' shoes."

Kate stared at her. What was she in for? Would the foreman give her a hard time, or would he accept her and her desire to contribute to the war effort?

Carolanne handed down her suitcase to a terminal employee. Kate thought she must have gone to one of those fancy finishing schools by the elegant way she moved. Carolanne held on to the step rail, took the employee's hand, and alighted out of the bus.

Kate stepped down without help. She'd been mounting and dismounting horses since she was six years old and had the balance of a trapeze artist. She walked with Carolanne to the front of the terminal, suitcase in hand. An American flag flew out front, and when the wind picked up it furled and whipped around the pole.

Kate slapped her hand on top of her straw cloche hat. "It's windy here."

"Not always," said Carolanne. "You aren't afraid of the wind, are you, Kate?"

"I've been through rougher weather than this. We get high winds and thunderstorms throughout the summer months. I'm not afraid in the least."

Kate's sunflower-yellow dress clung to her when the wind blew. She looked up at the tall buildings, admired the amount of glass and stone and the way ornamental cornices hung over the lips of roofs. Government buildings rose higher with decorative columns, triangular gables, and sweeping arches.

"They weren't kidding when they told me Washington looks like Athens."

"Where? Ohio?" said Carolanne.

"No. Ancient Greece."

"Oh yeah. I see what you mean. We got a lot of that here."

Kate looked at her new friend. "You're from Washington?"

"Last few years, yeah. Originally I'm from Schenectady."

"You're farther from home than I am. I bet you miss your family."

Carolanne shrugged and lugged her suitcase forward. "I just came from visiting my folks. It was my ma's birthday. Give me a week or two and I'll start bawling like a baby. Got a place to stay?"

Kate set down her suitcase and drew a newspaper clipping from her pocketbook. "I brought this with me. I'm sure to get a place in a rooming house."

Carolanne set her hand on her hip. "Think so? Let me see that." Kate handed over the clipping and Carolanne skimmed it. "Too expensive. You should try where I'm staying. It's a clean boarding-house for women working for the war effort. Some places have five girls to an apartment. Not Mrs. F. I've got my own room and the rest of the house to enjoy."

"I don't mind sharing. My sisters and I share a room."

"You won't have to. She should still have an opening. It was vacated the day before I left. Mrs. F. said she'd rent it out again." Carolanne paused and looked Kate up and down. "I think you're just the kind she's looking for."

Kate grabbed her suitcase and walked to the corner with Carolanne. "I'll try her. Thanks."

"How many sisters do you have?"

"Three."

"Brothers?"

"Two." Kate paused. "But we lost Brian when Pearl Harbor was attacked. Brad is somewhere on the *Nevada*."

"I'm sorry. Really I am. How have your folks gotten along without them?"

"It's been hard on Mother. I filled in as much as I could until Papa hired help. My parents bought a horse farm not long after I was born."

"Mine have a mom and pop grocery. I swept floors."

"Nothing wrong with that. I'm sure your folks appreciated it. I mucked stalls. I read there is a stable in Washington that is popular."

"Yeah, with the upper class that can afford it."

It had rained the day before, and puddles dotted the street. A taxi raced through one, the water he splashed missing Kate by inches. Her shoes were the only thing that got wet, and she looked down at them and smiled ruefully. If she'd been closer, the rainwater would have splashed over her new dress.

The light bell rang and turned red. They crossed to the other side, near the bistro the bus passed on the way in.

"Look at those guys," Carolanne said, popping another piece of gum. "Don't be surprised if they whistle at us."

Kate laughed. "I'll whistle back the same way I whistle at my horses."

A bewildered look fell over Carolanne's face. "What?"

"I whistle to my horses when they're out in the field, and they come running."

"You want those guys to come running, huh?"

Kate's smile fell and she blinked. "Oh, I see what you're saying. No, I didn't mean. . ."

"You got a lot to learn about living in a big city, country girl."

Carolanne chewed her gum, and Kate followed the direction of her eyes. Coming down the street, a fair-haired gentleman in a pinstriped suit and brown fedora smiled and picked up his pace.

"Yippee!" Carolanne threw out her arms. "There's my guy." She nudged Kate's shoulder. "Ain't he handsome? Works at the Department of the Treasury."

"Are you sure about that? He doesn't look the type."

"Why, sure I'm sure." She handed Kate a calling card. "Here's the address for the boardinghouse. Show it to Mrs. F. and tell her I sent you."

Kate glanced at the address. E STREET. MRS. FLANAGAN'S ROOMS FOR YOUNG LADIES. "Thank you, Carolanne. What if she turns me away?"

"Are you kidding? She needs the money." Carolanne raised her hand and waved at her beau. "You don't mind me leaving, do you?"

Kate smiled. "Don't keep your fella waiting."

"Thanks." Carolanne beamed. "I'll introduce you to him later."

In her heels and stockings, Carolanne rushed over to her guy and looped her arm through his. Together they walked off, and Kate was left to manage the rest of her journey on her own.

From under the brim of her hat, she spied the servicemen lounging at outdoor tables, smoking cigs and drinking Cokes. One in particular caught her eye, a handsome guy with sandy-brown hair, sitting alone reading a newspaper. He folded the paper and set it down. His eyes met hers. A flush swept over her cheeks. She knew what caused it but blamed it on the heat.

A skeeter-skate daredevil gave her no time to get out of his way. He flew around the corner and ran straight into her, knocking her suitcase right out of her hand. When it hit the sidewalk, it broke open, the handle snapped, and some of her clothes scattered. A bottle of jasmine perfume rolled across the pavement and cracked open. Kate's hands stifled her scream. Frank had given that perfume to her before he left, along with a sterling silver ring with a diamond chip.

One of the bistro waiters leaned into the boy's face. "Watch where you're goin', ya little hooligan."

"I'm all right," Kate said. "Don't scold him."

She crouched down and started gathering up her things. One of the male patrons seated outside the bistro whistled, and she narrowed her eyes at him.

The boy who caused the mishap scrambled from the pavement. "I'm sorry, lady. I didn't see you." He looked to be about eight, his hair tumbling over his forehead, the knees of his blue jeans smeared with dirt.

"Try to be more careful," Kate said. He was a kid, and by the sorry look on his face, she knew he hadn't a malicious bone in his body. "Maybe you could find an empty parking lot somewhere, get your pals together, and ride there."

The boy nodded. She smiled at him and handed him his cap. "I believe this is yours."

The boy took it from her hand, set it back on his head sidewise, then raced off with his skeeter skate intact.

The waiter huffed. "I ought to send for an officer. That would teach him."

"No harm done. He's a boy."

Shoving the last of her clothes into the case, she secured the latches. When she lifted her eyes, she came face-to-face with the sailor whose gaze had caused her to blush—long ago.

"Can I help?" he said.

Chapter 4

Kate sucked in a breath. She couldn't help it. Her eyes locked with Ronny's as she pressed her hands flat on the broken suitcase. Heat burned in her cheeks. It had been what she believed to be a flaw ever since she was old enough to notice boys. But this wasn't any boy. He was a hero in a summer-white uniform—with sultry eyes the shade of dark melted chocolate. She knew him. The eyes were a dead giveaway. She wanted to blurt it out but held back and waited for him to say something—anything that said he knew her.

"Miss, can I help?" he repeated.

Kate shook off the distraction. "Oh, I'm sorry. I didn't hear you."

A smile lifted a corner of his mouth. "I saw what happened. Good thing he knocked down your case and not you."

Embarrassed, she stood and left the suitcase on the pavement. "The handle's broken."

He looked down at it and bit his lower lip. "It's done for," he said. "You'll have to have it repaired." He hauled it up and maneuvered it under his arm.

Disappointed, Kate touched the dangling handle.

"Ronny Jordan." He held out his hand. Hesitant, Kate slipped hers into his. "You've got a strong grip for a girl," he said.

"I've worked on a farm all my life."

His sultry eyes widened. "So you're nowhere near a city girl."

"No, I—"

"I didn't insult you, did I?"

Kate let out a short laugh. "I'd be a pushover if you did."

She drew her hand from his and looked back at the front of the bistro. "Are you sure about helping me?"

He shifted on his feet. "Worried those guys will catcall? Ignore them."

"You're the second person to mention that today."

"Where're you headed?"

"A boardinghouse." She glanced at the card Carolanne had given her. "E Street."

"That's not far." Ronny positioned the heavy suitcase up on his shoulder.

"I'll walk you over. I won't let you carry this thing. It's too heavy. . .without the handle."

"Is it close, like you say?"

"The next street over. Let a sailor do his duty."

She gave him a gentle smile. "You probably have better things to do."

"You think you can handle this on your own?"

"I think so," Kate said. "I've mucked stalls, saddled horses, hauled water, chopped and stacked wood—"

Ronny's smile eased. "You don't have to say anything more. I get it. If you think you can lug this thing on your own, I'll not stop you."

Kate's mouth fell open. Pinpricks spread over her arms. She knew it would be a struggle to carry a suitcase without a handle down the street and find the boardinghouse at the same time. She could hail a cab but needed to save the money.

Ronny handed her the suitcase. Her knees buckled when she wrapped her arms around it. He touched his cover and walked away. She was alone with a broken suitcase in a strange town, and the man she once had a crush on was leaving.

Drawing in a deep breath, Kate took a faltering step toward Ronny. "Mr. Jordan. . .Seaman Jordan. . .whatever you're called. You're right. I can't do this on my own."

Ronny turned back as Kate juggled the suitcase in her arms. "I apologize and would be grateful if you helped me."

Ronny smiled and jerked his head toward the corner. "E Street is this way."

For the second time, he took the suitcase from her. He could have ignored her, walked off, and left her standing on the sidewalk. But he refused to. She saw in his expression that he was pleased to help. If only he had looked at her that way years ago. Maybe things would have been different.

"Let me know if I'm walking too fast," he said.

"A little slower, please. These heels weren't made for sprinting."

Ronny gave her an amused smile. "Don't know how you gals get around in those things."

She smiled back at him. "It takes practice." But navigating in high heels had not been a daily routine for Kate. Already her arches hurt. Heels were for church on Sundays. The rest of the week she wore work boots.

Stepping over a crack in the sidewalk, she looked down. At least in her heels her legs were as feminine as the next girl's. Perhaps more so, due to the exercise she got caring for the horses.

Ronny paused for her to catch up. "Sorry. I got ahead of you, country girl."

"I'm admiring the buildings," she said. "We've nothing like them back home."

"Where is home?"

"Pennsylvania." Her heart fluttered. Now that he knew, he'd figure her out. She hoped he'd have known the moment they first saw each other. Why hadn't he recognized the girl she had been? Had she changed that much?

"I've family in PA."

"Close family?"

"An aunt and uncle. I wish I had time to get up there to see them before I ship out again. The Navy gave me leave, but I'm taking a break from the war. . .seeing the sights."

Kate felt that old wound grow in her chest. "I can't say I blame you."

Along the street, Kate noticed blue stars in the windows of homes. A family member was away at war. Some stars were gold. A son or husband had died in the line of duty. Wrought iron fences lined the yards where roses grew, where those brave men once played as children. Two-story row houses lined the street, some stucco, some whitewashed, some redbrick with bay windows top and bottom. She took her handkerchief from her purse and dabbed her eyes.

Ronny slowed and walked close to Kate, and she stopped. "Before I drop you off on the doorstep, what's your name?"

"Oh, I never said, did I?" Kate's face flushed.

"Nope."

"Don't you remember me? The girl with spindly legs and freckles?"

Ronny's face lit up. "I knew you looked familiar."

"Really?"

"Yeah, really. You're Kate. I don't remember you having spindly legs and freckles. Freckles are *cute* on a girl." He glanced down. "And so are your legs."

Kate took a step back, looked at her legs, and then back at Ronny. "Is it customary for sailors to make comments like that?"

"I figured since we knew each other you wouldn't object to a friendly compliment," he replied. "It's a change from things I did and said when we were kids. Am I right?"

She tucked her handkerchief away. "All my life I've thought my freckles were dreadful."

He gave her a quick smile, and they moved on. "You can blame me, Kate. I was stupid at that age. What did I know about how to treat a girl?"

"Very little, as I recall."

"I get it. Sorry about that."

She bit her lower lip. "Forget it. It's in the past."

"But here we are now. Who'd have thought we'd run into each other?"

"I'm glad we did, Ronny. When I write home, I'll tell them about it. I'm sure Mrs. Mullins will be happy to hear it from my mother."

"Aunt Phoebe?"

Kate smiled and cocked her head. "She enjoys hearing news, and I don't mind until she starts to gossip. If a person wants to know anything about anybody in our little town, ask Mrs. Mullins."

"And you indulge her?"

"To be nice"—she leaned toward him—"polite."

Ronny laughed. "Are the old vets still hanging around the store?"

"They are."

"Is Mr. Cooper still living?"

"He is."

"I really liked that man. He sure had some stories to tell." They turned the corner, and Ronny jerked his head up to the street sign. "E Street."

"Already?"

"Your boardinghouse is a few doors down."

Kate looked past two stucco row houses to a third with a rose garden. A 1929 Model A was parked on the street. A sign hung from a light post by the gate. Kate stopped with Ronny and looked at the building top to bottom. Painted a pale yellow, it had a friendly look. Boxwoods grew below the porch. The windows were mullioned, trimmed in white. Sheer curtains hung across the glass.

A small dog in the lower bay window yapped. He sounded fierce, yet his tail wagged a mile a minute. "A terrier," Kate said. "Aw, he looks just like Toto."

"Yeah, but Toto wasn't a vicious guard dog." Ronny laughed.

"I prefer cats. But I won't mind that little fellow." Kate reached for her suitcase. "Thanks for helping me. It was real generous of you."

He kept the case on his shoulder and took a step closer. "Listen, Kate. I'm shipping out soon. Would you mind if I dropped by. . .to say, 'See you later'? We don't say goodbye in the Navy."

Before she could answer, the front screen door opened. Out stepped a stout woman in a colorful floral apron. Her dress had a flowered pattern too, and her shoes were black and clunky with thick heels. She opened a metal box and took out two bottles of milk.

"Good day." Kate hoped her tone sounded friendly.

The woman turned. "And to you too."

"Mrs. Flanagan?"

The woman balanced the bottles in her arms. "Who's askin'?"

"Kate St. Clare. Carolanne is one of your boarders."

"That she is. She's not at home. If you want to leave a message, you are more than welcome to." Mrs. Flanagan's eyes shifted to the damaged suitcase. "Oh, I see. Are you looking for a room to rent?"

"Yes, ma'am, I am. Carolanne recommended you."

"Do you have references?"

"From my pastor and Mrs. Mullins, the storekeeper back home. I have work, so I can pay."

"I'm sorry, I don't take in couples. Just single girls working in Washington for the war effort."

Ronny grinned. "We aren't a married couple, ma'am."

Mrs. Flanagan wiped her hands on her apron. "Well, come inside and we'll discuss it. I'm pretty picky about who I board." She turned to the front door.

"Mrs. Flanagan," Kate called out. "My suitcase handle is broken, and this sailor offered to carry it for me. Is it all right if he brings it inside?"

Mrs. Flanagan looked back. Her dog scampered out onto the porch and circled around her. "Come on up, Sailor. Set it inside the foyer." She picked up her pooch, who squirmed in her arms. "By the way, you can call me Mrs. F. It's easier than the long version."

Kate stepped through the gate and Ronny followed her. A cat leaped out of the bushes, ran up a post and onto the porch rail, then stretched and clawed the wood.

"Oh, that's Pekoe, my cat. Don't worry—she won't bite." Mrs. F. ushered Kate inside. "He's not waiting for you, is he?" she whispered.

Kate shook her head. "No, ma'am."

"I know they get lonely, but we've got things to talk about."

"I understand, and so does he."

Mrs. F. set her hand on the doorjamb and looked at Ronny. "I'm happy to give a man in uniform a sandwich and a pickle. I make my own soda bread and grow cucumbers in my garden. They make the best dills. How's a cheese and tomato sandwich sound?"

Ronny shifted on his feet. "Oh, I don't want you to go to all that trouble, ma'am."

Mrs. F. waved her hand at him. "It's no trouble at all. You came at the right time. I just finished making some. It'll only take me a minute."

Ronny swept off his cover. "Thank you, ma'am. I won't turn down an offer like that."

"I don't doubt your mother would be happy to know you're taken care of."

"She would, ma'am. But I lost her a few years ago."

"Ah, sorry to hear that." Mrs. F. raised her eyebrows. "Are you on furlough?"

"Yes, ma'am."

"Is Miss St. Clare your girl?"

Kate drew in a breath while standing in the shady foyer.

"No, ma'am. But. . ."

"Yes?"

"I'd like to see Miss St. Clare before I ship out. We're old friends. Would you mind if I come by?"

"That's up to Miss St. Clare. I'll be but a minute." With a lively step, Mrs. F. left for her kitchen. Kate took it as a sign she was happy.

She took a step closer to Ronny. She grasped how brief each encounter with him had been that one summer when she was fifteen. Here they had met again. Here he was leaving again—and too soon.

Kate lifted her eyes and smiled. "Well, this is a relief. Good thing I met Carolanne. . .and you. I would've been lost without your help, Ronny."

"Nothing happens by chance, Kate. Maybe we were meant to

meet again. Maybe it's part of God's plan, if you believe in that kind of thing."

"I was brought up to. My parents are strong believers. We lost my brother Brian and my fiancé at Pearl Harbor."

"Brian?"

"Do you remember him?"

His eyes clouded. "I'll never forget the guy. I'm sorry for your loss, Kate. . .and—"

The kitchen door swung out. Ronny and Kate moved apart. Those shoes of Mrs. F.'s might as well have been combat boots from the deep, hollow sound they made crossing the tile floor. She handed Ronny a bulging paper bag. "Eat hearty, and God bless you and keep you wherever you may be sent."

Ronny thanked her. He looked at Kate, and a lock of his hair fell over his forehead. "See you later, Kate." He pushed back his hair, put on his cover, and walked down the sidewalk.

"Ronny," Kate called, and he turned. "There's a lot I don't know about Washington. You will come back and show me around, won't you?"

Ronny smiled. "You bet, Kate. You'd find me on Mrs. F.'s doorstep even if you hadn't asked."

Kate's face beamed. "Then I'll see you later?"

Ronny gave her a reassuring smile. "You'll see me sooner rather than later."

He turned onto the sidewalk, and Kate rose up on her toes to watch him turn the corner. He paused and lifted his hand to her. Kate took a step forward and raised hers with a smile.

Chapter 5

As the screen door closed, Mrs. F.'s terrier sniffed and pawed at Kate's suitcase. His ears cocked and he moved back and whined. Mrs. F. shook her finger at the pup. "Quiet, Romeo." She smiled at Kate. "His whining is annoying, but he's learned to obey. You must have food in there, Miss St. Clare."

Kate crouched down to pet Romeo. He continued to sniff. "He probably smells Penny."

"Penny? Who's that?"

"She's my mare back home. I packed my riding clothes, and her scent must be on them."

The little dog nuzzled Kate's hand. She stroked his ears. "He's sweet. How old is he?"

"Oh, near ten years now. Come on, I'll show you the room."

Kate stepped beside Mrs. F. "Then you are taking me in, Mrs. F.?"

"I've a room and you seem like a nice young lady. Rent is five dollars a week due on Fridays. You're telling me the truth—you have a job and can pay?"

Kate nodded. "I am. It's a good job. . .for the war effort. I'll be standing in for one of our boys at the Navy Yard."

Romeo scampered off. He jumped into the window seat in the room next to the foyer and began barking. "He sees a squirrel. Believe me. He doesn't carry on at night. You won't be disturbed."

"I love animals. I was born and raised on a horse farm."

"Hmm. How interesting."

"Dogs and cats are not new to me, Mrs. F. I'm glad you have Romeo and Pekoe. They must give you a lot of joy."

"Oh, they do, Kate. Are your parents still living?"

"Yes, ma'am."

Kate followed Mrs. F. up a broad staircase, embracing her suitcase. Each step was carpeted in flowered Persian wool. She looked around. The house looked spotless. Not a mark or mar on wall or floor. The windows sparkled with the sun, and the light fell over yellow wallpaper.

At the top of the stairs, a mahogany table stood under an arched window. English ivy in a McCoy flowerpot thrived on top of a lace doily. The leaves were streaked, and the pot had a quilted design in aqua, something Kate had never seen. She admired it as they passed by. All they had at the farm were barrel planters near the front steps for summer marigolds and geraniums.

"This is so pretty," Kate said. She touched a leaf.

"Oh, I've had that plant for years. . .the pot too." Mrs. F. stepped away. "When I first saw that window, I was sold on the house. Mr. F. and I lived here together for twenty years before he went on to Glory."

"Do you think I could find a pot like that in Washington? I'd like to buy one for my mother."

Mrs. F. fanned her hand. "No need to buy one. I've more than I need down in the cellar. You're welcome to pick out one or two."

"I'll pay you, of course."

"I'll be glad you take something off my hands. When you get to be my age, you want to scale down the stuff you've accumulated over the years. Here's your room."

Mrs. F. opened the door and stepped aside for Kate. Pink floral wallpaper covered the walls. A four-poster bed, matching highboy, and dressing table hadn't a scratch or nick on them. Kate couldn't wait to sink into the thick mattress after the grueling bus ride. Her body ached. The Eastern Star pattern quilt reminded her of Mother sitting by the window, needle in hand, slipping thread through the fabric in tiny stitches.

Mrs. F. opened the doors to an armoire. "There's plenty of room for your clothes in here. You have a dresser over there. The mattress is new, and so are the sheets."

"It's a lovely room." Kate sighed. "It's more than I expected."

"You won't find those fold-up beds in closets in my house, Kate St. Clare. A girl needs a room like this."

Kate agreed. She knelt on the window seat and peered down into the backyard at the vegetable garden. Along the fence grew marigolds and an array of zinnias. The warm air buzzed with honeybees sucking nectar from a climbing rosebush. Monarch butterflies flitted over the flowers, and a nesting pair of wrens guarded a birdhouse.

Mrs. F. looked with Kate at the garden below. "For an old widow, I've done pretty well growing vegetables and flowers."

"You have a beautiful garden." Kate drew in the scent of the roses. "It makes me think of home."

A smile lifted Mrs. F.'s mouth. "I try to keep it up best I can. Everyone I know is growing a garden."

"I'd be glad to help."

"That would be kind of you, Kate." Mrs. F. drew away from the window seat and fluffed a cushion. Frowning at the wrinkles in the quilt, she smoothed them out with her hands. "Be gentle with this quilt, Kate. Fold it down at the foot of the bed at night and don't lay on it."

"I'll take good care of it."

"Carolanne's room is next to yours. The bath is down at the end of the hall. Fresh towels are in the hall cupboard. I bet you'd like a long soak in the tub. Did you bring any soap with you? If not, there's plenty."

"Yes." Kate opened her suitcase. "I brought two cakes of Camay."

"Ah, that is the best. Anything else you need, you tell me."

Kate blinked. "Thank you, Mrs. F. I think I'll be very happy here."

Mrs. F.'s brows arched. "My goodness. I've never had anyone get weepy over my rooms. That tells me you're the right person for it. I don't require you to sign a lease. Pay me weekly and keep the room clean. I don't like clothes on the floor. You can have use of the kitchen. Meals are included. I enjoy my girls joining me at meal-time. I hope you'll like my cooking."

"I'm sure I will, and I'll be happy to help in the kitchen."

"You can do the dishes. I make the best brisket and cabbage in Washington." She giggled. "I'm waiting for the White House to call and ask for my recipe."

Kate smiled. "Sounds scrumptious."

"I'll leave you to unpack. When you're done, come downstairs and I'll show you the rest of the house." Mrs. F. crossed over to the door. "By the way, there's paper, envelopes, and pens in the desk over there. Be sure to write your folks to let them know you're settled."

Kate nodded and turned to her suitcase. She unpacked her

clothes, set out her books, and placed Grandmother's Bible on the nightstand. A pigeon cooed outside the window, and her throat tightened. America at war, the hustle and bustle of Washington, the men in uniforms, all was just as she had expected. But the course of events ever since the bus pulled into the city surprised her to the point her heart swelled with emotion and tears moistened her eyes.

They had not met again by accident or chance.

Chapter 6

Kate and Carolanne approached the gatehouse. A guard stepped out of the booth and raised his hand for them to halt. Kate stared at the rifle slung over his shoulder. "Hi, Carolanne. Who's this?"

"Ain't she cute?" Carolanne said. "She's new. Fresh from the country a few days ago."

"Yeah. Well, I need a pass."

Kate opened her purse, pulled out a card, and handed it over. "Name. Building." He handed it back and smiled. "You're okay. A light welder, huh?"

She nodded. "Not professionally, but capable."

"I figured as much." He pointed to the left beyond the gate. "Go down that street past those pipes. The building is on the right side. Army-green double doors. Go up the stairs and to the office."

With a jerk of her head, Carolanne took hold of Kate's arm. She leaned toward the guard. "I know where she goes. See you later, soldier boy."

Tucking the card back inside her bag, Kate thanked him and went on. The business of war came from every angle. Hammering. The grinding of machinery. Clanging from inside the walls of buildings. Workers passed her, female workers. She glanced at her clothes. Surely her new boss did not expect her to show up in a pair of denim overalls on her first day.

A ceiling fan cooled the room she entered. Over the sound of a clacking typewriter, she gave her name to the secretary. "Sit down over there," the secretary said. "I'll tell Mr. Jones you're here." Kate could tell she dyed her hair rooster red, but that seemed all there was fake about her.

A middle-aged man stepped out from a side door. Absent of a suit jacket, he wore a gray vest and a white shirt with rolled-up sleeves. His tie hung loose at his throat. He pushed his palm over his salt-and-pepper hair and then placed his hands on his hips and looked at Kate as he chewed on an unlit cigar.

"You passed the first test, Miss St. Clare," he said. "You arrived on time."

"I was thinking I was too early. I guess my watch is a little fast."

"It's never wrong to be a little early. Late, and you'll have two warnings. The third, your pay is docked. After that, you're fired." With a swipe of his jaw, he moved his stogie from one side of his mouth to the other. "I see you've dressed right for the job."

She looked down at her dress. "I saw others in overalls, Mr. Jones."

"Everyone calls me Buck. Note: I'm not Buck Jones, the famous actor."

"I figured as much. He died last year, and you look perfectly healthy."

Buck patted his stomach. "I go to the gymnasium. Works out

the kinks I get on a daily basis from these females bawling about what the work does to their hair and nails. Come on, Kate St. Clare. I'll show you what you'll be doing."

He walked out the door and into a broad hallway. Kate followed him, her curiosity roused. She looked through the plate-glass windows at the women busy at work. Everything looked washed of color as if it were a black-and-white film.

"You're going to need to keep your hair back with a scarf. Hope you brought one. It was on the list. If not, maybe one of the other girls has an extra. But I'll have to dock a day's wages if you don't have one."

A day's wages. Carolanne was right. She had a taskmaster for a boss. She opened her bag, took out her headscarf, and waved it at him. "I have one, and I won't forget to wear it."

"It'd be easier if they made you girls cut your hair short. You wouldn't need to wear those things or get your pretty hair stuck in machinery. You can't wear jewelry either."

Kate touched her ring. She'd have to leave it in her room.

"You'll be given something easy to do. We don't do specialized welding. . .you know, the big stuff. We don't build ships here. We leave that up to Brooklyn and other places. We don't repair them either. We do the small stuff. Advancing will depend on how well you weld. You'll be given gloves and goggles. I expect you to wear them."

"I will, sir."

"You'll be using an acetylene welding torch. Do you know what that is?"

"Yes, sir," Kate said.

"You'll be quick but precise. Understand?"

Kate nodded. Buck opened a door to a locker room and handed her a key from a board of hooks. "You get locker seventy-eight. Keep it tidy and locked at all times, and don't lose the key. You lose it, you pay for a replacement."

He tilted his head in the direction of the locker. Kate stepped up to it, shoved the key into the lock, and opened it. She placed her pocketbook and lunch bag inside. She would have shoved the key into a pocket, but she wore a dress. She turned away and slipped it into her brassiere.

"The only time I'm in here is on these occasions," Buck told her. "This was one of the men's locker rooms before the war." He turned and pointed to a board fastened to the wall. On it were written the names of the drafted men and volunteers. "When this war is over, these men will be back." He looked at her. "You know what that means."

"Yes, we girls will lose our jobs," she said.

"No doubt about it." He grinned. "When all is said and done, you and all these other females will go home to the kitchen. A farm is it? Country girl. Milking cows and stuff. Making pies?"

"Yes, sir. . .I mean, Buck." She threw her shoulders back and locked eyes with him. "And I make a mean peach pie."

"Is that right?" He took the cigar out of his mouth and pointed it at her. "You might have to prove your brag one of these days, if you last."

"Maybe I will, if you keep me here." Sarcastic words flooded her mind. "Ever have a pie contest on the job?"

"That's a good idea." Buck put the cigar back in his mouth. "Might help with morale. So why did you leave home?"

"I want to help with the war effort."

"That's what they all say."

Kate looked at the row of gray lockers. "Do I need to buy the overalls?"

"There's some over there. Find your size and keep them."

"Thank you. . .Buck."

"You won't need them today. You're going to be shown the ropes." Buck pulled away from the lockers and walked toward the door. "Lock up. One of the girls will show you what to do."

Shouting outside the door caused Kate to fix her eyes on it. Buck stopped in his tracks. "Not again," he groaned. "Come on, Kate. You might as well see what I have to put up with."

He pushed the door open. Out in the hallway a group of women stood in a half circle with two others in front baring their teeth at each other. Kate wanted to cover her ears. The language that spewed out of one woman's mouth shocked her. Only once had Kate heard such foul words, when a pair of drifters came into Hope Valley to cause trouble. They harassed the old men sitting on the porch of the general store. It lasted a few minutes until old Mr. Cooper stood up and swung his cane with a fury. He knocked one man down the steps into the dirt. The other he poked with the tip and pushed him over a rocking chair. They scurried off, never to be seen again.

But here, in the hallway of the Navy Yard, the woman in a red scarf proved herself just as rank.

"Knock it off." Buck stepped in when she went for the other, fists flying, and smacked the girl in the face. Crying commenced.

Buck clenched his fists above his head. "I said, knock it off!"

The woman swung again and whacked the cigar out of Buck's mouth. "You didn't just do that, Milly." He stooped down, picked up his stogie, and put it back in his mouth. "That's the final straw."

Milly placed her feet apart and firm on the linoleum floor. She looked about eighteen, her face flushed and tense. "It's Betty's fault, Buck," she said. "She should learn to keep her mouth shut."

"Me?" the other woman cried. "I didn't say anything wrong. You started it."

The fight picked up with verbal barrages. "I said knock it off." Buck fumed. "All day I've got to deal with hurt feelings. You need to act like ladies instead of prizefighters. And the language coming out of your mouth, Milly, is enough to make my ears burn. This is the last time. Follow me to the office. Both of you."

"You're going to sack us?" Betty asked. She stood all but five feet tall, inches shorter than her assailant. Her scarf had been yanked off in the scuffle, and her brown hair crossed her cheek where a red mark showed. Kate met her eyes and gave her a sympathetic look.

She drew up to the bullied girl. "You should put some ice on that."

Betty touched her face. "Is it that bad?"

"It'll bruise if you don't."

"Okay, enough chitchat." Buck placed his hands on the girls' shoulders and turned them in the direction of the doors.

Betty winced. "Please, Buck. You know I need this job. I've got two kids and my husband is in the Army."

"Then you shouldn't have been fighting. Get a move on."

"She yanked off my scarf and called me a name I'll not repeat."

Buck sighed. "I never had this kind of trouble with men. Let's go. Time I sit you two down for a serious discussion."

He marched them through the doors. Betty looked back over her shoulder at Kate and shrugged. Kate stood under one of the windows, and as the group dispersed, Carolanne looked at her and smiled. "There you are, honey. Still up for it?"

Kate smiled. "I expect so."

"He's a brute, isn't he?"

"Hmm, he's rather brave to step into the middle of a catfight, if you ask me." Kate leaned close to Carolanne and lowered her voice. "You really think he's awful?"

"It's bad enough he supervises things down here, but I'd never want to be behind closed doors with that guy. Those girls will be lucky if they still have their jobs."

"Sounds like you've had problems with him before."

"Nothing I couldn't handle."

"He smells like stale cigars. The whole time he talked to me he had one moving around in his mouth." Kate fanned her face. "I can't stand the smell of cigars. It gets on men's clothes and skin. It's disgusting."

Carolanne wrinkled her nose. "And their breath. Ever kiss a man who smokes?"

Kate frowned. "Never."

"Like kissing an ashtray." Kate's newfound friend nudged her shoulder. "I bet you haven't ever been kissed."

"I'll never tell you either way." Kate walked on, smiling. She drew in a deep breath.

Carolanne tightened the knot on her headscarf as she walked beside her. "Don't worry," she said. "You'll do all right."

"As long as I steer clear of Buck, right? If I can handle an untamed horse, I can handle someone like Buck. I'm afraid of very little."

"I like your confidence, Kate."

"Thanks."

"You've really trained wild horses? I'd be scared."

"No reason to be if you know what you're doing."

"Ha, like men. A girl has to know what she's doing."

Kate fixed her eyes on the door at the end of the hallway. It looked cold, sterile, and she pondered what Carolanne said. It was a worldly way of looking at things, but greater words came into Kate's mind. A girl had to guard her heart—just as it was written. "Keep thy heart with all diligence; for out of it are the issues of life."

"Those are pretty words, Kate. Did you make them up?"

"They're from the book of Proverbs." She stopped walking and put her arm over Carolanne's shoulder. "I hope you're guarding your heart, Carolanne."

Carolanne sighed. "Country girl, you sure don't know the ways of the world."

"Sure I do, more than you know." Kate waited. Carolanne looked at her. Her eyes were prideful, but her cheeks were blushing with shame.

"What time did you get in?"

"Late," Carolanne admitted. "But I didn't do anything wrong."

"I didn't say you did. Just be careful with this guy."

They pushed open the door. It led into another hallway, bare and empty. "I had dinner last night with—*my fiancé*." Carolanne held out her left hand. A diamond set in silver sparkled on her finger.

"Wow wee." Kate sighed. "He proposed?"

"Yep. Pretty isn't it? I know we're not supposed to wear jewelry, but I had to show the girls today. I'll put it back in my pocket when break is over."

Kate grabbed Carolanne's hand and looked closer at the ring. "I'd say. It's a diamond."

"Didn't your guy give you a ring?"

"I guess he couldn't afford one like yours." She held up her hand. "It's a diamond chip."

"Hmm, cute."

"It's good enough for me. So, what's the date?"

"We haven't set one yet. But we already discussed plans to honeymoon in Niagara Falls."

"You're in love with this guy?"

Carolanne closed her eyes and smiled dreamily. "I'm over the moon for him. He's picking me up after work, taking me to the Willard Hotel for dinner."

"I saw the Willard coming into town. Swanky," Kate said with a grin.

A sad look passed over Carolanne's face. "Look, Kate. I apologize for leaving you the way I did. I should've had my guy help with your suitcase and drive you over to Mrs. Flanagan's. I feel real bad about it."

"I was fine. I had Ronny help me, and even if he hadn't, I would have made it on my own. Back home I ride the trails and have never gotten lost. . .not once."

"Ronny? He's that handsome sailor?"

Kate nodded. "He carried my case the entire way and knew the address. Funny thing is, we know each other from back home. It was years ago when we were kids."

"Well, what d'you know about that? Pretty romantic, I'd say."

Kate smiled.

"Your cheeks are turning red, Kate. You like him, don't you? He'd better call before he's shipped out, and put a ring on your finger."

Kate widened her eyes. "You're kidding me, right?"

A group of women headed past them through the door when the shift bell rang. Carolanne and Kate walked onto a military gray floor made of poured concrete. Ceiling fans whirled overhead. All the windows on the south side were open. Carolanne set her hand on Kate's shoulder and moved her forward. "Girls," she said. "This is Kate St. Clare, our newest cohort in sending Hitler and Hirohito to Hades in handbaskets."

Kate smiled, relieved by the warm greetings the ladies gave her. She knew then she would fit right in. At least she hoped so.

During the lunch break, Carolanne showed off her ring. The

sparkling stone impressed some, evoked envy in others. Some of the girls had husbands or boyfriends away fighting. A few were older women whose sons had gone off to war.

"I can't wait for this war to be over," said one of the girls. The others nodded in agreement. "I want my fella home."

"Me too." Betty had managed to escape Buck's wrath and sat beside Kate. "I read that some builders are planning communities called suburbs for when the men return. They can get VA loans and start families." She took a newspaper article out of her pocket and unfolded it on the table. "Look at this, girls." Everyone leaned in. "Family houses that will be cheap. Aren't they cute?"

"Where is that?" Carolanne asked.

"Not far from D.C. This one says it'll be called Viers Mill Village. But they won't start building until the war is over."

Carolanne frowned. "Gee, it looks like its way out in the country."

Kate placed her fingertip on the article's map and traced the road leading out of D.C. and Georgia Avenue. The lots lay in neat rows of Cape Cod bungalows. Each bungalow had windows to the left and right and a stout door in the middle. "It is far," Kate said. "You can see the hills and farms once you get out of the city. It's too bad," she said, and leaned back in the cold metal chair.

A woman wearing a Navy pin looked at her. "No, it's not. We're going to need homes. I plan to marry my guy and have lots of babies." The others giggled.

"But the farms will be taken up. You'll lose all that beautiful country."

"Of course that opinion would come from you, a country girl."

A woman in a blue scarf set down her peanut butter sandwich and folded her arms. Her hair was gray, her eyes milky. "Kate's right. Those little cracker boxes will be nothing more than shacks. You girls are getting all worked up thinking you're going to be living the highlife when you live in one of those. These *suburbs* are going to turn into *slum-burbs*. You watch and see."

Carolanne folded a piece of peppermint gum into her mouth. "What about you, Kate? Do you agree with Mrs. Wyatt? Where will you go after the war?"

Kate refused to be ashamed of her country roots. She lifted her chin and said, "Back to the farm where I belong. The city and this"—she pointed to the ad—"isn't for me."

"Not good enough for you, Kate?"

"I didn't say that. I'm happy you all will have nice homes to raise your families in. I can't see going through life without my horses."

The woman beside Carolanne laughed. "Without yokels, you mean. You'll never find a good husband out in the boonies." She looked at her workmates. "Not a rich one anyway."

Kate smiled and looked at the ring on her finger. "Where I come from there are plenty of good men. My fiancé was one. So was my brother."

Silence. They'd heard from Carolanne that Kate had lost two of America's heroes in the Pearl Harbor attack. They all had known loss—and the sad loneliness of a loved one far away.

To break the chill, Kate reached inside her pocket. "This is my horse, Penny." The picture passed around, and the women oohed and awed at the beautiful chestnut mare.

"You miss home, Kate?" Betty asked.

Kate nodded. "I'm going to try to stay busy and not think about it."

Milly had somehow been shown mercy. Buck had given her another chance after she begged him not to fire her. She sat at the end of the table and threw down her napkin. She glared at Kate. "You should've stayed home."

Kate glanced at Milly. "We all know why we're working here,

Milly. It's for the war effort."

"You can preach all you want that it's our patriotic duty. But I'm in it for the money and not ashamed to say so."

The other girls murmured and frowned. "The rest of us are here to help the men that went off to fight Hitler and Hirohito," Kate said. "If we lose this war, we won't be making anything except swastika flags and sun banners."

Milly stood. Chair legs scraped across the tile floor. "You think so. I guess leaving the farm and working at the Yard makes you feel better. You're so self-righteous, it makes me sick."

"That's enough of that talk." Carolanne smacked the tabletop with both hands. "Leave her alone."

"It's a free country."

Kate stood also. "It's all right, Carolanne. She's right. It is a free country."

Carolanne moved forward and looked Milly straight in the eyes. "Have you anyone fighting?"

Milly pressed her lips together. "Not now. He was killed."

Carolanne's face softened. "Sorry."

"I'm not. He was a good-for-nothing layabout. When he signed up I was glad to see the back of him."

The women murmured at Milly's cold comments. As for Kate, she looked at her in a different light. She was a woman broken, and she buried those feelings by hardening her heart. Mrs. Wyatt, on the other hand, tossed the rest of her sandwich in her lunch bucket and pointed an accusing finger at Milly.

"Then you have no idea how the rest of us feel. We miss our men. We pray night and day that they come home safe. We worry and cry ourselves to sleep at night. So lay off that kind of talk, like Carolanne said. The rest of us don't want to hear it."

Milly snapped her lunch box shut. "Fine."

"Let's not argue, girls," Kate said. "We're all suffering one way or another, and there's no point to any of this if we can't encourage each other."

Milly lifted her head, turned on her heel, and walked out.

That night Kate arrived home worn to the bone. Romeo leaped up at her, and Pekoe sat on the staircase staring. Four pink English roses set off their fragrance in a blue vase. Kate smiled, leaned down, and smelled them. She touched the soft petals.

Mrs. F. peeked around the kitchen door. "Those are from your sailor, Kate. He's in there." She jerked her head in the direction of the sitting room. "Don't keep him waiting."

Chapter 7

Kate checked her hair in the mirror before going in to meet Ronny. Sake's alive, she looked a mess. The scarf had mussed her hair, and she smelled like burnt acetylene. Her mascara still looked fresh. She grabbed her lipstick out of her pocketbook and dabbed it on. A soft peachy pink looked natural on her instead of the popular flaming shade, Red Majesty. She wore little at home. The girls on the home front were encouraged to wear lipstick and kiss each letter from home to their soldiers. She'd gotten her hands on two tubes, hoping she would have someone to write to other than her brother.

Drawing in a breath, she walked into the sunny sitting room that faced the street. Ronny stood from one of Mrs. F.'s overstuffed chairs, and Kate wondered what he would look like in civilian clothes. As handsome as in his Navy uniform, no doubt. But there was something alluring about his dress whites, the stripes and ribbons on his tunic.

"Sorry, I'm not dressed for company. I just got home from work."

His eyes moved to hers. "I think you look great."

She smirked. "Then you need glasses. I'm a mess. If you can wait, I'll go upstairs and change."

"I like you the way you are." He turned his cover in his hands. His eyes were warm and tender.

Kate glanced at the coffee table. A pitcher of lemonade and a plate of shortbread cookies were on it. "Mrs. F.'ll be hurt if you don't drink some of that." She moved to a chair and grabbed a cookie. "I'm starving. Too bad butter is rationed." She handed one to him. "These are pretty good even if they are made with that oleo stuff. Have one." She could see in his gaze he had no interest in food. It lingered elsewhere.

Ronny stepped forward. "Kate."

She glanced up at him and put her fingers over her mouth. The cookies were sweet, but she couldn't take another bite. His gaze mesmerized her. She gave herself a mental shake, lifted the pitcher, and started to pour lemonade in a glass. "It's hot today. You're probably thirsty."

"Kate. I don't want any."

She set down the pitcher. "Let me know if you change your mind. Thanks for the roses. I don't know how you knew they were my favorite—the color too. The girls at the shop will be so envious."

"I hear the girls get guff from some of the men."

"It's true—"

"Those of us in uniform appreciate you ladies. We can't win this war without you."

"They call us Winnie the Welder. Isn't that a hoot?"

The sight of him affected her. Whatever it was, it was a warm, comforting feeling. She'd never felt that with Frank.

"There's a dance at the USO tonight. I'd like to take you as my date." Ronny pushed his fingers through his hair. His sleeve inched back, and Kate saw a ragged scar on his wrist. Ronny didn't miss the direction of her eyes.

"Oh yeah. I guess I should show you this." He pushed his sleeve further back. "It's a war wound. I know it's ugly, and most women would be embarrassed to be seen with a guy who—"

"Not me. I find it heroic."

He dropped his arm. "Then you're one of a kind."

She gave him a gentle smile and glanced away. He had the sweetest way of complimenting her without sounding sappy.

He sat beside her. "Ever since we ran into each other, I can't stop thinking about you. I'm shipping out soon and won't be back for who knows how long."

"And you'd like to spend the time with me?"

"You bet I would. So. . .how about we cut a rug at the USO?"

"Yes," Kate said. "I'd love to go."

"Yeah? That's great. Can I pick you up at seven?"

"Seven is perfect. It'll give me a chance to transform myself." She laughed, kicking off her factory shoes. "I won't wear these. That's for sure."

Ronny stood. "What's your favorite song?"

" 'Stardust.' " Kate walked over to the door with him. "Sure would be nice to hear Artie Shaw, but he's playing for the guys in the Pacific."

"Goodman is playing. If he takes requests, I'll tell them to play it for you, Kate."

Kate gave Ronny a soft, cheeky gaze. "Be careful, Sailor. It's one of those 'hold me close' songs."

He smiled back. "I'd jump at the chance."

"To hear Artie Shaw, or to—"

"Hold you close." He stepped up to her and put his arm around her waist. "That would be the first thing I'd want to do."

Kate looked down. His words made her blush. She glanced up into his eyes. They captivated her. Long they looked into hers, until—Mrs. F. walked into the room.

"Thanks for the cookies and lemonade, Mrs. F." Ronny gave her a casual salute. "See you at seven, Kate."

After Ronny left, Kate rushed up the staircase to her room and flung open the armoire doors. She had brought little in the way of dressy clothes. As she skimmed through the hangers, she heard the front door slam. The tapping of those heels could only belong to Carolanne coming up the staircase. Kate pulled a dress out and held it in front of her, and then she turned. Carolanne's flushed face appeared in the doorway. She sighed and came in the room and lay across the bed.

"You're home early. I thought you were having dinner with your guy."

"I did," Carolanne said. She held up her arm and wiggled her fingers, admiring the ring.

"I've come home to change. He's waiting outside in the car." She sat up. "We're going dancing."

"Me too." Kate sounded just as enthused as her housemate did. She swung back to the armoire, hung the dress, and pulled out another. "Ronny's taking me to the USO."

"That's where Peter is taking me. We can make it a double date! I wish the Glen Miller Orchestra was going to be there. I love their music. So romantic."

Kate slipped out of her clothes. "I think so too."

"So are Tommy Dorset and Artie Shaw. A local big band is fine though. They'll play anything that's requested."

Kate smiled. "Don't you know Benny Goodman's orchestra's playing tonight?"

Carolanne yelped. "Wow wee! This is going to be better than I thought. I'm so glad we're going to double date, Kate. You like this guy don't you?"

"I barely know him, but yeah. . .I like him."

"Love can happen in a second."

"So I've heard. It's called 'at first sight.' "

A car horn honked. "Gee, I've got to hurry. Pete's waiting for me."

Off Carolanne went, and Mrs. F. knocked on the door. "I don't mean to bother you, Kate. But I thought you'd like to try this. . .since it's your first date with Ronny."

She held out a blue perfume bottle, and Kate read the label. "Evening in Paris! Oh, I can't."

Mrs. F. frowned. "Why not? You told me your perfume bottle broke on the way here. A young woman should smell her best, especially on a first date."

Kate's throat tightened. She grasped the bottle and put her arms around Mrs. F. "Thank you. I don't know where I would have ended up if not for you."

"Don't forget Carolanne. That girl pointed you in the right direction." She set Kate back and looked at her. "Let's hope she has enough sense to know what she's doing."

"You mean her engagement?"

Mrs. F. nodded. "Indeed I do. She's never introduced him to me or had him in the house. He waits out in the car for her or stands outside it leaning on the doors smoking like a fiend. He looks shady to me."

"Do you feel the same about Ronny? I think I could fall in love with him."

Mrs. F. lifted her head and gave Kate a sidelong glance. "If you haven't already. Now get yourself ready. He'll be here soon."

Kate pulled the stopper on the bottle and dabbed the scent behind her ears. Then she checked herself in the mirror. This would be her first real dance. Back home she'd been to a few barn dances. The musicians were locals, and when her generation brought swing dance into the picture, the older generation frowned, except for her father. He'd clap his hands and root them on. Mother would smile and quiet the disapproving old townswomen by encouraging the gentlemen to pull them out onto the dance floor.

Kate took out some writing paper and set it on the desk to remind her to write Mother when she got home. It would be late. She'd be exhausted from dancing, but she could not wait to tell her about Ronny, and how much she missed home.

Chapter 8

When a yellow cab pulled up outside the boardinghouse, Kate stood at the window. She watched Ronny leap out of the back and stride down the sidewalk. She hurried to the door and swung it open. His swarthy smile made her heart throb. This was not the schoolgirl crush she once felt. No, this was different. Love had no limit on time, but Kate wondered if this was what it felt like to fall in love. It seemed too early for such feelings, but maybe it was possible.

He pushed back his cover and looked her over. "Man, you're a picture." He sighed. "Why God thought me good enough to take out a doll like you, I'll never know."

Kate smoothed down the front of her dress. "So you think I look okay?"

"You look beautiful." He leaned in and said, "Wow, you smell beautiful too."

He held out his arm, and she placed her hand on it.

She glanced at his spit and polished uniform. He opened the

cab door for Kate and then slid in beside her. Kate looked out the window as the cab headed off of E Street onto Massachusetts Avenue. The city lights were brightening against a summer sunset. She couldn't see the horizon for the buildings, but above them a soft pearly pink shone, and the color washed over the white granite blocks. The sidewalks were crowded with people out for the evening.

Slowing, the cab pulled up behind other cabs in front of the USO building. Soldiers and sailors were exiting with their dates. Girls were decked out in bright colors and in deep floral patterns with ribbons and silk flowers in their hair. Excitement crackled in the air.

Ronny got out, and Kate scooted over to the open cab door. He paid the cabbie, told him to keep the change, and held Kate's hand. The entrance boiled over with people, but one distinctive laugh caught Kate's ears.

"You're such a tease." Carolanne's voice resounded through the others. "Stop telling me fibs, or I'll tell your mother," followed another giggle.

Kate leaned up to Ronny. "It's my friend Carolanne. Remember her?"

"The blond that was walking with you the first time I saw you?"

"Yes, that's her. She's been a good friend. That must be her fiancé who's making her laugh. You wouldn't think such a boisterous laugh could come out of the mouth of someone so pretty and elegant, would you?"

Ronny moved his eyes from Carolanne to Kate. "Want to say hi?"

"We hoped to make this a double date." Kate transferred her grip from his hand to his arm. "If we can get through this crowd."

He pulled her close and shouldered through the people. Carolanne turned, and her face lit up as bright as the bulbs surrounding the entrance. "Kate, this is Peter. Isn't he a dream?"

Peter nudged Carolanne's cheek with his hand. "You're the dream, doll."

Kate looked this guy in the eyes. Something shone in them that made her distrust him. He played the part of an affectionate fiancé, but to Kate the man had a sinister look about him. Everything on him looked expensive, from the watch he wore to his two-tone oxfords, to the tailored suit. Could he be that rich, or had he gotten his money from ill-gotten gains?

"And this is Ronny," Kate said, pulling him closer.

Carolanne smiled at Ronny. "Hmm, he's quite a catch."

Peter turned aside, not taking the hand Ronny offered. Kate frowned. "Something the matter that prevents you from shaking a sailor's hand?"

"Kate, don't bother," Ronny said.

"He won't shake your hand, but he'll step inside a USO dance?"

Peter sneered at Kate. "You don't understand. I don't shake just anybody's hand."

Carolanne leaned in. "Peter worries about germs. Don't you, Peter?"

"I do, but yours are an exception." Peter lifted Carolanne's hand and kissed her fingers.

Kate glared at him. "See you inside, Carolanne." She walked through the other couples with Ronny. "How can she be engaged to a man like that?" she fumed.

"Don't let it spoil our fun, Kate. He seems like a chump."

Inside the hall, she said, "I wouldn't let anything spoil our night, Ronny. I hope you're ready to work up a sweat in your neat Navy whites."

The band's drummer, Gene Krupa, pounded out a pulsating swing beat. As the crowd bounced on their heels, Benny Goodman stepped forward with his clarinet. Raspy trumpets, throaty trombones, and mellow saxophones struck up an electrifying four-four tempo.

Kate clapped her hands to the beat. " 'Sing, Sing, Sing.' I love this song."

"Come on, kid." Ronny's smile widened, and he thrust out his hand. "Let's cut a rug."

Kate's pulse raced, and she grabbed his hand. The dance floor teemed with couples, the men in uniforms, the girls dressed to the hilt. Perfume wafted in the air, the scent of men's soap and shaving lotion mingling with it. The war brought on dark days, but on nights like this, swing music lifted the spirits of everyone in the room.

Ronny whirled Kate out onto the dance floor. Her yellow skirt flared out above her knees and back down again, as they rock-stepped, drop-kicked, and triple-stepped. Ronny lunged to the side and pulled Kate against him. Her feet sprang from the floor and he held her all but a second before letting her go.

Their eyes met, and then he spun Kate out. She closed her eyes and felt the rhythm racing in her pulse. Together they flowed from one move to another. Breathless, Kate laughed as the horns led off. The drums beat out a fading tempo, and Ronny dipped her, held her inches above the floor with his lips close to hers. Her heart thumped in her chest to the pace of the dying drumbeat—from Ronny's closeness and embrace.

He pulled her up, and they drew in deep breaths. The crowd cheered, applauded, and urged the band on. "Again?" Ronny heaved a breath and held out his hand. Kate slapped hers into his, and he drew her to him.

The dance hall walls shuddered with more music, and the floor vibrated with the feet of the dancers as they danced to "In the

Mood." Kate's heart pounded along with each beat of each song, each swing and dip, and she wished the night would go on forever.

The doors were open, and after a while Ronny ducked Kate outside. He stuck his finger into his collar. "Man, it's hot in there. I'm thirsty."

"Me too," she said. A vendor on the sidewalk sold ices and drinks from a cart, and as Ronny dug into his pocket to pay the man, Kate looked across the street at the illuminated clock in the bank tower and sighed. When Ronny returned, she said, "We've been dancing for three hours."

Ronny handed her a cherry ice. "Worn out?"

"A little, but in a good way," she said.

Kate glanced back inside the dance hall. Couples were swinging and swaying to the music. She spotted Carolanne across the room. She stood off to the side with her date, watching the USO volunteers pick out the best dancers in a surprise competition. When Kate caught Carolanne's eye, she gave her a wave of goodbye. Carolanne nodded and lifted her hand.

Kate set her hand on Ronny's sleeve and moved close. "Take me home?" she said looking up into his eyes.

"If you want me to."

She leaned against his chest. "Take me home and sit on the porch with me. We can have cold drinks and look at the moon and stars."

"Mrs. F. won't mind?"

"No, she likes you."

He took her hand, and they headed to the street curb. Ronny hailed a cab and scooted in with Kate. Washington streets were quiet. Dark shades covered windows, and lights were dim.

Mrs. F.'s windows were open. The radio played mellow night music, and Kate laid her head on Ronny's shoulder as they rocked back and forth in the porch swing. "Moonlight Serenade" played. Ronny stood with Kate, took her in his arms, and moved his hand against the small of her back. His lead swayed her right to left, while his eyes settled on hers. Glenn Miller moved them through the song, the horns and the mellow clarinets flowing together in a dreamy chorus. Kate laid her head against Ronny's shoulder as her heart swelled. She moved her palm over his and felt his heart beating in his breast.

Ronny set his hands on Kate's shoulders. "I'm a man now, Kate, and know better. I hope you can forgive the past."

She looked up at him. "We were just kids."

"What would you do if I told you I love you? That I've always loved you?"

Kate whispered, "I'd say. . .I love you back and do this." She slipped her arms around his neck. They looked into each other's eyes as the song lingered on and came to a slow end. Ronny brought his lips close as Mrs. F.'s radio played Frank Sinatra singing "I Could Write a Book." With their eyes still holding each other's, they clung together. Kate whispered the words.

"It's true, isn't it?" Ronny murmured.

"I'd say so," Kate breathed out.

The kiss Ronny gave Kate seemed to raise her feet above the floor. Parting, Kate held on to him and said, "I hate war."

"We still have some time before I leave."

"Let's make the most of it," she said.

"Tomorrow night?"

"Every night," she breathed.

"I want to find you right here, on this porch, waiting for me."

Kate moved her hands to Ronny's shoulders, then to his hands. "Can we dance like this again?"

"It's a lot better than in a crowd."

The radio announcer came on and in a mellow voice told the time. "I'm due back by midnight," Ronny said. "I hate it, but I've got to go."

Kate nodded that she understood. "You don't want to get into trouble with an MP."

He kissed her hand. "You've got that right. I told our cabby to come back in an hour, and here he comes." Ronny kissed Kate long and soft. "Goodnight, Kate. See you in my dreams." Kate stood on the porch in the dark, reluctant for him to go. The cab swerved to the curb, and Ronny got in. It pulled away, and when Pekoe jumped up the steps and curled around Kate's legs, she picked her up and went inside where the music softly played on.

❧ Chapter 9 ❧

Saturday night couldn't come soon enough. A full moon hung in the night sky amid a spray of stars and the balmy air mixed with the scent of roses from Mrs. F.'s garden. Kate and Ronny stood alone on the front porch. White wicker chairs rested against the redbrick walls, and the porch swing swayed gently on the other end.

"Let's sit on the step," Kate said. "We can see the moon better from here." She lowered onto one, and Ronny drew down beside her. "You're leaving soon, aren't you?"

"When you're in the Navy, they send you where they want when they want. I've been called to Norfolk, not sure which ship yet."

"You'll be in the Atlantic?"

A smile struggled over Ronny's face. "Looks that way. Will you write to me?"

"Of course I will. I'll tell you all about the goings-on here in D.C. I can't promise it won't make you homesick."

He moved closer to her ear. She felt the warmth of his breath caress her neck. "I want a photo. I'll carry it with me everywhere I go and show you off to the guys."

Kate lowered her eyes and smiled. "Don't expect them to think too much of a plain girl like me."

He laughed. "Plain? You're the prettiest girl I've ever met."

Kate shook her head. She never thought of herself as anything but plain. Most days she wore jeans and riding boots, and tied her hair in a ponytail, not the elaborate Victory knots other girls were wearing.

She lifted her eyes and stared at the opal orb in the sky. "The moon reminds me of that dreamy song—'Moonlight Serenade.'"

"Think about me whenever you hear it, Kate." He turned her face to his. "We haven't had a lot of time together, but let's plan on it when I come back."

Tears escaped her eyes. Her heart ached thinking of him gone—gone for only God knew how long. "You will come back, won't you?"

"Sure I will."

"Ronny." Kate spoke his name softly. She pressed her cheek against his.

He picked up her hand and kissed it. "Don't worry about me, Kate. I promise I'll come back even if I have to crawl on my hands and knees."

She sighed. "Not a day goes by that someone at the Yard hears bad news."

His hand caressed her arm. "Hopefully it will be over soon. Then we can put it behind us."

"Rose Robertson came into the canteen the other day distraught. Her family got word that two of her brothers are POWs, and she hasn't heard from her guy. He's on the *Vulcan*, and she has no idea why he hasn't written or where he is."

Ronny's body stiffened. "The USS *Vulcan*. I've heard of that ship.

She's a repair ship. The fleet couldn't make it without those men."

"Rose worries about what it's doing to her mother. The girls try to comfort her."

Thoughtful silence came between them. A tree frog sang in Mrs. F.'s maple tree for its mate. Ronny finally broke the quiet. "Have you heard from your brother?"

"I got a letter from my mother the other day. Brad said he was fine." Kate turned to Ronny. "It was a miracle he survived the attack at Pearl Harbor. Poor Brian. It was different for him."

Ronny looked down at his hands. "Yeah, it sure was. I was on the *Arizona*."

Kate gasped. "You never said. . ."

"I don't know why I held back."

"I do, and I understand how difficult it must be to talk about it."

"Seaman Brian St. Clare—quick with a joke to keep our spirits up. We used to talk about Hope Valley. We didn't know each other well back then, but I remember he made deliveries for my aunt and uncle."

"So you knew Brian."

"No one picked on Brad when Brian and I were around."

"Please tell me about the attack."

"I doubt you really want to hear the details, Kate. It was as if we were in hell."

"I want to know my brother's sacrifice meant more than war bonds and ration books and rubber drives." She gripped Ronny's shoulders and swallowed. "I want to understand. Don't you see? I want to know everything you know."

Ronny's face paled. He touched her cheek and sighed. "I can't tell you everything I saw. . .not now. . .not ever."

She stared into his face. Then she kissed his cheek. "Then tell me a little."

He cupped her hands within his and held them to his lips a moment. Then, looking into her eyes, he said, "When I woke that morning, the sky was as blue as the ocean. It was empty. Not a cloud in it. Then in the distance as I stood on the deck, I could hear the humming of planes. I looked toward the horizon. So did others. We were all unconscious of the fact that within a few seconds most of us would be gone and the fleet destroyed. The ship's air raid alarm went off. We scrambled to general quarters. I watched torpedo bombers making their fast approach. Five headed right for our bridge."

"Where the officers were?"

Ronny nodded. "That's the first thing they targeted. The officers, our captain. They carried armor-piercing shells reformed into bombs. They bombed us from amidships to stern. Then they hit the bow area. Fires broke out. Black smoke billowed all around us. Men screamed, yelled out orders.

"I watched a Zero dive down toward the stern and release a bomb. I backed up against the bulkhead. It ricocheted off the face of a turret and breached the deck. They kept coming. More dropped. More hit our guns and our boys. That sound—that terrible buzzing sound those planes made. They screamed toward us. Deafening explosions. The last bomb ripped through the deck near the magazines. The forward magazines exploded. The turrets and conning tower collapsed. The ship ripped in half. Sailors were scrambling. Those of us that could pulled some to safety, the water being the only place to retreat, even though there was oil and fire on the surface. Brian was a good sailor, one of the best. I tried to save him. He was terribly injured, Kate. He called for your mother."

"Did he?" Kate's voice trembled. "And then—"

"I couldn't help him. He was gone before I could lift him. I helped another crewman out from under burning debris. So many guys were injured, and bodies were. . ." Ronny hung his head. "I can't go on, Kate."

She caressed his hair. "Thank you for trying. I know you would've saved him if it hadn't been too late. I love you for it, Ronny." She placed a tender kiss on his mouth. "Tell me about your medal."

"It's somewhere."

"I would like to see it someday."

"When the time is right."

"Someday your children and grandchildren will want to see it, and they will be proud."

"That's what Lieutenant Commander Fuqua told us. He was the damage control officer I served under. He deserved that Medal of Honor they awarded him and more. He kept a cool head. He led us in quelling the fires and getting survivors off the ship. A true hero and a great man."

"You are a hero and a great man too."

"Not me. The guys that didn't come back are the real heroes."

"I don't want you to go." Kate's voice quivered, and she dashed the tears falling down her cheeks. "You've been through too much too soon to forget, too soon to be sent back. Pearl Harbor should have been enough."

Ronny pulled her into his arms, and Kate snuggled into his shoulder. It hurt that he had to ship out, that they'd be separated, that she would spend each day worrying, praying, and hoping for his return.

Chapter 10

The travel clock on Kate's nightstand ticked away. She looked over at it. One in the morning, and already long before the sun came up a mockingbird chirped away in a tree. She lay awake thinking of Ronny and the dangers he would face. The distance that would be between them was unfathomable.

Footsteps rushed up the staircase. It had to be Carolanne coming in late. Kate turned on her side to face the window, to sleep and dream. A knock on her door and Mrs. F.'s frantic voice got her up.

"Kate, are you awake? I need you downstairs."

"I'm up." Kate slipped into her white chenille robe and opened the door. Mrs. F. stood in the hallway in her green robe and leather slippers.

"What's wrong?" Kate said, alarmed.

"It's Carolanne. Romeo scratched at my door, and I followed him downstairs." They both headed down the steps, Kate in her bare feet. "Carolanne is out on the porch. I can't tell if she's sick or had too much to drink. She's passed out cold."

Kate tightened her sash. "Carolanne doesn't drink, Mrs. F."

"Then she's sick."

Through the door and out on the porch, Kate and her landlady hurried to Carolanne. Curled up on the porch swing, she moaned. Kate shook her shoulder. "Carolanne, wake up. Come on, wake up."

"I'll get some smelling salts." Mrs. F. rushed back inside. Kate lifted Carolanne. Her face told Kate everything. Wet with tears, her mascara had made black rivulets down her cheeks. Her lips, once bright red from her lipstick, were pale. Carolanne opened her eyes and whimpered. Then she moved into Kate's arms.

"Oh Kate."

"What's wrong, honey?"

"He broke it off. He's dumped me."

Mrs. F. appeared with the smelling salts. "Good, she's awake. I guess she won't need these." She tucked the salts bottle into her robe pocket.

"Help me get her up, Mrs. F."

Together they got Carolanne off the porch and into the house. "What's happened?" asked Mrs. F. "Poor dear's been crying."

Kate looked at Mrs. F. "Her engagement ended."

Mrs. F. pressed her lips hard then said, "That man is the cause of this. I could tell he was no good."

Carolanne began to cry. "He is no good."

Mrs. F. squared her shoulders. "He's a womanizer. What a disgrace."

"I should've known from the start."

"Come on, dear. Sit down and tell us all about it."

"No." Carolanne groaned. "I want my bed."

Kate helped Carolanne upstairs and onto her bed. She set an extra pillow behind her and then sat on the bedside. "You don't have to talk about it if you don't want to."

Carolanne grabbed hold of Kate's hand. "I threw the ring at him."

Kate frowned. "Your diamond."

"Yes, my fake diamond," she blubbered. "He admitted it."

Kate handed her a tissue. Carolanne blew her nose.

"I'm sorry. Don't cry. Is there something I can do? Do you want me to get you some water or warm milk?"

Carolanne's face tightened. She pounded her fists and sat up. "You know what that jerk did? We went out to eat. . .you know, at that bistro. Some redhead came over to our table. She was all over him. When I told her to lay off my fiancé, he snapped at me. We had a row, and he told me to take a cab home. He threw the fare right in my face. Then, to make things worse, he got up and walked off with that girl. How could he do that to me, right there in front of everyone?"

What could Kate say? There wasn't much that would ease the anger and hurt her friend felt. Carolanne sighed. "I guess it was better I find out now rather than later. I rushed into this thing. I should have never gotten engaged so soon."

"You can't blame yourself, Carolanne," Kate said. "It wasn't you that did anything wrong. Peter's going to find out he made a big mistake."

"He'll telephone or come begging for forgiveness. You watch and see." She blew her nose.

"Don't take him back. If he did it once, he'll do it again."

Deep lines creased the edges of Carolanne's eyes. "You don't have to tell me. That girl knew him, called him by name and asked him why he hadn't called. I bet he has a bunch of girls on the side—including me. But not again!"

"If he does call or come by, what do you want us to do?"

"I don't want to talk to him. Tell him to get lost." Carolanne fell back on the pillow. "How has your time with Ronny been? I hope he's not acting badly."

"He leaves tomorrow."

Carolanne sniffed. "Did he kiss you yet?"

Kate felt that amazing sensation float through her. His was a kiss she'd never forget. "You know he did."

"Sad he's shipping out. That's one of the saddest things about being on the home front. Separation."

"I'll be all right. We promised to write to each other."

"Are you in love with him?"

Kate nudged her friend. "Don't tell me you can't tell. With what you know about romance, you should be writing an advice column for the lovelorn."

Carolanne laughed. "Me?" Then she gritted her teeth. "Yeah, tell them what mistakes not to make."

Mrs. F. stood inside the doorway with a tray. "How about some coconut cream pie, girls, and a glass of milk?" She set the tray down and smiled. "Pie makes me feel better whenever I'm blue."

Ruby light streamed through the window the next morning when Kate got up for work. She'd left it open all night, and the room felt cool. She glanced at her clock. Six. Ronny would soon be on his way out of Washington. He'd have a long journey ahead and then out to sea. She whispered a prayer for him as she stepped into the shower. The cool water revived her, and her heart swelled as she thought of Ronny. She had to make it to the station before seven. She could not let him leave without a *see you later* kiss and a promise.

Pekoe jumped up on the bed and curled into a ball. She squinted her eyes and purred. Kate slipped on a blouse, bent down, ran her hand over the sleek fur, and said, "Sleep here all you want, kitty. I won't be home till late."

Downstairs, she grabbed a muffin. Mrs. F. yawned from the kitchen table, teacup in her hands. "Work early, Kate? Have some coffee before you go."

"I need it. Thanks."

"You can have some sugar. I got it yesterday. What time do you have to be at work?"

"Nine." She filled a cup and gulped down the coffee. "I tossed and turned all night, thinking about Ronny. I've got to get to Union Station and see him off."

"Take the auto, Kate. It'll be faster."

"But I. . ."

"You can drive, can't you?"

"Well, yes, but it's your car. . .your prize car."

Mrs. F. twisted her mouth. "Dear me. You think I'm worried you'll dent it? The chances of that happening are slim. I've let Carolanne drive it. Why not you?"

"You're awfully kind." She threw her arms about the old woman's shoulders. "I'll put gas in it."

"Forget it. Wish that handsome sailor of yours well for me." She got up from the chair and reached inside her icebox. "Here, take this to him."

"What is it?"

"Cheese and lettuce sandwiches. No tomatoes. They make the bread soggy if you don't eat them right away."

Kate sighed. "He'll love them. I spied a tin of tea cookies. Do you mind if I take him some?"

As if swatting a fly from her face, Mrs. F. gestured to the cabinet. "Take the whole tin."

Kate threw open the cabinet door and brought down a yellow cookie tin. "You're sure? Don't you want the tin back?"

Mrs. F. laughed. "Tell him I want it back. That'll give him incentive to come home, second to you, of course."

Kate filled a paper sack, kissed Mrs. F.'s cheek, and headed out. Mrs. F. stood at the gate as Kate climbed into the Model A. "Turn the key, Kate, then the valve under the dash for the fuel."

"Never fear, Mrs. F. I know the rest."

"Do you? And what's that, exactly, if you don't mind me asking?"

"The spark goes up and the throttle down."

"You've got it. Godspeed, Kate."

Mrs. F. waved a hearty goodbye as Kate let out the clutch, and the auto sputtered down E Street for Union Station. Papa taught her to drive when she was fourteen. She handled their tractor well and other pieces of machinery. But to drive a polished Model A was a new experience. It sputtered and backfired while rolling down the lengthy Washington, D.C., streets, while other vehicles zipped past her.

Union Station seemed unusually busy that morning. She found an empty parking space outside the building and hurried inside. The enormous vaulted ceilings, the ornate plasterwork and frescos, distracted her only a moment.

"Richmond, Norfolk, now boarding!"

She had to hurry. He'd be on the southbound train. As she rushed, people bumped into her, skirted around her, and slowed her down. Her breath heaved. The domed ceiling echoed every sound. Men in uniform kissed their girls, hugged loved ones, boarded the trains that simmered on the tracks.

A station porter pushed a cart full of luggage, and Kate stopped him. "Gate 5, please."

"That way. You'd better hurry. It's about to pull out."

Clutching her purse under her arm and the bag in her hand, she rushed on. *Don't leave yet. Please don't leave yet.*

Steam. Whistles. The smell of oil. The low chugging of engines. Crowded platforms. People waving American flags. Kate hurried along the train, scanning the crowd for Ronny. Soldiers and sailors hung out the windows kissing their girlfriends and wives. They were smiling and speaking words of comfort to their ladies.

"I love you, dear. Don't worry. I'll be home before you know it."

"Take care of Mom, Dad. I'll write as soon as I can."

"Better start picking out a wedding dress. When I get back, we're getting married."

The next car down, she saw Ronny. She stopped and soaked in what she saw. Dressed in his whites, he stood out from all the rest, his profile against the jet colors of the train. The sun shone on the tips of his short brown hair and across the insignia patch on his arm.

She called out. "Ronny!" and lifted her hand. He turned his head, let go of the railing, and rushed to her.

"Kate!" He pulled her into his arms. "I didn't expect you—"

"I couldn't let you leave without saying, 'See you later.' I couldn't sleep all night thinking about you. I'm going to miss you, Ronny. I'm going to miss you so much."

Ronny kissed her. The conductor blew his whistle. "All aboard." Ronny looked back at him, then put his hands around Kate's face. "I've got to go. I love you, Kate. You understand. I love you. I think I always have, ever since the first day I saw you in pigtails."

Kate felt the burn of tears well in her eyes. "I love you too."

"Will you be my girl?"

Her heart skipped a beat and her limbs went weak. "Yes."

One last kiss, and then he picked up his seabag. Kate put her hand over his arm and walked with him to the step. "Take this. Mrs. F. didn't want you to leave hungry." She handed him the bag.

Ronny smiled and looked into the bag. "Boy, I'm going to enjoy these. Pretty soon I'll be eating K rations."

"Last call. All aboard."

Tears slid down Kate's cheeks. She whisked them away as sailors pushed past Ronny. Some waved a final farewell to family and friends. His fingertips moved from hers, and in he went. Kate skipped down to the windows. She had to see him one last time, burn his face into her mind. Steam buffed from beneath the train and onto her legs. The wheels squealed and she stepped back.

Ronny leaned out the window as the train pulled away and shouted something to her.

Kate didn't quite hear him over the din of the engine. "What?"

"Will you marry me?" he shouted.

"Yes! Yes, I'll marry you." She set her hand over her mouth and sobbed.

He waved. "See you later, beautiful."

Kate quickened her pace alongside the train, and when it picked up speed, she stood with her hand raised, watching it until it was long out of sight.

Chapter 11

June 1944

*K*ate folded her overalls and placed them in her locker with her scarf and goggles. The other girls were touching up their lipstick and brushing out their hair.

"What a day. When is this heat wave going to end?" Kate said to Carolanne. "We ought to stop by the creek on our way home and have a dip."

Up went Carolanne's brows. "In the creek? Hmm, I don't know if it's allowed." She giggled. "It'd be fun though. . .for you, Kate."

Kate smiled. "So let's do it."

"Not me, thank you. Not with all those slimy things in the water."

Kate pulled on her socks. "Don't tell me you've never done it, not even in Schenectady."

Betty laughed. "Are you kidding? I bet the only thing Carolanne ever dips her toes in is a milk bath."

Carolanne patted her hair. "I'll take that as a compliment."

Milly slammed her locker shut. "You would, Carolanne."

"What's it to you? Maybe you should try it sometime. Your skin looks like it could use it. How old are you anyway?"

Milly swung her legs over the other side of the bench. "None of your business."

Kate pushed her socks down to her ankles. "Your skin looks fine, Milly. But it's true what Carolanne says about milk baths."

Milly shrugged. "Who can afford it during wartime?"

"No one, really."

Kate finished lacing her shoes, deciding any further conversation with her friend would be outside the locker room away from Milly. Kate tolerated her as much as she could stand. Insult after insult, she bore it by not retaliating. Milly lived a lonely life without her husband, Smitty. He'd been in the North Sea aboard a transport ship when a German U-boat sunk it. It was the reason Buck let her stay on when just about any other employer would have fired her long ago. But as much as Kate tried, she could not break through Milly's hard veneer.

"Gee, Kate. You sure were quiet during work. Missing your sailor?" The insincere comment coming from the bully of the pack did not surprise Kate. "Miss the farm?"

Kate headed for the door.

"Don't worry." Milly stopped her. "You'll be back on your old homestead before long. We're here only for the duration. Once the war is over, we'll all be sent back to the kitchen. . .you to shoveling horse dung."

Kate struggled to smile, not to let the woman get the best of her. "When that happens, you should visit sometime. I might even let you ride Penny."

"Penny. Silly name for a horse. Is that all she's worth. . .a penny?"

Kate put her clip earrings on. "Penny is a thoroughbred."

"I'm of the opinion they should send those animals to the butchers. We're already rationed on beef. At least use them for dog food."

Carolanne took Kate by the elbow and walked out with her. "Don't let her get to you, Kate. She's afraid of what will happen when the boys return. She's got no husband and will need to find another means of income."

"I feel sorry for her."

"You're intimidated by her. You're not a rug to be walked over."

"I don't have it in me to be mean back. I'm not married, and yet I miss Ronny so much I could cry myself to sleep. I can't imagine what Milly feels."

"At least you have someone to miss," Carolanne said.

Kate looked at Carolanne. "You should meet my brother Brad when he comes home. You'd like him, and he knows how to treat a girl. He's not a wolf like Peter."

"You think he'd like a gal like me, Kate?"

"Sure, Carolanne. I know he would. You have a good heart, and Brad likes a girl with a good heart. I think you and he would be a perfect fit."

"Why didn't you say so before?"

"I mentioned Brad and you didn't seem interested. After all, he's serving and not around to take you out."

"I have a hard time sitting at home, that's for sure. I've been out with some guys since Peter and I broke off. But nothing serious. I'm glad I dodged that bullet."

"Maybe you could start writing to Brad."

"I'd like to. Do you have a photo of your brother?"

Kate opened her handbag. "I've got a new one in my wallet." She pulled it out and showed Carolanne her brother in uniform. "He looks older than when he first went in."

"Wowzer. He's handsome." Carolanne winked at Kate. "But not as handsome as your Ronny. Have you heard from him, kid?"

"I got a letter last week. He's doing okay, but you know our guys won't tell us everything they're seeing. I don't even know what ship he's on. I have to address my V-Mail to the Department of the Navy."

Carolanne leaned close to Kate. "Try not to worry, Kate. He'll come home."

"It's hard not to. I don't like it. The feeling is terrible."

"It's human nature, as long as you don't let it destroy you."

"Some people say that if we worry, we've lost our faith. I don't believe that. It pushes me toward God, to trust Him that everything will be all right. After all, Jesus took our burdens for us."

Carolanne's face softened. "Wow. I never thought of it like that. You talk about God the way my grandmother used to. She'd say, 'Carolanne, you'd better be in the habit of praying, because you're going to need it.' She was right."

Outside, the sunlight blinded Kate. She pulled down the brim of her hat and headed for the gate. "Let's walk today. I don't want to take the bus. The fresh air will do us good."

Washington skies soon clouded up with stretches of wispy clouds. Would it rain and break the heat wave? A Greyhound bus streamed by, and she wished she could be on it, that the wretched war would end and she could be home with Ronny. For the last year she had spent her days off at the Rock Creek Stable. The owners allowed her to ride free. She was skilled in the care of horses, so it was a good trade to groom them. The horses she rode were gentle like Penny and used to trotting over the paths above the mossy banks and rippling water. It saddened her in some ways that that was all the horses knew since there were no open fields for them to race over.

Down on E Street, rain began to fall. The girls hurried through the front door before getting soaked.

"A letter is on the side table for you, Kate," said Mrs. F. as she came into the hallway from the kitchen. "I wish it were from your Ronny. But it's nice to get a letter from home."

Kate snatched up the envelope. "I'll read it in my room."

Mrs. F.'s radio in the sitting room stopped playing the music she loved. An announcer came on and said that the president would be addressing the American people. Kate looked at Carolanne and Mrs. F. "Could it be the war is over? We better go in and listen."

"I suppose you girls haven't heard." Mrs. F. wiped her hands across her apron. Her hands shook and her face looked as pale as the pie dough she kneaded. "Our troops have landed in France."

The radio crackled. Mrs. F. sat on the settee with Romeo on her lap. Carolanne had the newspaper spread out on the floor. As for Kate, she sat in a chair near the fireplace with her legs bent up on the cushion. Pekoe snuggled beside her as rain pattered on the window. Her thoughts were mixed, and she realized it did no good to assume what Roosevelt was about to tell the nation.

A voice came over the radio. "Ladies and gentleman, the president of the United States."

Kate clutched her hands. *Please let it be victory, Lord.*

Then the words came that every American listening to the radio heard in their homes, in the stores, the barbershops, and pubs.

> *My fellow Americans: Last night, when I spoke with you about the fall of Rome, I knew at that moment that troops of the United States and our allies were crossing the Channel in*

another and greater operation. It has come to pass with success thus far.

And so, in this poignant hour, I ask you to join with me in prayer:

Almighty God: Our sons, pride of our nation, this day have set upon a mighty endeavor, a struggle to preserve our Republic, our religion, and our civilization, and to set free a suffering humanity. Lead them straight and true; give strength to their arms, stoutness to their hearts, steadfastness in their faith.

They will need Thy blessings. Their road will be long and hard. For the enemy is strong. He may hurl back our forces. Success may not come with rushing speed, but we shall return again and again; and we know that by Thy grace, and by the righteousness of our cause, our sons will triumph.

They will be sore tried, by night and by day, without rest— until the victory is won. The darkness will be rent by noise and flame. Men's souls will be shaken with the violences of war.

For these men are lately drawn from the ways of peace. They fight not for the lust of conquest. They fight to end conquest. They fight to liberate. They fight to let justice arise, and tolerance and goodwill among all Thy people. They yearn but for the end of battle, for their return to the haven of home. Some will never return. Embrace these, Father, and receive them, Thy heroic servants, into Thy Kingdom.

And for us at home—fathers, mothers, children, wives, sisters, and brothers of brave men overseas—whose thoughts and prayers are ever with them—help us, Almighty God, to rededicate ourselves in renewed faith in Thee in this hour of great sacrifice.

Many people have urged that I call the nation into a single day of special prayer. But, because the road is long and the

desire is great, I ask that our people devote themselves in a con-
tinuance of prayer. As we rise to each new day, and again when
each day is spent, let words of prayer be on our lips, invoking
Thy help to our efforts.

Give us strength too—strength in our daily tasks, to redou-
ble the contributions we make in the physical and the material
support of our armed forces. And let our hearts be stout, to wait
out the long travail, to bear sorrows that may come, to impart
our courage unto our sons where-so-ever they may be.

And, O Lord, give us faith. Give us faith in Thee; faith
in our sons; faith in each other; faith in our united crusade.
Let not the keenness of our spirit ever be dulled. Let not the
impacts of temporary events, of temporal matters of but fleeting
moment—let not these deter us in our unconquerable purpose.

With Thy blessing, we shall prevail over the unholy forces
of our enemy. Help us to conquer the apostles of greed and racial
arrogancies. Lead us to the saving of our country, and with our
sister nations into a world unity that will spell a sure peace—a
peace invulnerable to the schemings of unworthy men, and a
peace that will let all men live in freedom, reaping the just
rewards of their honest toil.

Thy will be done, Almighty God. Amen.

Kate, Carolanne, and Mrs. F. sat still and silent. Each of them had tears in their eyes. Kate's heart pounded as she drew in a deep breath and released it.

"Oh God help them," she whispered. Tears flooded her eyes. Could Ronny's and Brad's ships be a part of this dangerous mission?

"Kate?"

She looked at Carolanne. "Ronny and Brad are both in the Atlantic."

"And you think they'll be in the Normandy landing?"

"I'm not waiting." Kate sprang from her chair. "I'm going to church."

"Now?"

"Come with me if you want."

"I'll get my hat." Mrs. F. took her old straw cloche from the hall tree. She clapped it on her head as she pressed her lips together then said, "We'll go in my auto."

"I haven't been to church in a long time, Kate," Carolanne said. "But I'm coming too."

Chapter 12

Kate paused on the sidewalk in front of the granite brick church. She gazed up, awed at its immense size, luminous stained glass windows, strong columns, and massive door. It threw a shadow as far as the middle of the street. The door stood open. Its pointed arch caught the sunlight as it came through the breaks in the trees.

The churches in Washington were like gothic cathedrals compared to the humble white clapboard churches back home. Crowds gathered, ascended the steps, and walked solemnly inside. Unlike Sundays, there were no smiles on their faces. Worry creased every brow. Little conversation passed between them, only a few whispers.

With Carolanne on her left and Mrs. F. on her right, Kate fastened her eyes on the painted red door and its cast-iron works. With her friends, she stepped through it into the vestibule. The cool darkness of the interior forbade the heat from entering. Silence dominated the nave, except for a few coughs and faint sounds of weeping. Sympathy for the wives, mothers, sisters, and girlfriends overwhelmed Kate. She thought of Mother. She needed to call home and speak to her, comfort her somehow.

As the three slipped into a pew, Kate saw Betty Foster on the opposite side several pews forward. She was on her knees, her hands clutched and shaking, her eyes shut tight. Kate nudged Carolanne gently. "It's Betty."

"Should we—"

"I don't think so. Someone is with her. Probably a relative, and those must be her children seated next to her."

Throughout the night, people prayed on their knees and clung to each other in the pews. Burdened souls poured out their hearts to the Almighty. In despair Kate clung to her faith and pleaded for the thousands of lives facing their darkest hour—and for the life of her brother on the USS *Nevada* in the Atlantic, and for the man she loved and promised to marry.

✍

Mrs. F. kept her radio on over the next several days. The news coming out of Europe had Kate on pins and needles. She sat on the porch steps with a cup of coffee in her hands. Dawn had come and soft pink and blue clouds streaked the sky. Rosy hues splashed over the concrete sidewalks and curbs of the city.

The normal pace of a Wednesday had lessened as anxious people sat by their radios waiting for news. She could hear broadcasts coming from Mrs. F.'s open window, where the sheer curtains fluttered like butterfly wings in the soft June breeze.

"*Yesterday the United States Baseball League canceled all games across the nation,*" blared from the speaker. "*A patriotic gesture on the part of the players boosted the hopes and dreams of their fans.*" The kids in the neighborhood didn't understand and went on playing. The empty lot over on D Street attracted both boys and girls. Their dusty faces and clothes were a cheerful sight to be seen. Their laughter even more so.

The Allies have sunk several German U-boats in the Bay of Biscay. In France the 82nd Airborne Division has taken Sainte-Mère-Église, and the Canadian 50th Division has taken the town of Bayeux. In other news coming out of Europe, the Nazis have executed prisoners of war. This broadcast will continue as more news comes into our station.

The voice broke off, and dance music swelled. Kate's heart turned and twisted in her chest. *Ronny. Please, God. Protect him.* She closed her eyes to journey back to that night when he held her in his arms to "Moonlight Serenade"—their song.

She flinched when the screen door behind her squeaked open. "Come inside and have some breakfast, Kate. Carolanne is up."

"I'm not hungry, Mrs. F.," Kate told her. "Coffee is fine."

Mrs. F. sat down beside Kate. "It won't help Ronny or your brother if you don't eat. You have to keep up your strength, you know."

Kate looked at Mrs. F. and smiled. "Your coffee is as good as my mother's. It'll hold me over until lunch."

Mrs. F. shook her head. "Lunch at the canteen? Spam loaf and powdered eggs? That's not food."

"It's not so bad."

"Humph. It's not good, I wager."

"Would it make you happy to pack lunches for Carolanne and me?"

Mrs. F. slapped her knees. "Nothing would please me more." She stood to go inside. "Have you called your family yet?"

"Yes. I spoke to my parents last night."

"How are they holding up?"

"They're worried but strong in their faith. They're hoping to get word from Brad soon."

"Have you told them about Ronny?"

Kate hugged her knees and smiled. "Oh yes. When the war ends and he comes home, they want me to bring him to the farm. I'd love that." She looked over her shoulder at Mrs. F. "I came this close," she said, pressing her thumb and forefinger together, "to getting him on a horse. We never got the chance to go to the stables."

"I'm sure it did them good to hear your voice. I'd like to meet your mother. Maybe at your wedding, Kate."

"My wedding." Kate sighed. "He did ask me."

"And you said yes."

"I would have been crazy not to."

Kate sipped her coffee while the radio played on. Artie Shaw's clarinet hit a high note in "Begin the Beguine." Kate set the empty cup on the saucer beside her and rocked her knees. "I wish you could have seen us at the USO. I'll never forget that night."

Mrs. F. set her hand on Kate's shoulder. "There'll be other nights like that, Kate. Now come on. You pay me every week for room and board. If your mother finds out you haven't been eating, she'll be upset. Why add to her worries?"

Mrs. F. looked out across the street. "Oh dear. The Miltons have a gold star in their window."

Kate looked in that direction too. Gold stars were becoming more and more common. "It wasn't there yesterday."

Mrs. F. sighed. "I don't know how much good it will do, but I'll take them over breakfast."

Kate pictured Mother standing at the stove flipping pancakes. She always had a smile on her face when cooking. Papa would head out to the barn after downing a huge stack smothered in syrup.

He'd let the horses out into the field unless the night had been warm enough for them to linger in the meadow.

Kate missed caring for the horses, and on mornings like this, she longed to be home. But time and again the newspapers, radio, and newsreels told her the most patriotic thing she could do was to support the war effort by working a job a man had to leave. The pay was good, and she had extra to send home. Heading back to Hope Valley would need to wait.

She got up and smoothed down her dress. "It's going to be a long day. I won't be home until late. They've stepped up production."

Mrs. F. put her hands on her hips. "We'll have a nice meal tonight. I got my hands on a good brisket, and I'll fix us a real good supper. Something you can look forward to."

When Carolanne breezed out the front door, Kate hugged her surrogate mother goodbye and they set off for the Navy Yard. She and Carolanne walked down to the bus stop. Since the invasion, the usual riders they stood with were quiet. Even the streets with all the usual traffic seemed subdued.

Carolanne talked less. Kate occupied her mind with Ronny. She sent V-Mail every week and said prayers every night. The news coming out of the Atlantic equaled the brutality coming out of East Asia, and as much as she tried, she could not help but fear for him and her brother.

"Kate!" Buck's booming voice startled her. "What's wrong with you? You're not concentrating." Buck shook her shoulder. "You missed welding that piece all the way to the end. You can't be making those kinds of mistakes."

She set down her torch and lifted her goggles. "I'm sorry, Buck."

He leaned down. "Don't let it happen again."

Nodding, she picked up her torch and lowered her goggles. "I promise to be more careful, Buck."

"Make sure you are, or you might find yourself out of here." Buck set his unlit cigar between his teeth and began to walk away. Then he turned and placed a hand on her shoulder. "I shouldn't have said that, Kate. It's not a firing offense. You're one of the best workers in the shop. So try not to let worry affect your job."

Kate looked up at him. "Thanks, Buck."

Buck walked back to his office. The other girls were silent with their eyes on their work. Kate knew she deserved Buck's reprimand. If she failed to do her job, it could cost lives. She adjusted her goggles and forced thoughts of Ronny from her mind. *Do it right, Kate. Do it right for him, and for Brad too.*

Chapter 13

That evening when the sun sank low, Kate walked home beside Carolanne. The temperature had only gone down a few degrees. People sat out on their porches or on the front steps. Soothing music flowed from radios. Kids played games on the sidewalks.

As they turned the corner, Kate stopped and touched Carolanne's arm. "Look at that."

Up ahead, a woman in a floral dress ran down a pair of brick steps. A man in a drab green Army uniform exited a cab and set down a duffel bag. The woman reached him, and they fell into each other's arms.

Carolanne sighed. "If that ain't a sight for sore eyes, Kate, I don't know what is."

A soft smile lifted Kate's mouth. "I'm happy for them. You think they're husband and wife?"

"With the way he's holding on to her, I say they are, or soon will be."

The couple went inside the stucco townhouse, his arm around her waist and her head on his shoulder.

"It's a sign, Kate," Carolanne said.

"I believe it. The boys will be home soon. . .all of them."

The front of Mrs. F.'s house glowed with magenta sunlight. Inside, Kate set down her purse and took off her hat. Pekoe curled around her legs. She crouched down and scratched the cat's ears. Mrs. F. poked her head out from her kitchen door. "Mail came. I haven't sifted through it yet, but you girls look to see if there is anything for you. There's a box for you, Kate, from your mother."

Kate rushed over to the box sitting beside the table in the foyer. She pulled it open, lifted a card, and smiled.

"My mother thinks of everything," she said to Carolanne.

"What is it?" Carolanne bent over the box.

"She's sent me fabric squares. They're for quilts. And look, a little sewing box." She opened the lid. "Needles. Thread. Just about everything I need."

"I hope I got something," Carolanne said.

Picking up the stack, Kate thumbed through the envelopes. "A letter for Mrs. F. One for you, Carolanne. It looks like a bill though." Kate handed Carolanne her mail.

"You're right. It's from that store downtown—Woodward and Lothrops. I couldn't resist the polka-dot blue dress I saw in the window."

On top of the stack lay a letter-size manila envelope. Kate's name and address was typed and showed through the slot on the front. The three-cent eagle stamp had "Win the War" on it. The return address—WESTERN UNION TELEGRAM.

Something dreadful clawed in her chest and up her throat. It attacked her heart, and she felt it quiver. She covered her mouth, and tears blurred her vision.

"I've got an idea," Carolanne said. "Let's go shopping on Saturday. I can't wait to see the new styles coming out. Nothing like a new outfit to distract the blues."

Kate said nothing. She stared at the envelope and then looked at Carolanne.

"Kate, what's the matter? What's happened?"

Kate showed her the envelope. "I'm afraid to open it, Carolanne. Will you?"

"Sure, honey. Hand it over."

"It can't be about Brad. My parents would get the telegram if it were. Ronny would have made his aunt and uncle the ones to be notified, not me." She shook her head. "I don't understand."

"If it's about Ronny, he must have made you a beneficiary, since his parents aren't living and he has no siblings. That, and the fact you're engaged to him."

Beneficiary. Engaged. Kate swallowed and went into the sitting room. The windows were open and a warm breezed blew inside. Mrs. F. had left the radio on, and Bob Hope told a joke in the evening broadcast that incited rounds of laughter. "How do you do, ladies and gentlemen? This is Bob Mosquito Hope with the USO somewhere in the South Pacific."

Kate drew in a breath and crossed the room. Any other day she would have laughed too, but not now. Her nerves were on edge. She turned off the radio and sat down.

The silence that followed added to the tension racing through Kate. Her heart drummed in her temples. She wanted to have faith and be strong, but others had faith and strength too, and they had gotten the worst news imaginable.

Carolanne sat down next to Kate and put her hand on her shoulder. "Do you want me to read it aloud, honey?"

Kate nodded. "Yes. Please, Carolanne."

Carolanne slipped her finger through the envelope and pulled out the telegram. She unfolded it and looked at it. Kate watched her eyes, her expression, and drew in a breath. "Please, go on. Read it out loud to me."

Carolanne looked at Kate. Sadness etched her face. She swallowed and then read, " 'It is with regret we must inform you that Petty Officer 2nd Class Ronald Lee Jordan USN, since the sixth day of June during the Normandy Invasion, has been reported. . .' "

Kate slapped her hands over her eyes. "Stop! I don't think I can hear anymore. He's dead."

Carolanne moved closer beside her. "He's not dead, Kate. It says he's missing in action." Carolanne showed Kate the telegram. "See. Look what it says. It doesn't mean he's gone. They'll find him."

"Missing in action means they don't know. I don't know."

"Maybe the rest will tell us something." Carolanne pointed to the words on the telegram. ". . .has been reported missing in action while in service of his country. The Department appreciates your great anxiety, but details not now available and delay in receipt thereof must necessarily be expected. To prevent possible aid to our enemies and to safeguard the lives of other personnel, please do not divulge the name of his ship or station or discuss publicly the fact that he is missing. From the office of the Vice Admiral. . .Chief of Naval Personnel. . .' "

Grabbing the box of tissues on the corner table, Carolanne handed one to Kate. "He could have been wounded and is in a hospital in France. He could have lost his dog tags. Maybe he can't speak the language. He could have been—"

"Captured? The next worst thing to death. A slow death." Kate pictured Ronny taken by the Nazis. Pushed into line. Abused, beaten, and marched off to a prisoner of war camp. She'd read enough in the newspapers, seen enough in the newsreels, to know what they would do to him. He'd starve. He'd fall sick. They could shoot him and dump his body in a mass grave.

As these painful thoughts attacked her mind, she broke down. Tears ran down her face. Her throat tightened and she gasped.

Carolanne put her arms around her. "There is hope, isn't there? A lot of hope."

Kate swiped the tears from her cheeks. "I'll wait for him. . .pray for him."

"And I'll hang right in there with you, honey."

"I'm not supposed to discuss this publicly, so we can't say anything to anyone at the Navy Yard. I'm going to tell Mrs. F. though. She has a right to know."

"You have my word on it, Kate." Carolanne squeezed Kate's hand. "I'll wait with you. Okay?"

Kate nodded and slid the telegram back in the envelope. She'd write home that night to Mother but not say a word about the news she received.

✿

Letters were written and the envelopes sealed and stamped. Kate knelt beside her bed, hoping her tears would be enough to bring him back. Her mortal being had no such power. Yet the balm of prayer brought a quiet peace into her soul.

As the night deepened and the moon rose higher, she grew weary. She could hear a mockingbird serenade her from the tree next door. She went to the window and looked out. She could see it silhouetted in the moonlight, hear the beauty of its song. She closed the curtains and turned. Mother's letter lay unopened on the nightstand.

"Oh Mama. I wish I could call home and tell you what's happened. I wish I could hear you pray for Ronny. I know you do for Brad. Dear Brad."

She sat on the bedside and opened the letter. Mother's fluid handwriting had a happy note to it. Slowly, to absorb every word written, Kate began to read.

"Dear Darling Kate," she read aloud. "Your father and I have happy news. Brad has been given an honorable discharge. He'll be coming home to us within the next week. We are praising God that he made it through Normandy and has been awarded the Navy Cross. It is joyous news, isn't it, darling? I've no doubt you'll be getting happy news soon about Ronny. Mrs. Mullins brags about him all the time, and she's so pleased you and he are 'an item.'"

The rest of the letter contained news about the girls finishing out the school year with good grades. Penny's foal had arrived. Mother included a snapshot of a husky colt they named Admiral. Kate lay back on her pillow and stared at the photo. She ran her finger down the length of the colt's white streak. Her eyelids grew heavy, and soon sleep came. . .with dreams of Ronny exiting a cab and her rushing into his waiting arms.

Chapter 14

Waiting proved to be excruciating. It deprived Kate of sleep and made her restless. War work occupied her time, but her thoughts drifted the moment she set down her torch.

Did Mother sense something wrong? Was that the reason she sent a box of fabric squares and encouraged her to make a quilt? Mother's gesture encouraged Kate, but as she told Carolanne, "I still cannot get the stitches even," and pricked her fingers, her thoughts fixed on Ronny.

Summer ended with mighty thunderstorms pushed by cold fronts that came down from the northwest. Autumn arrived in all its glory, and by the end of October, the trees had lost most of their leaves due to rain. Only the leaves on the pin oaks clung to their moorings.

Everyone seemed to be growing weary of the war. Rationing had started to take its toll months ago, and the black market prospered like it did in the days of Prohibition. Misty drizzle fell in November, the skies gray and dreary with short breaks of sun.

Kate sat on the bench in the locker room and drew off her rain boots, glad the last day in the workweek had arrived. She went out onto the factory floor and grabbed her welding torch and goggles. But before she could begin, Buck's secretary walked over.

"Buck wants to see you upstairs, Kate."

Kate set down her goggles. "Do you know why?"

"Yeah, I do, but I'm not allowed to say." She walked away, and the door glided shut.

"Yikes, Kate. What's he want, I wonder?" Carolanne said.

Kate scooted back her chair. "I'll let you know."

Buck's office always smelled of cigars. The smell sickened Kate. When she entered, she wrinkled her nose. He sat at his desk smoking a cigar, looking like Winston Churchill. Perhaps he meant to.

"Have a seat, Kate." He dumped ashes onto a plate.

Kate lowered into the hard wooden chair. "Is something wrong, Buck?"

"Yeah, there is. You knew when you took this job, if a serviceman came home, he'd get his job back. You do remember that, don't you?"

Kate gripped the arms of the chair. "Yes, I remember."

"I'm letting you go, Kate, but only for that reason."

She stared at the floor. "I see." Then she looked at him. "Can't you give me something else to do?"

"Sorry, Kate." Buck drew on his cigar and blew smoke rings. Then he leaned over his desk. "Listen. All the other girls are going to face the same thing. Guys that were drafted are required to serve one year, so they'll want jobs. It's only right we give them back. You served your country. Now it's time for you to go back to the farm."

Kate stood. "I never did get to bake that pie for you, Buck."

"No, you never did."

She held her hand out to him. His hand wrapped around hers.

"Tell Carolanne I want to see her." Kate nodded and headed back to the floor. She wiped her hand along the front of her overalls, disgusted by Buck's smelly mitt. Now he wanted to see her best friend.

Carolanne had her eyes fixed on the piece she was working on. Kate set her hand on her shoulder. "He wants to see you."

Pulling off her goggles, Carolanne's mouth fell open. "What's going on?"

"His secretary may not tell you, but I will. He's let me go."

Carolanne's face turned pale. "Golly, Kate."

"It's okay. It's so a serviceman can have his job back."

Carolanne huffed and tossed down her goggles. The other girls looked at her. "You think so. I'm not so sure. I think he's getting rid of us because he never has liked the idea of women doing this kind of work."

"I think he's telling the truth, Carolanne, no matter how he thinks of us. We were the last ones hired."

"So we're the first ones out?" Carolanne slapped her hands over her hips. "What'd he tell you? Go back to the farm? Well, I don't want to go back to sweeping up a store."

Betty spoke up. "It's not the end of the world, Carolanne. Maybe you can find another job in Washington."

Off Carolanne stormed, through the door and up the metal stairs to Buck's office.

❦

Kate and Carolanne left the Navy Yard with their chins up. Kate paused on the street and pointed to a passing cloud. "You see that silver lining, Carolanne? We're going to find ours. It's not so bad to leave the Yard. The war will end and life will be better."

Back at the house, Mrs. F. blew her nose. "I've called a cab," Kate told her. "I'm heading home." She put some folded bills in her landlady's palm. "It's the rest of the rent for the month. Please don't argue and take it. I left my address on the table in the kitchen."

"If you get another telegram—"

"Forward it to me, please."

Kate finished packing and went down the hallway to Carolanne's room. "See you, *honey*. I'll think of you whenever I hear that word."

Carolanne let out a cry and threw her arms around Kate. "Take care of yourself, kid. Gosh, I'm gonna miss you."

"I'll miss you too. Come see me, okay?"

"Sure."

"We did a good job helping with the war effort. We should be proud."

Carolanne nodded and wiped the tears from her face. "You're right about that."

Romeo whined. Kate patted his head and went down the steps. Mrs. F. followed her out onto the porch when the cab pulled up. The handle on Kate's suitcase had been repaired, and as she gripped it, she thought of the day she ran into Ronny. The pang of missing him deepened as she paused on the porch and went down the steps. If by chance he were to return to Washington, he would not find her on E Street.

"You will tell Ronny where I am, Mrs. F., if he happens to come back? Give him the address at the farm and tell him everything that's happened."

"Of course I will, dear." Mrs. F. kissed Kate's cheek. "Don't worry."

Carolanne stepped out onto the porch dressed in her blue polka-dot dress and matching hat with a camel hair coat draped over her shoulders. She put on her sunglasses. "I'm leaving too."

"You're going back home?"

"I don't really want to go back to working in the store. But what else is there for me to do?"

"Why don't you come home with me? It'll give you time to find your bearings."

Carolanne threw out her hands. "You're the best friend a girl could ever have." Then she turned to Mrs. F. "Don't worry, Mrs. F. I left the remainder of my rent on the table. I want you to have it for all you've done for me." She leaned over and kissed the landlady's cheek.

"You look like you're headed for Hollywood, Carolanne," said Mrs. F.

"Nah, the farm with Kate. I'm leaving with my head up, looking like a million bucks." She looked Kate up and down. "You look pretty as a peach, Kate," she said." You'll have every soldier's head turning at the station."

"That would be a dream come true if it were Ronny."

"Maybe we'll run into that wolfish Peter. He'll see what he missed in dumping me."

Carolanne went down the steps in her open-toed shoes and joined Kate at the gate. Holding their heads high, they walked down to the curb. The cabbie opened the door for them, and they got inside.

The cab pulled away and rolled down the street. Kate looked out the window. *Come home, Ronny. I have to fulfill a promise.*

❧ *Chapter 15* ❧

Kate set her head against the window of the bus, closed her eyes, and pictured her family. Papa would be training the new colt, Brad mucking out the stalls. Mother cutting her homegrown pumpkins to make filling for pies. The girls would be sitting in the kitchen separating the seeds. How they must have grown since she'd been away.

Although it came as a blow to lose her job so soon, Kate greeted the change with joy. For it to be perfect, Ronny would be beside her. No word had come of his whereabouts.

The bus slowed into the station. Together with Carolanne, Kate stepped out onto the platform. Porters tipped their hats, and the stationmaster recognized her, welcomed her home. Patriotic garlands hung from the station roof, and Kate smiled. She felt proud of her brothers and Ronny. Of all the men serving. She prayed their sacrifices, whatever they may have been or would be, would be honored down through the decades.

"Can you walk in those shoes?" Kate asked Carolanne.

Carolanne glanced down. "Pretty sure I can. How far is home?"

"A half mile."

"Well then, let's get going."

Before sunset, Kate saw the farm in the distance. "It hasn't changed." She led Carolanne to an opening in the split-rail fence, and as they lugged their suitcases, Mother came out on the porch then hurried forward.

"Papa, it's Kate. Brad. Girls. Your sister is home!"

There were hugs and kisses. Mother shed tears. Jan, Jean, and Amber threw their arms around Kate's legs. Kate hugged each of them and paused to look at their faces. "You three have grown, especially you, Amber."

"I've never seen so much happiness in a family," said Carolanne.

Kate grabbed her. "Mama, Papa, this is Carolanne. She's my best friend I wrote to you about. We worked together and lived in the same boardinghouse."

Carolanne gave them a shaky dip. "Pleased to make your acquaintance."

Kate smiled. She remembered Carolanne had said the same to her when they met. Papa nodded and Mother took Carolanne's hand. "You are most welcome to our home."

Coming around the corner of the barn, Brad stopped and threw down the bridle in his hand. He ran forward. He looked older, his brown hair lighter from days under the ocean sun, his skin swarthy. The emotion of that moment, when Kate embraced her brother, overwhelmed all. Kate put her arm through his. "Come here, Brad. I want you to meet my friend Carolanne."

The gleam in Brad's eyes when he laid eyes on the swanky girl from Schenectady could not be missed. Kate saw a shy regard in her friend's eyes when she lifted her sunglasses.

From inside the barn, Penny neighed. "She knows I'm here." Kate peeled Carolanne away from Brad and hurried into the barn. She stroked Penny's nose, hugged her neck. "You remember me, don't you, girl? And look at that babe of yours."

Carolanne stood back. "Come meet her," Kate said.

Hesitant, Carolanne stepped up to the stall and reached out. Penny sniffed her. "She's as pretty as her picture." She turned to Kate. "That photo you showed me of Brad doesn't do him justice. He's handsomer."

Ushered into the house, they sat down for a feast. After the dishes were cleared, washed, and put away, the family talked late into the night. Finally Mother sent the girls off to bed.

"Papa, Mama, I'll be getting up at dawn," Kate said. "Before I go up, I have a present for you, Mother." She opened her suitcase and took out a box tied in string.

Mother smiled. "How kind." She untied the string, opened the box, and unwrapped a red McCoy pot. "Oh! A McCoy. The real thing. It's beautiful, Kate."

"It's a small one but so pretty. Mrs. F. had some like this one, and when I admired hers, she offered me one to give to you."

"I've never seen one this color." Mother stood and hugged Kate. "I'll treasure it, Kate, and I'll write a thank-you letter to Mrs. F."

"I knew you'd like it." Kate yawned. "Sorry, I'm so sleepy. I'll say good night."

She kissed her parents' cheeks and left Brad and Carolanne sitting alone in the living room in front of the fire.

Kate watched the snow fall outside her window. "Dear God, when will I get word about Ronny? Is he safe? Is he alive? Please, Father. I love this man. I want to live out my life with him.

Please bring him back to me."

She stepped away from the window. Her eyes wet with tears, she looked at her sisters. Each slept peacefully in the double bed. Carolanne slept in the spare room. The house was quiet.

She smiled and laid an extra quilt over the girls. Amber stirred, and Kate hushed her. What did the future hold for the three of them? At least they'd grow up free. The cost heavy—Brian gone from their lives, Brad and Ronny sacrificing the best years of their youth to fight an evil that cost the lives of millions.

When Kate told Brad about Ronny, he hung his head in sorrow. He told Kate there was nothing she could do but wait and pray. He was a comfort to his sister—and to Carolanne. Anyone that doubted love at first sight had never experienced it. Kate had, and so had Carolanne and Brad.

She had a photo of Ronny in a frame, his eyes so brave and true that when she looked at it her heart pounded. If she hadn't made the decision to take the job at the Navy Yard, they might not have met again. So much good came from a single decision, including gaining a best friend in Carolanne and contributing her skills to the war effort by mending, fusing, and cutting with a little oxy-fueled torch.

Without a sound, she slipped out of the room. She paused outside her parents' bedroom door. Then she tiptoed down the hallway to the staircase. The stairs creaked as she made her way down to the first floor and to the hall tree where she had hung her winter coat. She slipped it on and then tugged on her wool-lined boots.

She picked up the family's old brass lantern, raised the wick, and lit it. The flame grew inside the globe and brightened. She pulled back the latch to the front door and stepped out into the wintry night. Turning up her coat collar, she plodded across the yard toward the barn. Golden lantern light fanned over the snow. Reaching the barn, she stepped inside. Her mare rallied from the floor of hay, looked out from her stall, and snorted. The colt slept.

Kate hung the lantern and went to Penny. She ran her hand down the length of the horse's nose and sighed. Penny made a low sound of contentment and nudged Kate. She set her head against the horse and cried. "Oh my love. Where are you? I need you."

The barn door creaked, and she thought it must be the wind. The other horses stood in their stalls. Their stallion, Commodore, pounded his hooves and shook his mane. Kate went to him, took a sugar cube out of her pocket, laid it flat in her palm, and gave it to him.

Again, the door creaked, and Kate turned. "Who's there?"

A figure moved forward, etched by the lantern light.

As the figure stepped inside, Kate realized it was a man. She stepped back and reached for the hay fork that stood against the wall.

"Hi, Kate. Wanna cut a rug, kid?"

Kate's heart leaped. She sucked in a breath and dropped the hay fork. "Ronny?"

"We don't have a big band to dance to. Still, we could dance slow."

"Ronny!" She ran forward and into his arms. "Ronny," she breathed against his neck. "You're here." She ran her hands through his hair. "You're alive. You're safe." Tears ran down Kate's cheeks— tears of joy and not sorrow. "I prayed and prayed."

He rubbed his cheek against hers and then kissed her—long and soft. Passion and joy were in it, the bond of love in their embrace. He touched her face, caressed her hair, and whispered, "I love you, Kate." They held on to each other, forbidding anything to separate them.

Ronny went down on his knees and brought Kate with him.

They fell back against a mound of hay and stayed in each other's arms as morning shone through the cracks in the barn roof.

"What happened, Ronny? You were listed missing in action. We didn't know if you were alive or. . .dead."

"Normandy is what happened, Kate. I suffered a concussion from a bomb that exploded near me. For months I was laid up in a French hospital. I lost my dog tags and was unable to speak. What happened to me that day is what a lot of guys suffer after seeing battle."

"I didn't know. That's so horrible, Ronny." She cuddled up to him. "I'm so glad you're here. How did you get home?"

"I was transferred to a hospital in England and then back to the U.S. I served my time and was given an honorable discharge and the Navy Cross." Ronny turned to her and smiled. "Hey, kid. Didn't you get a telegram from the Navy Department telling you I was coming home? You looked surprised when I came through the door."

"It would have gone to Mrs. F.'s house. She said she'd forward whatever came, but maybe it got lost."

"Well, what about that old broken suitcase? Did you ever get it fixed?" he asked.

She turned her face up to him. "Yes."

"Good, because you're going to need to pack. I'm going to marry you, Kate. And when I do, I'm going to take you to a quiet place in the mountains for our honeymoon."

Smiling, Kate sat up and leaned on her elbow. "I'll never forget the day you asked me, while the train was pulling away. I stood there until I couldn't see the train anymore, and when I got that telegram, my heart just about burst."

"I'm here now. I made it."

"Yes, thank God, and I can't wait to tell everyone." She started to get up, but Ronny pulled her back.

"Before you do, I've got something for you." He sat up, and from his pocket he pulled out a small black velvet box. He opened it, took out the ring, and slipped it on her finger. "It's to seal my promise. I hope you like it."

The moment Kate threw her arms around his neck, the barn door opened. "Kate! There's a telegram for you." Papa rushed inside holding a manila envelope. "Says it's from the Navy Department. . .probably about Ronny."

Kate and Ronny burst out laughing and sat up. Papa, standing in front of them, wide-eyed, crossed his arms. "Well, praise the Lord and pass the ammunition. Look who it is!"

Author's Notes

Dear Reader,

My mother, Rose Robertson, whom I mention in the story, used to say there is a silver lining to every cloud. Ronny and Kate found theirs. So did Carolanne and Brad.

Look up, and you just might find yours.

V-Mail, Short for Victory Mail
Among my father's papers, I found a sheet of paper labeled V-Mail. It was a poem from his mother dated August 29, 1943, commemorating the anniversary of his enlistment, sent to the USS *Vulcan* 7th Division through the fleet post office in New York City. V-Mail was the chief method of correspondence with soldiers stationed abroad. It reads as follows:

Dear Son,
Today being the anniversary of your enlistment, I have written another little poem. I hope you like it. Remember, I am no poet, so here goes.

> *"To You My Son"*
> *I*
> *One year ago this very day,*
> *a young and gallant boy said*
> *farewell to his home and*
> *friends and sped to the call.*
> *II*
> *He knew he had a job to do.*
> *His country to defend. So what*
> *could be better than the good*
> *ole USN.*

III

We all are very proud of him
and all his buddies too. For
they are doing a fine job, and
will bring the Victory thro.
Mother

Victory Gardens

These gardens were a wonderful way to show support for the troops and feed a family during a time of rationing. There are videos on YouTube from that era showing how people grew their gardens. They consisted of vegetables and fruit, and the women of the household learned the art of canning, like my grandmother Bessie Robertson, who had five sons and two future sons-in-law serving in the military.

Popular WWII Big Band Leaders and Their Music

Big Band music lifted the spirits of servicemen and those on the home front. As Kate and Ronny discovered, swing dancing requires skill and stamina. The USO sponsored dances, and Big Band orchestras made appearances on the home front and abroad. Swing was banned by the Nazi Party in the late '30s. They labeled it degenerate, but the "swing youth" rebelled and continued to listen and dance to swing. Brutal suppression followed. German youth were arrested, and many were sent to concentration camps. As for the Allies, the music played on.

Glenn Miller: America suffered a great loss when Glenn Miller went missing over the English Channel in December 1944. His music was the most popular swing music from 1939 to 1943.

"Moonlight Serenade": I chose this song for the title and because of the lyrics, which express the romance of the time.

Benny Goodman: He was known as the "King of Swing."

"Sing, Sing, Sing": To me this was the most electrifying and definitive song of the swing era. When it was recorded in 1937, it became a blockbuster and is still played today as the quintessential song of World War II.

Artie Shaw: Shaw was another popular American band leader during the swing era. He was a clarinetist, composer, writer, and actor.

"Begin the Bequine": Another romantic dance song of the 1940s. In case you're wondering what *beguine* means, it's a popular dance of the Islands of Saint Lucia and Martinique that somewhat resembles the rumba.

"Stardust": This was my parents' song. It was written by Hoagy Carmichael in 1927, and lyrics were added by Mitchell Parish in 1929.

"I Could Write a Book": Written by Richard Rodgers and Lorenz Hart and first recorded in 1940.

The phrase "Praise the Lord and pass the ammunition" is taken from a patriotic song of the same name written by Frank Loesser in 1942, describing a prayer from a Navy chaplain as he joined in the fight against the enemy during the Pearl Harbor attack.

 **Rita Gerlach** lives in central Maryland with her husband and two sons. She is a bestselling author of eight inspirational historical novels, including the Daughters of the Potomac series, of which the book review magazine *Romantic Times* said, "Creating characters with intense realism and compassion is one of Gerlach's gifts."

Only Forever

by Lauralee Bliss

"The LORD does not see as man sees; for man looks at the outward appearance, but the LORD looks at the heart."
1 SAMUEL 16:7 NKJV

Chapter 1

Springville, New York
Spring 1943

*W*hat a dreadful sight. Sheets and blanket tossed in a heap on the bed. Overalls and a soiled shirt dropped atop dirty sneakers on the floor where feet once flung them away. How her heart prayed this was just a dream. Maybe when she awoke one morning, the war would be over and her family reunited to laugh and share in good times again. Marilyn Pearl blinked, hoping to find her only brother, Rob nestled beneath the cover of Grandma's crocheted blanket, snoring away, until Dad rang the bell to summon them to early morning chores on the farm.

But no. The nightmare persisted. Rob was gone. Two weeks ago he walked off with several buddies to join the Army. She watched through glazed eyes as the train pulled away, bound for Buffalo. The new recruits, bearing wide grins and shiny eyes, hung out the train windows and waved with enthusiasm to their families. Rob waved too, his smile reaching from ear to ear as if he couldn't wait to be a part of it all. To him this was an adventure of a lifetime. But his departure left Marilyn feeling hollow inside.

Marilyn tried to swallow the thick lump of sadness clogging her throat. Rob would expect her to be brave. He would want her to carry on in his absence with her head held high, her heart determined to live while he did his best in the fight against their country's enemies. Everyone's lives had turned upside down since Pearl Harbor over sixteen months ago. Goose bumps still rose on Marilyn's skin at the message broadcasted over the radio, along with the dreadful sights and sounds on the newsreels in the theater of ships on fire and brave men dying terrible deaths. The country stood frozen, stunned by it all. Then came the nationwide mourning. Dad had hung black ribbon and displayed the flag as did everyone in Springville. Rob in particular seemed affected by it. He constantly listened to the radio for updates on the war effort. Then came the news over the ensuing battle in the Pacific. Rob would pace about, letting the chores go undone, instead talking with friends and classmates who wanted to join up and defeat the enemy.

Then one night Rob announced at the supper table that he was joining the Army. Marilyn expected Dad and Mother to heartily object. Dad sat stone-faced and silent. Mother wiped her eyes with a handkerchief. Marilyn thought at first he might be pulling their leg. When she realized he wasn't, she then prayed he would change his mind. She asked why he had to go.

"It's my duty," he said, plain and simple.

And that was that. Now he was gone for who knew how long. Gone to face a terrible enemy on the battlefield. Gone to witness the sights and sounds of war. Gone, and all of them changed forever.

"Marilyn, I need some eggs to make the pancakes," Mother said from the hall when Marilyn appeared out of Rob's room. She noted Mother's stately frame, clothed in a dress sprinkled with flowers and covered by an apron with frilled edges. Mother's thick bobbed brown hair was so unlike her own blond locks.

The busyness of life left little time for grieving. There was lots to do with Rob gone. Dad would likely have to hire someone to help with the planting and the cattle. She had twice as many chores these days, it seemed. But Marilyn could not forget Rob's look of defiance and his willingness to leave behind all he knew to fight the enemy. Shouldn't they all be as determined here on the home front to keep on living? Even if it proved difficult?

Marilyn grabbed the basket from Mother and hurried down the stairs and out to the chicken coop. Warm breezes blew, tousling her hair and brushing against her face. How glad she had been to see the flowers unfold from the cold ground that had seen another harsh winter here in western New York.

Just then she caught sight of the rounded form of a robin as it flew to the ground, landing on a pair of skinny golden legs. It hopped about in search of worms. "Hello!" Marilyn greeted the symbol of springtime, and the robin looked up at her, cocked its head, and flew away. The sight made her rejoice. Just as winter hadn't lasted forever, their family wouldn't be separated forever either. God would bring forth a new season, just like the spring. In the meantime, He would protect dear Rob and bring him home when the time was right. Until then she would occupy herself as the Bible said.

Marilyn greeted the flock of chickens and pawed through the straw to find several eggs. The sun streaming into the coop aided in the search. At least the day had not dawned dark and dreary. That would have intensified her melancholy this day. With the rays of sun, just like God's rays of love shining in the midst of uncertainty, hope stood fast.

An engine sputtering to life alerted Marilyn to Dad starting up the tractor for plowing the nearby fields. With the snow nearly gone and the temperatures warming, work to prepare the ground for the summer crops had begun in earnest. Mother had already worked the garden soil to plant the early spring vegetables of lettuce, carrots, and beets. She allowed Marilyn to tend a portion of the garden last year, and Marilyn had grown an enormous pumpkin and several other squashes, some tomatoes, and rows of green beans. The pumpkin had earned the grand award at the fair last year before being turned into pies and baked goods, with Rob exclaiming over the pumpkin pie at Thanksgiving—his favorite. Just the thought of him enjoying the pie from the fruit she had lovingly grown brought a sudden tear to her eye. It made her determined to continue growing vegetables, perhaps another pumpkin to bake tasty treats and send them to him and the men come fall, should he be away that long.

As Marilyn returned to the house, carrying the basket of eggs, a familiar black truck rolled up the long dirt road. Tires spit up mud along the way. She recognized the driver immediately—with his straight brown hair and large wire-rimmed glasses. Dear Arthur McNamara. No doubt he wanted to find out how things were going since Rob left. He always seemed to be around for every major calamity in her life. Sort of like the sun after the passing of a storm, never failing, always present. Slowly he exited the truck, bearing a distinct limp from his weakened left leg as he ambled over to her. The weakness came from a brief tangle with polio as a youngster. Many people had been stricken by the disease, including President Roosevelt. The handicap kept Art from joining the fight, which was fine with Marilyn. She could use a friendly face during these difficult times.

"How are you doing?" he now asked, thrusting his hands deep into his trouser pockets. The patchwork sweater he wore set off his broad shoulders.

"I'm doing all right," she said, uncertain how else to answer.

He followed her into the house where Mother greeted him with a pleasant hello and then busied herself making pancakes. In no time Art was served a tall stack with a heap of butter dripping down the sides.

Art drew up a stool, sat down, and picked up the nearby pitcher to pour a hefty amount of syrup over it all. "There's a lot of talk in town. Everyone is upset about the war and the men leaving."

"As they should be," Mother said, flipping pancakes on the griddle. "These are terribly unsettling times."

"I wish I could do something to help," Marilyn mumbled, sitting down beside Art and resting her cheek in her hand. "I feel so useless with Rob gone."

"There's plenty to do around here," Mother said, giving her a knowing look.

"I know I want to grow more pumpkins. You remember that one I grew last year, Art."

"There's a reason it won the ribbon," Art said between bites of pancake. "It was enormous."

"I think it would be nice to send Rob something tasty once a pumpkin gets big enough. Maybe pumpkin bread or muffins or something. He could be home by Thanksgiving in time for pumpkin pie too. Don't you think, Mother?"

Mother sighed "I don't know, dear. All we can do is pray. But I'm not sure those terrible men who began this whole thing will just lay down their weapons and give up. I'm afraid it could be a very long conflict."

This was not something Marilyn wanted to hear. She wanted the family together again as soon as possible. She glanced over to find Art looking at her solemnly through his glasses. The deep brown eyes appeared kind and compassionate. If only they hadn't known each other forever, she might have considered him as a possible boyfriend. But Art could never be that. Instead, he filled the role that Rob had left behind. The brother looking out for the sister. The brother that would go with her on tramps into the woods, looking for neat plants or fishing at the nearby pond. The brother with ideas about life when she didn't understand. The brother with a friendly smile or a kind word. That would do nicely in this time of need.

"Speaking of growing pumpkins. . . I saw something interesting in the store today." Art set down the fork and took his time limping back out to the truck. When he returned he thrust a big piece of paper into Marilyn's startled hands. "Mr. Winston had several of these plastered on the store windows. I saw this and thought of you."

Marilyn stared at the poster of a woman dressed in overalls and a red kerchief, holding an oversized basket of vegetables in one hand and a hoe in the other. The printed words shouted out:

"War Gardens for Victory! Grow Vitamins at Your Kitchen Door!"

"Maybe this is something you could do," Art suggested. "I saw a couple of other posters Mr. Winston had received. I think it's a campaign the government is starting up. Growing a vegetable garden."

"But I already grow a garden."

"Most don't. You could teach them. Look what you did with that pumpkin. The vegetables raised can help the men and our country. I think maybe this is something worthwhile you could do."

Marilyn gasped. The flame of purpose that had gone out suddenly burst into life.

⚘

Marilyn's long fingers tightened around the poster, her blue eyes widening, her head nodding in a way that made her blond hair bounce up and down at her shoulders. Arthur stared for another moment, considering her attractive features, before diverting his attention to his breakfast. If Marilyn knew how much he loved her, he feared she would send him away for good. He'd loved her as long as he could remember. He would defend her to the last. Even when they were in grade school and she cried when a boy had stolen the sack containing her lunch, she never knew that he'd ordered the boy to give it back. And then he watched her, with her tearstained face, eat the peanut butter sandwich on white bread, and he felt like a hero.

Years had passed since then, and each year Marilyn had grown more beautiful. But time had failed to change the relationship between them. They remained good friends, but that was all. Art would think so much about their wedding day that he nearly took the money he had earned at the store and bought a ring to ask for her hand under a starlit sky. But he hadn't quite drummed up the courage to go that far. The money remained hidden in his dresser drawer. He feared, as most men did, that she would say no. Then all would be lost, and he'd look like a fool for trying.

As the years went by, he continued to watch over everything that concerned her and act the role of a good friend. And right now she was broken up over Rob joining the Army. He had to do something to lessen the sorrow and the long days without her brother here. God had drawn his attention to a poster hanging in the store window of the mercantile where he worked. Memories of Marilyn with her winning pumpkin and accompanying ribbon flashed through his mind. He asked his boss, Mr. Winston, if he might borrow the poster.

Now in her excitement Marilyn began crinkling the precious poster. He ought to say something, like the poster was borrowed and he needed to return it. But he didn't dare disrupt her sudden joy. He liked seeing her so excited.

"So what is this, really?" she asked, scrutinizing the poster. "It says here in small print to send away for more information on how to begin a community-wide Victory garden project."

"We're going to need to save the food supplies for the men. Some supplies are already hard to come by. Families need to start growing their own during this hard time, and you know everything there is to know about gardening. You could be the one to start a Victory garden project here in Springville."

Her cherry-red lips curled into a smile. He would never admit to anyone except himself that he truly wanted to taste those lips one day. *Do best friends ever kiss? Or is that strictly for lovers?*

Marilyn suddenly lurched to her feet. "Where's the writing paper?" she asked her mother. "I'm going to write a letter immediately and tell them we need help here in Springville. I'm sure lots of families will plant gardens. We can grow vegetables like pumpkins. And Rob's company can get pumpkin bread. That would let them know we care and are supporting them."

Marilyn had been brought out of her sadness to the glory of life, like a dormant tree of winter springing forth in bud on the breath of a warm wind. Art silently congratulated himself for hearing God and being a bearer of hope by way of a simple advertisement. While it may be a Victory garden of vegetables she hoped to spread, he prayed for a Victory garden of married life within her heart one day soon.

But now she busied herself with writing the letter to the government and asking Art how she should word it. He offered suggestions, like telling them about her brother's sacrifice for the war effort, her gardening skill, and her willingness to help others learn about gardening. With each suggestion he gave, her lips curved into another delighted smile, accompanied by a rosy tint to her cheeks to complete the attractive picture. When she finished writing, she stood to her feet, cleared her throat, and read the letter out loud.

"It sounds lovely, dear," Mrs. Pearl said. "I could type it up on your father's typewriter."

"Oh, would you? Thank you, Mother!" She twirled on one heel, the dress she wore spinning about her. She then stopped and looked down at her apparel as if to read Art's thoughts that were concentrated on the way the dress spun around her legs. The next words surprised him. "I can't wear this anymore." She batted at the dress.

"What do you mean?" Art asked.

"I mean I need to put on my overalls, like that poster shows. I've got work to do in the garden today, just as soon as I mail the letter. It's going to be the best garden ever, and everyone will want to come see it."

"A good idea." Art stood, wobbling. The muscles in his bad leg would spasm if he sat too long in a certain position. He massaged the cramped muscles and shook his limb to loosen it. For most people a bad leg would seem the end of life. But for Art, who knew little else since he was only two years of age when the polio struck, the handicap had become a part of him. Mother used to tell him that when he got to heaven, God would give him a new leg, and he could run as he pleased. Until then he remained content with his lot.

Now he said, "I'll be glad to help and—"

"No, no," she interrupted in such a way that he stepped back. "What I mean is, you need to plant your own garden, Art. If this is to be a community project, every family needs to participate."

"We have a garden." He didn't think any more needed to be done in the garden at this time, since Mother finished planting it. "But I can grow a few pumpkins," he added, joyful at seeing the smile return to her face.

"Swell!" Marilyn clapped her hands. "This is turning out to be a good day after all."

Art heard the distant tap, tap of the typewriter as Mrs. Pearl typed up the letter to Washington. "I'll post the letter while I'm in town so you can work in the garden," he added.

"Oh Art. What would I do without you?"

His heart leapt in his chest. *That's why you need me in your life.* He thought of the best thing she could do for him, chief of which was a resounding "Yes!" to the engagement ring he planned to have in his pocket one day. Maybe while in town he ought to stop by the store and check out rings, if that wasn't too presumptuous. High time he put faith to these thoughts of his. God was with him, and He spoke loud and clear about faith. Surely the Lord would guide him in the most important steps of life, such as marriage. Then would come the walk down the aisle of the church as husband and wife, to the cheers of family and friends, and onward to a perfect life.

⚜

Two weeks later Art gunned the truck toward the Pearl farm. On the seat beside him rested a large envelope, postmarked Washington, D.C., with Marilyn's name clearly written on it. He knew what it must be and couldn't wait to give it to her. Thankfully, during his work at the store the letter carrier stopped by, and Art thought to ask if there was any mail for the Pearl family. Lo and behold, the carrier's bag contained the large envelope from the United States Department of Agriculture.

The truck lurched to a stop before the house. Art was barely able to exit the vehicle with his infirmity, too eager to give his sweetheart the revered envelope. "Where's Marilyn?" he breathlessly asked Mrs. Pearl, who was sweeping off the front porch.

"In the garden, of course. What's all the excitement?"

"I think she got a response to her letter about the Victory garden project." He walked as fast as his leg would allow until he spotted the fair woman on her hands and knees, digging a small hole in the soft earth with a spade. "Marilyn!" How he loved saying her name. It was like a song. She stood in response, dirt covering her knees, her face ignited by the rays of the sun. He waved the envelope in the air.

Marilyn raced over. "Oh wow. Is it for me?"

"Yes. From the government."

She wiped her hands on her overalls before taking the envelope. "I can hardly open it, my hands are shaking so much."

Art stood by expectantly, enjoying the look of wonder and delight on Marilyn's face, though a part of him was curious to know what the government had sent.

She scanned the contents. "They are looking for people to set up a gardening committee in each major town." She held up a flyer. "They are asking every family to plant a garden to help in the war effort. And now is the time." She then took out a hefty booklet. "They even sent a leader's manual on Victory gardens! Why, they must think *I'm* in charge! Holy cow."

"So they want you to head up a committee in Springville?" Could it be that his Marilyn would be trusted with such an important duty and be famous all over town?

"They want it done, that's for sure. It's for victory, they say. A Victory garden for our brave men. For Rob." Her voice trailed away as she looked over her garden. "I must finish the early planting as quickly as possible if this is to be the garden display for everyone to see. I will need to show the folks how to plant one. And then there will be all kinds of nice pumpkin bread and pies to send to the men."

The happiness in her voice, accompanied by the rich smile, made his heart sing. No, he wasn't celebrating an engagement, as he so wanted. But to see her happy after the last few weeks of sorrow since her family was turned upside down by Rob's departure spurred hope that one day her happiness would turn to the two of them. And if it took a Victory garden to bring victory to them as a couple, Art would embrace it with everything in his heart.

Chapter 2

*M*arilyn, it's for you! A man from Washington, D.C. I think he may be from the government. Hurry!"

Marilyn nearly dropped the basket of clothes she had plucked off the outside line. A man from the government was calling her? What on earth could he want? She couldn't have possibly done anything wrong. Quickly she laid down the basket and went into the hall where Mother stood holding out the ebony receiver and stick phone to her. Marilyn grabbed both with shaky hands, holding the receiver to her ear and speaking into the mouthpiece. "Hello?"

"Do I have the pleasure of addressing Miss Pearl?" came a deep voice.

"Uh, yes, this is Marilyn Pearl."

"My name is Quentin Hardy, and I've just been informed that you are interested in creating a Victory garden committee in the town of Springville. Have you received our literature yet?"

"Yes, yes I have." Her fingers began to cramp from gripping the stick phone. "I already have friends who are interested and—"

"Excellent! I will be arriving in the area in a few days and would very much like to meet with you to talk about starting a committee and spreading the word about the Victory garden project. It's one of the main ways we are going to defeat our enemies, as I'm sure you are aware. Would you be able to meet with me to discuss this?"

A sudden bout of nerves, coupled with breathlessness, made the words difficult to say. "Y–Yes, of course! Anytime."

"Excellent. How about Thursday around two? Is there a good place in town to meet?"

"Yes, oh yes." Marilyn managed to choke out the name of a popular hangout in town that served burgers and pop, to the soft chuckle of Mr. Hardy on the other line.

"Fine, fine. I'll see you then."

Marilyn could hardly replace the receiver, so overcome was she at the call. Mother stood in the doorway staring, her hand over her heart. "It wasn't bad news, was it? I can't for the life of me think of why someone from the government would be calling. Unless something happened to Rob. . . ." Her words became garbled under the emotion of their meaning.

"Oh no, Mother. It was a Mr. Hardy, wanting to meet with me and talk about the Victory garden idea. Isn't that wonderful?"

Mother nodded and, with a loud sigh of relief, collapsed into a chair. "I'm so glad it's just that. I suppose I worry too much."

Marilyn wished she could have told Mother what was happening during the call rather than have her be so anxious. As far as they knew, Rob had yet to be called up to active duty. He was still training somewhere in Alabama. But they knew orders could come at any time, and he would likely head for Europe or maybe even the Pacific—no one really knew. But for now she put aside any thoughts of poor Rob in the middle of some terrible war to consider the meeting to come. The simple letter she had sent must have some-how intrigued Mr. Hardy enough to come all the way here to talk about the Victory garden project. *Thank You, God. Only You could make this work out so well.* And with that she hurried upstairs to put on her overalls. Time to work in the garden, especially with an official arriving in just two short days.

Mother's voice echoed up the stairs. "Marilyn! The basket of clothes!"

She sighed and sheepishly returned to pick up the basket. The goal of a Victory garden in every home here in Springville sent her feet flying, and her heart filled with purpose. She needed something worthwhile in life, and now, thanks to Art, it appeared on the brink of reality with the pending arrival of Mr. Hardy.

After putting the clothes and towels in their proper places, Marilyn hurried to don overalls and a checkered shirt while consid-ering the meeting to come. And not just any meeting, but one with a government official. A wave of anxiety washed over her. What if this Mr. Hardy thought her too young? What if she made a fool of herself during the meeting? What if she couldn't think of the words to say? She dare not try to do this alone. She could use moral sup-port and knew just the person to ask.

Once more she hurried downstairs to the telephone. "So what do you think, Art?" Marilyn asked after telling him about the call from the government while trying to keep her hands from shaking.

"Wow. I had no idea someone would be calling you about your letter."

"Isn't it swell? Mr. Hardy's going to tell us exactly what to do. We'll get a committee set up then tell everyone how to plant a gar-den. I just know we'll grow lots of vegetables to help the men and our country."

She heard a loud whistle and smiled to herself over Art's way of expressing his excitement. He agreed to be there for the meeting if it would help, and Marilyn assured him it would. In all honesty, she had no idea what she would do without his help. Art had been a part of her family's life forever, it seemed. They had grown up together. Sometimes, though, she caught him eyeing her strangely. Like when she came to church one Sunday wearing a light blue dress and Mother's nice hat. He stepped back when they greeted each other, his face beet red, and she thought he fumbled to hold on to the church pew. Or maybe it was all her imagination. She had no romantic interest in an old-time chum like Arthur McNamara. It would be like having a relationship with a relative. She shook her head. Art would always be that good friend and substitute brother while Rob was off to war.

Just then a horn sounded. Marilyn rushed outside to see a car rattle down the country lane over the rocks and dirt. She stared in shock when she glimpsed the faces of the town councilman and his wife beaming in her direction. Mr. and Mrs. Tompkins! She looked down at her dirt encrusted overalls and sighed. *Oh dear.*

"There she is!" Mr. Tompkins exclaimed. "We had to come out here and tell you. I just got an important call from a Mr. Hardy about the Victory garden project."

Marilyn stared in stunned surprise. "He called you?"

"Yes indeed, young lady, and I gave him your phone number and told him you're the one wanting to set up the Victory garden project in the community. What an excellent idea, by the way. Very plucky of you."

At that moment she felt neither the pluck nor the confidence to take up the call suddenly placed on her. In fact, she felt more like a plant withering in the hot sun. "I think it's a good idea to help the men and our country," she managed to say. "Mr. Hardy and I had a conversation about it, and we are meeting later this week to go over the details."

"How nice. Seeing as you're dressed for work, let's take a look at this garden of yours, shall we?" All at once another fellow came out of the back seat of the car wearing a suit and toting a large camera. "I brought along a reporter from the *Springville Journal*. He wants to do a story about your ideas for a garden."

He wants to do a story about me? Marilyn nearly gasped out loud. "There's not much to take pictures of right now," she said faintly, wishing she was wearing that cornflower-blue dress and Mother's hat with the blue ribbon. "It's still early and hardly anything is growing."

"No matter. Just to have a picture of the planted rows and maybe one or two of you with a hoe in your hand will look excellent in the newspaper."

The reporter nodded in agreement.

Marilyn could not believe all this was happening. She felt dizzy and short of breath, wondering what else lay around the corner. She led the way to the modest garden plot, thankful the rows appeared straight. To her delight the abundant sunshine last week had warmed the soil enough for the first of the lettuce seedlings to emerge. Mrs. Tompkins squealed in glee while the reporter snapped picture after picture and even knelt down on the ground to take some close-ups.

"This is marvelous," cooed Mrs. Tompkins. "What have you planted so far?"

"Lettuce, radishes, beets, and carrots." Then she added, "But you must come to the shed where Dad built a greenhouse. There I've started the late-season plants." Confidence began to build as she guided them to behind the rear shed where Dad had pieced together a greenhouse. "In here I'm growing tomatoes, squash, and, of course, my famous pumpkins."

"What do you mean by 'famous' pumpkins?" Mrs. Tompkins asked.

"I should have said 'award-winning.' Come, I'll show you." Excited by their wide eyes, Marilyn led the merry trio back to the house where Mother stared in shock before quickly undoing her apron.

"Why, hello!" Mother greeted.

"Hi, Sally," Mrs. Tompkins said. "We're interviewing Marilyn and learning more about her Victory garden plans. Isn't this exciting?"

Marilyn was grateful Mother invited them into the living room while she fetched the blue ribbon from the state fair. When she returned, Mother was serving tea and her delicious French breakfast puffs. "This is the grand award I won at last year's state fair for growing the largest pumpkin," Marilyn said proudly. "This made me consider how much I could help the men if I grew even more pumpkins to make bread and muffins and cookies to send."

The reporter took pictures of Marilyn and the ribbon from different angles and then set down the camera to scribble in a pad.

"This is simply lovely," Mrs. Tompkins said with a sigh. "You have a wonderfully talented daughter, Sally. You must be so proud."

Mother smiled and nodded. "Marilyn succeeds at everything she puts her mind to."

Marilyn watched the reporter write that statement down also. She couldn't help the warmth of pride trickling through her. After they had all drunk their tea and eaten the cinnamon-and-sugar-coated muffins, the Tompkins stood to their feet, as did the reporter.

"We hate to go," gushed Mrs. Tompkins, "but there are a few other places we want to visit where we've heard of folks starting up their gardens. I must say, this is the best news our community could possibly have. Toodle-oo!"

Marilyn and Mother both stood near the front door as the trio paraded on by and out to the car. As Marilyn watched them leave, she tingled with excitement. Everything was moving at such a fast pace, it seemed difficult to grasp. She couldn't wait to tell Art what had transpired, and all because he had seen a poster in the store window one day.

"Dear me, look at you," Mother said, shaking her head. "Standing there with these important people, and you dressed in dirty dungarees."

"I worried too, but they were fine with it. Especially since the article is about the Victory garden."

Mother chuckled as she gathered up the dishes. "You do beat all, young lady. What will happen next around here?"

Marilyn had to wonder too.

Art had just finished up his work hours at the store and stood ready to buy the evening edition of the paper when the Tompkins burst in, their faces shining. Mr. Winston, the proprietor and his boss, smiled in return and asked what all the hubbub was about.

"Did you hear we have an important official coming all the way from Washington?" Mrs. Tompkins's high-pitched voice rang out. She never failed to gather a crowd, and shoppers began to scoot over from the neighboring aisles to hear the news. "They have taken a great interest in our town and want to come here personally to help form a Victory garden committee. A reporter for the *Springville Journal* went with us to interview Miss Marilyn Pearl about the project and take pictures. Isn't it exciting?"

Art stared in stunned amazement. His Marilyn had just been

interviewed by a reporter? He glanced at the papers neatly stacked in a wire rack, envisioning Marilyn's smile adorning the front page with the words OUR OWN SPRINGVILLE DARLING OF THE VICTORY GARDENS PROJECT. He wondered how she would handle such fame. Nothing like this had ever happened to her before.

"Well, how about that?" Mr. Winston said. "It's about time our communities are finally being noticed by those hotheads in Washington. I've been saying all along it's the ordinary citizen that's going to win this war." He sighed. "And we need to prepare. Just today I was told there would be limited delivery of canned goods. Once I'm out of my principal stock, then what?"

The jubilation on the faces of the Tompkins quickly melted into frowns and narrow eyes. "I don't understand," Mr. Tompkins said.

"Food shortages are already happening. So it's good that young gal is raising up the gardening idea. Why, me and the missus have planted a garden for many years now. Everyone needs to do it. I'll be glad to continue advertising about it here at the store. And I will see to stocking more gardening tools and seeds."

Art's mind spun with this news, and certainly Marilyn's did too. All this seemed good and right, but it could also spiral into things no one anticipated. Like unexpected fame and fortune. It could be good in a way, he reasoned. Were they not to be lamps on a pedestal? To shine their light in the darkness, especially at a time like this? What could be darker than a country at war after the devastation of Pearl Harbor and ready to wage horrific battle on foreign soil? Still, he felt the need to ask Marilyn if she was all right with the way things were progressing and if she could face the spotlight of fame.

"Of course I can!" Marilyn answered with her nose in the air after

Art's arrival at the Pearl farm.

Art rather liked her impudent way of expressing her feelings, with the late afternoon sun shining on her upturned face. "It just all seems to be going pretty fast," he began. "I mean with Washington calling and then the Tompkinses rushing out here with a reporter."

"We need to start planting now. Why, the lettuce in my garden is already up. I'm glad everyone is interested."

Art couldn't argue with that. A news story plus the meeting to come would surely get the project up and running. "Have you read over the Victory garden leadership guide that came in the mail so you're ready for the meeting?"

"A little. I suppose I should read it all, but with everything else happening. . ." She paused. "How about I give it to you, Art, and you can tell me what's in it? I have so much to do right now, I dearly need the help. It just looks so long and complicated. I'd only need to know what's most important though."

"Well I—"

"Oh, and don't forget I need you to come on Thursday for the meeting with Mr. Hardy. It's at two o'clock. You have to help me remember everything. It's too much for one person to think about, and I don't want to be alone."

Art enjoyed hearing her needful plea, even if at first he was taken aback by the expectation of knowing the contents of the leadership manual. But leaders of all kinds had assistants to do their work for them. Maybe this was what he was called to do for now. Even if his heart wished things were different and he could instead become a husband to a beautiful and talented wife. He took the booklet to add to his duties then followed her out to the garden and the rows of newly sprouted plants. Art chuckled softly, seeing God's hand at work. No one was more fitted for instruction in gardening than Marilyn. Her enthusiasm could rapidly spread like the wind throughout the town and help others with the goal of growing vegetables.

Marilyn whirled. "Do you see anything wrong? If there is, please tell me right away. I'm sure that government official will want to see my garden. I could also have lots of people coming by here. Maybe I could do some classes, like holding a school. A Victory garden school where everyone can learn how to prepare the soil, till it, plant it, things like that."

The ideas streamed out of her like the water she now poured out of a watering can. While it was good to see her alive with ideas flowing, he only hoped it would not become a burden that she wished she'd never had to carry.

"I think the garden looks fine. God is using your gifts to do something great. I mean, the idea a government official is coming here for a meeting, and with a war going on. How did he know to call you?"

"Mr. Tompkins gave this Mr. Hardy my name. But I wonder how Mr. Tompkins knew I had sent away for the literature?" Art felt the warmth crawl into his cheeks just then, realizing he'd told many customers in the store about Marilyn and the Victory garden project. For now she looked at the watering can and added, "I hope I can do this."

"You can. Just take it one step at a time. It's like planting a garden. We need to make sure we know everything first. Like the information in the booklet. Then we think up new ideas, which you're already doing. We can hold a few community meetings, maybe at the church so everyone can attend." He paused. "Did you ever think you might speak to a hundred townsfolk about planting a garden? Or that a picture of you and your garden would appear in the paper?"

Her hand trembled as she set down the can. "No. All I did

was grow a pumpkin and send my dear brother off to war. I didn't want to sit around moping, waiting for news. I had to get busy with something. Anything." She blinked her long eyelashes over perfect blue eyes and nodded. "I guess if you think I can do it, then I can." She hesitated, and he caught her staring at him. "You know, Art, if you hadn't brought me that poster, no one would know anything about this. I mean, you were the one who got everything going."

The bells of appreciation rang loud and clear. For the first time, hope began to rise. His heart pounded as he wondered if this might be the signal to invite her to share lunch with him. But then she took up the watering can once more and headed for a rain barrel set up beneath the gutter of the barn. In a flash, his courage to ask her on a date fluttered away. "I was only doing what I felt God wanted me to," he said as he followed her.

"And you have. It's as plain as day. How else could everything be working out so well?" She lifted her full watering can up out of the barrel. "And no matter what, it will be good for us and for the war effort. I just know it."

Art sighed. *I just pray it will eventually turn out good for us too, dear Marilyn. After all these years of waiting, maybe we will come together as we work on this gardening idea. And maybe it will grow more than just vegetables. Maybe we will grow a lifetime together.*

❧ Chapter 3 ❧

Marilyn went through three wardrobe changes before she decided on the dress she wanted to wear for the meeting with the government official. First she tried on a plaid affair, but it appeared far too busy. Next came one with fancy trim across the neckline and bodice. She put that one aside also and finally selected a simple green frock without any decoration. Green reminded her of the leaves of springtime and seemed appropriate. Now she brushed out her shoulder-length hair and accentuated her lips with bright red lipstick. Mother stepped into the room to look her over, nodding in approval at the choice of dress, and helped retie the ribbon about her waist into a prettier bow. Mother's hands trembled as she did, leading Marilyn to wonder if she too was nervous.

"Now, you know how to address someone important," Mother said to her. "Since we don't yet know the gentleman's official title, 'Mister' will suffice. Be courteous, don't talk out of turn, and be sure to thank him for coming."

Marilyn nodded, fluffing out her hair with her fingers then turning sideways to examine her profile in the mirror. "Oh Mother, the bow sticks out way too far, don't you think?"

Mother readjusted it before patting her arm. "Have you everything you need, dear?"

"Yes. I'm so glad Art is going with me. He will help me understand everything that's being said." She inhaled a sharp breath. "I just hope I can do this."

"Of course you can. The Lord wouldn't have given this to you if He didn't think you could. You're very capable."

Marilyn couldn't argue with a godly observation, though the compliment did little to lessen the anxiety over her newfound duties—from answering Mr. Hardy's phone call to entertaining the highfalutin Mr. and Mrs. Tompkins when they arrived unexpectedly at her home to receiving comments at the market from neighbors who had heard of the official coming from Washington to see her. Another neighbor came by yesterday asking for pointers in readying the soil for planting. "I know you're right. I mean, already folks are showing a great deal of interest in gardening. That's a good thing, isn't it?"

"Yes indeed. And you are helping people become a part of it all rather than sitting idly by while our dear Rob and others do all the work. I can't begin to tell you how many times the phone has rung with neighbors excited about what is happening. Everyone is coming together in this. You're changing Springville for the better, Marilyn."

While she wished Mother's positive words strengthened her confidence, she remained jittery and unable to swallow down her breakfast oatmeal. She knew she must eat something to be her best during the meeting, and finally managed a slice of bread with Mother's homemade strawberry preserves. *This is the day to rejoice and not to dread*, she told herself.

A horn sounded in the front yard. Art was there in his coal-colored truck, ready to take her to town. Marilyn took up a pad of paper and a pencil, gave one last glance at her reflection in the mirror, and sighed as she wiped a small speck of jam off her chin. "Say a prayer for me, Mother."

"You know I will," she said, waving at Art who waved back.

Marilyn settled into the passenger seat. Art depressed the clutch and shifted the stick to maneuver the truck. "Are you okay?"

"Why? Don't I look all right?"

Art turned bright red and apologized. "I meant you look lovely. I just wanted to make sure you're ready for this. It's a big day."

"I hope I'm ready. It's not every day one gets to sit down with an important person."

"I know you'll do swell. I read over the manual like you asked."

Her face brightened, and she straightened in her seat. "What did it say?"

"It mainly gives ideas on gardening that you already know. What tools you need, what seeds to buy. What places work best for a garden plot. How you know the soil is fertile enough for planting. How to ready the soil and water it. Then once you have vegetables, how to can, dry, or store them in a root cellar."

"I know all that, thank goodness. So there's nothing new?"

Art shook his head. "Not in the gardening part. If anyone knows how to manage a garden, it's you. You grew the prize Springville pumpkin, don't forget. Can't do any better than that."

Marilyn managed a small smile. She could always count on Art for a compliment that helped her feel better.

"But," Art continued on, "you should know the parts of the manual on how to get others involved. Like heading up a committee. There's a lot of information on that. Being a leader of an organization is much different than just caring for your garden. You are responsible for everyone else's garden too. What the community does will reflect on you."

Suddenly Marilyn felt a needle of doubt pop the balloon of confidence. The air began rushing out of her. "Do you. . .do you think this Mr. Hardy will ask me questions about why I want to be the leader of this project?"

"He will try to find out if you're capable, which makes sense. But you've already grown a successful garden. You've also had opportunities to spread the word—"

"Yes, I have," she interrupted. "I did a newspaper interview and met with several who are looking to plant their first gardens. It was exciting, actually."

Art smiled, and suddenly she saw his free hand creeping over to pat hers. Or would he try to hold her hand? He only gave a slight squeeze before returning his hand to join the other on the steering wheel. "Be sure you share those ideas, and you'll be fine. And say these words—'I know that every Victory garden is a blow to the enemy.' You will impress this gentleman from Washington for certain."

Marilyn relaxed a bit, the balloon of confidence regaining some air. She tried not to tap on the car door with her fingernail. In no time the familiar buildings of Springville began to appear, with trees lining the street. Soon came the church, the post office, and the main business district. Finally they came to the favorite eating spot in town where the meeting would take place. Art found a parking place down the street, and she smiled as he limped around to open the car door for her. She tried not to give away what she was feeling at the moment, with nerves as tense as violin strings and dampness collecting beneath the hair at the nape of her neck.

Art held open the door to the joint. The place was jumping,

with every booth taken. Young people jabbered away while sipping pop and eating hamburgers. Only two unoccupied revolving metal stools at the counter remained. Marilyn searched the crowd for any sign of a well-dressed man in a suit and hat with a briefcase in hand but saw no one matching that description. She blew out a sigh that fanned the blond bangs across her forehead, wondering how in the world she of all people was elected to meet with Mr. Hardy.

"Might as well take those seats," Art suggested, pointing at the stools.

"I hope he can find the place all right," she fussed. "What if I messed this up, Art? What am I going to do?"

"Stop worrying." He ordered two chocolate malts. Marilyn smiled. Art knew her favorite drink to calm her jitters, like a big brother would. A tear entered her eye at the thought of Rob. He would likewise try to calm her in the midst of a trying situation. Soon his training would be over, and he would likely be called up to the front. How she wished he could just come home. At least the gardening project gave her something to focus on rather than her brother's stark absence. Who knew what mess she might be in without this project—or Art, for that matter. Marilyn cast him a sideways glance before taking a long sip of the cold, chocolaty concoction that relieved her parched throat. If it weren't for Art, she might have been wallowing in a pit of depression and feeling sorry for herself. He had given her a sense of purpose.

"Thank you," she suddenly said.

"Sure. I know you like chocolate milkshakes."

"No. I mean thank you. . .for being you." And suddenly her hand reached over and gave his hand a squeeze.

Art sat in shock. Could this be happening? Could his dreams be coming true, right here, surrounded by all of Springville while he and Marilyn sipped chocolate malts? Could it be that God was using these glasses of sugary sweetness to open the eyes of Marilyn Pearl?

Until he heard her say—

"No brother could have done more to help me. I get so worried about Rob and this project and everything, but you're always right here to guide me. Thank you so much."

Art felt his solid reaction of love melt into a puddle of disappointment. *I don't want to be a brother. I don't want to be a friend either. I want to be your husband.* But anyone looking at them sitting side by side on stools, swaying to the left and right, sipping malts, could hardly construe this as a romantic encounter. They did appear as best chums enjoying a fine outing. For all intents and purposes, they *were* best friends. Or maybe just best siblings, according to Marilyn's viewpoint. Nothing appeared ready to change either. What else was there but to continue doing what he had always done and wait patiently. Like plants in a vegetable garden, God's love for each of them and a love for one another would grow if given the proper soil, temperature, and amount of water. Friendship was fine—if it led to better things in life.

For now Art brushed aside any romantic notions and took out the *Victory Garden Leader's Handbook* he'd been reading. "As I said in the truck, you know most everything. Just stay calm."

She gazed fixedly at the door, her fingernails tapping on the counter, waiting for someone official to enter. "What if he doesn't come?"

"Then we're going to ask around here to find out who wants to put in a garden and help the cause. We will set up a meeting of the committee next Sunday, after church maybe. I think we can do it without the government coming in to defend the idea."

Marilyn sighed. "I guess I shouldn't have gotten my hopes up. I wish Mr. Hardy had never called me. I knew it was too good to be true and—" She stopped in midsentence. The blue eyes he thought lustrous and amazing grew to the size of silver dollars. She flew to her feet.

Art looked over to see a tall, broad-shouldered man wearing a black hat and dressed in a dark pinstriped suit enter the establishment. In one hand he held a briefcase, in the other, the latest edition of the town newspaper. He watched as this fellow and Marilyn exchanged smiles. Art frowned. To him it was like witnessing an enemy invasion into Marilyn's life. He knew he had no reason to jump to such a rash conclusion. The man was only here to encourage the Victory garden project. He hoped and prayed.

"Miss Pearl?" the man inquired in a deep voice.

"Yes, oh yes," Marilyn said breathlessly, pushing a bit of blond hair behind one ear. "I'm Marilyn Pearl."

"Quentin Hardy." He looked over at Art, who still occupied the stool next to Marilyn's empty one and gestured with the newspaper. "Would you mind sitting elsewhere? The young lady and I have some important matters to discuss."

Art sheepishly abandoned the stool, which Mr. Hardy occupied while Marilyn happily took the other stool. He only heard bits and pieces of the discussion at first. Marilyn pointed to her drink, and Mr. Hardy signaled the server to also bring him a chocolate malt. Her red lips curved into a smile on her blushing face, and her eyes sparkled as Hardy chattered away. Watching them converse, Art felt his fingers and shoulders tighten. Marilyn already had an affinity for the stranger. And no wonder. The fellow made her feel important. He gave her purpose. Although, looking at the manual he'd scooped up from the counter, Art reasoned he'd also had a fair hand in helping put Marilyn on the right path.

"Oh, and you must meet my assistant, Arthur McNamara." Marilyn tugged on his shirt sleeve.

Art suddenly found himself propelled into the middle of the discussion with Hardy offering him a hearty handshake. Art shook the man's damp, cold hand.

"Art is like the vice president of the committee," Marilyn went on, "although I haven't formally asked him." Her large eyes silently looked Art's way as if begging him to accept.

"I see the lady here would like you to serve," Quentin Hardy acknowledged. His brown, nearly black eyes narrowed even as his lips smiled. For some reason, Art disliked the man's bemused expression. It gave him a nefarious look, although Art could hardly know why. Maybe he simply disliked the idea of a stranger occupying Art's rightful place beside Marilyn at the counter.

"Art assisted me with understanding the Victory garden leader's manual you sent," Marilyn added. "He has many excellent ideas."

Hardy's dark eyes again turned to survey Art. "Well then, I'd say you're someone we need to have working on the project. As time goes by and we see how the war effort is slowly eating away common resources, it's important that both men and women pick up the hoe, so to speak, and help sow worthy ventures to help our nation and the men."

"So how long have you been with the Department of Agriculture?" Art asked. He thought it a good question, after all, with the handbook and the Victory garden concept coming from that department. It might also give him information as to the man's sincerity for the project. He didn't imagine that many from the government cared about a humble community in western New York.

"Ahem." Hardy cleared his throat. "You must mean the Garden Commission. Why, many years. Of course it began long ago on my aunt's farm in Wisconsin and—"

"I live on a farm!" Marilyn interrupted with glee. "That's why it seemed perfect for me to help with this project. I also grew the largest pumpkin in last year's state fair."

"So I read in the paper. And having farming experience makes your position that much more presentable, especially to those who are uncertain where to begin." Hardy began withdrawing some documents from his briefcase. "Of course, in any venture, there's always paperwork."

"What paperwork?" Art asked.

Hardy gave him a quick glance before pushing the papers toward Marilyn. "This gives me permission to oversee the formation of the committee and answer any questions you might have."

"I think it's a good idea to look over the papers first, Marilyn," Art suggested. "Maybe even have a few officials in town read it. Like Mr. Tompkins from the town board."

Marilyn frowned. "It's just to set up the committee. You know with anything having to do with the government, there's always something to sign."

"After all, I too have to show the higher-ups I was here," Hardy said with a chuckle, which Marilyn joined in.

Art felt a strange sensation rise up within him. Something about this Hardy fellow irked him, but he couldn't quite put his finger on it. He and the man now exchanged stares until Hardy suddenly took back the papers and stuffed them into his briefcase.

"On the other hand, I think I may be getting the cart before the horse here. Before we do anything more, I should like to see firsthand what you've accomplished with your garden, Miss Pearl. These boring details can wait." He placed his hat on his head and stood to his feet.

Marilyn likewise jumped to her feet. "Of course! I'd be delighted to have you see it."

Art was glad Marilyn decided to ride back to her house in his truck rather than sharing anything more with this Hardy fellow. He had no confidence of honor within the man. They had yet to see any credentials. The man appeared polished like someone from Washington might, with black hair slicked back and wearing a good suit and shiny shoes on his feet. But it mattered more what was on the inside, and so far he'd seen nothing that eased his misgivings. Perhaps he was simply worried that another man might steal away the only girl he ever loved. He refused to let that happen. He opened the car door for Marilyn, watching her hair flounce around her shoulders. She formed a silent *thank you* with her lips and plopped down in the passenger seat.

"What a wonderful man," she said with a sigh. "Imagine having a prestigious job in the government. And then coming here to Springville, of all places!"

"Actually we don't know much about him." Art slipped behind the driver's seat and started the engine.

Marilyn's eyes turned to slits, with her face pointed skyward and her arms folded. "Oh for heaven's sake. He said he came from a farm in Wisconsin. He's with the Agricultural Department! Or the Garden Commission. Or something."

"That's the point. We honestly don't know who he is or what he intends to do." Art drove out of town and into the countryside toward Marilyn's house. Out of the corner of his eye he saw her silently stare out the window, her arms remaining folded. He knew he ought to try and keep quiet and see what happens. But privately he wished he'd never shown Marilyn the poster on the Victory garden project. It had opened a door he now wished he could slam shut.

He pulled into the yard, followed by Hardy in his automobile. Marilyn flew out of the truck. Mrs. Pearl came out onto the porch to greet them. "This is my mother, Sally Pearl," Marilyn said breathlessly. "Mother, this is Mr. Quentin Hardy."

"Welcome to our farm, Mr. Hardy."

Hardy was all smiles as he swept off his hat and bowed. "Delighted to be here. You have a caring and smart daughter, Mrs. Pearl. It's wonderful to see such enthusiasm for this project. I know that with her helping hand in the Victory garden project, we will get plenty accomplished." He glanced about the place as if taking it all in—the house, the outbuildings, the animals, and every so often, Marilyn herself. A distant *chug-chug* alerted them to Marilyn's father hard at work in the fields with the tractor, oblivious to the stranger in their midst.

"Mother, I plan to show Mr. Hardy my garden." Marilyn smiled shyly then led the way, nearly skipping along the path, her blond hair bouncing about her shoulders. As they walked, she explained to Hardy her gardening skills with special importance placed on the prize-winning pumpkin that became their Thanksgiving pie and other baked treats.

"You grow me a pumpkin like that and I will pay you handsomely for it," he declared.

Marilyn stopped in her tracks. "Are you for real?"

"I mean every word, Miss Pearl. My cook can make a variety of excellent baked items."

"You have a cook?" A dreamy mist cloaked her blue eyes, and Art had a strange feeling about what she must be thinking. A cook meant money. More than Art would ever see in his life, no doubt. But he must be certain not to turn green like a plant either.

"Oh yes, a cook, a gardener, a cleaning woman." They walked past the barn and out to the field where the new vegetables stood nicely in tidy rows. Marilyn pointed out the lettuce, beets, and carrots. "It's too cold yet for the pumpkins, but I have started them."

She then showed him the miniature greenhouse Mr. Pearl had helped build and the tiny late-season plants she had begun.

"I am most impressed by your skill, Miss Pearl. The garden looks absolutely perfect. A great display for the committee to share around town. Just as I read in the newspaper. You are a wonderful woman, Marilyn. I look forward to seeing what will happen with this project in Springville."

Marilyn glowed. She lifted her head, squared her shoulders, and recited, "Well, you know, every Victory garden is a blow to the enemy."

Hardy gave her a broad smile and nod at the quote from the leader's manual. Just the way they exchanged silent communication via a wink, a smile, and a nod made Art cringe. And then the way Marilyn's eyes had misted over. He saw his dreams for Marilyn and himself fading under the ways of a stranger who had captivated her with flowers of a different sort—his fancy words. But Art had invited it all to happen by showing her that poster. He had no one to blame but himself.

Chapter 4

Marilyn didn't know at first if she should confess her frequent dreams of the meeting with Quentin Hardy, but finally she did. Her best friend, Alice Stanton, managed to coax the story out of her as they went for a bicycle ride near the pond, a pretty area bordering the town of Springville. Marilyn wanted to see if Alice would be planting a Victory garden so she might have something important to tell the man from Washington when next they met. It seemed right to try and get friends to do their part.

They stopped beside the pond and were admiring the pretty sight when the conversation turned to Quentin Hardy. "So is he interesting, this man from Washington?" Alice asked after Marilyn described the meeting at the soda fountain and again when he came to survey her garden.

"More than interesting. He's breathtaking. And I have to tell you. . .I can't get him out of my mind."

"Is he that good-looking and all?"

Marilyn laughed. "Not just that, but he works for the Agricultural Department!"

"Oh. Is he coming back?"

Marilyn nodded. Quentin Hardy told her upon leaving that he had business to tend to but would return for the first official meeting of the Victory garden committee in a few days. Before then Marilyn was to find others to serve and maybe even close friends who had established gardens as proof of the venture. "So how is your garden coming?" she asked Alice.

"You mean, Alice, Alice, quite contrary, how does your garden grow?" Alice giggled at her wit. "I dug out a little piece of ground, if that counts."

Marilyn pushed her gently on the arm. "Well, it's a start."

Alice nodded. "I also did what you said and planted the lettuce seeds. Nothing much is up yet, but I planted them."

Marilyn wished Alice had better news, but at least she could say her friend had begun a garden of sorts. And Art had come through for her, his garden bursting with lettuce, peas, radishes, and collard greens, along with tiny pumpkin plants already sprouted in pots set inside a temporary greenhouse he had nailed together. The way Art was pitching in to help warmed her heart. *Thank You, Lord, for bringing Art into my life and giving him the heart to stand with me in this.*

"I did hear from Karen and Lisa that they had gardens already going."

Marilyn looked over at her friend. "Why didn't you tell me?"

"My goodness, aren't you the eager beaver."

"I just can't wait to put Springville on the national map. No one knows or cares about our town here in New York State. It's time people knew that we are true Americans who will do what we must to help our fellow man. I need to call Karen and Lisa and see if they can come to the meeting to set up the town committee. The more we have at the meeting who have started their gardens, the better it will be in helping others start theirs."

"I think you also need important people involved too. Like people in the community who have more influence and can help get the project going. Mr. Harris has the largest farm in the area. Mr. Winston, I'm sure, will supply the gardening tools. And then there's folks like Mrs. Carlson, whose twin boys joined up. I'm sure any family who sent a loved one to war would like to be a part."

Marilyn could barely keep from jumping up and down. "What swell ideas. Thanks! I will ask them. We need to have older and younger folks working together from all over town." The Tompkinses should have been first on her list, what with them arranging for the reporter to interview her just before Quentin Hardy arrived. They would give the whole effort an air of legitimacy. She sighed, amazed at how God was orchestrating this endeavor. And just at a point in her life when she began questioning the Lord's will after the horror of Pearl Harbor and then Rob running off to join the Army. Every day the radio blared the grim news of war on several fronts in the Pacific, North Africa, and Europe. No one really knew what the future held, adding to the vulnerability and the fear. Marilyn licked her lips, thankful for this mission that she felt called to do. No longer were fear and sadness her constant companions. She had a purpose to fulfill.

Marilyn now looked over at Alice whose bright red hair reflected the sun's rays, complementing the blouse and slacks she wore for the bike ride. Marilyn looked down at her usual overalls and plaid shirt. Yesterday she asked for Mother's help in creating a patriotic outfit to wear to the first meeting of the Victory Garden Committee. Mother suggested a red-and-white-striped material to make into a blouse, matching it with her blue flared skirt. Red, white, and blue were perfect patriotic colors that everyone was sure to admire. Particularly Quentin Hardy.

A strange feeling drifted over her. Why would she care about impressing Quentin Hardy? The man could be married with three children, for all she knew. Though she didn't recall seeing a wedding ring. At least she should try to temper her feelings until she knew more about him.

"Hello in there!" exclaimed Alice. "What are you thinking about now? You look like you're somewhere else."

"Oh nothing. Well. . ." She hesitated. "I was trying to recall if Quentin Hardy wore a wedding ring."

"Oh Marilyn, really!" Alice shook her head.

"I know. Silly of me."

"I'll bet Art isn't too happy to hear you're mooning over this man from Washington."

Her comment cut Marilyn to the quick. She whirled to stare at her friend. "What do you mean by that?"

"I have it in good confidence that Art is head over heels for you. But I'm sure you already knew that. Unless you're blind."

Marilyn laughed. "Art and I have known each other since we were in diapers. We're good friends."

Alice shook her head and smiled. "Honey, wake up and smell the coffee! The man loves you."

"Of course he does. And I love him too."

Now it was Alice's turn to stare.

"It's not what you think," Marilyn corrected. "Art's not my boyfriend or anything. He's like an older brother. He's been a part of my family forever. Why, Mother still makes him pancakes when he stops by on Saturdays. He knows our farm better than I do."

"I don't know. I think you need to get your head out of the clouds and see what's happening."

Thankfully Alice ceased the strange chitchat and gossiped about other news around Springville. They then mounted their bicycles and continued the ride. Yet Marilyn could not get the words about Art out of her mind. Maybe she should set the record straight and see where she and Art stood. And if need be, correct the notion that their relationship meant anything more than simple friendship.

They road along the streets of Springville on their bicycles until Marilyn parted ways with Alice on Main Street to take a side trip to the soda fountain. Oftentimes Art hung out there, talking to people after his workday finished at the store. She wondered if he had told any of his friends about the two of them. Like what Alice had mentioned—that somehow he was in love? That she was his girl? Though she couldn't believe it. Art only wanted to help, to be there when called on to do something great or small. He proved steadfast and sure, especially with the Victory garden idea. Marilyn noticed the poster in the window for the meeting to be held at the church and smiled.

She spotted several of Art's friends at the counter sipping pop, but there was no sign of the brown-haired man with glasses.

"Hi, Matt," she greeted. "Has Art been here?"

Matt shook his head. "Haven't seen him in a few days. I hear he may be helping his aunt at her house. She had some fixing up to do."

"Oh." Marilyn felt disappointed. She had to know if God was trying to speak through Alice. She'd never considered Art a boyfriend type. For so long they had done fun things together. Or talked about life, like the news in their families or about the town. Over the last few years, the conversations centered more and more on the news unfolding in the world—the rise of Hitler and the Third Reich, the attacks on Great Britain, the terrible days following Pearl Harbor that drew the nation into this conflict. Never had

Art let on that he might have feelings for her. All those times they sat in his truck or on the front porch, he'd never tried to kiss her. Why, they'd never even been out on a date! They were, as she told Alice, more like siblings, supporting each other when life loomed dark and dubious.

Marilyn sighed, ready to return to her bicycle where she'd left it at the curb, when she noticed a well-dressed man walking briskly along the sidewalk. Quentin Hardy!

"Well, if it isn't the best rose in the Victory garden!" he announced.

Warmth swept into her cheeks and neck. "Hello, Mr. Hardy."

"Come now, I think we know each other well enough to be on a first-name basis. Quentin James is my name, but I prefer James." His white teeth sparkling in the sun caught her attention. "Glad we ran into each other, actually. I have some information here I was going to drop off with the Tompkinses. Do you know where they live?"

"Yes, over on Maple Avenue. I'd be glad to show you."

His smile grew brighter. "Splendid. So are we set for the meeting? How does everyone seem to feel about the project?"

"I've talked with a few people. I know my best friend Alice planted lettuce. And she had an excellent idea for inviting those who might have an interest in gardening, such as Mr. Winston who sells tools."

Quentin James Hardy paused in midstep. "Well then, it's a good thing I ran into you. You see, I've stumbled upon something extraordinary. An excellent deal on tools and seeds. Everything we need to plant successful Victory gardens."

"Really?"

"Oh yes. As part of the government, we can make deals with companies to offer good bargains." James pulled out a paper that listed the items for sale—from assorted seeds to tools, gardening gloves, everything needed to start a vegetable garden.

Marilyn reviewed it. "Why, I think my dad paid nearly twice as much at Mr. Winston's store for a hoe last year."

"You see? I can tell already you will be an excellent representative for these products. What do you say about passing a few of these around and telling everyone what an excellent bargain we have on the tools we need?" He handed her some advertisements.

"With such good prices, everyone should be able to put in a garden." She glanced at her humble black bicycle with the basket on front. "I came here on my bicycle, you see, and I don't want to lose the papers. . . ."

"I see. I can wait on meeting the Tompkinses. We can put your bicycle in the trunk of my car, and I'll gladly take you home."

Marilyn agreed with a huge grin. Maybe all her dreams about Quentin, now James Hardy, were not for naught. From his debonair smile to the way he offered to help with this project to the ride, she couldn't imagine anyone better to lead the way in all this. After putting her bike in the trunk, he talked nonstop about his work and the fair prices he had found for tools and seeds. "Not that I want to besmirch your town mercantile for wanting to make a profit. But with the extreme importance of this project, and the way this will assist the war effort, we need to find good prices."

"Will you be talking about this at the meeting?"

"Yes, but I'm a stranger in your town, Marilyn. It would be better to have someone who lives here with a passion for seeing this project get off the ground, someone who understands the importance of everyone helping out, to head up the project. Each one of us has loved ones who may at any time face bullets and bombs for our country's sake."

Sadness and fear swept over her at the thought of dear Rob

facing a foreign enemy amid the whistle of bullets and shrapnel that could wound and kill. The thought made her muscles tense and the back of her neck break out in a cold sweat.

James went on. "We all need to do whatever we can to help. And I believe the person to lead this project is you." He paused and stared at her. "Forgive me. I can see my words were lacking in tact and understanding."

"I'm just worried about my brother. He will be done with train-ing soon. Then he'll likely have to leave. After that, no one knows what will happen." She wiped away an unexpected tear slipping down her cheek. "What if I never see him again?"

Suddenly the man's large hand rested on hers, not warm as she expected, but cool and moist. "This is very difficult, I'm sure. Which is all the more reason we have no time to waste. The growing season is here; the time is now to defeat the enemy. Remember the posters? Like 'Your Victory Garden Counts More Than Ever.' "

Marilyn nodded, wiping away the final tear and sitting straighter in the seat with her gaze focused ahead. With James by her side, she knew she could make this all work out for good in honor of Rob and the men. It was the very least she could do.

Hardy. Art's hand closed around the glass of lemonade on the table when he saw the car come to a stop in front of the Pearl residence. *Fawning all over Marilyn with more of his gobbledygook.* When he arrived at the Pearl farm, Marilyn was nowhere to be found. Mrs. Pearl served him lemonade and freshly baked nut bread, explaining that Marilyn had gone bike riding with Alice. Seeing the image before him, he couldn't help the tension in his fingers as he gripped the lemonade glass. *Why is she with Hardy then? Did she use Alice as an excuse to be with him instead?* When he saw Hardy take out her bicycle, he quickly chastised himself. He had no reason to think after one encounter that Marilyn would fall for some government official who was only here to see the Victory garden project off the ground. But watching them exchange smiles and the way she tossed her head, making her blond ponytail swish, his questioning continued.

When Marilyn saw him, she stopped short. Her blue eyes widened, her mouth forming a small O. He wondered what caused the reaction. Or was it embarrassment that she had been caught with Hardy? *Stop it, Art.*

"Well, if it isn't Mr. McNamara," Hardy said, offering his hand. Art shook it lightly. "We are making plans for the big meeting in two days. Will you be there?"

"Of course. Wouldn't miss it."

"Please have some lemonade with us," Mrs. Pearl invited as she came out onto the porch. Hardy seemed to study the scene before him, looking at the half-empty glass of lemonade, then at Art, and finally shook his head. "I'm afraid I'll have to take you up on your kind offer another time, ma'am. Duty calls." He bowed slightly, smiled, and lifted his hat to bid them farewell, his gaze bearing down on Marilyn before he left.

Art blew out a sigh, thankful the man had seen fit to leave so quickly. Marilyn took a seat beside him, flopping a pile of papers on the table.

"He has so many interesting plans."

Art gave a quick glance at the papers to see products and accompanying prices that caught his eye. "What's this?"

"James mentioned something about good prices on the tools and seeds we need for the gardens."

Art perked at the name. "James?" He watched her face take on a pinkish hue.

"I guess Quentin is too difficult to say. It's his middle name."

Art frowned. The time had come to draw her attention away from the man. At least Art had her to himself right now. He cast the paper aside to inquire about her visit with Alice. Her finger began to trace the length of the chair's armrest, and the pinkish color of her cheeks deepened to red. "Oh, we were just catching up on all the news. I wanted to know too if she had done anything about a Victory garden. She said she planted some lettuce. And Karen and Lisa have planted gardens too."

"That's good. Word is already spreading, it seems, especially with the upcoming meeting. I'm glad Alice planted a garden. I don't think she has ever touched dirt in her life. It gives hope for everyone else." He ended the observation with a chuckle.

The comment brought a smile to Marilyn's cherry-red lips. "She had some good suggestions for others who may want to get involved. Although I wonder if we should invite your boss, Mr. Winston. Especially if James can get such good prices on tools and seeds. It might make him feel bad."

Art barely heard her words as he watched her. Marilyn made the outfit of overalls and a plaid shirt look attractive. He liked the way she had done up her hair into the big fluffy ponytail. But his thoughts soon turned to his boss, Mr. Winston, and the lines of disapproval crisscrossing the man's face on the news of a competitor looking to take customers away from his mercantile. "I agree it's best not to tell him right now. Although there needs to be thought given on how the whole town can come together during this time, including the store owners. You don't want to cast them aside." As an employee of Mr. Winston's, Art wouldn't want to suffer the consequences either.

Marilyn sighed. Then he noticed her blue eyes staring at him. "I'm glad you're a part of this, Art. You always have such good ideas.

I mean, if it weren't for you, we wouldn't be having a meeting or Victory gardens or anything."

And if it weren't for me, James wouldn't be here either. He frowned at the thought.

"What's the matter?"

Now it was his turn to lend color to the conversation by way of his warm face. "I'm just glad we can work together for the good of the war effort."

Marilyn began to squirm in her seat. She wiped her hands on the knees of her overalls. "I—I was wondering something, Art."

His heart began to pound, waiting for her next words to spill out.

She leaned back and closed her eyes, allowing the sun's rays to kiss her face. "Oh, how do I say this? I don't even know where to begin." Her head lowered to rest her gaze on him for a moment before looking off into the distance. "It was something Alice said to me. I didn't want to believe it. She asked me if—"

The door to the porch banged open. "I just wanted to see if anyone needed more lemonade before I gather up the glasses," Mrs. Pearl said.

Marilyn lurched to her feet. "We're fine, Mother. I, uh, I just remembered. I–I'd better go see to the chickens. I forgot to gather the eggs yesterday."

"Then you'd better do it," her mother admonished.

Marilyn said a quick goodbye and dashed off toward the chicken coop quicker than a rabbit through the grass. Disappointment filled him. What was she going to ask him? Curiosity flowed like a river, ready to pour over like the falls of the mighty Niagara several hours north. Only he hoped he wouldn't get caught in the water's flow and find himself dashed on the rocks when he did learn her thoughts. Maybe it would be something good for a change, like about them and *not* Quentin *James* Hardy. Whatever it was, he wished he had the moment back.

Art picked up the paper once more that offered tools and seeds for the Victory garden project. Lots of things with cheap prices. Information his boss would very much dislike. And just then, maybe he was glad he didn't know what Marilyn was about to say. There was no reason to further cloud an already uncertain time. Things were difficult enough.

Chapter 5

*A*rt checked his appearance in the hall mirror before picking up a briefcase that belonged to his dad. He might as well look the part of a businessman, even if he felt nothing of the sort. He rather liked his job working at the mercantile. At times his leg would ache from muscle spasms, and Mr. Winston would arrange for him to sit and manage the cash drawer until the pain subsided. But Art refused to play the role of an invalid. He'd done the required exercises every day now for years that allowed him to avoid wearing a clunky metal brace. He was happy not to be permanently paralyzed, even though Mother talked often of the time he was sick, and she worried that her dear boy would never walk again. He'd managed pretty well to overcome it all, except for some lingering weakness.

Now he took up the case containing pencils and paper to take notes, and a copy of the Victory garden leader's manual, ready for the important committee meeting this afternoon. He told Marilyn he would pick her up and take her to the church for the meeting. It seemed strange to return to the same place where just last evening they had sung many beautiful hymns and listened to good preaching. Now the reverend and his wife would be present to lend a spiritual note to the gathering. Art liked the idea of a holy man among them, especially where Quentin James Hardy was concerned. Why the man got him hot under the collar he didn't know. He prayed it wasn't just jealousy.

He headed for the truck and wrestled himself into the seat. Herein was another praise—that he could get around despite the weakness in his leg. While many in this area rode bicycles with the increasing gas shortages, he had the truck for visiting and going to work. Dad found someone to exchange gasoline for electrical work, which Dad loved to do, and that helped in this time of rationing. He pushed his glasses farther up his nose and turned over the engine. On the way to Marilyn's house, he pondered the meeting to come and what this Hardy fellow would say and do. He shouldn't try to guess motives, but he also didn't want to let his guard down either. He would remain neutral, he supposed. *Look and listen to what's going on and offer a quiet prayer.*

Marilyn looked lovely standing there on the porch when he pulled up, dressed like Old Glory in a red-and-white-striped blouse and blue skirt, accessorized by a nice straw hat decorated with red ribbon. The bounce in her step matched her smile, and for a moment he wished he could skip right along with her.

"This is a great day!" she exclaimed, settling in beside him. "I was up half the night trying to decide what to say."

Art looked over at her. "What do you mean? I thought that Hardy fellow was going to run the meeting."

"I was told by Mr. Tompkins to have a small speech ready. A president will need to be elected too, and that person will need to say some encouraging words." She rearranged her blue skirt. "It makes sense I could be elected, you know. Anyway, I plan to talk about Rob and the pumpkin pie he loved. I brought along my ribbon for the pumpkin I grew last year." She held it up. "James was very impressed by it, so I thought it would be helpful."

Art blew out a sigh when she said the man's name as if her tongue enjoyed rolling it out in endearing fashion. "What else are you going to say?" he asked, trying to change the subject before his dismay leaked out.

"I will suggest what plants can be grown. And if anyone wants, Mother said it would be perfectly fine to have folks come over and see our garden."

Art nodded. Marilyn did have a good head on her shoulders, and a pretty head at that, with fine blond hair he would love to run his fingers through. He saw her rearrange the blue skirt again and then glance out the window at the trees and houses. "I'm getting a little nervous," she said with a gasp. She opened her pocketbook to withdraw a handkerchief. "I hope I don't get sick."

"You'll do fine. God has prepared you for such a time as this," he said, quoting Esther. He then remembered their last meeting and the abrupt way it ended. He wondered what she was about to tell him that day before her mother interrupted. How he would love to draw it out of her, but he knew her mind and heart were concentrated on the day's events, as his should be.

Marilyn sucked in her breath as he pulled into the parking lot. Art hoped to see friendly townsfolk descending on the church, eager to learn how to help the men in arms and their country. When they entered the sanctuary, he was pleased to see a fair number already gathered to hear about the plans, looking on expectantly from their places in the pews. Quentin Hardy stood in the front of the church, glancing through some papers. He flashed Marilyn a smile, which seemed to vanish when he caught sight of Art, or maybe it was just Art's imagination. Art considered joining them to hear what they were saying but reluctantly took a seat in the front pew as a spectator.

Just then the Tompkinses entered with Mrs. Tompkins laughing boisterously over some remark. Everyone shifted in their seats, straining to see. Mr. Tompkins went to shake the hands of many in attendance, as if he were running for political office. He then strode to the front of the church and raised his hands. A hush fell over the assembly.

"Thank you for coming to hear about the Victory garden committee we are forming. Thanks to young Marilyn Pearl here, we are making a bold move as a community to help our boys and our country."

He went on to offer a short description of the program while Art carefully watched Marilyn's expression. She sat as stiff as a statue in the VIP seats, clutching a piece of paper that likely contained her speech. Her gaze never wavered, her cheeks bright red to match the stripe in her blouse and the ribbon in her hat. Art felt as nervous as she. He wished he could hold her and whisper words of encouragement. Instead, he offered a prayer for peace.

"Now I'm pleased to introduce to you the girl who came up with this marvelous idea: Marilyn Pearl."

She stood stiffly and strode to the podium, her hands trembling. Her voice came forth steady and strong, speaking about her great fondness for growing vegetables and especially pumpkins. She held up the blue ribbon and went on with her idea of baking treats for Rob and the company as well as growing vegetables for those in need. "And with that, I turn it over to Mr. Hardy of the U.S. Department of Agriculture, who will say more about the program."

Quentin Hardy smiled big, waved his hand, and to Art's shock, deposited a small kiss on Marilyn's cheek. Art nearly flew to his feet, his shock quickly replaced by anger. It took all his effort not to dash up front and tell Hardy in no uncertain terms to keep his hands off Marilyn. He barely heard any of the man's words as he stared at Marilyn and the way her face glowed in the man's presence. She looked enraptured. He took off his glasses to polish them on a handkerchief, all the while wondering how he should respond to this uncomfortable situation.

"Now it's time to select the committee board." Hardy glanced over at Mr. and Mrs. Tompkins, who looked on expectantly. "I believe its right to put into place those who support this venture and who have the will to see Springville become a place of victory. Unless there is an objection, I hereby nominate Edward Tompkins as president. All those in favor?"

Art sat there with his mouth open. Everyone but Marilyn and him raised their hands. The once jovial look on Marilyn's face disintegrated, replaced by wide eyes and a flushed face. Hardy then proceeded to select Mrs. Tompkins as the secretary and Marilyn as treasurer. Art saw her shake her head ever so slightly, knowing she didn't want to be treasurer, even with the applause radiating throughout the building. Marilyn's gaze turned to the wooden floor below while her fingers crinkled her speech.

"Finally, as the treasurer will soon be sharing with you, I have an excellent vendor that will give good prices for those needing tools and seeds for their gardens. After the meeting we will hand out the advertisements. The money can be given to the treasurer either today or in the coming days so the equipment may be ordered as quickly as possible."

Hardy stepped away, and Mr. Tompkins took on the role of the newly elected president. He asked by a show of hands who had already planted a garden. Many had, to Art's surprise. "So are we going to tell all our neighbors and friends that planting season is here?" The audience responded in the affirmative. "Then I thank Mr. Hardy for giving us what we need to have a successful Victory garden campaign. And with it, we will do our part to win victory over our enemies."

Cheers broke out along with more applause. Marilyn remained in her subdued position, clapping halfheartedly, her gaze elsewhere. Art knew exactly what she was thinking: *Why wasn't I elected president?*

Why wasn't I elected president? Marilyn tried not to feel disappointed as she politely clapped along with everyone else, though the smile she gave felt forced. She'd been chosen treasurer, of all things. It didn't make sense. After all, the idea of having a Victory garden committee here in Springville came about because of the letter she had written and an interview she'd given to the local paper. Her gaze focused on Art, who looked directly at her. He was the first to tell her about the project and the first who believed in her. And there he sat among those in the pews, not seeking a title or anything else prestigious. But right now, his humble example did little to change her own discontent at not being selected. After all, she felt she'd earned the leadership role. She had the excitement and the garden and the notoriety of being a headline in the town newspaper. Instead, the honor had been given to the one who held influence in the community—a member of the town board.

Suddenly James Hardy strode up, startling her. "You don't look happy, Miss Pearl."

"Oh, I'm fine," she fibbed. "It's just. . .I know nothing about being a treasurer. I'm a gardener and—"

He smiled. "Well everyone is supposed to be a gardener. That is our plan. The role of treasurer is quite simple but also important.

We need someone to manage the money within the organization."

Marilyn looked up at him and the serious expression on his face. "Why do we need money?"

"Every organization needs money. Tools and seeds are needed for the gardens. You will be responsible for collecting the money and giving it to me to buy what we need. Every person here received a brochure outlining the products for sale. I gave you some advertisements earlier in the week."

"I'm just not sure how I'm going to do all of this. . . ." Her voice trailed off, and she wished with all her might that she could tell him what a dreadful mistake he'd made. She may be young, but she did know about gardening, much more than the Tompkinses, in her opinion.

"You are invaluable to the community, Marilyn. Mr. Tompkins will need all the help he can get. But you must see how important it is that a powerful and influential voice in the community heads up this committee. It gives the project a sense of legitimacy. But"—James paused—"every boss needs an assistant; someone he can rely on to make good decisions. You are that important person, Miss Pearl. The one he can count on, and I can count on too." His dark eyes seem to burrow into hers. "Do I have your loyalty to the project?"

"Of course."

"Good. You had me worried." He pulled several papers out of his briefcase and a pen. "I also need your signature on this paperwork so we can move on with what needs to be done."

She signed it, just as Art came up behind them. His thoughtful presence proved comforting at that moment. Art had always been a comfort in times of trial. Though he, like James, probably thought her foolish to bemoan not being selected president.

"I'm here to see what needs to be done," Art offered. She saw something in his eyes. Compassion, maybe? Like he understood her disappointment?

James looked at him. "I'm sure the new treasurer will be looking for people to help sell the necessary items for their gardens and collecting the money. Are you good at sales?"

"I work at the mercantile and—"

"Excellent! I would say you have a qualified assistant to help where needed, Marilyn. Here's more brochures for those who were unable to make the meeting." He handed a pile to her. "We need these distributed to as many people as possible so they understand what we are doing. And depending on what they need, we can show them the excellent tools and seeds we offer for half the normal cost."

Marilyn heard Art issue a loud sigh and say, "I'm not sure why we need this when Mr. Winston carries similar items in his store—"

"It's simple. An entire town needs to plant the gardens. I have the resources to secure what they will need and at good prices. This is far too large an operation for a simple town merchant to supply."

"It makes sense to me," Marilyn interrupted. "I'll be glad to hand these out and collect the money and orders," she said to James.

Art said nothing. She knew he would defend the place where he worked, but right now she was more concerned about her status as the new treasurer. Maybe if she did well in this position, she might become Mr. Tompkins's assistant. That would be like a vice president, which was just as good as president in her opinion.

After she left the church, Art suddenly came up behind her. His quickness surprised her, as usually he was fairly deliberate in his walking on account of his leg. "Are you really going to collect money for that man?"

"Of course. It's my responsibility as treasurer, like he said."

"I'm just not sure about this. I don't like it either that we aren't allowing Mr. Winston to order the tools and seeds. He runs a good business in town. He supports people's livelihoods. It makes sense."

"You're just saying that because you work for him. I'm the official treasurer. And James wants to go through the government where the prices are much better."

Art stared at her with dark brown eyes that reminded Marilyn of a hound dog begging for a bone. Only she had no idea why he would beg. But she also realized she shouldn't push him away. She needed him to help her figure out this new role of treasurer. She just wished he'd come along the way he'd always done rather than question everything. The doubting made her jittery and even irritated. "I know you want to support Mr. Winston. But we need to rely on those who began the program, like James and the Department of Agriculture. But if you want to ask Mr. Winston if he can supply the neighboring farms, that would be fine."

"Yoo-hoo! Marilyn!"

Marilyn whirled to find Mrs. Tompkins waving at her. "Congratulations on becoming treasurer, young lady. What a nice thing to have happen."

Marilyn forced a smile. "Thank you."

"We need to work together to see the Victory gardens happen in our town. And Ed would like to use your garden as an example of what folks need to do. Hopefully your parents won't object to having folks stop by and take a look."

"That would be fine. And for those who weren't able to make it today, Mr. Hardy gave me brochures for tools and seeds so folks can order the supplies. I need to get these out as soon as possible and collect the money for supplies."

Mrs. Tompkins took a handful of papers. "Fine, fine. I'll start sending folks over to your farm then. I just know we are going to have an excellent program with all of us working hard to make it happen." For a moment Marilyn thought the woman might squeeze her cheek in appreciation, but she only waved and returned to her husband's side as he chatted with some townsfolk. Marilyn noticed Mrs. Tompkins point back at her. She couldn't help feeling a sudden twinge of nerves. "I think I'm going to have visitors to the farm very soon," she murmured to Art. "Will you still help with this?"

"You know I will."

Relief flowed over her. How she needed to hear that. "Thank you so much."

Just then an older couple, Mr. and Mrs. Fielding, greeted Marilyn with money and a completed order form in hand. "We want to buy a hoe, rake, and some seed packets. And these prices are much better than at the mercantile."

Marilyn's heart sang as she accepted their order with grateful thanks. When they asked her when to expect the delivery, she looked to Art, who was busy saying hello to another neighbor. She never thought to ask James how or when the materials would be delivered. But knowing the time was short, likely he would see to it that the items arrived quickly. "Uh. . .just come to my house in about a week or so, and I'm sure the items will be there."

The couple smiled and walked off. Marilyn made a mental note to ask James about the delivery date as she stored the money in her pocketbook. "We got our first customer!" she told Art when he returned to her side. He nodded before gently reminding her they probably should head back to the farm and prepare for visitors. Oh, how she needed him by her side. Maybe Alice's words were true. Maybe he did care for her, and maybe she ought to consider if she also cared for him.

❧ Chapter 6 ❧

*Y*ou are wonderful. I knew I could rely on you.

The words reverberated in Marilyn's mind every day since she presented James Hardy with the money she had raised from the families of Springville to buy the tools and seeds for their gardens. A whole one hundred dollars had been collected, which was more than she'd ever had in her possession. James Hardy was all smiles, promising a quick delivery of the needed supplies. Marilyn agreed to have the items come to the farm. Mother didn't object, saying the products could be stored in one of the older sheds until neighbors could claim their purchases. Everything was working out perfectly. Except for—

Arthur McNamara. From the moment James arrived, Art seemed set against anything and everything James said or did. Art claimed that his boss, Mr. Winston, grew irate over the business being conducted outside his mercantile. Marilyn knew Art would side with his boss. If only he could see beyond to the common good—the growing enthusiasm within the community to plant Victory gardens. That's all that mattered.

Today Marilyn worked in her garden, hoeing out the weeds between the plants that had grown new sets of leaves in the warm weather. The plants reminded her of God's faithfulness as she tended them each day. She believed God would continue prospering it all if she proved faithful in what she had been given. If only Art could see this rather than sowing seeds of doubt and confusion.

As if Art had heard her thoughts, his dark truck came rolling up the lane. Marilyn sighed, hoping no more contentious issues would be brought up. She hadn't the strength to deal with it anymore. In fact, she would prefer to keep him at arm's length. Yes, he had been helpful in the past, but right now he was trying to choke out what had sprouted.

He limped over to her, his hands tucked inside his pockets. "The garden's looking good."

She nodded and kept hoeing. Out of the corner of her eye, she saw him step back and stare in wonder.

"Have I done something wrong, Marilyn?"

She forced the hoe deeper into the soft earth to wrench out a stubborn dandelion. "I'm just trying to dig out the weeds. But you might as well know, I think God is doing a great work here in Springville." She paused. "Sometimes, though, I wonder if you really want this project to succeed. You said you would help me. Not make it fail."

His eyes widened behind his spectacles, and a soft voice responded. "Why would I want this to fail? I wanted you to do the Victory garden project in the first place." He braved a step forward. "But I do believe we need to be cautious when a stranger comes—"

"There you go again." She jammed the hoe back into the ground to loosen another weed. "You never have anything positive to say.

Especially about James. I think maybe you're jealous of him or something."

The silence fueled a feeling of triumph. She had hit the nail on the head.

"I'm sorry you think that," he finally said.

"Well, I do. James wants this project to succeed. And look what's happened. The Tompkinses have organized many of the folks to start gardening. The delivery is coming soon. I can't help it that folks decided James's prices were better than Mr. Winston's. People want to save money these days. You can't blame them for that."

Silence once more filled the air until Marilyn broke it with more glowing reports of how everything was working out with the Victory garden project. And he of all people should have more faith. "You're always talking about praying and asking God to take control of things."

"I hope He is. Without Him we are nothing."

She whirled, frustration building within. "Of course God is in this! Look at what's happened."

"Okay. I don't want to argue, Marilyn. I only want what's best. If you don't think I can contribute anymore to this project and I'm hurting more than helping, I'll step back."

He turned, and Marilyn watched him amble back to the truck. Suddenly it felt like a repeat of Rob leaving the family. The emptiness. The fear of the unknown. Her heart sank. "Wait, Art!"

He turned to face her.

"I know you've done a lot to help. I just don't want you questioning everything I do. It. . .it makes me nervous."

"So if I agree with you on everything, all is well?"

Marilyn stared with her mouth wide open. The truth be known, that is exactly what she wanted. An assistant at her beck and call. Hadn't that been the way from the very beginning, ever since he brought home the poster? But her pride drowned out the sound of conviction in her heart. "Oh, honestly, you just confuse me. I have enough to think about with my brother gone and all we're going through as a country with this awful war. We need to work together." She stood poised to blurt out the thing that had left her beyond curious since the day Alice brought it up. The idea he might love her. If one could call it that. How she wanted to ask if this was his way of showing love.

Art mumbled something about an errand he had to run and headed for his truck. Marilyn decided to let him go, thinking it was probably for the better. Maybe now there would be peace and not turmoil. She returned to the soil, trying to drive away the picture of Art standing there wearing a look of dejection. Again she pulled out weeds, knowing this was what she must do to allow the tender plants of the Victory garden project to grow. To keep focused on the task set before her and not let another's opinion ruin everything. Even if Alice's words might be true. That Art might be doing this out of love.

The sputter of an engine on the road again interrupted her task. This time hope soared. Maybe Art was returning to make amends. Everything would be well, and then she could find out where things stood between them. She heard Mother calling for her. Marilyn set down the hoe and took off for the house.

The bright face of a delivery boy from town with a bouquet of red chrysanthemums met her startled gaze. "These are for you, Marilyn," he said with a smile.

"Thank you." She took the bouquet, uncertain what to think. Trembling fingers opened the card that came with them.

I think you're wonderful. I hope these flowers prove it.
–James Hardy

"Aren't they pretty," Mother cooed.

Marilyn stared at the note, stunned. No one had ever given her flowers. Not that she had anyone of interest to do it. Especially after today's encounter with Art. Flowers never seemed a part of his nature.

"Who are they from?" Mother inquired.

"Uh. . .from James. I mean Mr. Hardy."

"The man from the government? Why in the world would he be giving you flowers?"

"I'm not sure." Seeing Mother's raised eyebrows, she added hastily, "I'm sure he's giving them to all those who've helped with the Victory garden project. Mrs. Tompkins is probably receiving flowers too."

Mother said nothing as Marilyn arranged the flowers in a vase and set it carefully on a table. Wonder and amazement filled her. Just then the phone rang, making her jump as she rushed to answer. "Hello?"

"Hello, Marilyn? This is James Hardy."

Her heart began to pound. "Oh James, thank you ever so much for the lovely bouquet. I was very surprised."

"Bouquet?" His puzzlement sent a dart of concern through Marilyn until she heard his calm coolness return through the receiver. "Oh yes, the flowers. You must excuse me, there is so much going on here."

"Oh, I'm sure, and—"

"I just wanted to see if there have been any final orders for gardening tools."

"No, I haven't gotten any more orders, but—"

"Well, we won't worry about it. You did collect a hundred dollars, and that in itself is quite admirable. If I had a vacancy on my staff here, you would be hired on in an instant. I never had such a hard worker for a noble cause."

Marilyn inhaled a deep breath. Did he just say she could come work for him in Washington? "I don't know what to say."

He chuckled. "Not that I have any vacancies at the moment, but you would be highly considered if I did. Perhaps you should consider being a part of the Women's Land Army. We need enthusiastic women to help at the nation's farms while the men are fighting."

"Really?" Just the thought of being part of an army moved her. If Rob could join, then why shouldn't she?

His deep voice brought her back into the conversation. "But you will let me know if you have any more buyers."

"Oh yes. And I told them the orders will be coming soon, right?"

"Yes, yes, very soon. Sorry, but I must run to a meeting. Happy to hear you received the flowers."

Marilyn offered a quick goodbye before hanging up the receiver. Her head began to spin. Just the idea that James wanted to hire her for a position or even recommend her as part of an army made her want to dance. She rushed back into the kitchen. "Mother, you'll never guess! Mr. Hardy just told me I should join the Women's Land Army!"

Mother nearly dropped the pot of water she was holding. "What army? What are you talking about?"

"A women's army here in this country. To help on the farms while the men are away. He said I was one of the most enthusiastic people he's ever met and believes I would do well."

"Why, I don't know what to think, Marilyn. Except your father and I need help right here on our farm with your brother away. Plus there's all the activity with the Victory garden. I'd say you're quite busy serving now. Wouldn't you?"

Marilyn couldn't argue with that. But the mere notion that James thought her worthy enough for such prestigious roles sent waves of joy soaring through her. How good it felt to be wanted and appreciated. It made the tension of the past week and Art's sad expression all melt away.

❧

Art felt terrible after the confrontation with Marilyn. For so long they had nursed a close friendship, and Art had felt certain it might be moving toward a place where he could finally ask her on an official date to pursue a deeper relationship. But all the dreams had been neatly driven away—and he knew by whom. Why some man from Washington could drive a wedge between them after all these years of friendship went beyond his sense of reasoning. Or why Marilyn would find the man so appealing in the first place. She did Hardy's bidding without question, even with Art doubting the man's intentions, and refused to hear anything to the contrary. It puzzled him to no end.

All this weighed heavily on him while he assisted a customer at the mercantile with her grocery selection. As the war went on, the shelves grew barer. Customers grumbled over the lack of canned goods and other foodstuffs and having to use ration cards to purchase items such as sugar and coffee. He heard talk of the garden project and customers starting theirs for fear of the lack of food. But he also heard his boss, Mr. Winston, complain about the man from Washington who had stolen his business. The mercantile still had plenty of tools and seeds left out back because of the orders for Mr. Hardy, and his taking away business left a dark cloud over the establishment.

Art glanced around the store and spied Marilyn's best friend, Alice Stanton, looking at fabric and thread. He wondered if the two girls had talked any and if she might know what was happening in Marilyn's heart. He walked over to where Alice was examining some fabric and greeted her.

Her hand flew to her neck. "Oh Art! You startled me."

"Sorry about that. Finding everything okay?"

"I'm trying to decide which material would look better for a skirt. What color do you like?"

Art selected the light blue fabric, the color he loved best on Marilyn, if the truth were known. He thought of her sweet, smiling face then and her light blue dress and hat with the blue ribbon. He asked Alice if she'd seen Marilyn recently.

"Not since the meeting at the church. She always seems so busy." Alice tipped her head to one side as she surveyed him. "Are you two getting along all right?"

He shrugged and turned to rearrange the notions on the shelf. "I'm not sure."

"Hmm. I thought you might be having some difficulties."

Surprised by her comment, Art turned to her. "Why would you say that?"

"Oh, just something she told me. How she was thinking a lot about that man from Washington. I told her to think about other possibilities. Like maybe you two have something going. Do you?"

Art sighed. How he wished he could tell Alice everything held in a deep lake of wishes in his heart. But nothing like that came out. "We've been good friends. But it seems she doesn't even want friendship anymore."

"I wouldn't take it to heart. Marilyn knows what a good friend she has in you. And in me. This government man will move on to other towns."

Art prayed she was right. Not a day went by when he didn't think of Marilyn. If only he could make up for the way they had parted the other day. To renew their friendship and maybe more. They had been close for so long. Even Alice recognized it. But Marilyn seemed emphatic last week that he caused her more heartache than joy. That maybe they shouldn't be together. But the mere idea of life without her seemed inconceivable, even if the door had shut and all his hopes and dreams appeared to have faded away.

For several days he went through the workday with less cheer. He tried to keep Marilyn from occupying every thought, but it proved impossible. She seemed to be everywhere and in everything he did, from rearranging the tools out back—reminding him of Hardy driving away business—to seeing the blue fabric that reminded him of his favorite dress, to noting a bottle of perfume he wanted to buy her for her birthday. He sought to release the burden to God's tender care. After all, God cared for the flowers of the field and the birds of the air. He cared about this situation too.

The door to the store suddenly banged open and Mr. Fielding marched in. From his pinched eyes and red face, his feet heavy on the wooden floor, Art could see he was not in a pleasant mood. The man had been known for outbursts in the past and today looked to be no exception.

"Can I help you, Mr. Fielding?"

"I'm real upset, Art. I don't have those tools I ordered. It's been three weeks since I gave that young Pearl gal five whole dollars for a hoe, rake, and seeds. I called her mother, and there's been nothing. I was told maybe next week. But it's been three already."

Art felt his anxiety suddenly rise. "I'm sorry to hear that."

"I've got to get that garden planted. So I'm here to buy the tools and seeds I need. If you see that Pearl gal though, you tell her I'm upset about all this."

Art said he would as he helped the older man select the tools he needed and some seed packets. The man's words about the equipment not yet arriving disturbed him. Art blew out a sigh. No matter what Marilyn thought of him interrupting her life, he had no choice but to see her and find out what was happening before angry townspeople descended on the Pearl farm.

⚜

Art's fingers gripped the steering wheel when he thought about the confrontation to come. When he arrived at the farm, Mrs. Pearl seemed surprised to see him. He hoped Marilyn hadn't told her about their disagreement. Even so, he pressed on, asking if they had received any deliveries of tools and seeds from the government.

She shook her head. "Not a thing. I'm surprised Marilyn didn't ask that man about it. She talked to him a week ago."

Art frowned. "Mr. Fielding came into the store today quite upset. The season for planting is getting later, and he had to buy the tools and seeds at the mercantile. He's already out five dollars and now had to spend more."

"Oh dear. Go right now and ask Marilyn what she said to that man. She's at the greenhouse."

Art thanked her and headed outside, taking slow, deliberate steps, not so much from the spasms in his muscles as from fear of the unknown. A week ago he had been driven away from this place. Now that he was back again, Marilyn might see him as some foreboding shadow trying to derail her every move. But he must intervene, despite being put off by these circumstances. He sensed danger now—the same danger he felt the moment that Hardy fellow set foot in their humble town.

He found her potting plants. "Hi, Marilyn."

She whirled about. "Oh, hi. What are you doing here?"

"I spoke to Mr. Fielding. You remember, he was the first one to buy tools and seeds and give you money. He wants to know where they are."

She shrugged and went back to repotting young pumpkin plants into bigger pots. "It takes a while to get them, I guess."

"Marilyn, this is serious. When did Mr. Hardy say they would come in?"

"I'm not sure. He didn't give me an actual date. He said 'soon.'"

"Well, it's been over three weeks since Mr. Fielding gave the money, and he had to buy the tools and seeds at the mercantile today. I'm concerned that if he's upset, others will be too, and they could come here demanding their goods or their money back."

Marilyn's eyes widened as she wiped her hands on a cloth. "But I don't have the money. I gave it to James."

"You need to call him and find out when everything will be delivered."

"All right, I will. I'm sure there's a logical explanation for the delay, with the war going on and everything." She brushed by him, her head held high, and marched to the house. Art followed, determined to know what was happening. She swiped up the stick phone to make the call.

"But this is the number I was given," Marilyn said into the mouthpiece. She paused, her face turning bright red, then mumbled a feeble "Thank you" before hanging up. "I don't understand. The number he gave me now belongs to some woman from Kentucky."

Art wiped the perspiration beading up on his forehead. "Where is the Victory garden manual? Maybe there's a number in there we can call."

Marilyn left for her room and returned with it. Art flipped through the pages and called the Department of Agriculture. He asked for a Quentin Hardy and waited.

"I'm sorry, but no one by that name works in the department or with the Garden Commission."

"But he must. Quentin James Hardy? He came with materials from your department about the Victory garden project. He took a hundred dollars from the citizens of Springville to buy tools and seeds."

"I'm sorry, but there is no one here by that name."

"All right, thank you for checking." Art hung up to see Marilyn's eyes wide, her lips moving but no sound coming from within. "They have no idea who he is," he told her softly.

"No! That can't be! Art, what am I going to do?"

He had no answer.

Chapter 7

Marilyn's world appeared to be collapsing all around her with no way of stopping it. She thought Rob's departure would be difficult enough. Now she was plagued each day by irate townsfolk asking for their seeds and tools. She tried several times to reach Quentin James Hardy with the phone number he had given her, but to no avail. The woman in Kentucky finally told her to stop calling or she would alert the switchboard operator to cease accepting calls from her area. Art suggested she again call the Department of Agriculture and at least report the shenanigans. Marilyn felt her nerves on edge, her palms sweaty, her heart thumping as she spoke to the man in charge.

"Did you see his credentials?" the official asked when she told him what happened.

"No, I didn't. He seemed to say all the right things. He had the paperwork and brochures."

She heard a sigh come through the receiver. "It's unfortunate this happened. But there are shysters roaming about trying to cheat people out of their hard-earned money, using the war effort to cash in. Very sad, but it is happening. That is why you must see any credentials." The official apologized and took down the needed information in the hopes it might lead to the man's whereabouts.

Marilyn slowly hung up the receiver, feeling no confidence that anything would be done. *Why did this have to happen?* Nothing alerted her to the man's evil intentions. Shouldn't the president of the committee, Mr. Tompkins, also be looking into this and making inquiries? This wasn't just her fault, after all. It began with Art showing her that poster and then the Tompkinses, who passed on her information to Quentin Hardy. Now she had no idea what to do.

A knock came on the door. Marilyn retreated, not wishing to see any more angry people demanding their money. She peeked through the parted curtains to see a wide-eyed Alice with compassion written on her features. Marilyn slowly opened the door for her best friend. "I guess you heard."

"It's all over town."

"I can't believe this happened. Why?"

"I don't know, but Mr. and Mrs. Tompkins are very upset. So are some other folks."

Marilyn frowned. "Mr. Tompkins is the president. He gave James my phone number. I wish Art had never showed me that poster and gotten my hopes up." She rattled on, telling Alice the hurtful things stored up inside, none of which really made sense once she said them.

Alice stared at her so hard that Marilyn was obliged to look aside. "You can't blame others for this. It wasn't anyone else's idea to sell tools and seeds. You gave out the brochures and collected the money, which you then gave to that man."

"I. . ." Heat filled Marilyn's face. She turned away, realizing

Alice had hit a hurtful spot. Tears bubbled up in her eyes. "I trusted that man. He said all these wonderful things when he was actually here to cheat the town." A tear slipped out. "Now I can't reach him. He's gone. What am I going to do?"

"I don't know. But if I were you, I think a good start is fixing your relationship with Art. And telling him you're sorry about the way you've been acting. The man loves you so much, Marilyn. He would do anything for you. And you could dearly use his help right now. Do you realize how much other girls would give to have a man like that stand with them, no matter what?"

Marilyn considered what Alice said long after she left. It reminded her of another great Love who stood by her through everything. Her Savior, the One who gave Himself so she might be set free. There were no excuses but a chance to make things right by seeking those who truly cared for her. Like praying to God and seeking forgiveness. And talking to Art. Still, it didn't rescue her from this awful situation. She didn't have a hundred dollars to pay back everyone. No one would ever trust her or even acknowledge her again. She would be an outcast, and the Victory garden project would be dried up and dead.

For several days Marilyn wandered aimlessly about the farm. All the plans, the dreams, the hopes of having something worthwhile come of this venture came raining down in a violent storm of deceit. How would she ever bear up under it all? Her joy at seeing her plants grow in the garden evaporated. She had even forgotten to water the newly transplanted pumpkin plants, and many had begun to wither. Life itself had dried up.

With a halfhearted gesture, she refilled the watering can from the large rain barrel to try and save the plants. Just then she heard a whistle. Dad was coming across the field. Marilyn had said little to him about the goings-on with the Victory garden idea. He'd been busy trying to plant the new corn crop. But from the look on his face, Marilyn realized he knew that folks had come by looking for tools and returning empty-handed with nothing for their hard-earned money.

"I hear you've got yourself in one big pickle, eh, girl?" he asked, chewing on a grassy reed poking out of his mouth. "Wish your mother had told me what was going on long before this. I would've told you never to trust anyone from Washington."

"Oh Dad, what am I going to do?"

He pulled out the reed. "You need to get that money back for those folks. That's what you have to do."

Marilyn stared at him blankly. "But how? I have no idea where the man went. And it takes forever to earn that much."

"Best find yourself a job somewhere so at least you can start earning something. I don't have that kind of money, you know."

"But the man stole it—"

"You gave it to him. It's up to you now." He walked off with his hands stuffed into the pockets of his overalls.

Marilyn exhaled a loud sigh and turned away. Everyone was disappointed in her, and she most of all. Right now she felt droopy like the plants, dying for water to quench the thirst. She gave the plants a long drink from the watering can and could almost feel them bursting to life. *God, I need water right now. I'm drying up under all this. I've made a mess, and only You can make it right again.* She felt a bit better after putting the matter into God's hands, even if the circumstances had not changed. She thought back to the conversation with Alice and how her friend spoke of Art and his love. She wondered now, after all that had happened, if Art would even speak to her again. She didn't deserve it. She'd followed blindly after some conniver from the moment they met. She'd taken the man's fancy words and flowers rather than embracing the truth.

Marilyn then heard the familiar rumble of an engine and knew it was Art's truck. For a moment she wanted to run away and hide in the back of the shed, not only for the things she had done to him and to others but for what she had done to herself. Her feet shifted. She glanced at the shed, considering a hiding place, then decided to stand her ground. If she didn't start by facing Art, how would she ever face anyone again?

Marilyn glanced out of the corner of her eye to see him limping across the field toward her. He had done so well in life, bearing the cross of infirmity bravely like a soldier of the battlefield, refusing to allow disillusionment to cloud his purpose. He never let the pain or other problems of childhood polio affect him. Or if it did, he kept it well hidden. He was God's soldier in more ways than one.

"Hi," he greeted.

"Hi." She turned back to watering the garden. "I can't believe I neglected this. The plants almost died."

"It's looking okay. A few plants have withered, but you saved most of them."

Marilyn tossed aside the can and faced him. "Art, I'm sorry for what I've said and done these last few weeks. You were trying so hard to warn me, and I ignored it all. I ignored God's warnings too."

"It's okay."

A wave of sudden tears in her eyes made his quiet figure shimmer like sunlight on water. "No, it's not okay. You tried many times to give advice. Instead, I let this robber take everything. Now I owe money I have no way to repay. The whole town is angry at me. And I'm sure you're angry too."

"I'm not angry. I blame myself too. I. . .I kept things hidden, you see."

Marilyn stepped back at these words. "Huh?"

"About how I felt. I. . .well, you might as well know. I adore you, Marilyn. I'm in love with you. I have been for as long as I can remember. I should have told you though, even if you didn't want to believe it or accept it. Maybe I held back because I thought I could never be good enough. . .with my leg and all. . .but—"

Marilyn wiped away a lone tear that managed to escape down her cheek. "Alice knew all along. She told me. I just. . . I just saw you like Rob. A brother to me. But you most definitely are *not* Rob. You've tried to rescue me more times than I can say. You've been there with me through everything. I think you really are closer than a friend."

He stepped forward. She felt her nerves on edge. He was no longer Art, the friend she'd known since childhood. He was Art, the one who wanted to be there for her and care for her. Like Christ did for His bride. When he reached out to draw her close for a deep kiss, everything changed. The problems with the Victory garden remained, but she and Art had become what they were meant to be. Together.

⚘

Was this a dream? Marilyn in his arms? Her lips begging for a kiss as much as his? Could this really be happening? Or would it slip away? When they parted and she stepped back, he saw the small smile on her lips and knew everything would be all right. At least with them. But soon the smile melted into an expression laced with anxiety. The problem at hand had not gone away. He'd placed more calls to the Agricultural Department about the incident, informing them the whole town was out one hundred dollars from this thief. The official assured him they were looking into it. But a long-distance promise did nothing to liberate them of the consequences and irate townspeople who ventured into Mr. Winston's store, lamenting over their lack of tools and seeds. Most of them ended up rebuying at the store because they still had gardens to put in. Even with this terrible situation, they would not be dissuaded from their civic responsibilities to help in wartime. How Art wished that God would miraculously bestow the hundred dollars to give back to these dear folks. It seemed like such a simple prayer to answer. Then everything would be set right again, and he and Marilyn could live happily ever after.

Art reached out and took hold of her hand, drawing her close. "I'm sorry all this is happening, Marilyn. But I believe God is going to make something good come of it. I'm just glad that nothing will separate us. Two are better than one. We need to be together in this."

"I wish I had a hundred dollars," she said softly.

"I was just wishing that too." Their eyes met and so too came a pair of weak smiles.

"I don't dare go to church or anywhere in town," she said with a soft moan. "Everyone hates me."

"They don't hate you. I've talked to many of them. They only want to know what to do. They like the gardening idea, especially as the shelves in the store are becoming empty of canned goods. They know things will get worse before they get better. They realize it's time for everyone to roll up their sleeves and grow and can their own vegetables."

"I thought maybe they would hate the whole idea of a Victory garden after losing their money. No one would want to help."

Art shook his head. "You forget the spirit of our town, Marilyn. We stick together through the hard times as well as the good. It's what makes us strong." He paused. "And I haven't given up. You can't either. All will be made right in God's timing."

The words seemed to ring hollow as she moved off, her head down, shoulders slumped, appearing defeated. They walked around the farm some more, stopping at the pens of the goats and pigs and the chicken coop before heading to the fields.

"I don't understand how someone like James could take advantage of others like this," she said softly. "What makes people mean like that?" She pressed her lips together and looked off into the distance.

"It's like everything that began this war, Marilyn. There are those with a lust for power and for things, neither of which satisfies. Do you think everyone with two good legs is happier than I am with only one working one? I see plenty of unhappy people walking around on fine legs. We can't trust in what we have but only in God who satisfies. Until that Hardy fellow realizes the money he stole will never bring him happiness, he will keep right on traveling to towns and looking for willing victims of his schemes. I just pray someone can stop him before he does any more harm."

Marilyn leaned over the fence, and they both gazed into the green pasture where the cattle peacefully grazed. Life could appear so calm, camouflaging the harsh reality of sin standing in the shadow, ready to steal away peace. Art wanted so much for peace to be restored.

They chatted for a bit longer before ideas began fluttering through him, ideas of how he might be able to help restore some peace into the situation. "Do you still have a list of those families who bought tools from Hardy?"

"Yes. Why?"

"I'd like to have it if I may."

She shrugged and led the way to the house and her room where she kept the document. He told her of some errands he must run and made haste for his truck.

Returning to town, he went straight for the mercantile where Mr. Winston was restocking brooms in a container. "What are you doing here, Art? This is your day off."

"I know. I was wondering if anyone else had come in looking to buy tools after not receiving their order from Mr. Hardy."

"I saw a few folks. I saw the Tompkinses too, and they are very angry. But they still plan to do what they can. I mean, going through with the Victory garden project."

Art was happy to hear this news but unhappy that anger still radiated throughout Springville. "I have a list here of those who paid for tools from Hardy. Can you tell me if any of these people have come in and bought tools from you?" Art went over the list with Mr. Winston and found about eight who had. Several others came in to do other shopping but only complained. Art knew now what he must do. It would be a great undertaking, but he was determined to be as God would have him—a peacemaker during a time of war. If that was possible.

Not long after he left the mercantile, he was visiting Mr. Fielding at his home. "Times are hard," the man said gruffly. "I don't like losing five dollars. Especially to some thief."

"And we are trying to get it back, sir. We just want to know if you are still on board with the project and with the boys, despite what's happened. It's all Marilyn ever wanted when she began this idea, even if Hardy used her and this town. To help her brother Rob and the others. The thief may come to steal and destroy, but we are going to stand strong against him."

Mr. Fielding nodded, and they shook hands. "Won't have no thief ruining my life and keeping me from helping," he added. "Or the enemy wins."

Art stopped by several other homes and was able to check off most of the names. To his relief many were able to let go of the money issue for now and allow the government to search for the culprit. Most of all, they appeared willing to exonerate Marilyn from blame. "She was," as he was told by the crotchety Miss Givens who bemoaned her loss of seven dollars, "used by that terrible man." Miss Givens had stared at him and, with her strong voice, vowed never to let some thief rob her of her patriotic duties. She then showed Art the nicely sown garden with rows of healthy-looking vegetables.

Art could not be happier, even if the circumstances still remained. He hoped and prayed the town would come together as one. He prayed too that Marilyn would be able to release her burden and do what was most difficult—forgive herself and move on. Then maybe love would have a chance.

Chapter 8

*E*very day Marilyn knelt and prayed about the situation with the gardening supplies and the stolen money. And every day she heard nothing. She had yet to set foot in town since Hardy took the money and ran, worried about the reaction she might receive from those who once trusted her. Instead, she found her solace in the garden that flourished despite the trials she faced. But Mother did ask when she would return to church. Marilyn wanted no part of the public eye right now. The whole situation had left such a terrible stain, she couldn't face anyone or anything. For Art's part, he refused to leave her. He came by as often as his work schedule would allow, although he did tell her on their last visit that he would need to cut back on travel because of the gas shortage. Marilyn understood, but when days would pass without seeing him, the yearning for his friendly face grew. As did the memory of their kiss, which she replayed many times in her mind. A new door had opened within her that she never wanted to close again. If only she didn't have the episode with Quentin Hardy clouding everything. She tried once more to find out information from the Agricultural Department. Someone had been assigned to investigate, but there was no further information. No news meant bad news and a continued burden without any resolution.

Suddenly there came a rumble and the familiar truck rolling up the lane. Art was making a big sacrifice with the gas shortage to come see her, especially when she didn't deserve it. Many times in the past he'd tried to check her rambunctious ways, only to have her toss his concerns and suggestions aside. But she refused to spend this time depressed. He hadn't used the precious gasoline to come here for that.

Marilyn put on a smile when he walked up carrying a fistful of bluebells. "How sweet, Art. Thank you." And sweet the flowers were, given by a man not looking to steal her emotions like James Hardy had, but one who showed her a pure heart.

His eyes narrowed. "You don't look so good. Are you all right?"

"Oh, you know. Feeling sorry for myself." She trudged back to the house to put the flowers in water. "I wish things would change."

"I worry about you. Which is why I need to get you away from this place. So I've come to invite you to the church picnic later this afternoon."

A wave of panic shot through Marilyn. She turned away. "I can't do that. I can't go anywhere. The whole town is angry. Oh, why did this have to happen?"

"Marilyn, you need to go. It's important. If you don't step out now, you'll never be able to."

Just the thought of a multitude of eyes staring, with looks of disapproval accompanied by whispers about stolen money, sent fear coursing through her. "I can't do it."

Art sighed. "I think it will be very good for you. Moving forward brings healing like nothing else right now." He took up her hand. "And I want you healed from this."

"I'll be all right." But she knew she wouldn't be. Not for a long time. Too much had happened. She'd let herself be carried away with the Victory garden project and all the prestige it held, stumbling about blindly without a thought to her actions or the deception that had played out.

"You're going to have to face the world one day, Marilyn. You can't stay hidden here the rest of your life." He turned away and headed back for his truck.

"Where are you going?"

"I need to go back to town. I'm helping out with the picnic. I'd love to have you come and help me. It would be very good for you."

Marilyn wanted to but shook her head and watched him walk off slowly, his head bent, his hands dug into his pockets. Now she feared she'd lost him too along with everyone else in town. None of this was right, but she didn't know what to do except pray, so long as God was still listening. Especially with things so bleak.

Marilyn plodded back to the house and into the kitchen, where she found Mother making a huge pan of baked beans. "I guess you're going to the picnic."

"It's a lovely day for it, don't you think? Can you fetch the tablecloths out of the drawer, please? I don't know how many will come to the picnic, but I'm sure we'll need most of them."

Marilyn walked over to the linen closet and took out the tablecloths, all different colors, many embroidered with flowers by Mother's loving hand. She thought of the picnic, with everyone laughing and enjoying fried chicken, Mother's baked beans, and the sound of musical instruments. Here she was, caught in a web of her own making with no way to break free. And all because she'd trusted a man with an endearing smile and persuasive speech. She thought of the words in the Bible, of the deceiver who offered words of light but that were actually lies. Lies had besieged Springville, hiding the light of the Victory garden project that would help the men and the country.

An hour later Marilyn heard a car pull into the driveway. It was Mother's friend, Kathleen Miller. Thankfully she had not ordered any of the tools or seeds, but Marilyn still felt strange when the woman stood before the screen door bearing a steaming dish in her hands. "Hi, Marilyn."

She said it so brightly, accompanied by a wide smile, that Marilyn felt her legs weaken. She opened the door and invited the woman in. "Uh, Mother is in the kitchen."

Mrs. Miller nodded and headed inside, dish in hand. All at once another car came up the driveway. Marilyn stared, wondering what on earth was going on. Mother must have decided to have her friends meet here before going on to the church picnic. She began to shy away, heading for the stairs, when she heard Mother call for help. *I can't do this, God*, she told herself. *I can't.*

"Hi, Marilyn!" greeted another voice from the entryway. This time it was Mrs. Fielding, whose husband first complained about the lack of tools he'd ordered. Her heart began to pound. Her palms broke out in a sweat. But Mrs. Fielding too went into the kitchen and began chattering away with Mother. Unable to bear anymore, Marilyn slipped upstairs to her room. She gazed at her sad appearance in the mirror, noting the dark circles under her eyes. She threw cold water on her face and took a brush to her hair. No sense looking like a vagabond with all Mother's friends roaming about. Like Art said, she had no choice. She couldn't hide forever. Could she?

Marilyn gazed out the window to find a steady caravan of cars and people on bicycles making their way up the road to the large gate that led to the fields. Everyone had food and drink. Dad began setting up extra tables while others spread tablecloths on the grass. She stared at all this in confusion and wonder until a knock came on the door.

"Marilyn?"

It was Art. She hurried to open it. "What is going on, Art? Why are all these people here? I don't understand—"

"We decided to bring the picnic to you."

"What?"

Art took her hand in his. "I talked to the families about Hardy and what he did. They were angry Hardy took the money, yes, but angrier still that he tried to stop a project that was bringing us together in a time of need. And I will say not one of them blames you. And to prove it, they agreed to bring the picnic here to show their support—not only for you but for the Victory garden project. For our men. For our country."

Marilyn stared in shock. Tears filled her eyes, and he offered her his handkerchief. She took it with thanks and blew her nose. "I don't know what to say."

"Just be yourself. That's who we all love anyway. Come out and say hello."

She held her breath and did as he asked, holding on to his arm, allowing his strength to lead the way. When she ventured outside, everyone turned and smiled.

The reverend of the church held up his hand, and silence fell over the assembly. "Everyone, thank you so much for coming out today," he said. "We have seen sin try to disrupt our town and steal our joy, but we will not let it gain the victory. Victory instead is our town coming together for one common cause during a time of need. Marilyn Pearl came to us with a great and exciting plan for Victory gardens to feed not only ourselves but others. That is just what Christ would do too. Feed the hungry and give to the poor.

We have her to thank for helping us see what is most important. Marilyn Pearl has done so much for our town. She truly is our Victory garden heroine."

Applause surrounded Marilyn, and suddenly she felt weak-kneed, grateful for Art beside her, his hand squeezing hers. "Can you say something?" he whispered. "God will give you the strength."

Marilyn said a quick prayer under her breath. Now was the time to speak about the burden she carried in her heart. The emotion clogged her throat. She cleared it away as best she could. "Th–thank you. It's hard to speak." She looked over at Art, who nodded. "You may not know, but I did not want to be seen anywhere. I—I knew you would all be upset at having your money lost. I can't blame you. I'm sorry I didn't do all that I could to make sure it was safe. I hope that somehow you might be able to look beyond all this and forgive me. I will still do everything I can to make sure you get your money back—"

"Don't worry about it," someone shouted.

Marilyn shook her head. "I do worry. It is your hard-earned money and—"

Art squeezed her hand and stepped forward. "Marilyn, we know how much you worked on this project. And what it means to you. You didn't do this for yourself. You did it for others. For the men fighting against evil. We wanted to make sure you understand that. If the government finds Hardy, we will rejoice. But if not, we will still rejoice because that's what friends do. In war and in peace." And suddenly she felt his lips kiss her cheek as everyone applauded.

The reverend asked the gathering to bow their heads as he offered a prayer over the food. Marilyn could not believe this was happening. It seemed like a dream, but a good dream, one she never thought would come true. Yet the power of love and forgiveness in the townsfolk who gave her smiles and tables brimming with food showed her a loving God who works all things together for good. Even through something bad. And in this she learned what true victory was all about.

❧

"Looks like you have several winners in the making," Art said with approval. Marilyn bent down to part the large leaves, revealing several plump, tangerine-colored pumpkins growing on the vine. The garden itself had already seen a harvest of lettuce, beets, and carrots, and now the beginnings of the warm-weather vegetables. From all around Springville folks were coming to tell her of their yields. The growing conditions had been God's gift, with just the right amount of rain and sunshine. Their visits made her heart sing for the first time after many weeks of trying to work through the varying emotions of the Victory garden project.

"I heard from Rob," she said. "He's finished boot camp and is soon heading for Europe for training exercises with the British soldiers." She liked the way Art's brown eyes focused on her as they sat down in the grass.

"Are you worried?"

"Yes. I pray for him every night. I pray for lots of things. But mainly about the money I owe the town."

"I wish this wasn't so hard for you. Many of the families that bought those tools and seeds already have good gardens. You need to put it aside."

Marilyn ran her hand through the grassy shoots, feeling the feathery heads. "I know I should. There's been no news from the Agricultural Department. But I suppose they have their hands full with everything going on in the war effort and don't have time to track down one menace."

"We need to trust that God's justice will take care of Quentin

James Hardy. And who knows? Maybe it will be the catalyst that turns him from his evil ways and causes him to pursue the goodness of God. He's not beyond God's hand."

Marilyn nodded. She looked up to see Art staring at her with the same look of affection he always gave before his lips came calling. These days they held hands frequently in town and shared the same straw at the soda fountain. It seemed many of their friends had likewise linked up, with Alice now going out with one of Art's friends. Everyone was seeking companionship in these hard times.

"I was wondering something though," Art said.

Marilyn straightened, fearing the words he might say. She hoped he hadn't had a change of heart. She prayed he was here to stay, no matter what.

"I thought maybe we could go steady," he said softly.

She laughed out of relief. "I thought we were already! Like for years!"

Art laughed loudly, and Marilyn joined in. It was true that neither of them had ever had another love interest. It was as if they were always meant to be together, even with the ups and downs that life seemed to bring. He leaned over for a kiss to seal the commitment, which she accepted with all her heart.

"Then if we've already been doing this for years, what about the next step?"

Marilyn sucked in her breath. "You mean?"

"Only if you feel ready. I won't rush you. I'm fine. I've waited this long." His eyes said it all, how long he had truly waited while Marilyn did her own thing, not realizing his steadfast love that refused to let go, even in the most difficult of circumstances. It amazed her how hard he worked to bring the town together after the news of Hardy making off with the town's money. He had done it all out of love, not only for her but also for a town that refused to retreat in the face of battle. Even if that battle sometimes came from within.

"Art, I have something to say. You know, on that day of the picnic when I was called a heroine—"

"You are," he interrupted.

"No. The heroine desperately needed rescuing by the hero. Or she would have been caught up in the tower of her room forever, never forgiving herself."

Art laughed, and Marilyn looked at him inquisitively. "Well, aren't you glad that stories can have happy endings? I know we don't really have an ending quite yet. There is still the war going on and unanswered questions. But we have each other and God, and a cord of three strands is not easily broken."

Art encircled her with his arms, and Marilyn rested her head on his shoulder. The faint rays of the sun kissed the garden and fell over them on its journey to the horizon. Even in times of war, peace could still be embraced. And that was the greatest victory of all.

Lauralee Bliss has always liked to dream big dreams. Her dream of being a published writer was realized in 1997, after several years of hard work, with the publication of her first romance novel, *Mountaintop*, through Barbour Publishing. Since then she's published over twenty-seven books, both historical and contemporary. Lauralee is also an avid hiker, completing the entire length of the Appalachian Trail, both north and south. Lauralee makes her home in Virginia in the foothills of the Blue Ridge Mountains with her family. Visit her website at www.lauraleebliss.com, and find her on Twitter and Facebook Readers of Author Lauralee Bliss.

Blue Moon

by Johnnie Alexander

For Peggy Clemmer,
whose friendship is a treasured gift.
(Wanna go see a movie?)

Be ye kind one to another, tenderhearted, forgiving one another,
even as God for Christ's sake hath forgiven you.
EPHESIANS 4:32 KJV

❧ Chapter 1 ❧

Near Norris Dam, Tennessee
October 31, 1944

The final notes of the melancholy song faded into a silence broken by static and the energetic voice of the radio announcer. "There you have it, folks, 'Blue Moon' as brought to you by the inimitable Billie Holiday. We brought it special just for you, ladies and gentlemen, boys and girls, because tonight is one of those rare, unusual nights. Don't let your parents send you to bed, kids. Tell them to take you outside to see the—"

Kathleen Forrest turned off the radio in an elaborate wooden cabinet that stood below a framed landscape of cloud-covered mountains. A gold-plated label attached to the frame read: Appalachian Morning.

But the label didn't identify the specific range. When Kathleen traveled south from her rural Ohio home, she might have gone past these particular peaks. Somehow that thought comforted her—especially during her occasional bouts of homesickness.

Her roommates didn't share her curiosity in the painting or its inspiration. Then again, they'd been born and raised in these mountains. Not here in eastern Tennessee, but in Virginia and Kentucky. Kathleen was the outsider. The northerner.

Strange. She'd never thought of herself as a northerner—a Yankee—before coming to this secluded wilderness to do her patriotic duty.

She might have stayed home if she'd been warned how boring that duty would be.

And how lonely.

Though maybe that was her fault. Betty Sue had practically begged her to go on a double date this evening. But Kathleen, all too aware that Betty Sue only asked her because their other two roommates were on patrol tonight, had refused. Though that wasn't her only reason for saying no.

Eventually a displeased Betty Sue had left without a date for her current boyfriend's cousin.

Kathleen didn't like disappointing her friend. Disappointing anyone. But she'd have been miserable if she'd gone on that double date. She couldn't do it. Not tonight.

"Blue Moon," the tune that had played before Kathleen turned off the annoying radio announcer with his endless prattle, seemed to echo in the dimly lit room. She hummed a couple bars and sang a phrase or two though the melancholy music and lonesome lyrics pressed against her already low spirits. At least the song ended with hope—the dream of finding that special someone.

A dream Kathleen once had but now seemed designed for other girls. Flirtatious beauties like Betty Sue.

Kathleen wandered to the window and drew aside the curtain. She peered beyond the nearby mountains to the dark autumn sky. A few stars shone, strong and bright, in the ebony darkness.

"Maybe I should have said yes." Kathleen turned and smiled at

Liberty, her three-year-old German shepherd. The dog, black and gray with tan markings, lay on the rug in front of the wood-burning stove. "But then you would have been home alone. What fun would that have been?"

Liberty stood and stretched, then padded to Kathleen, who knelt and cupped the shepherd's long muzzle in her hands as a mischievous idea came to her. "What do you say, girl? Do you want to see a blue moon?"

Liberty's ears perked, and her tail swished as her entire body wagged a jubilant yes.

"We'll have to be quiet." Kathleen pulled on a jacket and grabbed Liberty's leash from the row of hooks by the door. "We're breaking the rules."

A low sound emitted from Liberty's throat, a strange cross between a moan and a lighthearted growl. Kathleen patted the dog's shoulder and fastened the leash to her collar. "Don't be a worrywart. We won't get caught. I know the patrol schedule, remember? And neither Babs nor Milly ever deviate from it."

A big mistake, in Kathleen's opinion. But her superiors at the Tennessee Valley Authority's Public Safety Service weren't interested in her opinions. More than once she'd been reprimanded for not being in a particular spot at a particular time. But if night after night after night she didn't vary her routine, an enemy saboteur could easily figure out the best place and time to sneak into the facility. She'd never let that happen on her watch.

The reprimands weren't fair. Neither did they persuade her to stick to one repetitive pattern.

She turned out the remaining lights then opened the cabin's door wide enough for her and Liberty to slip through the gap. Noiselessly they ambled along the hard-packed lane, which was loosely covered in fallen leaves and pine needles, toward the dirt road. The bright moon and stars shone enough light to see by, although Kathleen could have made her way along the familiar path in total darkness. At least she liked to believe so.

After checking for traffic—not that she expected any this late— Kathleen and Liberty crossed the road leading to the dam and wended their way through the trees. About ten minutes later, they emerged from the woods and skirted along its edge till they reached one of Kathleen's favorite spots.

The downward sloping woods separated the broad Clinch River from the block of cabins that housed a few of the Women Officers of Public Safety, or WOOPs, as they were often called, and others who either guarded or worked at Norris Dam. The first of several dams constructed by the TVA, the Norris stretched across the Clinch and provided electrical power to the defense-related industries in the area.

Now that most of the young men had either volunteered or been drafted to fight the Germans and the Japanese, the specially trained WOOPs guarded the TVA's vital facilities and installations.

The ground on this side of the tree line sloped to the banks of the Clinch, while the dam, to Kathleen's left, held back tons of water in a mighty reservoir. The slope was broken up here and there by jutting rocks and massive boulders. One of these, about halfway down the hill, had a natural backrest where Kathleen could enjoy a few private moments. Not that she had many opportunities to be alone. Even though they weren't a military unit, her intense training had included gun handling and marksmanship, combat training that included judo, and security protocols. That had been followed by several weeks of training with Liberty.

But when she had the chance and the weather cooperated, Kathleen and Liberty came here. Whether their visits were during the day or in the midst of the night, her aching heart found peace as she gazed at the river and the mountains rising beyond it. God's presence seemed near, and His everlasting love wrapped around her. She had little else to hold on to.

When they'd settled against the boulder, Kathleen pointed to the moon. "There it is, Liberty. Isn't it beautiful?" She leaned closer, placing her ear near the dog's nose. "What's that? It doesn't look blue to you? That's because a blue moon isn't blue, silly. It's just the second full moon in one month. That makes it kind of rare."

She stared at the silver orb, round and full and streaked with shadows. "As rare as true love."

The tune played in her mind again, pulling an inexplicable longing from her heart. No, not so inexplicable. Like Billie Holiday, Kathleen didn't have a dream of her own. She didn't have someone to love, and no one loved her.

Not anymore.

Perhaps if the Japanese hadn't bombed Pearl Harbor and plunged the United States into war, she'd have married the man of her dreams and settled into a comfortable, domestic existence. Instead, she'd kissed him goodbye when he left for basic training, wrote him every day, and memorized every letter he sent her.

Until his letters stopped coming.

More than a year had passed since she'd received his last one—little more than a cryptic note written in a shaky hand. Sometime during those long months, she stopped writing to him.

He still wrote to his parents though. Grandma used to pass along news from his mom in her letters to Kathleen. Until Kathleen asked her to stop. She didn't want to know secondhand, thirdhand information about him.

That didn't stop her thinking about him though. Or praying for him. Every single day.

She placed her arm around Liberty's shoulders and rested her cheek against the dog's neck as she softly hummed the haunting melody.

A cloud drifted in front of the moon, hiding its reflected light. A few moments passed. Suddenly Liberty stiffened. Kathleen straightened and stared in the same direction as her dog. A movement on the other side of the river caught her eye. Kathleen reached for her .38 then remembered she hadn't brought the gun with her. After all, she was only going for a walk. She wasn't on patrol.

The cloud drifted away, and there in the moonlight someone stood at the river's edge. A woman and a dog.

Kathleen relaxed. "Shhh, girl," she whispered as she gave Liberty the hand signal to *down*. "It's only Milly and Frankie. They mustn't know we're here."

Liberty lay down and rested her nose on her front paws. But her body remained stiff as she tracked the movements at the river's far shore. Kathleen slunk as low as she could and did the same. Milly and Frankie, a huge German shepherd named for President Roosevelt, walked along the river, apparently oblivious to their presence.

Kathleen couldn't help smiling to herself. Milly would be furious if she knew they were hiding from her, watching her, and that neither she nor Frankie had detected their presence. Though it seemed odd that Milly was on that side of the river. By now she should be on the north side of the dam. Kathleen's nerves tingled. Why had Milly deviated from her usual schedule?

All of Kathleen's senses sharpened as she puzzled over Milly's out-of-the-ordinary behavior. The smells of decaying leaves and aging river life grew more pungent as the breeze blew from the reservoir behind the dam. She could almost hear the beating of her heart and every breath that Liberty took. But the closer Milly and Frankie got to the base of the dam, the more Liberty relaxed.

Kathleen decided to wait at least fifteen more minutes, to give Milly and Frankie plenty of time to cross to the opposite side of the immense structure, before leaving their hiding place and going home. Her back ached from crouching, so she straightened and rolled her shoulders.

To pass the time, she started to hum "Blue Moon" again, but the melancholy melody had raked her heartstrings too much for one night. Instead, she quietly sang the words to "Boogie Woogie Bugle Boy." The upbeat tempo got her blood flowing and her head bobbing. She followed that with a whispery rendition of "Don't Sit Under the Apple Tree."

She was on the last verse when Liberty's ears perked up. The hackles on her neck rose beneath Kathleen's hand.

Kathleen's song faded as her body tensed. Once again, a cloud obscured the moon, leaving the river in shadows. But Kathleen could detect no movement, could hear no sounds above the croaking of the frogs and toads near the river.

Liberty sat then twisted her body to face the woods on their side of the dam.

"What is it, girl?" Kathleen whispered. "Do you see something? Someone?"

Maybe Babs was out here, though she shouldn't be patrolling the tree line. Her assignment was farther upriver.

A shadow moved. Or was Kathleen's imagination working overtime? Liberty emitted a low growl, and Kathleen grasped the dog's collar. "Shhh."

She stared at the spot then blinked, trying to differentiate between the depths of darkness beneath the trees. Another movement, and the shape came into focus.

Someone stood at the edge of the woods.

❧ Chapter 2 ❧

*R*oger Craig squatted at the base of an old maple, careful to avoid rustling the dead leaves that surrounded the thick trunk. The clouds were doing him a favor tonight as they drifted in front of the moon and hid its reflected light. Earlier that evening someone mentioned it was a rare blue moon. Roger would have preferred a quarter sliver instead. He'd argued with his superiors about waiting for a darker night. But they insisted he do what needed to be done.

He'd had no choice. Tonight was the night. So be it.

When the moonlight appeared again, Roger lifted binoculars to his eyes and focused on the base of the dam on this side of the Clinch River. He planned to set a couple charges where they'd make the most impact while he stayed as dry as possible. No need to slip into that dark water.

He'd place the rest of the charges inside the structure then hightail it out of there. And disappear.

He trained the binoculars on the road built on top of the dam. No traffic. Not that he'd expected any. Due to the blackout regulations, most people were inside their homes this late at night. His only concern, more an annoyance than a credible threat, was being seen by one of the women who patrolled the dam and the riverbanks at night.

WOOPs, they were called, the pants-wearing women who'd stepped up to take the jobs vacated by the young men who'd gone overseas to fight America's enemies. So many young men who risked their lives to stop evil from coming to their homeland. Too many who had already died.

The war needed to come to an end. Soon. Now.

This mission wouldn't do much to bring peace, but Roger would be a step closer to returning to the European battlefields if he succeeded. He'd do whatever it took for that to happen.

He lowered the binoculars and patted the canvas bag that rested against his hip. Its substance and heft calmed the nervous energy surging through him. His senses were on full alert, ready for any deviation from his meticulous plan.

Preparation and practice often meant the difference between success and failure. He'd memorized the dam's blueprint until he was confident he could navigate the catwalks and inner crannies with confidence. He'd been out here every night for two weeks to observe the security routine. And he could set the charges in his canvas bag with his eyes closed.

Patience. The third key to success.

His haunches ached, and he shifted slightly to redistribute his weight. The bag scuffed against dry leaves, but the whisper of noise barely rose above the breeze nudging the maple's orange and yellow branches.

Even so, Roger stilled his breathing and relaxed his muscles. For a long moment, he remained silent, though he suspected he could walk straight to the dam in the light of the blue moon without anyone being the wiser. Those so-called WOOPs-de-doo officers, even with their guns, could do little to stop an operative trained in defensive measures. Though they did have those military dogs. Sharp teeth Roger respected. But the patrols wouldn't be on this side of the dam for at least another hour.

The unexpected appearance of the one—Millicent Turner was her name—who'd shown up across the river hadn't disturbed his plans. No one could foresee every anomaly, and he'd almost expected something like that to happen. She probably had an overly ambitious superior who hoped to catch Roger in the act. A typical wrench in the works to keep him on his toes.

Another cloud obscured the moon. Now was his moment.

He returned the binoculars to the bag then slowly stood, bracing himself against the trunk of the maple while the cramping in his legs eased. He pulled the wool cap further down his forehead, adjusted the bag's strap that hung across his body, and rested his palm for a moment on the holster of the Colt Government pistol he wore at his right thigh.

In his mind's eye, he visualized the path he planned to take to the dam. The boulders that jutted from the slope at irregular intervals were his guide. He'd stay between them and the tree line, moving from one outcrop to the other until he reached his destination. Even in the darkness he could distinguish the first boulder, about thirty-five, maybe forty yards away. As he stared at it, the hairs on the back of his neck raised.

He brushed away the strange sensation and sprinted toward the boulder. He'd only covered a few yards when an apparition appeared and bolted toward him.

Roger dropped to the ground, drawing his gun in one fluid

motion, and aimed. A shout disturbed the night air—"Liberty!"—and a second figure appeared.

Time slowed as Roger's mind registered the running apparition as a dog, and he lowered the barrel a fraction of a second before the gun's report echoed between the mountains.

But not low enough.

The dog yelped and fell, whimpered, and pawed at the air.

"Noooo." The second apparition, a woman, ran toward them.

If this dog was Liberty, then the woman was—

Roger jumped to his feet and hurried toward the dog. His mind whirled, thoughts and emotions colliding, but he didn't have time to sort through them. Not now.

Help the dog. Calm the woman. If at all possible, hide his identity.

Those were his new objectives.

But the woman didn't stop by the dog as he'd expected her to do. Instead, she ran straight toward him. He stood his ground and held up his hands. "I didn't—"

She barreled into him, knocked the gun from his grasp, then grabbed his arm with both of her hands. The next instant, he flipped and landed on his back. All the air whooshed from his lungs.

While he struggled to catch his breath, she rolled him onto his stomach, dug her knee into his back, and bound his hands with what must have been the dog's leash.

He didn't attempt to free himself or to overpower her. Guilt gnawed at him for shooting the animal. If she died—

But he couldn't do much about that now. Better for his captor to think she had him securely tied so she'd tend to her dog. He twisted his head to follow her movements.

She retrieved the gun, and for a moment he feared she planned to conk him on the head with it. But the dog whimpered, and she scurried to the injured animal.

"Liberty," she whispered. "Don't move." Her voice cracked. "Don't die."

Roger deepened his voice and feigned a southern accent. "Put pressure on the wound."

"Don't tell me what to do." She removed her jacket then pressed it against the dog's shoulder.

The woman's body shook, and Roger sensed she was doing her best to keep her grief in check.

"I didn't know 'twas a dog till it was too late," he said.

"Too late?" She turned toward him, and he averted his face. Maybe, if he was careful, he'd get out of this without her recognizing him. He tasted dirt and spat.

"She was attackin' me."

"And I'm arresting you." She shot the words at him with more venom than he would have thought possible.

He rested his forehead against the dirt and peered at her out of his peripheral vision. Moonlight, no longer shielded by the dark clouds, shone on her and the whimpering dog. Her hair, as dark as the shepherd's, fell to her shoulders in loose waves, framing an oval face with delicate features. An attractive face even though her jaw was clenched and her skin stretched tight across her bones.

A familiar face. One he'd never expected to see again.

She removed her belt and tightened it around the blood-soaked jacket as a siren sounded in the distance.

He had to get out of here before the wrong type of help arrived. Before she got a closer look at him. But how could he leave her alone with the wounded dog?

While she focused on stopping the blood, he wiggled his

fingers. She'd been in too big of a hurry to notice how he'd positioned his hands. Or maybe the WOOPs officers weren't trained in those techniques. One hand then the other slipped from the leash. Even though it was probably too dark for her to notice he was no longer bound, he held both hands behind his back and gripped the leash.

The siren grew louder, and she raised her head in that direction. "Help is coming." She walked toward him, gun in one hand, and picked up his canvas bag. Without thinking, he leaped to his feet and grabbed the strap.

His quick movement startled her, but she quickly recovered and pointed the gun at him. He averted his face and let go of the strap. Perhaps it was more important to conceal his identity than the contents of the bag.

At least to him.

Though her eyes were shadowed, he sensed they widened with the shock of what she'd found inside. "What were you going to do?"

He kept his head lowered and shrugged.

"Sit down."

He sat.

"Don't move. Not even a muscle. Or I'll shoot you. I swear I will."

"I believe you, ma'am. I surely do."

With her eyes fixed on him, she carried the bag back to the dog and sat beside her. The gun wavered but not enough for him to believe she wouldn't shoot him if he made a wrong move. With her other hand, she found the flashlight he'd tucked in an outer pocket of the bag and turned it on. She waved the beam toward the road on top of the dam.

Back and forth. Back and forth.

Roger pulled up his knees, rested his forearms on them, and

lowered his head. He'd failed at his mission. He'd shot—perhaps killed—Kathleen's dog. And now he'd have to suffer the consequences.

And the indignity of being caught by the WOOPs-de-doo who was never supposed to know he was here.

Who now had even more reason to hate him.

Chapter 3

*K*athleen relinquished the saboteur's pistol and canvas bag to the first military police officer who reached her. "I think he planned to blow up the dam. He's got black stuff all over his face." She glanced at the man, but his back was to her. Against the darkness of the trees, he almost seemed a ghostly silhouette instead of a living, breathing person.

He stood with his feet apart, his hands clasped together behind his head. Making no attempt to get away. Making no effort to explain himself. She furrowed her brow, staring at his outline, made bulky by his thick jacket and woolen cap.

The MP looked in the bag and whistled. "Never expected anything like that to happen around here."

"I don't know why not." A second officer removed handcuffs from his utility belt while striding toward the stranger. "Think of the industries that'd shut down if this dam went ka-pooey. Could mean the difference between victory and defeat."

Kathleen exchanged a glance with the MP then knelt beside Liberty, near enough to feel the shepherd's warm breath on her cheek. "He shot my dog." Blood soaked her jacket, and Kathleen struggled to hold her emotions in check. It wouldn't do to appear weak in front of these men. No need to give them a reason to criticize the WOOPs guards.

Liberty's tongue slid across Kathleen's jaw, and Kathleen ran her fingers over the dog's head.

The first MP knelt on Liberty's other side. "How bad is it?"

"The bleeding won't stop."

"Sir, I'm taking this dog to the doc." Without waiting for a response, he scooped Liberty into his arms and lumbered up the slope to his jeep. A couple more vehicles, sirens sounding, crossed the dam road and pulled up nearby.

Kathleen glanced at the other officer. She could barely make out his features in the darkness.

"Go." He gripped the stranger's upper arm. "Someone will get your statement later."

"Thank you." She raced toward the jeep and climbed into the back seat with Liberty. The MP called someone on his radio as he sped along the winding road to the veterinary clinic at the dog training compound. The trip took about ten minutes, but each of those minutes seemed like an hour. When they arrived, the MP braked to a hard stop. The clinic door flew open and the vet, Dr. Lawson, hurried toward them.

The next few moments passed in a blur. Dr. Lawson and the MP rushed Liberty into a small operating room. Kathleen caught glimpses of metal instruments and a surgical table before a woman wearing a white lab coat over a lavender dress—Kathleen couldn't remember her name—escorted her and the MP out the door.

Kathleen turned and peered through the door's observation

window. "I should be in there," she murmured.

"You'd only be in the way." The MP cupped her elbow and led her toward the waiting area. When they passed a set of restrooms, he stopped and examined his blood-streaked hands. Kathleen stared at her own. Blood—Liberty's blood—stained her fingers, and a dark smear moistened her blouse.

Her stomach roiled. She gagged then pushed through the restroom door.

After retching the meager contents of her stomach and scrubbing her hands raw, Kathleen returned to the waiting area.

The MP wasn't there, but another officer stood by the front desk. Kathleen's shoulders tensed as she noted the insignia on his uniform. They'd never met, but she'd seen him a few times before. Even though the WOOPs weren't military, he'd been one of the dignitaries at her training graduation. She stood at attention but didn't salute.

"This isn't the time or place for formalities." He extended a hand. "I'm Major Everett Rafferty."

"Officer Kathleen Forrest."

"I was at headquarters when the report came in. That gunshot created quite the stir."

"I can imagine, sir."

"I've been briefed that your dog was hit. But you—" He wagged his finger toward her bloodstained clothes. "Not yours, is it?"

"No, sir."

"Good, that's good." He gestured toward the seating area. "Please have a seat, Officer Forrest."

She chose a chair that faced the hallway door. She wanted to know the instant Dr. Lawson emerged from surgery. To see the expression on his face. To know before he spoke if he had good news or bad. Her fingers gripped the seat, and all her muscles stiffened. Her only defense against her crumbling emotions was to hold herself rock steady.

Major Rafferty angled a nearby chair and rested his hat on his knee as he sat. "I'm sure the doctor will do everything he can to save your dog. From what I understand, he's quite competent."

Kathleen no longer trusted her voice. She nodded, her focus on the door.

"It was an unfortunate mistake."

The words settled into her consciousness as the seconds ticked by. Surely she'd misunderstood, but they echoed in her skull. She frowned.

"A mistake?" Her voice rose, but she couldn't suppress her anger any longer. "He deliberately shot her."

"My apologies." He brushed imaginary lint from his trouser leg. "I only meant. . .never mind. We'll talk about it in the morning."

"Talk about what?" Her tone bordered on insolence. So did her question. Obviously both her TVA Public Safety superiors and the Army would want to know every single detail of what had happened. But all she could think about was Liberty lying on that surgical table. The blood drying on her blouse. The wretched taste that lingered in her mouth.

"What happened tonight should not have happened," he said.

"I agree."

He made a humphing noise, and Kathleen shifted her gaze to his. Distinguished speckles of gray lightened his dark hair, and deep wrinkles creased the outer edges of his eyes. His inscrutable expression caused her stomach to roil again. And her mind to regret any hint of disrespect.

She deliberately softened her tone. "At least we caught him."

"Security is of the utmost importance in this matter."

"I know."

"The gunshot will be explained away. A training accident or

some such nonsense." His gaze hardened. "You're to tell no one about the man you saw. You're to answer no questions from anyone but me without my express permission. Do you understand?"

As he spoke, Kathleen leaned back in her chair as if pushed there by the force of his words. She purposely relaxed her grip on the seat, flexed her fingers, and folded her hands together in her lap. Her mind raced with the implications.

"But what about my boss at the TVA? He'll want to know—"

"He'll be briefed."

"How do I explain about Liberty?"

"You don't."

"But my roommates—"

"Can't know anything." He leaned forward. "If I can't count on your discretion, I will detain you."

Kathleen scooted her chair farther from his as her eyes widened. "Sir," she said, swallowing and lowering her gaze, "that won't be necessary."

"Good. I've already made more comfortable arrangements than a cell. Please don't make me regret my trust in you."

Kathleen pulled her shoulders inward. Something else was going on here—something deeper than thwarted sabotage. She snuck a glance at the major. He'd picked up a magazine from a nearby table and lazily flipped through the pages.

Her pulse quickened.

Why was he here?

Had the TVA even been notified?

Why the secrecy about what had happened to Liberty?

So many questions but no answers to any of them. Or perhaps, in her worry over Liberty, she wasn't thinking straight. Of course military security wouldn't want everyone in the valley to know that the dam had almost been blown up by a saboteur.

An English-speaking saboteur with a southern accent. Her nerves tensed again, and she scraped at the cuticle on her thumbnail.

An *American* saboteur.

The man they'd caught was a traitor who'd plotted to cripple the research facilities, munitions factories, and the aluminum plants that depended on the power that the dam provided them. A heartless scumbag who'd tried to kill her dog.

If only she had never left the house—hadn't been beguiled by her loneliness into seeking out the blue moon. Liberty would be sleeping at the foot of Kathleen's bed instead of enduring the pain and stress of surgery.

Except if they hadn't been on the riverbank, no one would have apprehended the saboteur. He'd have been free to complete his traitorous mission.

Hot tears stung Kathleen's eyes, and she swiped them away before the major saw them. A heavy ache expanded in her chest until she thought her ribs would explode. If Liberty died. . . But no, she couldn't allow herself to finish that thought. They'd been a team for almost a year now, and the dog was her best friend. The shepherd seemed to understand Kathleen's every mood, and of course she could never divulge any of the secrets that Kathleen whispered into her large ears.

Kathleen shifted in her chair, twisting away from the major, who now seemed engrossed in his magazine. She rested her head against the back of the uncomfortable chair while her heart cried to God the words she didn't know how to say. Prayers for her dog. Prayers for protection from danger. Prayers for this endless war to end.

Oh God, would it never end?

Four months ago, the Allies had invaded the Normandy beaches. Optimism had swept the country as the immense army marched across Europe. But now it seemed that Hitler and the Nazis had dug in their heels for another stand.

A stand that might allow the war to make its way here.

Kathleen shook her head to clear her thoughts. The man had appeared from the trees, a dark shadow amid dark shadows. Liberty's growl had been enough proof that the man wasn't a figment of Kathleen's imagination. Per protocol, she'd unleashed her dog, who'd bounded toward the man.

Startled by the gun's flash, Kathleen's body responded while her mind needed a few seconds to comprehend the situation. For the first time, she'd used her judo moves outside of training. There again, her body knew exactly what to do while her thoughts were in turmoil.

As soon as she had the man subdued and under control, she'd returned to Liberty.

She brushed her hands against each other as if ridding herself again of the blood she'd already washed away.

Early in the war, Germans arrived at the shores of Long Island and the coast of Florida by submarine with plans to blow up a number of targets, including the Aluminum Company of America's plant in nearby Knoxville.

Operation Pastorius, as it was known, failed when the German agents were captured. Six of the eight were executed.

As far as Kathleen knew, there had been no other threats to American soil. Until now.

She raised her head, struck by a disturbing thought.

Where there was one saboteur, wouldn't there be others? The stranger had been caught, but what other nefarious schemes had been planned?

She'd had a false sense of security, thanks to her training and her dog. But that security ended with one single gunshot. And Liberty had paid the price for her foolishness.

The outer door of the clinic opened, and the MP who'd placed the handcuffs on the saboteur entered. Except he wasn't wearing an MP armband. Or an MP uniform. In the darkness and in her concern over Liberty, Kathleen had assumed he was with the military police. Just like the soldier who had carried Liberty to his jeep.

But this man wore Army khakis with only an officer collar insignia. Nothing to indicate his specific rank. Kathleen wavered between getting to her feet and staying seated. He must have noticed her hesitation, because he held up a hand.

"No need to stand, Officer Forrest." He nodded to the major, who closed his magazine and placed it on the table. "How is Liberty?"

Kathleen shifted her gaze from Major Rafferty to the newcomer. "She's in surgery. We're waiting for news."

"I'm sure Dr. Lawson will do everything he can for her."

"I hope so." She prayed so.

His encouraging smile faded as he turned his attention to the major. "I'd like to have a little chat with Officer Forrest, if you don't mind. In private."

"And if I do mind?" Major Rafferty responded in a flat tone.

The newcomer's slight shrug suggested embarrassment at the request. But something in his demeanor—perhaps the set of his jaw or the intensity of his gaze—made Kathleen suspect he wasn't actually asking the major for permission.

Who could this man be?

The major slowly stood, as if to work out the kinks in his joints as he did so. "I'll be outside. Stretching my legs."

"Perhaps you'd wait outside the operating room instead. Stop the doctor if he heads this way."

Rafferty made a disgruntled noise, but he didn't object.

"Thank you, Major." The newcomer stood aside for the older man to pass then shut the hallway door behind him.

Kathleen gripped her seat again as he sat in the chair vacated by the major. He leaned forward and the smile returned. His eyes were soft and friendly.

"No need to be nervous. I'm Special Agent Rusty Minshall with Army CIC. That's Counter Intelligence Corps."

"I know what it means." *But not how you're here so quickly.* It made sense that CIC would investigate sabotage, especially on a vital target like Norris Dam. But why were they already at the base?

"Good. Then you'll understand why I need to talk to you."

"Major Rafferty said I shouldn't talk to anyone but him."

"I'm sure he meant well by giving you that advice. It's true, you could be arrested if you told your coworkers, your roommates, even your family about what happened tonight."

"Arrested?" The knot forming in Kathleen's stomach turned to mush. She covered her mouth and prayed she wouldn't be sick again. Not that she had anything left in her stomach to vomit.

"Nobody wants that to happen," Minshall said. "But I do need you to answer a few questions. And I need you to tell me the truth."

"I'm not a liar."

"Good." He stood and placed his hands behind his back.

Kathleen felt small and insignificant as he towered over her. No doubt that was exactly what he intended. She lifted her chin and straightened her shoulders.

"How did you know about tonight's operation?"

She blinked and shook her head. "I. . .I didn't. What do you mean, 'operation'?"

"Officer Forrest, I ask the questions. You answer them." His earlier friendliness had disappeared, and his lips pressed together in a straight line as he glowered at her.

"I didn't know about any operation."

"Then why were you and your dog on the riverbank?"

Kathleen looked down and clasped her hands in her lap. How could she explain something she didn't understand herself? If she told the truth, he'd think she was a sentimental lonely heart. What if she got kicked out of WOOPs because of a nostalgic whim? Heat rose up her neck and burned her cheeks.

"The truth, Officer Forrest. Please."

"We went for a walk." She raised her eyes to his. "That's all. We often sit in front of that boulder and look out over the river. It's a nice view, and tonight was a full moon. I wanted to see it."

"You couldn't see it from your cabin door?" Suspicion laced his tone.

She met his gaze without wavering, but the beat of her heart thumped against her ears. "I couldn't see it reflecting on the water."

He remained still, appraising her, as her heart pounded. "You were surprised to see the trespasser?"

"I was."

"I believe you." He walked to the hallway door, placed his hand on the knob, then turned back to Kathleen. "You'll be escorted to my office in the morning to give a formal statement. Until then, you will tell no one of our conversation. Not even Major Rafferty. Understood?"

"Yes, sir." Though she didn't understand at all. Who had more authority, the major or the CIC agent? Nothing in her WOOPs training had prepared her for a situation like this. *Stick to the truth.* That's all she could do. Besides, she hadn't done anything wrong. Quite the contrary, in fact.

"Good." Minshall opened the hallway door, took several steps inside, then returned. A congenial smile softened his expression. "Dr. Lawson is waiting for you. He appears pleased."

Kathleen jumped to her feet and, out of habit, smoothed her skirt. Her hand passed over a stiff spot, and she recoiled from the dried blood. A shudder raced up her spine.

"Are you all right?"

"Yes, sir. Thank you, sir."

He tilted his head toward the open door. "Go."

Kathleen hurried past him and along the corridor. Thinking about and stewing over the strange conversation would have to wait. All that mattered now was seeing Liberty. If Dr. Lawson hadn't been standing in front of the operating room door, blocking her way, she'd have sailed right past him. Instead, she halted and took a deep breath.

"How is she?"

"Sleeping." Dr. Lawson placed a comforting hand on Kathleen's shoulder. "She lost a lot of blood, but barring an infection or anything unusual, she should be back to work in a few weeks."

The heavy weight Kathleen had borne on her shoulders since the shooting suddenly lifted like a hot air balloon. She wanted to throw her arms around the veterinarian's neck but hugged them to herself instead. "May I see her?"

"For only a moment," Major Rafferty said. "It's been a long night for all of us."

Kathleen smiled her thanks then went through the door and straight for the table. Liberty lay beneath a blanket, as still as if she were frozen except for the almost imperceptible rise and fall of her chest. Kathleen rested her hand on the dog's side.

"I'm sorry," she whispered. "We shouldn't have been there." *Except then the dam would have been blown up.* She closed her eyes, unwilling to pursue those thoughts again. "I'm sorry."

Chapter 4

A jail cell or "more comfortable arrangements"? Why were those Kathleen's only two options when all she wanted to do was to wake up in the morning in her own bed to find the night's events had been nothing but a horrid dream? She had promised Major Rafferty that she'd tell her roommates nothing, but he'd been unyielding. She wouldn't be going home tonight.

Despite the late hour, Anita Rafferty had waited up for them. The major disappeared after a curt "good night" while his wife pointed out the bathroom then ushered Kathleen to a tidy bedroom filled with sports and military memorabilia. An overnight bag rested on the foot of the bed.

"An MP dropped that off for you," Mrs. Rafferty said. "If you want anything else, then do your best to do without. It's what we all must do in days like these."

She left the room and disappeared down the hall.

Kathleen unzipped the bag and examined its contents. Her

nightgown. A clean uniform. A few toiletries. Only the basics.

Had the MP who brought the bag also packed it for her? Gone through her drawers and her personal belongings?

She sat on the side of the bed, elbows on knees, and buried her face in her hands. What difference did it make who packed the bag? All that mattered was Liberty. She'd be fine.

And a saboteur had been caught.

Thank You, Father. Thank You.

Kathleen sat a moment longer as her eyes grew heavy, and then she shook off the stupor before she fell asleep in her ruined clothes. That she couldn't do. Not when they were stained with Liberty's blood.

She pushed herself off the bed and carried the bag to the bathroom. When she returned—face washed, teeth brushed, and wearing her nightgown—she pulled back the covers and slipped beneath the crisp sheets.

When she reached to turn off the lamp, she found a plate covered by a napkin and a tumbler of water on the table. Beneath the napkin were two oatmeal cookies.

Kathleen's mouth watered. It'd been hours since she'd eaten, but her stomach still felt queasy. She nibbled the edge of one of the cookies, then devoured it and the other one. Anita Rafferty might not be the most welcoming of hostesses, but she definitely knew how to bake a great-tasting cookie.

Chapter 5

*R*oger paced the small room, back and forth and back and forth. No doubt someone watched him through the one-way mirror. Not that he cared. After spending a sleepless night in a hard bunk in an even smaller cell, he needed to stretch his muscles. Besides, counting steps was preferable to thinking.

About the wounded dog and the ferocious girl.

About the mess he'd made of the operation.

He intertwined his fingers and pressed his hands against the back of his head as he crossed the room again.

This had been his chance to prove himself. To show he could do what needed to be done. That he was ready to get back in the game.

The plan had been simple. Straightforward even. If it had succeeded, he'd soon be on his way to where the real fighting happened. Where he'd be now if not for. . .

No.

He wouldn't let himself fall into that rabbit hole. Not now and not here. He eyed the mirror. Not when someone watched him. Appraised him. Sought out his weaknesses.

Bottom line, Kathleen Forrest and her blasted dog weren't supposed to be there. He'd seen the duty rosters. He'd spied on each WOOPs-de-doo officer as she walked the dam's perimeter. He'd done his due diligence.

And yet Kathleen had been there.

How had she known? Who had let the secret slip?

That was the person responsible for wounding her dog. Not him.

His stomach churned as he relived the horrific moment when Liberty jerked and fell. When the blood oozed onto her coat. When Kathleen pressed her jacket into the wound while she blinked tears from her dark eyes.

He had to give her credit. She'd taken him down as if he were a rag doll.

Not that he'd fought her. He'd learned the WOOPs training included judo, but she'd still taken him by surprise. Another mistake he'd made—underestimating her abilities.

Maybe he should have retreated. With her dog wounded, possibly dying, she might not have followed him into the woods.

But he couldn't leave her.

He couldn't let her know who he was either, but he couldn't—wouldn't—leave her.

A key sounded in the door then opened.

Special Agent Rusty Minshall.

Roger nodded then shifted his eyes toward the mirror.

"No one's there," Minsh said.

"You sure about that?" Roger asked, dropping the southern accent he'd used when talking to Kathleen.

Minsh gestured toward the table. "Have a seat."

"Is that an order?"

"No."

"I'd rather stand." Roger shoved his hands into his pockets to keep them still then leaned against the wall.

Minsh laid a folder on the table and pulled out a chair. Instead of sitting, he propped one foot on the seat and rested his elbow on his thigh. "What happened out there?"

"How's the dog?"

"Still alive. Dr. Lawson is optimistic she'll be back on duty in a month or so."

"That's good." Roger wiped his palm along his face and unshaven jaw. "I didn't want to. . . She came right at me."

"That's what she's trained to do."

Roger stared at the mirror then took his seat. Despite Minsh's assurance, Roger was skeptical that no one stood on the other side.

Observing. Listening.

Minsh glanced back at the mirror then sat in his chair. He pulled it close to the table and leaned forward. "You have something else to say?"

Roger met his boss's gaze, gauging the man who could keep him stationed stateside for the duration of the war. He lowered his head and shielded his lips with his hand. His voice was barely audible. "Did you change the duty roster?"

"Is that what you think?" Minsh's tone was normal, as if he wanted to prove to Roger that his suspicions were unwarranted.

But Roger couldn't ignore his training. He'd give nothing away until he had a few answers of his own. "She wasn't supposed to be there. Not on that side of the dam. Nobody was."

"The duty roster wasn't changed."

"Then why was she there? And why was Milly Turner on the

other side of the river?"

"Operations like this have a way of being leaked. Someone may have hoped to stop you to further his own agenda."

"I had a similar thought." *An overly ambitious desk jockey. Probably angling for a promotion.* "That would explain Officer Turner's change of routine."

"But not Officer Forrest's behavior."

"Have you talked to her?"

"Only for a few minutes." Minsh slid the folder toward Roger. "She'll be here soon, but everything you need to know about her is in here."

"I already know all I want to know." More than Minsh knew he knew, that was for sure.

"You know her marksmanship scores? Her times on the obstacles course?"

"Why would I need to know any of that?"

"You have a new assignment." Minsh tapped the folder. "And Kathleen Forrest is your new partner."

Roger's stomach caved as if he'd been punched in the gut. A hundred retorts zipped through his head, none of them appropriate. He lowered his head and focused on returning his breathing to something resembling normal. When he felt calmer, he looked Minsh straight in the eyes.

"Do you have the authority to send a WOOPs to Europe?" He tried for an even tone but failed. Whatever Minsh had planned, Roger wasn't going to like it. "In case you've forgotten, she's civilian. Not military."

"Your next assignment is only a few miles away."

Roger shook his head and refrained from pounding his fist on the table.

"Look," Minsh said. "I know you want to go back—"

"You *promised* I'd go back."

"And you will." Minsh's voice hardened. "But not yet."

"If she hadn't been there, I wouldn't have failed."

"Last night has nothing to do with keeping you here. Something odd has come up. And I need my top man to figure it out."

Flattery. That's all it was. Still, Minsh's conciliatory tone eased the disappointment a hair or two.

An assignment only a few miles away, he'd said.

"What is it, one of the plants in Knoxville?"

"I'll brief you and Officer Forrest together. Like I said, she'll be here soon." Minsh glanced at his watch. "I'm going to grab a cup of coffee. Want one?"

"Sure."

"While I'm gone," Minsh said as he headed for the door, "familiarize yourself with Officer Forrest's file."

Roger didn't answer. When the door closed again, he ran his hand across the folder and let his mind drift to a place he usually avoided.

April 30, 1942.

Southern England.

Another night of a rare blue moon.

🌿

Alone in the dining room, Kathleen ate a breakfast of one egg, over easy with the edges burnt, hash browns that weren't quite done, and a cold biscuit served with honey. Mrs. Rafferty busied herself in the kitchen and refused Kathleen's offer to help in any way. The major was either gone or in hiding.

After forcing down the meal, Kathleen wandered into the adjoining parlor and studied the two framed photographs displayed on the fireplace mantel on either side of a black wreath.

Each photograph was of a young man wearing a military uniform, one Navy and one Army. A black satin ribbon hung along the side of each frame.

Kathleen's heart dropped to her stomach. A similar ribbon adorned the photograph of her brother that had the place of honor on the family's spinet piano.

"I see you've met my boys," said a voice behind her.

Kathleen faced Mrs. Rafferty, who wiped her hands on the floral apron covering her shirtwaist dress.

"Excuse me, ma'am?" Had she misunderstood, or did Mrs. Rafferty believe she'd known the young men? "I've never met your sons."

"That there's the only way to meet them now." Mrs. Rafferty strode to the mantel and pointed at first one photograph then the other. "That's James. Drowned when the Japs bombed Pearl Harbor. And that one's Joseph. Killed by the Nazis at Normandy."

Kathleen involuntarily stepped back, as if to make room for her hostess's pungent grief. The woman's sorrow seemed to mushroom, a palpable presence in the room.

"I am so sorry." The words tasted stale, helpless, in Kathleen's mouth. She hadn't wanted to hear them when her brother was killed. How much more difficult must they be for a mother who had lost two of her sons? "I mean—"

Mrs. Rafferty held up both hands. "Don't bother." She adjusted the nearest frame, moving it a fraction of an inch then returning it to its original position.

Kathleen stepped away, intending to return to the bedroom.

"My husband called." Mrs. Rafferty caressed the satin ribbon. "He will be here in a moment to take you away."

Take me where?

"Thank you." *I guess.* "I'll get my bag."

Kathleen hesitated, but Mrs. Rafferty didn't respond. The photographs of her sons held her in their grasp. There was no room for a stranger within the triangle they created—a mother and the military portraits of her deceased warrior sons.

Chapter 6

Roger shook away the memories of that April blue moon then opened Kathleen's personnel folder. The top page provided the basics, the facts he already knew. The color of her hair. The color of her eyes. Her date of birth.

But reading them, even in this official document, caused his chest to tighten. He'd done everything he could to avoid seeing her while on this assignment. But God must have had another plan.

The photo staring back at him, though a black-and-white print, was a good likeness. The expression in her eyes showed eager anticipation, as if she were on the brink of adventure. She'd had that same expression the first time he'd taken her to explore the caves in southern Ohio. It was one of the things he loved about her. Her zeal for living. Her courage.

But that didn't mean he wanted her for a partner on whatever assignment Minsh had planned for him. He couldn't be responsible for her safety. It was too cruel for God to expect him to be.

Shooting Liberty was an accident—one he deeply regretted—but still, an accident. As he'd been told often enough since being reassigned stateside, accidents happened. He wasn't supposed to blame himself for something over which he had no control.

Much easier said than done.

He flipped through a few more pages then stopped at the training section. She'd excelled at the gun range and on the obstacle courses. No surprise there. Kathleen's grandpa never shooed her back into the house when he went hunting or fishing. Both she and Kenny, her brother, learned the skills of an outdoorsman in the Ohio hills where they were raised.

Roger rotated his shoulder. No need to look at her martial arts training scores. She'd proven her ability to handle herself, and his body had paid the price. His back still ached where she'd slammed him to the ground.

The last section in the file was a psychological evaluation. Heat swept up Roger's neck, and he closed the folder. Reading the evaluation seemed an invasion of Kathleen's privacy. He wouldn't do it. He *couldn't* do it.

No shrink could tell him anything he didn't already know about the woman he loved. What he didn't know, well, at one time he'd expected to spend the rest of his life getting to know. A life they'd live together.

Now?

He didn't know.

Except that Kathleen deserved a hero. And he was nothing but a goat.

After showing their identification at two separate checkpoints, Kathleen followed Major Rafferty into a back door of the headquarters building. Beyond another checkpoint, a series of closed doors lined a long hallway.

The major knocked on one of the doors, opened it, then stepped aside for Kathleen to enter the room before him.

Special Agent Minshall quickly stood as Major Rafferty followed her into the room.

"I wasn't expecting you," he said to the major, ignoring Kathleen.

"The security of Norris Dam is under my purview."

"The dam is under the authority of the TVA Public Safety Office."

"And the U.S. Army has an interest in its security. As you very well know."

Kathleen followed Major Rafferty's gaze toward the man sitting on the other side of the rectangular table. Her body stiffened and heat flushed her cheeks.

Roger?

After all these long months, they were in the same room. Only a few feet from each other. She wanted to laugh. To cry. Instead, she stared at him, seeking an explanation in his eyes for his silence. His gaze never left hers as he stood. A gaze that revealed no hint of recognition.

Major Rafferty continued speaking, his expression as unyielding as his tone. "I think I have a right to meet your 'saboteur.' Especially since I wasn't given the courtesy of being notified of your intentions."

"That doesn't mean you didn't know, Major."

"What are you insinuating?"

"We already discussed this. Ad nauseum." Minshall raised his hands as if to ward off any more of the major's criticisms. "Since you're here, you might as well stay. Officer Forrest, you can sit here." He gripped the back of one of the chairs.

Kathleen reluctantly took a seat across from Roger, unsure of where to look or what to do.

His hands were clasped on top of a closed folder. He'd dropped his gaze, but Kathleen didn't want to look at him. Or to imagine what he was doing here. This Roger was a stranger to her.

She glanced at Major Rafferty as he sat beside her. He probably meant his tight-lipped smile to be reassuring. But she didn't find it comforting.

Minshall lowered a black shade over the one-way mirror, then turned the knob on a speaker hanging near the ceiling in one corner of the room. He joined them at the table, taking a seat beside Roger.

"Major Rafferty, Officer Forrest," he said, "I'd like to formally introduce you to Agent Roger Craig. He's also with the U.S. Army CIC."

The Counter Intelligence Corps? Since when?

Last Kathleen knew, Roger was regular Army. Though he hardly looked like a soldier now. Even though he wore a uniform, the whiskers lining his jaw were thicker than a five o'clock shadow, and his brown hair needed a trim.

But perhaps he'd lied to her about his military service. As he'd lied when he told her he loved her.

Roger spread out his hands, an apologetic gesture, and suddenly she was on the riverbank again as the saboteur approached her after firing at Liberty.

She blinked. It couldn't have been. Not Roger.

"You." Her voice caught, and she averted her gaze. She didn't want to do this. Not here. Not in front of Major Rafferty nor Special Agent Minshall. But her mind couldn't reconcile how all these pieces fit together.

Roger—the man she loved. The man she expected to marry.

The soldier who'd left her with promises to come home then broke her heart.

Roger, a CIC officer.

A saboteur.

She finally found her voice. "What are you doing here?"

"My job."

"You shot my dog." Her voice trembled. Because of Liberty's injury. Because of Roger's detached demeanor.

"I didn't want to," he said, shaking his head. "She came at me and. . . I'm sorry."

That phrase again. Meaningless words. Especially from him.

"This is exactly why I should have been informed," Major Rafferty cut in. "Then an incident like this wouldn't have happened."

"You're here as a courtesy, Major," Minshall said. "If you wish to stay, I'd advise you to keep your opinions to yourself." The two men glared at each other, and then Minshall turned to Kathleen. His eyes softened. "How is Liberty?"

"I don't know," Kathleen said, unsettled by the change in the agent's mood. An undercurrent of tension lurched between him and the major. As if they were enemies instead of fighting on the same side in this war. "I'm going to the clinic when we're done here."

"We've got some paperwork to take care of. Then I'll take you there myself." Minshall shifted toward Roger. "Agent Craig, you'll accompany us."

The room shifted beneath Kathleen's feet. "He can't go."

"But he will."

"He shot Liberty. He tried to blow up the dam." Kathleen crossed her arms, holding herself as tight as possible. She shouldn't talk this way to an Army officer. Especially not one in counterintelligence. But she wanted answers.

Not from Roger—he'd only lie to her—but from Minshall. "Why isn't he locked up in a cell?"

"What makes you think he wanted to blow up the dam?" Minshall asked. "Last night you told me you knew nothing about his operation."

"I saw the explosives in his bag."

"You don't really think. . ." Roger leaned forward. "Those were dummy charges. Designed to create a lot of noise and smoke but no real damage."

"But why?"

Major Rafferty let out a cheerless laugh. "Don't you understand, Officer Forrest? The CIC was testing our security procedures. Trying to find a flaw in how we do things around here."

The wayward pieces fell into place, forming a picture she didn't like. Her heartbeat quickened and she stared at Minshall. "You mean, you were testing the WOOPs?"

"Testing *all* the security," the agent said. "The WOOPs and the military."

Kathleen shifted her gaze to Roger and lifted her chin. "And Liberty and I stopped you."

"You weren't supposed to be there," he said.

"I threw you."

"You surprised me."

"Perhaps that was her intent," Minshall said. "Tell me, Major. Did you really know nothing about our operation? Or did you arrange for Officer Forrest to be on that riverbank at precisely the right time to stop it?"

"Think what you will," Major Rafferty said, a smug smile crossing his face.

Minshall grunted then turned to Kathleen. "Did you lie to me last night, Officer Forrest?"

Kathleen's face reddened, but her gaze didn't waver. "I did not."

"You simply decided to take your dog for a walk," Minshall said. "To get a look at the full moon."

She snuck a quick glance at Roger, but he shifted his gaze away from her.

"That's why you were out there?" The accusatory tone in Minshall's voice pushed against Kathleen like a giant invisible hand. "You didn't know about the operation? You just happened to be there?"

"How could I have known?" she blurted to stop the onslaught of questions. One corner of Minshall's mouth tilted upward. "I just. . ." Her voice gave out. If only she could slip under the table and disappear into a magic hole.

"It was a blue moon," Roger said quietly. Kathleen raised her eyes, but he still avoided looking at her.

"A blue moon?" Minshall furrowed his brow. "You mean like the song?"

"Officer Forrest's reasons for being at the river," Major Rafferty cut in, "don't change the fact that she did exactly what she was trained to do. She protected the dam from potential sabotage. Nor does it change the fact that because of the CIC's mission, which was executed without my knowledge or permission, a valuable dog was injured and could have been killed."

"You're right, Major," Minshall conceded. "The CIC regrets what happened to Liberty, and we commend Officer Forrest for her remarkable courage and skill."

He pulled a manila folder from a briefcase beneath the table and handed it to the major. "This is the paperwork granting my request to have Officer Forrest temporarily assigned to a special unit I'm putting together. The TVA has already signed off on it."

Kathleen's eyes widened. She'd expected to be assigned a desk job in administration while Liberty recovered.

Typing reports. Filing papers. Making coffee.

Nothing as exciting as working with CIC. Her spirits rose then sank. Minshall's special unit obviously included Roger. How could she work with him after what he'd done?

"How did you. . ." Major Rafferty frowned as he flipped through the folder.

Minshall gave a nonchalant shrug. "Called in a favor."

The major tossed the folder onto the table and stood. "I wish you the best with your new assignment, Officer Forrest."

"Thank you, sir." *I think.* Any other time, she'd be ecstatic for an opportunity like this. But how could she work with Roger?

Minshall closed the door after the major then eyed Kathleen and Roger. "I have a hunch about you two. And my hunches are seldom wrong."

"What kind of hunch?" Roger asked.

"I don't think last night is the first time you met."

"That's true," Kathleen said. "We grew up in the same county. In Ohio."

Minshall leaned across the table and rapped the folder between Roger's hands. "You couldn't have told me that when I gave you this?"

The writing on the folder's tab was no longer hidden beneath Roger's hand. Kathleen read the name and gasped.

Kathleen Jean Forrest.

She glared at Roger. "You read my file?"

"Minsh made me." For the first time since she entered the room, he smiled. "It's impressive. So's your judo."

Minshall raised his eyes to the ceiling then swiped his palms over his face. "If last night was some kind of misbegotten rendezvous between the two of you—"

"I had no idea he'd be there," Kathleen said.

"You know that's not true," Roger said at the same time.

"Guess you wouldn't have fired your gun. . ." A broad grin crossed Minshall's face. "Wow, I wish I'd seen her throw you. We could go out to the training area—"

"C'mon, Minsh." Roger gave him a disgusted look. "I didn't try to get away. If I'd wanted to, believe me, I could have."

"Sure, Craig, sure. You keep telling yourself that." Minshall checked his watch then placed a few forms, including a Declaration of Secrecy, in front of Kathleen. "We've got about an hour before the briefing. After you sign these, we'll go to the clinic."

Kathleen scanned the papers, which seemed to be filled with legalese about the consequences if she ever told anyone about her temporary assignment with the CIC. But secrecy had already become a way of life. She'd just have to trust that the papers didn't require her to give the Army her firstborn child when all this was over.

When she finished, Minshall slid the documents into his briefcase.

"Ready to go to the clinic?" he asked. His tone was light and airy, as if they hadn't spent the last half hour in some kind of weird interrogation.

"I'm more than ready," Kathleen said.

Minshall jabbed Roger's arm. "Coming, Agent Craig?"

Kathleen wished he'd say no. But Minshall's tone had made it clear that the question was more a command than a request. She couldn't imagine why the special agent wanted Roger to accompany them. Some kind of strange penance, perhaps?

She shoved all her confusion, all her hurt and her questions, deep down inside. The past was over, and the future held too much uncertainty. All she could do was focus on today. On this moment.

On seeing Liberty.

Chapter 7

Kathleen gripped the jeep's door handle as Minshall pulled to a stop in the alley behind the vet clinic. Almost immediately the back door opened and the woman who'd assisted Dr. Lawson the night before greeted them and led them inside. They followed her to a room with cages of varying sizes stacked against two walls. Most of the cages were empty.

None of them held Liberty.

"She's over there." The assistant pointed beneath a metal table in the opposite corner. Liberty, with a white bandage wrapped around her shoulder, leg, and chest, lay beneath the table on a pile of blankets. "A cage isn't for the likes of such a good girl."

Kathleen immediately knelt before her dog. The shepherd raised her head, whimpered, then shifted her position.

"I'm here, girl," she said softly as she caressed the dog's muzzle. "I'm here."

Liberty mouthed Kathleen's hand and tried to stand.

"Don't get up," she crooned. "You need your rest. Lie down."

Liberty obeyed but pushed her head against Kathleen's hand. She scooted forward, but the effort seemed to take all her energy. She whimpered again and lay still.

"She's in pain," Kathleen said.

"I gave her a sedative. It helps." Dr. Lawson entered the room and shook hands with Minshall and Roger. "But she's glad to see you. That's a good sign."

"I'm glad to see her too. She's going to be all right, isn't she?"

"I believe so. The bullet grazed her shoulder. A bit too close to the bone, but nothing time won't heal."

"That's good news," Minshall said. "Think she'll let you pet her, Rog?"

Kathleen shifted her gaze between the two men. Minshall's tone seemed to contain a dare while Roger stood against the door with his hands in his pockets, almost as if he wished he could be anywhere else than where he was.

"I think you should try," Dr. Lawson said. "She threatened to attack you because she saw you as a threat. It's important she see you now as a friend."

Roger looked doubtful. After a moment's hesitation, he straightened. "If you say so."

Minshall clapped Roger on the shoulder, a broad smile spreading across his face. "I knew you weren't a coward."

Roger scowled at him then caught Kathleen's gaze. "You know her better than anyone. How should I do this?"

Kathleen wished she didn't have to answer him. But neither did she want the others to know that she and Roger had been more than neighbors.

"Sit beside me." She shifted so she held Liberty's head in her lap. "If she believes we're friends, she won't harm you."

Roger took a step forward, and Liberty raised one lip to reveal several sharp white teeth.

"You sure about that?" he asked.

"It's okay, girl. He won't hurt you. I promise." Kathleen smiled at the dog. "Because if he does, I'll toss him again."

"Ha." Roger lowered himself beside them, his movements slow and easy.

Kathleen's shoulders tensed, though she tried not to show any signs of nervousness. Minshall was right that Liberty needed to see Roger as a friend. It didn't matter that he'd broken Kathleen's heart or that being close enough to get a whiff of his aftershave caused her pulse to race. When he settled on the floor, it was if they were back home again. Sitting beside each other in the porch swing or dangling their feet over the wooden bridge behind Grandpa's barn. Her head screamed at her to jump up and run away, but her feet wouldn't move. Besides, in her heart of hearts, she wanted to stay.

How had it come to this?

The question caused the ache in her heart to spread because the answer was so simple. Kenny died, and Roger had stopped writing.

"Hello, Liberty," he said quietly. He didn't try to touch her or pat her. Instead, he hunched, making himself as small as possible, and kept his voice low and even. "You came at me something fierce last night. In the dark, I wasn't sure what you were. If I'd known. . ."

He raised his gaze to Kathleen. She sensed he watched her, but she kept her head down, knowing he meant the words for her.

"She would have attacked you," she said softly. "Gotten you down and held you there till I commanded her to let go."

"Guess I'm lucky you're the one who dropped me instead." His tone held the familiar lilt of his gentle teasing.

She wanted to lean into him, to have him place his arm around her shoulder, and to rest her head in the curve of his neck. To have him pull her close and kiss her temple, her jaw, her lips. The way he used to before he went away.

But that yearning couldn't be indulged. Not with Dr. Lawson and Special Agent Minshall in the room. And not even if they weren't. Another barrier now existed between them. An invisible one, born of Roger's silence all these long months, one that separated them more than anything else could have done. A barrier she didn't understand.

Liberty nuzzled Kathleen's fingers then stretched her neck forward to sniff Roger's leg. He held out his hand, palm up, fingers extended. A nonthreatening invitation for the shepherd to smell his scent. One she accepted.

Kathleen rubbed Liberty's neck and Roger lightly scratched the underside of her jaw. After a moment or two, she licked his fingers then dropped her head in Kathleen's lap and closed her eyes.

"She's exhausted," Roger said. He suppressed a yawn then snickered. "So am I. Think there's room for me under that table?"

Kathleen wasn't sure if he was talking to her or to Liberty. She chose not to answer but buried her face in her dog's fur. They'd be making her leave soon, but she didn't want to go. Not yet.

Roger gave Liberty a final pat, which she accepted with a contented sigh, then used the table to pull himself up.

"You all right there, buddy?" Agent Minshall asked.

"Fine." Roger blurted the word, but he didn't sound fine. He sounded like Grandpa did when his joints were stiff and he hadn't moved them in a while. "Where to now?"

"Back to headquarters." Minshall exhaled a heavy sigh. "Sorry, Officer Forrest. We've got a briefing to attend."

Kathleen kissed the top of Liberty's head and gave her a final pat. "I'll be back when I can," she said as she carefully eased the shepherd from her lap and onto the pile of blankets. "Get well."

As she started to rise, she realized Roger had extended his hand. She took it, both reluctant and eager to do so. Once she was on her feet, he gave her fingers a gentle squeeze before letting go.

A message? Or habit? Maybe an apology. She didn't know. But she couldn't hold his gaze, couldn't get lost in his eyes, not now. Not at this moment when she wanted to fall into his arms, when she wanted to yell at him, when she wanted to crawl under the table with Liberty and never come out.

If only they could go back to the days before Kenny's death, to before Pearl Harbor. To the days when they hid messages to each other in the crook of the old apple tree. To the days when they loved each other.

To the days before they were strangers.

Chapter 8

Roger rubbed his hand over his unshaven jaw while he waited for Minsh to begin the briefing. He'd showered last night after his return to headquarters, eager to wash the dirt from his face and body. Wishing he could wash away his regrets just as easily. After shooting Liberty and seeing Kathleen, he couldn't bear to see his reflection in the mirror. Not even to rid himself of the tiresome whiskers that disguised his features during his mission. Then this morning, he hadn't had the time.

Too many people had too many questions. Minsh had deflected most of them, citing secrecy. But Roger still believed someone had been behind the one-way mirror in the interrogation room. Apparently not Major Rafferty. Someone higher up in the chain of command, perhaps? He might never know.

Minsh spread out a map on his desk, smoothing it over folders, books, and even the telephone. Kathleen, sitting in the chair next to Roger's, scooted forward.

"This is Knoxville." Minsh pointed to the city. "And this is Norris Dam. Either of you know what's located along here?" His finger swept across a spot south of the dam.

"That's Oak Ridge," Kathleen said. "Though around here, some folks call it the Reservation."

"What else do you know about it?"

Kathleen shrugged. "Only that it exists. The entire compound is surrounded by barbed wire." The skin between her eyes scrunched together, and her lips pressed into a confused frown. "Is that where I've been reassigned? To patrol the fence?"

"Nothing that simple," Minsh said. "You and Agent Craig are Oak Ridge's newest residents. You're going undercover."

Roger frowned as his pulse quickened. He'd jump at the opportunity to go undercover on his own. But he didn't need a partner. Especially not a partner named Kathleen Forrest.

"To do what?" he asked.

"Find a killer."

Roger humphed. "Isn't that a job for the police?"

"The death may have been from natural causes."

"So. . .there may not be a killer?"

"That's what we need to find out. And soon."

Roger shifted his gaze to Kathleen. She remained sitting on the edge of the seat, her back straight and her eyes glued to the map. But he sensed she wasn't seeing its lines and dots. Her cheeks were pale, and her hands were clasped tight in her lap.

Maybe she would back out. He could do the assignment alone. Then he'd have no one to worry about but himself.

"Important research is going on at that place," Minsh said. "Research that could end the war. Only a few people—and I'm not one of them—know all the details. But I can tell you this. We're in a race with the Germans and the Japanese. You're both bright enough to imagine what they're trying to do."

A bomb.

Roger blew out air. Kathleen stared at him, her eyes wide. She probably had the same thought as he, but she also had the good sense not to say nothing.

Minsh handed Roger a folder. "That has the details of a series of incidents that have occurred out there recently. Mishaps that could be nothing more than simple accidents."

"Except. . . ," Roger urged.

Minsh released a heavy sigh. "Security is extremely tight at the Reservation. The people who work there, who live there, they know not to talk. As extra insurance, quite a few are recruited as informants. They're given a stack of envelopes addressed to the ACME Insurance Company and a drop-off location."

"In other words," Roger said, "they tattle on their coworkers. Their neighbors."

"The FBI calls them 'creeps.'" Minsh made a face, his expression both amused and reproachful. "But yes, if they overhear someone saying something out of turn, they write a letter."

"And now one of them is dead."

Kathleen's face turned even whiter at Roger's blunt choice of words. *Good. She doesn't need to be part of this.*

"Sharper than a bowie knife—that's you, Rog." Minsh settled back in his chair and swiveled from side to side. "And the reason I want you inside that fence."

"Sir." Kathleen's voice wavered as she held up a hand. Like a child in a schoolroom. Surely Minsh could see she wasn't cut out for anything like this.

"You don't need permission to speak, Officer Forrest."

She nodded slightly, folded her hands again, and took a deep breath. "Why me?"

"I'm taking a page out of our English cousins' playbook."

"Sir?"

"Women make great spies." Minsh held out his hands. "British intelligence sends specially trained women to work with the French Resistance. To engage in all kinds of espionage. Men are suspicious of other men. They're not necessarily as distrustful of a woman."

"But I've had no special training."

"You know how to handle a weapon." Minsh glanced at Roger. "You've proven yourself more than capable of disarming a threat."

Roger glared, but Minsh only laughed.

"Plus, you're intelligent and, forgive me for saying so, easy on the eyes. That can be a big advantage in these types of situations."

Kathleen blushed, and Roger had to force his tense muscles to relax. Minsh had paid Kathleen a compliment. So what? He'd only said what was true. What Roger had always known about her.

"What exactly are you asking us to do?" Roger asked.

"We need fresh eyes. The informant mailed one of those ACME letters about a week prior to his death. We believe he was on his way to mail another, but he didn't make it to the drop-off point." Minsh gestured toward the folder. "Like I said, all the information we have is in there. Also his photo and a copy of the letter we received. Spend the rest of the afternoon studying all of it."

"What about our being Oak Ridge's newest residents?" Kathleen asked.

"You're moving there in the morning." He handed envelopes to both of them. "Those contain your security badges, the addresses to the dorms where you'll be staying. Even some money. If a sabotage ring is at the Reservation, we need you to find it and shut it down."

"That sounds imposs—overwhelming." Kathleen shifted her gaze to Roger.

In her eyes, he read her doubt of their success, her hope that they would solve the case. And beyond all that, he saw her fear that she'd be the one to fail.

He knew that look. He'd seen it in her brother's eyes before his last mission.

"I can do this alone," he blurted.

"Not a chance," Minsh said. "You're both going."

"I've got more experience—"

Minsh held up a hand. The hard glare in his eyes warned Roger to drop the subject. Fine. But that didn't mean he had to be happy about it.

"What's our cover?" he asked, forcing a neutral tone into his voice. A thought occurred to him, and he braced himself. "Don't tell me we're pretending to be married."

"That wouldn't have been a bad idea," Minsh said, his expression softening. "Our informant, his name was Michael Cooke, worked as a pipe tester at the Y-12 facility. We're sending you in to do the same job. That way you might just see what he saw, hear what he heard."

"Y-12? What's that?"

"Part of the secret. Anyway, the letter that Cooke sent to ACME was about 'incidents' with the pipes. He had a couple of suspects but didn't name them. Apparently he didn't want to cause any trouble for someone who wasn't guilty."

"And then he died." Kathleen's voice was low and full of sympathy.

Roger moved to take her hand then stopped himself. He flexed his fingers then caught Minsh looking at him, speculation in his eyes.

"What about Kathleen," he said. "What's her cover?"

"She doesn't actually have one."

Are you kidding me?

"I don't understand," Kathleen said.

"I called in a favor and got you a desk in the Castle on the Hill. That's the Army's administration building. But mainly you're to blend in. Your first task is to deliver a, let's call it a condolence basket, to Michael Cooke's widow. She probably won't talk to you, but you might glean something. You also need to be seen around town with Roger to give his cover more credibility."

"Won't people find it strange if I'm not working somewhere?"

"Who's going to know you don't?" Minsh asked with a shrug. "People out there do their jobs. They don't talk about them. No one's going to ask you what you do."

"But how are we going to find out anything important?" Kathleen asked. "Especially if everyone is so secretive."

"If it was easy, I wouldn't need an undercover team." Minsh stood, the signal for Roger and Kathleen to go. "Become friends with your suspects. Do what they do and go where they go. Have some fun while you're at it, but don't let your guard down. Either of you. This is our one shot to find out if our suspicions are warranted. And if they are, we need to apprehend whoever is responsible before they try anything else."

Roger clutched the folder as he followed Kathleen from the office. But he wouldn't remove the barrier he'd put between them. Their relationship was strictly professional. And he'd do everything possible to ensure it stayed that way.

Chapter 9

What happened?

Two little words that Kathleen couldn't bring herself to say to Roger. Especially when she wasn't exactly sure what she wanted to ask.

What happened to us? What happened to you?

After the briefing, Special Agent Minshall had escorted her and Roger to a small conference room where they could review the folder of information he'd given them. At least the upholstered chairs were more comfortable than the metal ones in the interrogation room.

But this was the first time she and Roger had been left alone together. Now was the time to ask. To get the unspoken tension between them out of the way. But the dryness in her mouth, the searing ache in her heart, closed around the words. The two simple words.

"Let's see what we've got in here." Roger opened his envelope and slid the contents onto the table. Kathleen did the same with hers.

"I've got two badges," she said. "This one is a Townsite Resident's Pass." Both badges had her photo, the same one used by the TVA for her WOOPs ID.

Kathleen scanned the information. Her height, her weight, her age, even her eye color was listed along with an ID number. "It tells me what gates I can use to get in and out."

"Mine does too. What's the other one?"

"It's for the administration building." She grinned. "The Castle on the Hill. Sounds like a fairy tale."

"Except it's real life. Don't forget why we're going out there."

The rebuke wasn't harsh, but it still stung. She wasn't likely to forget something so important, and he didn't need to treat her as if they were strangers. The old Roger, *her* Roger, would have known her failed attempt to lighten the tension was due to nerves, not incompetence.

To hide her uneasiness, she picked up the card with the addresses for the administration building and her dormitory. "I'm in W-5. On Tennessee Avenue."

Roger glanced at the card. "Shouldn't be too hard to find. Looks like it's close to the Castle." He took a pen from his pocket and handed it to her. "Go ahead and sign those badges. Then we'll get started on this." He rapped his knuckles against the folder, seemingly ready to get down to business.

If that's the way he wanted it. . . Kathleen signed her badges and held out the pen.

"Keep it. You may need to take notes."

Great. Even in the world of undercover work, women were expected to take care of the details. She should have known when Special Agent Minshall said part of her role was to support Roger's cover that neither man considered her an equal partner in this mission. Her WOOPs training could only get her in the door. She needed to prove her value before they'd see her as a vital part of the team.

They sat on the same side of the table while reviewing the folder's contents. There wasn't much. The letter to the ACME Insurance Company. A few incident reports that may or may not be important. A photo of Michael Cooke, probably the same one used for his ID badge.

"Here's the report from the auxiliary police unit." Roger laid the paper between them so Kathleen could read along with him.

"His body was found outside the bowling alley." Kathleen pointed to the line in the report.

"Minsh said the drop-off point to send the letter was close by." Roger leaned back in his chair and stared at the ceiling. "I wonder how close."

"We can see for ourselves tomorrow," Kathleen suggested.

Roger slowly nodded, seemingly deep in thought. Kathleen finished reading the report. Cooke, a diabetic in his late twenties, had been classified as 4-F. Ineligible for military service yet wanting to serve his country, he'd gained the skills needed to work at the Y-12 plant. The death certificate noted he'd died of natural causes in connection to his diabetes. No one would have questioned the cause if Cooke hadn't been an informant.

After a few moments, Roger sat forward. A self-satisfied smile curved his lips. "How's this for a plan."

"I'm listening."

"First we'll go to the bowling alley. Scout it out. Then we'll deliver that condolence basket to the Cooke family. See if they can tell us anything."

"Why would they?"

"You'll have to gain their trust."

"Me?"

His eyes softened, and for a moment Kathleen felt herself being drawn into the enchantment he'd always woven around her. Then he blinked, and the magic disappeared.

He pushed away from the table and gathered the documents into a stack. "Find a common interest," he said gruffly. "Anything to keep a conversation going. And don't be afraid of silences. Most people are, so let them start talking first."

"That seems so. . ."

"Manipulative? Cruel?"

"Maybe not cruel, but unkind. Offering friendship that's not real."

He faced her, his eyes cold and unreadable. "It's not too late for you to back out. I can do this on my own."

"No." Kathleen bit her lip and shook her head. "Special Agent Minshall—"

"Just call him Minsh, would you?"

"*Minsh* said you need me."

"He never said that."

"He implied it." She stuffed her badges and the money back into the envelope. "You might as well get it through your thick skull. I'm going to Oak Ridge with you tomorrow whether you like it or not."

The door opened, drawing her attention. Minsh shifted his gaze from Kathleen to Roger and back again. Kathleen self-consciously pushed back the hair that had fallen into her eyes.

"Trouble?" Minsh asked.

"Not from me," Kathleen said quickly.

"Rog?"

"I'm fine."

"Good. Let's talk about tomorrow."

Kathleen resumed her seat, although what she wanted most to do was throw Roger onto his back again. What did she have to do to convince him that she could do this job? Deceive a grieving widow into believing she was a friend?

God, please help me. How do I do that?

The answer, immediate and whisper soft, flowed through her. *Be ye kind.*

Yes. A thousand times, yes. That she could do.

Chapter 10

Roger peered through the bus's dusty window at the three monkeys on the large billboard outside Solway Gate. One had its paws over its eyes, the center one's paws were over its ears, and the third had its paws against its mouth. A large cutout on top of the billboard featured Uncle Sam rolling up his sleeves with his hat to his side. The text scripted across the monkeys read:

WHAT YOU SEE HERE
WHAT YOU DO HERE
WHAT YOU HEAR HERE
WHEN YOU LEAVE HERE
LET IT STAY HERE

Minsh hadn't been kidding about the Reservation's emphasis on secrecy.

Earlier that morning the special agent had driven both Roger and Kathleen to the Knoxville station, about twenty-five miles from Oak Ridge. Getting on the bus at Norris might raise questions, he'd said, after he'd walked in on their argument.

An argument that shouldn't have happened. If only he could tell Kathleen how he had failed. But then she'd despise him. He couldn't bear to see that kind of disappointment, that depth of bitterness, in her eyes.

Neither could he walk away from her again without facing up to his mistakes. When this assignment was over—he'd tell her then.

For now they both needed to focus on their mission.

On the drive to Knoxville, Kathleen had told them what she'd learned about the town since coming to Norris. It wasn't much.

When the government bought the rural land a couple of years ago, for less than it was worth, the affected families weren't given much time to move. They'd been forced out of their homes and off their farms. Businesses were boarded up and schools were closed.

Construction started almost immediately, and people came from throughout the U.S. seeking employment. The population had boomed, and new, cheap housing was still being built.

When they arrived at the station, Roger went inside first, and Kathleen followed a few minutes later. Per Minsh's instructions, neither one spoke to the other but simply boarded the green bus to Oak Ridge and settled in for the ride.

When the bus—Roger heard another passenger call it a cattle car—finally lurched to a stop outside the gates, two guards boarded. All the passengers seemed to know the drill. Roger held out his badge for the guard as if he did this every day. He refrained from looking at Kathleen, who sat in one of the seats lining the side of the bus, and hoped she resisted any urge to look at him. It was a common mistake with new recruits. That look for reassurance.

Minsh had given her a crash course in the finer points of

undercover work after supper last night. Hopefully that training would be enough for them to complete their assignment before anyone suspected why they were here.

And then Roger would hold Minsh to his promise. Soon, he'd be back in France. Maybe even in Germany. Though in recent weeks the end of the war seemed to be slipping further away. The euphoria surrounding D-day had waned as Hitler's anticipated surrender didn't materialize. How much longer could the tyrant hold out? Surely not for another long, harsh winter.

When all the badges had been checked, the guards got off the bus and the driver passed through the checkpoint gate. At Kathleen's bus stop, she made her way past the heater located in the center of the bus and departed with a few other women. Not once did she turn around.

Minsh had coached her well.

An hour or so later, Kathleen eyed with suspicion the narrow wooden planks leading from the bus stop to the cafeteria. Agent Minshall had warned her of the pervasive brownish-red mud and the cracks in the boardwalks, but she'd thought he was exaggerating.

He wasn't.

No wonder so many of the women wore boots and carried their shoes. Or that the shoe repair shop on Jackson Square was open twenty-four hours a day.

That tidbit she'd gleaned from the dorm mother, Miss Reba, who'd greeted her when she arrived at her new home away from home. The petite woman, who wore her silver hair wound in a knot at the nape of her neck, reviewed the rules—no men allowed in the rooms, no cameras or liquor allowed on the Reservation—then gave her an update on the social activities offered in the community.

Once she was alone, Kathleen had quickly unpacked. The first-floor room was simply furnished with a narrow bed, a dresser, and a desk. The window looked out onto another dormitory separated from hers by a strip of weed-infested grass. After hanging her dresses in the tiny closet, hidden behind a long curtain instead of a door, she'd left for her rendezvous with Roger.

Where they were to pretend to meet for the first time.

If only that were true.

Kathleen took care that her heels didn't slip between the boards as she made her way to the cafeteria. She was almost to the entrance when a woman wearing a nurse's uniform approached. Kathleen startled then averted her gaze. But not soon enough.

"Miss Forrest? Is that you?"

Kathleen turned and pasted on a smile. "Mrs. Rafferty. I didn't know you were a nurse."

Mrs. Rafferty looked her up and down as if making an assessment. One which Kathleen apparently failed, given the stern expression on the woman's face.

"I got my training during the Great War," she said then frowned. "Though I can't say there was anything *great* about it. Young men died then, and young men are dying now."

"Hopefully this one will end soon."

"It could end today, and my sons would be just as dead."

Kathleen wanted to offer sympathy. But what could she say that would provide any comfort? She could tell Mrs. Rafferty that her brother had also been killed. But what good would that do?

Everyone grieves differently, Grandma always said. Those without God often turned bitter. Sometimes those with God did too.

"My husband told me you worked at the dam." Mrs. Rafferty's suspicious tone caused Kathleen's nerves to tingle. "What are you doing here?"

So much for people not asking questions.

Kathleen focused on keeping her expression soft and nonconfrontational. "Why, Mrs. Rafferty," she said lightly. "Look what it says right up there." She pointed at a nearby billboard.

It read: Who, me? Yes, you! Keep mum about this job!

Mrs. Rafferty glanced at the billboard then shifted her hard gaze back at Kathleen. "You ask me, there's something fishy about you being here. I don't like fishy. It smells."

"I have a job here now," Kathleen said. At least that was technically true. "I can't return to patrolling the dam until my dog recovers. . ."

Her voice wavered. She had no idea whether Mrs. Rafferty knew why she'd been forced to play hostess, to have an unexpected overnight guest in her home. Agent Minshall seemed to want to keep Major Rafferty as much in the dark as possible about her new assignment. Had the major told his wife about the incident on the riverbank?

"Yes?"

"Please excuse me. I must be going."

"Of course." Mrs. Rafferty moved to one side, and Kathleen walked past her.

As much as she wanted to turn around, she resisted the urge. Shoulders straight, head high, she continued along the wooden sidewalk. But she felt the arrows of Mrs. Rafferty's frightening glare piercing her back with every step.

Chapter 11

The housewares on display in the window of McCrory's Five and Dime weren't nearly as fascinating as the scene happening across the street. Roger could see Kathleen's reflection in the glass as she talked to the nurse who had abruptly stopped her.

Kathleen wasn't supposed to know anyone on the Reservation. But the conversation had gone on too long for him to believe the woman was a stranger. If only he could get a better look at their facial expressions. Or hear what they were saying to each other.

When Kathleen walked away, her posture was stiff. Uneasy. Before the nurse stopped her, she'd been paying attention to where she stepped. Now she seemed to be making a point of appearing self-confident.

Which meant she wasn't.

The nurse stared at Kathleen's back then plodded along in the other direction.

Roger counted to ten then crossed the street and entered the cafeteria. Kathleen stood inside the door, her back against the wall, and her arms wrapped around her body. She glanced his way, immediately dropped her hands to her side, and walked toward the end of the cafeteria line. He caught up to her at the tray station.

"Hi," he said casually.

She graced him with a smile. "Hello."

"I'm new here," he said. "What do you recommend?"

"Eating somewhere else."

"Is the food that bad?"

Kathleen shrugged. "My dorm mother suggested I stock up on peanut butter and crackers."

They kept up the easy banter while adding food to their trays, and then Roger followed Kathleen to a secluded corner table.

"Looks like we beat the dinner crowd," Kathleen said. "Did you know this place is open all day and all night?"

"Something else your dorm mother told you?"

"She seems to be very helpful."

"What about that nurse you were talking to?" Roger waited for Kathleen's reaction. "Was she being helpful too?"

Kathleen stiffened, but she held his gaze. "You saw us?"

"I was across the street."

"She's Major Rafferty's wife. I spent the night with them—the night that, you know, *that* night."

The night I shot Liberty. At least she'd been kind enough not to say the words out loud.

"I didn't know she worked here. Or anywhere," Kathleen continued. "She wanted to know why I was here."

"That doesn't seem very Oak-Ridgian of her."

"I think she was just surprised to see me, that's all." Kathleen picked at her fried potatoes with her fork. "She's lost two sons. And she's bitter."

"You seemed upset when I came in." He didn't like pushing her for answers. But he also needed to know she was okay. That she could handle whatever they might have to face.

"I guess it felt like some kind of a test." She stared at him, and he felt himself getting swept up in the depths of those deep brown eyes. Like he used to.

He took a sip of water.

"Do you think Special Agent, I mean Minsh, do you think he set me up? To see what I'd do?"

Roger considered her question for a moment then shook his head. "I can't see Minsh doing something like that. If he didn't trust you, you wouldn't be here."

"If nothing had happened to Liberty, I wouldn't be here."

"Maybe not. But like your grandpa always says, God works in mysterious ways."

A small smile crossed Kathleen's face, and a teasing glint appeared in her eyes. "You're not supposed to know my grandpa."

He returned the smile, unwilling to let the moment go too quickly even as he knew it must. Traveling down memory lane would be a mistake.

"Don't tell Minsh on me."

"Never."

Roger cleaned his plate while Kathleen appeared to toy with her food. She was probably dreading the visit with Michael Cooke's widow. He wasn't looking forward to it either. "What do you say we do the condolence visit first? Then we won't be thinking about it while we're at the bowling alley."

"What if I say the wrong thing?"

"You won't."

She gave him a grateful smile and placed her napkin on her tray. "I'm ready whenever you are."

"Afterwards maybe we can find you that peanut butter."

"And crackers?"

"And crackers." Roger placed his hand at the small of Kathleen's back as they walked toward the exit. Then he caught himself and shoved his hand in his pocket. Touching her that way—as they went to church, to a movie—was an old habit. A familiar habit.

But not appropriate behavior for two people who had just met. Another slipup to keep from Minsh.

Chapter 12

Roger stood by the punch bowl, pretending to be interested in the dancing going on around him while sipping the red concoction. The community hall was a rectangular building, quickly assembled just like every other building in the town, that lacked any architectural appeal. But no one seemed to mind. The cubicle girls who worked at the secretive Y-12 plant, most of them in their late teens or early twenties, and the young GIs assigned to the Reservation cared more about each other's appeal.

The band, consisting of a piano and an instrumental combo, performed on a raised platform while tables and rows of chairs lined the walls. The music pulsed through the crowd as the partners swung one another around to the tunes of Glenn Miller and Jimmy Dorsey.

The door from the foyer opened, and Roger's heart sped up. Several people entered, three soldiers and their dates, but Kathleen wasn't among them. He downed the rest of his punch then ladled more into his cup.

Perhaps he should have gone to her dormitory and walked with her to the dance. He'd almost suggested that when they agreed to meet here tonight. But his mouth had gone dry and the words wouldn't come. This wasn't a date. Picking her up would have made it seem too much like one.

They hadn't yet talked about the past. He'd expected her to ask—had even braced himself for her anger, her tears—but so far she hadn't said a word. Only looked at him with that cool, appraising gaze. The one that made him want to throw himself at her feet and beg her forgiveness.

But he couldn't do that. No more than he could go back in time and change the decision that had gotten him to now.

To this time and this place—eager to see her walk through that door. Fearing what would happen to his heart when she did.

As if on cue, the door opened again and Kathleen appeared alone in the doorway. She'd changed into a royal-blue dress with a sweetheart neckline and scalloped trim. The matching fabric belt emphasized her petite waist. Her black pumps were amazingly clean, a detail that made him smile. It didn't take a highly trained CIC agent to know she'd worn boots to the community center and changed into the shoes after she arrived.

He set down his cup and slipped along the wall, keeping an eye on her as several couples jitterbugged between them. She'd stepped farther into the room, casting her eyes about.

Looking for him? He hoped so.

A slender man wearing a bright red handkerchief in his suit pocket approached her and said a few words. Roger repositioned himself to get a clear view among the bobbing and weaving of the dancers. The man gestured toward the dance floor. Kathleen hesitated and swept her gaze around the room. Roger, without knowing why, ducked behind a trio of matrons who were discussing a gazillion recipes for vegetable soup.

When he looked back at the doorway, Kathleen was gone. His mouth went dry, but then he spied her. Dancing with Red Hanky. Smiling at him. Hanging on to his every word.

Roger started toward them, ready to claim her from the interloper, then stopped and took a deep breath. He hadn't intended to ask her to dance. The community center was simply the place to be on a Friday night. But now?

When the song ended, Roger maneuvered among the couples till he stood behind Kathleen. After acknowledging the crowd's applause, the band played the opening notes of the next song.

"Shall we?" Red Hanky held out his arms.

Roger stepped forward. "I think this dance is mine."

Kathleen's eyes rounded in surprise, and her gaze shifted between him and Red Hanky, whose eyes shot daggers at Roger. Not that he cared. As long as Kathleen didn't dance with him again.

She rested her hand lightly on Roger's arm. "Maybe the one after this."

He swallowed his disappointment and faked a smile. "I'll hold you to that."

"Make me no promises."

I'll tell you no lies. One of the silly exchanges they'd often had with each other.

Red Hanky quickly whisked her away, and Roger returned to the refreshment table. He grabbed a cupcake, swallowing a huge bite without tasting it.

"She turned you down?" said a voice behind him.

Minsh. Always showing up when he wasn't wanted.

"What are you doing here?"

"Seemed a good time to check on my. . .helpers."

"Helpers?"

"Some words shouldn't be said in public. Words like"—he lowered his voice to an almost inaudible whisper—"agents."

Roger shoved another hunk of the cupcake into his mouth then brushed off his hands. "How'd you know we'd be here?"

"Followed Kathleen from her dorm." Minsh helped himself to a couple of cookies.

"Does she know that?"

"I doubt it." Minsh tilted his head toward an empty table, and Roger followed him to it. When they'd settled in the wooden chairs, Minsh looked out over the dance floor. "Any progress?"

Roger shook his head. "It's not been a good day."

"What happened?"

"She's gone."

Minsh gave him a quizzical look. "The widow?"

"Kathleen's writing the report." Not that there was much to tell. They'd gone to the Cooke home, a trailer in Happy Valley, but no one was home. Even more disconcerting, the place appeared deserted. No curtains hung at the windows. No boots were lined up on the front steps.

A neighbor woman, busy hanging clothes on a sagging line, had darted suspicious stares their way. But Kathleen had managed to thaw the woman's chilly demeanor with her warm smile and pleasant manner. They learned Mrs. Cooke had packed up as many of the family's belongings as possible and returned to their home somewhere in Georgia. Kathleen had given the basket to the neighbor.

"Did you go to the. . . ?" Minsh asked.

"The 'mailbox' is around the corner from where he was found." It was possible, even probable, that Michael Cooke intended to hide another letter to ACME at the drop-off point. But despite their best efforts, neither he nor Kathleen had found anything around the premises of the bowling alley to indicate what had really happened on that fateful night.

Minsh tapped out the rhythm of the song the band was playing on the table. No one watching them would guess they were discussing an undercover investigation. "What's next?"

"I start my new job testing pipes tomorrow morning at seven."

"Keep your eyes open."

"You didn't need to say that." Roger stood as the band played the song's final chorus. "This dance is mine."

"I'll be here when it's over."

In other words, *Come back to the table, and bring Kathleen with you.*

"Understood." Roger scanned the floor for Kathleen. Red Hanky was saying something, and she seemed completely engrossed.

How could she?

Why couldn't she?

Roger forced a smile and joined them. As he approached, Kathleen stiffened, but her expression didn't change.

"Are you ready to swing?" he said with as much cheer as he could muster. No need for her to know she was turning his insides to jelly by dancing with another man.

"Are you?" she responded.

Red Hanky laughed but had the decency to exit. Though not until he'd gotten a promise from Kathleen for another dance before the evening ended.

"Nice guy?" Roger asked as he walked away.

"Seems to be."

"Any idea what he does here?"

Kathleen pointed at the poster on the wall warning everyone of the need for secrecy. "I couldn't very well ask."

The music started, one measure and then the next. Kathleen's face reddened, and she bent her head.

Of all the songs.

He reached for her hand then slipped his arm around her waist. She nestled her head in his shoulder as the haunting strains of "Blue Moon" swirled around them. At least the band didn't include a vocalist to sing the poignant lyrics.

They moved across the dance floor in unison with the other dancers. But Roger hardly noticed them. The last time he'd held Kathleen in his arms as they danced to this song, she'd worn an off-the-shoulder dress with frills and lace. He'd been wearing his Army uniform.

Their last night before he shipped out. The last time they'd been together until their paths crossed again on the riverbank near Norris Dam.

Despite its sadness, its longing, "Blue Moon" had become *their* song. They were each other's love, each other's dream—only waiting for the war to end to start their lives together.

But then. . .

"April 30, 1942."

Kathleen spoke so quietly, Roger barely made out the words. But he didn't need to hear them to know what she said.

Unlike him, she wasn't thinking of their last date together before he shipped out, but the last time two full moons had appeared in the same month.

She'd still been home then, working in her grandparents' general store. He'd been in England with the wave of U.S. servicemen who were stationed there. That was before he'd been shipped to Salerno, Italy, and took part in Operation Avalanche. Before Kenny died and before Roger had been transferred to CIC.

They'd known the blue moon would appear that April night, the first in about three years. They couldn't be together, but they could gaze at the blue moon at the same time and know the other one was doing the same. It'd been a poignant night for both of them, full of longing and missing and hopes for better days.

He drew her closer, rested his chin against her temple, and felt her soft breath on his throat.

"I'm sorry," he murmured.

"Me too."

"I'd take his place. If I could."

Her head jerked up, bumping into his jaw. Tears glistened in her eyes. "Do you think. . ." She shook her head then rested her forehead against his shoulder. His grip tightened around her waist. An involuntary gesture but one he didn't regret.

He breathed in the familiar scent of her shampoo, the floral fragrance of her perfume.

The song ended, the brass instruments drawing out the last plaintive note.

Roger stilled, but he didn't let her go. She stirred in his arms, but he held her close. "Not yet."

He took one more deep breath, soaking in her essence, then released her. She avoided his gaze but didn't flinch when he took her by the elbow.

"Minsh is here."

She merely nodded and let him guide her to the table. Minsh stood and pulled out a chair. "How good to see you again, Kathleen," he said as if they were old friends. "Having a good time?"

"I am." She gave him a huge smile, although her eyes glistened with unshed tears.

Minsh pretended not to notice. "Hope you'll save a dance for me," he said as he took a seat next to her.

"If you'd like."

Roger started to pull out the chair on the other side of Kathleen, but Minsh held up a hand to stop him. "Why don't you get us all something to drink before you sit down? Kathleen looks thirsty."

"Sure." Roger reluctantly returned to the refreshment table. If Minsh wanted a moment alone with Kathleen, that was fine with him. Though they were supposed to be a team. Minsh shouldn't have anything to say to Kathleen that he wouldn't tell them both.

While he filled the glasses with the red punch, he snuck a glance back at the table. He could see Minsh's face but only Kathleen's profile. Minsh was all smiles as he and Kathleen chatted.

Punch overflowed the cup and dripped onto Roger's hand. Aggravated with himself, he grabbed one of the napkins and dried his hand. One of the matrons stepped up to help.

"Sorry about the mess," he said.

"Don't worry about it, dear. It happens to the best of us. Now you just take your drinks and go on. Have a good time and let me take care of this."

Roger sheepishly filled another glass then returned to the table.

"Have a little accident?" Minsh teased.

"Nothing too serious." Roger handed out the glasses then took his seat. He was acting like a jealous schoolboy. Unacceptable for a soldier. For an agent. They had a job to do, and he couldn't let his feelings for Kathleen get in the way of that.

His feelings.

They'd betrayed him tonight. He'd done his best for over a year now to put aside all thought of her. To convince himself that he was over her. But it wasn't true. He never would be.

A few moments later, Red Hanky returned to claim Kathleen for another dance. "This is Percy Ford." She introduced Roger and Minsh.

After the men shook hands, Percy led Kathleen away. Minsh leaned toward Roger. "You can thank me now."

"For what?"

"Who do you think told the band to play 'Blue Moon'? I figured it meant something to the two of you." Minsh sat back with a self-satisfied grin and pounded his thumb against his chest. "Your old buddy here called in a favor. Wouldn't mind hearing why that song is so special."

"You don't know what you're talking about." Roger spoke as offhandedly as he could.

"Sure I don't. Though I've got to say, if I were in your shoes, that gal wouldn't be dancing with anybody else." Minsh stood to leave and clapped Roger on the shoulder. "Don't stay out too late. Your shift starts mighty early in the morning."

Yeah, he was looking forward to that. Eight hours of testing pipes in a plant full of secrets. And then what? Somehow he and Kathleen needed to solve this case, say their goodbyes, and go their separate ways.

If only it could be that simple.

Chapter 13

Kathleen took her place in line at the cafeteria. What a long, frustrating day. True to his word, Minshall had arranged a desk for her in the Castle. Tucked away in her tiny corner, she'd typed up detailed reports about yesterday's visit to the Cooke home and their investigation at the bowling alley.

Not that she had much to say about the latter. If only they'd been able to find a clue. Or a lead to a clue. She spent the rest of the day reading every single word in the reports Minshall had given them.

Roger hadn't fared much better. After his shift, he stopped by her desk while she was reading—again—the information Minshall had given them. But he hadn't stayed long.

Kathleen picked up a tray and sniffed the unappetizing odors coming from the kitchen. If only she had made it to the store for that peanut butter.

A masculine voice spoke close to her ear. "Hello, beautiful. Come here often?"

Percy.

Kathleen shifted to face him and smiled. "Only when I'm hungry."

Percy chuckled, and his eyes crinkled with humor. "What would you say to dining somewhere else?"

Heat flushed Kathleen's cheeks. "I don't know. . ." *Roger might not like it* collided with *It doesn't matter what Roger thinks.*

But what about Minshall? He'd told her to be herself, to spend time with other people. Did that mean she should she say yes?

This spy stuff was driving her crazy. How could she be herself when she couldn't forget, even for a moment, why she was really here at the Reservation?

"We can go to Rosie's Diner. I promise you the food is a thousand times better."

"I'm not dressed to go out."

"You look gorgeous to me." He offered his arm. "Shall we?"

Kathleen accepted his arm, and they walked toward the cafeteria exit. They were near the door when Roger entered. A momentary darkness appeared in his eyes, but then he smiled and said hello.

Maybe she'd imagined that darkness. Even hoped he'd be upset at seeing her with another man. Though what did that say about her? Nothing good. Except, much as she hated to admit it, she wanted him to still have feelings for her. Just as she still had feelings for him.

How could she not? One didn't throw away love, not that easily, not when it was built on respect and wonder and shared times— both laughter and tears—and also those times of quiet and boredom and contemplation.

But he hadn't offered any explanation for his silence. Just that one muttered "*I'm sorry*" at the dance last night. An apology that could have meant any number of things.

Sorry he'd shot Liberty. Sorry for Kenny's death. Sorry for not writing.

Maybe a sorry she didn't know about—perhaps an apology because he'd fallen in love with someone else and didn't know how to tell her.

If only the band had been playing a different song. Then she might have found the courage to ask him why. Although perhaps then the "*I'm sorry*" might not have been said.

The song had seemed to pull them both back into other, happier, times. For her, a peaceful time when all of Europe's problems were an ocean away. And then there had been that night in 1942 when they'd arranged to be under the glow of the April blue moon at the same time.

She'd gone alone to the pasture behind her grandparents' home and sat on the boulder in the curve of Deer Creek. Tully Jane, their gray-brindled mastiff cur, had gone with her. Keeping watch, just as she'd done since Kathleen and Roger had found her, a bedraggled pup, dumped on the side of the road.

"Kathleen?" Percy said. "Roger asked you a question."

Kathleen mentally shook away the memories and pasted on a smile. "Sorry. I was thinking of Tully."

"Who's Tully?" Percy asked.

Kathleen ignored Percy's question and turned to Roger. "You asked me something?"

"Tully." His eyes softened. "Is that old girl still alive?"

"She doesn't wander too far from home these days. Every time I get a letter from Grandma, I'm afraid it's going to have bad news."

"She's lived a good life." A small smile creased his face, and Kathleen followed his thoughts to the hot summer afternoons when the three of them—Kathleen, Roger, and Kenny—had used the old tire swing to jump into the creek. Tully stood guard, keeping a close watch, ready to jump in if she needed to rescue one of them.

Roger's gaze shifted to Percy, who stared at them with a curious expression on his face. "Have you already eaten?" Roger said quickly. "That's what I asked you."

"When you were lost in your thoughts," Percy added.

"We're going to Rosie's Diner," Kathleen said, mentally kicking herself for mentioning Tully's name. "Would you like to join us?"

Percy gave an involuntary jerk but quickly recovered. "I'm sure Roger has other plans."

"I do," Roger said. "Big plans. Besides, third wheel and all that. You kids have fun."

Percy hurried Kathleen away before she could respond. His steps quickened until they were out of the cafeteria and on the wooden boardwalk leading toward Jackson Square. Despite his efforts at small talk, he seemed agitated.

After they were seated and the waitress, an older woman wearing a giant brooch on her ample bosom and dangling earrings, had taken their orders, Percy seemed to study her. Kathleen grew uncomfortable under his steady gaze, but she refused to be intimidated.

"Is something wrong?"

"I'm wondering who you are." Percy said. "We didn't get much chance to talk last night."

"You're not asking me what I do here at Oak Ridge, are you?"

"Of course not. I wouldn't want a letter sent to ACME accusing me of prying."

He knew about ACME? How could he? Unless. . .was he an informant?

"ACME?" she said, as innocently as possible.

"Surely you know all about them. About their creeps."

"No. Can't say that I do." At least that was true. She knew very little about the inner workings of that fictitious insurance company.

"It doesn't matter." He played with the saltshaker, moving it this way and that. "I only want to know more about you. Where you grew up. What you did before the war took our lives away from us."

"There's not much to tell. My parents died from an outbreak of influenza when I was ten. My grandparents took me in." No need to tell him about her brother. Or where she lived. "What about you?" She gave him a flirtatious smile. "At least what you can tell me."

"Lived all of my life in these mountains. Seen lots of changes."

"Such as the building of this place?"

"I used to hunt these ridges until the government bought up all the land. Hunted over where Norris Dam now is too."

"It must have been hard on the families that had to move."

"No use crying over what can't be helped."

"I guess not." Though she'd be devastated if the government took her grandparents' farm.

Their food arrived, and they traded childhood stories while they ate. After Percy paid the bill, they wandered past the storefronts, stopping occasionally to look at the window displays. The theater marquee announced the double bill of *Double Indemnity*, starring Barbara Stanwyck and Fred MacMurray, and *The Invisible Man's Revenge*. The first movie had already started.

"Have you seen either of those yet?" Percy asked.

"No, I've been too busy."

"Will you be 'too busy' tomorrow night? If not, we could go together."

Once again, Kathleen felt paralyzed by indecision. What was the right thing for her to do? What did she *want* to do? Maybe she should talk to Minshall before accepting another invitation from Percy. "I may have other plans."

"Tell you what. I'll come by your place around six. If you want to go, we'll go. If not, I'll slink away like a brokenhearted hound dog." His face drooped though his eyes sparkled with humor.

Kathleen laughed at how pitiful he looked. "Okay. Tomorrow at six."

"Great. What's your address?"

"I'm in the W-5 dorm."

"On Tennessee Avenue, right? I know where it is."

They continued past a tea shop and an insurance office that had closed for the evening. The boardwalk became less crowded the farther they walked, sometimes in silence and sometimes engaged in idle chatter. When they stopped at a quiet intersection, Kathleen looked over her shoulder. The marquee lights were a bright but distant rectangle, and they were all alone in this desolate part of town.

Percy stepped closer and hovered over her. "Who's Tully? Isn't that the name you said earlier?"

Kathleen had avoided mentioning the brindled mix again. He must have known she wasn't being completely open about her family. But she could say the same about him. Both had been careful with how much they shared even while laughing at their youthful antics. He seemed to be an only child. Though he probably thought she was too.

But there seemed little harm in answering.

"She's my family's dog."

"A dog." His smile reminded her of a barn cat playing with a field mouse. It lacked warmth, and his gaze seemed calculating. "Strange, though."

"What is?"

"That Roger fella. Seemed like he knew all about that dog. But last night I got the impression the two of you didn't know each other all that well. Didn't you tell me when we were dancing that you'd only met him that day?" He smiled that false smile again.

"Or maybe I misunderstood."

He was right. She had told him that. Now what was she supposed to do? Again, she wanted to kick herself. And Roger too. They both had messed up. Why, oh why had she ever mentioned Tully?

Because she'd been lost in the past. A place she'd wanted to stay.

"It's not that hard of a question."

Another of Minshall's off-the-cuff lessons popped into Kathleen's head: *Turn the tables. If someone puts you on the defensive, do the same to them.*

"You know how it is," she said. "There's so much we can't talk about that Roger and I talked about our family pets last night."

"Seemed more to it than that."

"Did it?" She shrugged as if bored with the conversation. "I was wondering something myself. About you."

"What's that?"

"That ACME Insurance Company you mentioned. And, what was it you said—'*creeps*'? What's that all about?"

He studied her under his dark brows, but she did her best to keep her gaze steady. To not squirm even as every muscle in her body urged her to run as fast and as far as she could. She'd already proven her mettle when she threw Roger. What harm could Percy possibly do?

Chapter 14

Roger refrained from looking at his watch as he stood in the shadows outside of Kathleen's dormitory. Only a few minutes had passed since he last checked the time. *Where was she?*

Maybe Percy had taken her to the movies. Or perhaps they'd gone to one of the tennis court dances. That seemed to be a popular pastime.

Face the facts, old buddy; they could be anywhere.

When Kathleen hadn't shown up by eight thirty, Roger went to the diner. The waitress, who wore earrings that nearly reached her shoulders, remembered Kathleen and Percy. But they'd left an hour ago. Maybe two.

Roger left the diner and headed back to the dormitory.

They'd goofed up—both of them—talking about Tully. But that only mattered if Percy was the man they were after. How likely was that? Not very, and yet the unlikely odds knotted Roger's stomach.

Nothing about this assignment was "likely." For instance, why was Percy so interested in Kathleen anyway?

Sure, it was easy to get lost in those deep brown eyes, and her lips. . .The memory of kissing those enticing lips about did him in.

Roger glanced at his watch again.

He needed to think like an agent, not a jealous ex-boyfriend. Even from that perspective, Percy's interest seemed too much. How many times had Roger caught Percy eyeing them, scrutinizing them, at the dance last night? Enough times to make his skin crawl.

Kathleen shouldn't have gone to the diner with the scumbag. Something was wrong, and Roger needed to figure out what. Since he couldn't find Kathleen, he needed to find Percy Ford.

But first he had to be absolutely sure Kathleen wasn't inside the dorm. She could be getting acquainted with her neighbors in one of the other rooms or chatting with the dorm mother. Only one way to find out.

He slid along the side of the building, intending to climb through the window if he had to, when a thin beam of light appeared through a crack in the curtains. It wavered then went out. A moment later, the window opened, and a shadow emerged. Roger pressed himself against the building. The figure, dressed entirely in black, scanned his surroundings, climbed out of the window, and took off in a crouching run in the opposite direction.

"Hey, you!" Roger shouted.

The figure turned, straightened, then raced toward the woods beyond the dormitory. Roger bolted after him but lost him in the trees. He stood a moment, waiting for his heart to stop pounding, and assessed his situation. All was quiet. Apparently no one else had heard his shout.

He stayed close to the building and climbed through Kathleen's open window into the dark room. He shut the curtains then turned on the light. Clothing hung from the partially opened dresser drawers, and the contents of the desk drawer were scattered across the floor. The mattress was askew on the bed.

The mysterious intruder had been looking for something. But what?

Had Kathleen somehow given herself away to the very person they were looking for? If so. . .Percy. It had to be him.

But if Percy had been here, in this room, then where was Kathleen? And what had he hoped to find?

Roger turned out the light and listened at the door. Nothing. He quietly opened it then scurried through the empty hallway to the lobby. He knocked on the door of the apartment belonging to the dorm mother. What was her name? Reba. Kathleen had called her Miss Reba.

When she finally answered, dressed in a housecoat and slippers, he pushed his way inside and shut the door.

"Young man," she exclaimed. "What do you think you're doing?"

"Asking for your help."

"Would you like a cup of tea?"

"What? No!" Roger shook his head and pulled out his CIC ID card. "Kathleen Forrest isn't in her room. Do you know where she is?"

"Kathleen Forrest. Yes, that's the new girl." Miss Reba examined the card. "What does she have to do with the CIC?"

"I'm not at liberty to tell you that, ma'am."

"I haven't seen her, but now I know how she got a room so quickly. We have a waiting list, but she didn't have to wait at all."

"I need to find her."

"In that case we can check the register."

She led the way to a tall stand in the lobby that held a large logbook. After placing a pair of pince-nez glasses on her nose, she examined the open page.

"It doesn't look like she's checked in this evening. Maybe she forgot."

"I don't think so. Do you have a phone?"

"Is Miss Forrest in some kind of trouble?"

"I'm not sure. I hope not."

"Come with me." Miss Reba led him back to her apartment and closed the door. "If all these girls knew I had a phone, it'd be like Grand Central station in here from dawn to midnight. So I keep it secret except for emergencies." She opened a hidden door in the wall near a closet and pulled on a string. An overhead light came on. "It's in there. You'll need to plug it in. I can't have anyone hearing it ring when I don't want them to."

The phone sat on a tiny desk that also held a cup of pencils and a pad of paper.

He closed the door, dialed Minsh's number, and prayed the agent would answer. He did, sounding as if he'd been asleep, on the eighth ring.

"Kathleen's disappeared."

"What?"

"She went to Rosie's Diner with that Percy Ford, and no one has seen her since."

"Where are you?"

"In her dormitory. Someone was in her room. Tore the place up."

"She was at the diner, you said."

"That's right."

"Meet me there. I'm on my way."

Roger grabbed a pencil from the cup and scribbled the number to CIC headquarters on it. He found Miss Reba at the kitchen table, sipping a glass of juice, with her Bible open.

He handed her the paper. "If Kathleen comes back, if you hear anything from her or about her, anything at all, call this number."

She placed the paper on top of the Bible and folded her hands over it. "I'm praying you find her, young man. Please let me know when she's safe."

He nodded then ran out the front door and toward the diner. He had no idea how they could find Kathleen unless they found Percy first. That's what they had to do. Find Percy.

Chapter 15

Kathleen groaned and tried to sit up. But she couldn't raise her arms, and even the slightest movement caused her head to pound with the worst headache she'd ever experienced.

Where was she? And how had she gotten here? Her memory seemed blurred, fuzzy. But she needed to think. That man, what was his name? Marshall? Mitchell? No, it was Minshall. He'd talked to her about tac something. Tac, tac. Tactics. That's what it was.

Assess the situation. Adapt to the situation. Act on the situation. She could do that.

Her head still ached, the pain so debilitating that bile rose into her throat. She swallowed it then drew in a deep breath and slowly let it out.

Assess.

The surface beneath her was hard, unyielding. The floor? No. Somehow, she knew she was higher than that. She was on a table. A short, narrow table. Like the one in the examining room where she'd been given her physical when she applied for the WOOPs training.

She tried to move her hands again, but they were strapped to the sides of the table. More straps bound her chest and her ankles.

But why?

She took another slow, deep breath, and then another as the memory flooded back. She and Percy standing in an alley. Talking about Tully. Talking about the ACME Insurance Company.

Then a nurse had emerged from the darkened alley. Kathleen gasped. "Mrs. Rafferty." She shifted her gaze to Percy and back again. "What's going on?"

Percy squeezed Kathleen's upper arm and pressed a revolver against her ribs. "You shouldn't have come here. Sticking your nose where it doesn't belong,"

"I'm not—"

"Shut your mouth." Mrs. Rafferty grabbed Kathleen's other arm and pulled a hypodermic needle from her pocket. "You've got nothing to say that I want to hear."

Kathleen struggled to get away, but Percy thrust the revolver into her side. "Don't make me pull the trigger. Not yet."

The needle pricked her skin, and a burning sensation flowed into her vein. She blinked as the blood seemed to rush to her feet. Her head felt woozy, and her knees wobbled. Her legs, no stronger than jelly, could no longer hold her. She sank to the ground and closed her eyes.

"Carry her inside," Mrs. Rafferty said. "Then go to her room. Make sure there's nothing there that could incriminate you."

"She was never onto me, Ma. I'm too smart for the likes of her."

The sound of skin slapping skin resounded against Kathleen's eardrums. "Do what I tell you," Mrs. Rafferty had said. "Then come back here, and we'll see to it that you have an alibi."

Percy had said something else as he slung Kathleen over his shoulder. But she hadn't been able to make out his words before the darkness descended around her.

Kathleen fought against the straps as she shook away the horrible memory. She seemed to be alone in the room, but who knew when they'd return? Or what they'd do with her when they did.

She slowly, very slowly, twisted her head toward a tiny lamp emitting a weak circle of light on a nearby counter. She closed her eyes and willed herself not to drowse off again. She needed to stay awake. She needed to find Roger.

To tell him about Percy and his ma. The major's wife.

Chapter 16

Roger tried to appear inconspicuous as he hung around outside the diner. Minsh seemed to be taking his sweet time getting here. But without him, Roger didn't know what to do. He'd already checked out the nearby businesses, those that were still open, to see if Kathleen and Percy stopped inside any of them. Fortunately he still carried a photo of Kathleen in his wallet that he could show around. But no one remembered seeing her.

Roger had been back at the diner several more minutes when a nearby horn sounded. Minsh parked the jeep in front of the diner then came around the front of the vehicle and opened the passenger door. Roger glanced inside then did a double take. "What is she doing here?"

"Called in a favor." Minsh smiled, but worry darkened his eyes. "I figured she was our best chance at finding Kathleen."

"Is she well enough?"

"If she's not, then we'll need a miracle."

"I think we need a miracle either way." Roger knelt on the boardwalk and held out his hand. "Are we friends now?"

Liberty, wearing a pristine bandage around her shoulder, stepped gingerly from the jeep onto the wooden boardwalk. She leaned toward Roger and sniffed his hand.

"We need to find Kathleen," he said. "Can you do that for us?"

She gently licked Roger's fingers.

"Guess she's forgiven you." Minsh handed Roger the dog's leash.

He scratched the top of Liberty's head and breathed a quick prayer. Several hours had passed since Kathleen had been in the diner. He'd heard miracle stories of dogs finding missing persons. *Please, God. Let this be another one.*

Minsh clapped him on the back. "This is going to work."

Roger took Liberty into the diner where only a few customers still lingered. He led her to the booth the waitress had pointed out to him earlier—the one where Kathleen and Percy had sat.

"Find her, girl," Roger said quietly. "For both of us."

Liberty sniffed around the booth then eagerly wagged her tail. She headed out the door, head raised, and hurriedly limped along the boardwalk toward the movie theater. Roger followed slightly behind, giving her as much slack in the leash as she needed to work.

Her nose dropped again in front of the theater but only for a moment. Then she was on her way, trotting as quickly as she could with her bandaged leg and chasing a trail only she could follow.

When they'd gone a few more blocks Liberty circled a spot near an intersection. She sniffed the ground, back and forth, back and forth, then led Roger down the side street to the back of the building. She whined as she pawed the door.

"Where are we?" Roger asked.

Minsh waved his flashlight across the building then rested the beam on a sign above the door. "It's a medical clinic."

"What would Kathleen be doing here?"

"Let's find out." Minsh drew his gun and tried the knob. The door was locked.

"Allow me." Roger dropped Liberty's leash, pulled a leather packet from his pocket, and chose a small implement. Within a few seconds, he'd picked the lock.

He opened the door then stepped back for Minsh to go in first. But before either could enter, Liberty maneuvered in between them and raced along the corridor.

"Liberty," Roger whisper-shouted. "Get back here."

She ignored him and placed her front paws on one of the closed doors. Her pitiful whine tugged at Roger's heart.

Minsh took up a guard position, scanning the hallway and the doors, while Roger joined Liberty and opened the door. A dim light shone in the room, enough for Roger to see someone lying on the examination table. Liberty moaned in pain as she tried, and failed, to jump onto the table.

"Liberty?" Kathleen's voice, small and weak, sounded in the darkness, Roger heaved a deep sigh and realized he'd been holding his breath. "What are you doing here?"

"She's looking for you."

"Roger?"

"I'm here." He reached for Kathleen's hand, and his fingers brushed against a buckled strap. He switched on the overhead light then quickly set to work to free her. "What happened?"

"She drugged me."

"Who?"

"Anita Rafferty."

"The major's wife?"

"And Percy." Her voice seemed to gain strength the more she talked. "He called her 'ma.'"

"Percy Ford is the major's son? That doesn't make sense."

"I think he killed Michael Cooke."

"Don't worry about that right now. Are you hurt?" He reached behind her back to help her to a sitting position.

"A headache, that's all." She rubbed her temples then reached down to scratch Liberty's head. "She found me."

"She sure did."

"And so did you."

Roger gazed into her eyes, allowed himself to get lost once more in their depths. Who was he kidding? He didn't want to live without her in his life. But would she give him a second chance?

"We need to get out of here," he said. "Can you walk?"

"I think so."

She slid from the table while Roger supported her. When she was steady on her feet, he retrieved Liberty's leash and handed it to her.

"Let's go find Minsh."

"I'm right here." The special agent appeared in the doorway, his hands raised in surrender. "With company."

"We got them all now, Ma." Percy had one hand on Minsh's shoulder and a gun pointed at his back. Liberty growled as he guided Minsh further into the room and Mrs. Rafferty sauntered in behind them.

"You better hold on to that dog," the woman warned. "Or she'll get another bullet in her hide."

"Don't you dare hurt her," Kathleen said.

That's my girl. Roger casually reached for her hand then held Minsh's gaze. "How did this happen?"

"Embarrassing, isn't it?"

"Enough talking from you." Mrs. Rafferty trained Minsh's gun on Roger and Kathleen. She glanced at Percy and let out a heavy sigh. "When I helped you clean up that first mess, I didn't expect you to get into another. They can't all look like natural causes."

"I know these hills like the back of my hand," Percy said. "Lots of places to hide bodies where they won't ever be found."

"You're forgetting one thing." Roger slowly turned his gaze from Minsh to Percy and squeezed Kathleen's hand. "We have a WOOPs-de-doo gal on our side."

Simultaneously Minsh smacked the back of his head into Percy's face and swiveled away from his pistol while Roger made a tackling leap, knocking Percy off his feet.

Liberty, obeying Kathleen's signal, latched onto Mrs. Rafferty's arm. She screamed and dropped the gun. Kathleen scooped it up.

"Get her off me," Mrs. Rafferty shrieked. "Get her off."

"Leave her," Kathleen commanded. Liberty immediately let go and returned to Kathleen's side.

Mrs. Rafferty, tears streaming down her face, cradled her injured arm. "How could you?" she bellowed at them. "You've taken everything from me. Everything."

As Roger and Minsh pulled Percy to his feet, Mrs. Rafferty put her head down and charged Kathleen like a bad-tempered bull. Without a moment's hesitation, Kathleen grabbed the woman's uninjured arm and threw her head over heels onto the floor. She quickly rolled her over then placed her knee in the older woman's back.

Roger chuckled and elbowed Minsh. "That's my girl."

Chapter 17

*L*iberty lay at Kathleen's feet while she stood with Roger and Major Rafferty on the viewing side of the one-way mirror that looked into the interrogation room at the Army headquarters near Norris Dam. Mrs. Rafferty, her injured arm in a sling, and Percy Ford sat at the table opposite Special Agent Minshall and a one-star general.

Kathleen wanted to tell Major Rafferty how sorry she was for all his losses. But *I'm sorry* never seemed enough. What other words were there?

Be ye kind. . .

She wanted to be. But she didn't know how.

They listened a while longer while Anita Rafferty broke down in heartbreaking sobs then went on wild tirades against the military then sobbed again. Her grievances were many, and they were painful.

Her family had lived in the Eastern Tennessee mountains for generations, only to be swept off their property "as if we were no better than trash" when the land was needed to construct the Norris Dam. Though bitter, they'd resettled nearby and done the hard work of starting over and setting down new roots. But this land was needed too, for the building of Oak Ridge and the mysterious work that went on behind the barbed wire fencing.

As if that wasn't enough, the Great War, the one that was supposed to end all wars, had claimed the life of her first husband and Percy's father. Now another war, the one responsible for taking her heritage—Percy's heritage—had also taken the lives of her two younger sons.

Percy's testimony wasn't as emotional as his mother's. His acts of vengeance against the military that had taken so much from his family and caused his mother such deep heartache started out small then became more daring. The disabling of a machine. The theft of tools. A small fire in a warehouse.

His mother had encouraged his exploits.

Then he realized he was being watched, and he confronted Michael Cooke outside the bowling alley. He'd only meant to scare the man off, but Michael wouldn't listen. He didn't care "what I'd lost, only about what I was doing."

Percy had come prepared with a hypodermic needle containing liquid cyanide. His mother had given it to him "just in case." After injecting Michael and making sure he was dead, he'd found the letter to the ACME Insurance Company in Michael's pocket and burned it.

"I believe I've heard enough," Major Rafferty said when Percy finished telling his story. "Officer Forrest, I ask you to accept my apologies on their behalf for what they did to you. What they tried to do to you. I am sorry."

"Thank you, sir. That means a lot." She blinked away sudden tears. The words, though often trite and cliché, did mean something.

"I'm sorry too. For all you've gone through."

His lips pressed together into a grim smile. "Thank you. I pray a brighter future for you. Both of you." He nodded at Roger and left the room.

Roger placed his arm around Kathleen's waist. "Maybe we should go too."

"Where to?"

"I was thinking about this boulder. It's on the bank of the Clinch River near the dam."

"Sounds nice."

"One rule, though." Roger's eyes twinkled. "No judo."

"As long as you don't shoot my dog."

Chapter 18

Near Norris Dam, Tennessee
November 1945

*K*athleen placed Roger's latest letter with the others he'd written since his return to Europe a year ago. Each month's letters were tied together with a brightly colored ribbon and stored in a cedar box her grandpa had made for her when she graduated from high school.

They'd had long talks before he left—at the boulder, on hikes through the mountains, and even under the table in Dr. Lawson's veterinarian clinic during Liberty's convalescence.

Roger told her how he blamed himself when Kenny died as the Allies fought the Germans on the beaches of Salerno during Operation Avalanche. In the confusion of the battle, they'd been separated. Roger still believed that if they'd stayed together, Kenny wouldn't have been killed. Unable to forgive himself for the death of his best friend, he became convinced that Kathleen wouldn't forgive him either.

Then on August 6 of this year, they'd learned the secret hidden behind the barbed wire fencing surrounding the Reservation. An atomic bomb, nicknamed Little Boy, was dropped over Hiroshima. A second bomb, Fat Man, fell on Nagasaki a few days later. President Roosevelt mentioned Oak Ridge by name in his address to the nation. Until then, many of the residents had been unaware of the research and production taking place in the Secret City.

Kathleen packed the cedar box in her trunk among her clothes and a few other personal items. The war had ended months ago, but public safety officers were still needed to patrol Norris Dam. She'd stayed, mainly to avoid saying goodbye to Liberty for as long as possible. The German shepherd belonged to the military, so she had to be left behind.

Yet the time had come for Kathleen to return to her Ohio roots. Her grandparents were eager to have her home, and they'd soon be celebrating Thanksgiving. Roger should be back soon too. Then they could start dreaming of the brighter future that Major Rafferty had been gracious enough to pray for them.

Kathleen took one last look around the room where she'd lived for the past couple of years, then closed the trunk lid and locked it. Hopefully she'd already cried all the tears left within her so she could leave now with at least a little bit of dignity. No need for the soldier driving her to the bus station in Knoxville to see her blubbering all over herself.

She slipped on her jacket and went outside to wait on the porch. The autumn air was crisp and fresh, with a hint of winter chill in the gusts that scraped the bare tree limbs against each other. She was going to miss these mountain mornings. But oh, how much she was looking forward to sharing cups of hot cocoa with her grandma on mornings even colder than this one in the weeks to come.

The sound of an engine interrupted the quiet. A few seconds later, a military jeep rounded the curve in the road and pulled into the drive leading to the cabin. It parked, and the back door opened. Liberty jumped out and ran toward Kathleen, her tail wagging furiously.

A bittersweet pang dug into Kathleen's heart. Saying goodbye the day before had about broken her. She wasn't sure she could go through that again. So much for no crying and a bit of dignity.

She knelt, burying her face in the dog's warm neck, and let her tears dampen the coarse fur.

"No hugs for me?"

A tremor shot through Kathleen's spine. She looked up, and more tears flowed. In an instant she was in Roger's arms, her cheek pressed against his as Liberty barked and danced around them.

His lips traveled along her jawline then covered hers in a kiss that took her breath away and made her weak at the knees. Her fingers caressed the nape of his neck as the kiss ended and began again.

"Don't I get a hug too?"

Kathleen reluctantly broke off the kiss and peered beyond Roger's shoulder. "Minsh! What are you doing here?"

"I brought your man back to you." He gave her a brotherly kiss on the cheek. "And your dog."

Kathleen wrapped her arms around Roger's waist. "Does this mean we're traveling home together?"

"We sure are." Roger pulled her into a side hug.

"I'm grateful to you for that, Minsh. More than you can imagine." Kathleen scratched Liberty's neck as the dog leaned against her leg. "It was nice of you to bring Liberty too, but I wish you hadn't. It's awfully hard leaving her."

"Who says you have to leave her?"

"The Army. They think she belongs to them."

"Shows how much they know." Minsh's smile widened, and his

eyes took on that familiar self-satisfied look.

"Don't tell me," Roger said, "you called in a favor."

"I called in a favor."

"I told you not to tell me."

Kathleen looked from one to the other. She didn't want to get her hopes up only to have them dashed. But. . . "What kind of favor?"

Minsh pulled a yellow slip of paper from his shirt pocket and held it out to her. "Liberty belongs to you now. All legal and everything."

"I don't believe it."

"Believe it." He glanced at his watch. "If you're going to catch that bus, we'd better be going."

While the two men went inside the house to get Kathleen's trunk, she sat on the edge of the porch and unfolded the paper Minsh had given her. Liberty settled beside her and stretched her long body against Kathleen's leg.

The paper looked real enough. The document listed Liberty's breed, name, date of birth, and registration number, and proclaimed Kathleen Forrest as her legal owner.

Thank You, Father. She raised her face to the heavens. *Thank You that this war has ended. That Roger and I are taking Liberty home with us. And thank You with all my heart for the gift of blue moon nights.*

Dear Reader,

When I started looking for ideas for this collection, I was beyond the moon excited to learn about WOOPs—the Women Officers of Public Safety who were hired to patrol the Tennessee Valley Authority's facilities and installations. However, the little bit of information I learned way back then was about all I could ever find. I sincerely doubt that any of the real women of WOOPs lived in cabins near the dam, or that they would have been reassigned to the Army Counter Intelligence Corps. But I'm glad my heroine had both those experiences!

It's also highly doubtful that any acts of sabotage ever occurred at the Secret City. However, many families who were displaced when the government bought land to build Norris Dam were forced from their homes again when land was needed to build Oak Ridge.

My research for this novel included a visit to this historic city, where I spent a delightful morning at the newly opened history museum. That afternoon I drove to Norris Dam and later stopped in at the Museum of Appalachia. I had a great time during my brief stay, thanks to the lovely people I met.

In addition to reading books and scouring websites, I listened to several of the oral interviews preserved by the Atomic Heritage Foundation and Los Alamos Historical Society. These are featured on the Voices of the Manhattan Project website at https://www.manhattanprojectvoices.org.

Though I tried to be as accurate as possible when I could be, I was purposefully vague on a few details. And I made up some stuff too! Even so, I hope you enjoyed this story and hope that Kathleen, Roger, and Liberty will live on in your hearts for a long time to come.

Best wishes,
Johnnie

Acknowledgments

I'm writing this section—a very important one to me—at 1:42 on a Saturday morning. A few moments ago, I typed "The End" on the manuscript, so I'm feeling euphoric and weary. The story went places I didn't expect, and once again I fell in love with imaginary characters who visit me for a while and then slip away (though they're never forgotten).

I am so thankful God gives these characters to me and that I get to tell their stories.

I'm thankful too for the very real people who share their knowledge, resources, and experiences with me so that my characters are rooted in real places and real events. I especially want to thank the following individuals:

- Cyn Taylor sent me helpful internet links and encouragement. Her husband retired from the Oak Ridge National Laboratory (ORNL) in 2017.
- Carrie Booth Schmidt introduced me to her dad, David Booth, whose parents worked at the Y-12 plant. We had a great time Zooming together one morning. Carrie's grandmother is one of the women featured in the photo on the cover of *The Girls of Atomic City* by Denise Kiernan.
- Lloyd and Betty Stokes welcomed me when I visited the Oak Ridge History Museum. They were very generous with their time, and Mr. Stokes gave me a tour of the very impressive museum housed in a 1940s-era community recreational hall.
- Emily Hunnicutt is the daughter of Ed Westcott, the

official Oak Ridge photographer who took the photo that appears on the cover of *The Girls of Atomic City*. Emily and her husband, Don, were also gracious and welcoming when I met them at the Oak Ridge History Museum.

A special shout-out to my fabulous agent, Tamela Hancock Murray. I'm so grateful to have you beside me on my writing journey. (Nine years and counting! Can you believe it?)

Thank you to the Barbour team for your dedication to publishing top-notch historical collections and the opportunities you provide to so many authors. Special thanks to Ellen Tarver, the gifted editor who opens my eyes to my blind spots.

Thanks to Rita Gerlach, who brought this collection together, and also to Amanda Barratt and Lauralee Bliss. I've had a great time working with each of you.

As always, love and joy to Bethany and Justin, Jillian and Jacob, and Nate and Bre. And hugs aplenty to my adorable, mischievous, heartwarming, miss-you-when-I'm-not-with-you grands: Jeremy, Jedidiah, Kaydi, Josiah, and Presley.

Johnnie Alexander creates characters you want to meet and imagines stories you won't forget in a variety of genres. An award-winning, bestselling novelist, she serves on the executive boards of Serious Writer, Inc., and the Mid-South Christian Writers Conference, cohosts Writers Chat, and interviews other inspirational authors for Novelists Unwind. Johnnie lives in Oklahoma with Griff, her happy-go-lucky collie, and Rugby, her raccoon-treeing papillon. Connect with her at www.johnnie-alexander.com and other social media sites via https://linktr.ee/johnniealexndr.

Dream a Little Dream

by Amanda Barratt

Soli Deo Gloria

Chapter 1

Hollywood, California
November 15, 1940

Sunset Boulevard. One could almost smell the mystique, the luxury in the tropical air. Bright signs, sleek autos, breathless anticipation. The playground of the fabled, the waiting room of the unknown.

Rosemary James had never been to Hollywood, despite having grown up just five hours north. Right out of high school, she'd started work at the public library. There'd never been room—or money—in her life for something as frivolous as a vacation.

But here she was—for one week, before she returned to Ainsley Falls to work through the Christmas holidays so the head librarian, Mrs. Edwards, could visit her brother in San Francisco.

She'd already used up six days. Sunned herself on the beaches and taken the bus tour through Beverly Hills. Sat in darkened movie theaters, eating handfuls of buttery popcorn, while stories of romance and adventure spun their way across the silver screen. Dined on sandwiches in her hotel room in the evening while reading *Gone with the Wind* for the third time. Played tourist at

Grauman's Chinese Theatre, putting her feet in the footprints of the stars. Jean Harlow. Shirley Temple. Clark Gable. Ginger Rogers. Fred Astaire. They'd all made their mark on the slabs of cement bedecking the walkway, and the sight of those prints had dazzled her.

She'd savored every moment of her week in Tinseltown, the brevity of the visit magnifying every moment into something sweet and golden.

Next on her list—a soda at Schwab's Drugstore. Not that she had aspirations of becoming the next Lana Turner, whom dubious gossip reported had been discovered there. In a simple navy suit, hair wind-mussed, she'd attract no attention, least of all from an agent or producer. But she'd heard Schwab's had great ice cream and sodas. Since she was on vacation until tomorrow, she'd treat herself.

In the minutes since the taxi driver dropped her off, she'd lingered on the sidewalk, taking in the sights. Now she approached the front door, the large sign in curving white letters prosaically declaring SCHWAB'S PHARMACY.

She pushed open the door, the scents of sweet ice cream and fried food hitting her in a wash of warm air. The place was crammed with people. Men in suits lounged on counter stools, digging into sandwiches. Women sipped sodas in frosted glasses, red-burnished fingers daintily holding straws. White-aproned waiters and waitresses took orders behind the counter, sliding filled plates and glasses topped with ice cream to waiting customers.

Quite the crowd for late afternoon. A glance around the room's perimeter revealed not one empty seat at either counter or tables.

Rosemary squeezed in line behind a couple holding hands and staring into each other's eyes. She clasped her fingers tighter around her faded clutch purse. In order to live off her meager funds, she had watched every penny. No splurges. Her hotel—one of the cheapest she could find—cost dear enough.

The line inched forward. The couple ahead ordered a hot fudge sundae and a cherry soda. Two teenagers exited their spots at the counter, and a waitress hastily cleared the space. The man stepped aside to let his companion through, and she slid onto the stool with a smile. Their intertwined gaze made Rosemary's heart cinch. Paul never looked at her like that.

She never looked at him like that either.

"What can I get you, miss?" the young man behind the counter asked.

Rosemary scanned the menu board.

"A chocolate milkshake, please."

"Alrighty then. That'll be forty-five cents."

She opened her purse and counted out the coins, passing them into his palm. He thanked her, and she moved out of the line to the end of the counter to wait for her order. During her week of vacation, she'd become accustomed to traveling alone. Sitting at a small diner table, taking careful bites, with only occasional glances at the empty seat across from her. Except for brief conversations with the cleaning woman at the hotel, the ticket man at the movie theater, and waitresses at restaurants—and that one time on the beach when she broke down and started talking to herself—the week had been void of words. She didn't mind silence. But the abundance of it, a lone woman surrounded by vacationing couples and families, chafed at the empty space inside her.

"One chocolate milkshake," called a brunette waitress.

"That's me." Clamping her purse beneath her arm, Rosemary took the glass. It was cool and moist against her fingers, filled to the brim with rich chocolatey liquid. A straw poked from one side. Her mouth watered at the wafting chocolate scent.

She thanked the waitress and scanned the room again. Every seat at the counter and every table had occupants. She bit her lip, hesitating. Now what?

A laughing couple carrying white paper sacks brushed past her and headed for the door. Rosemary watched them, admiring the woman's trim red dress.

A jolt hit her from behind. The slick glass slipped from her fingers and crashed to the ground. Chocolate splashed the floor, dotting her black pumps and the skirt of her suit. A dozen gazes turned toward her.

"Quit blocking the walkway, lady." A man in a white fedora flicked her a glance of annoyance. He sidestepped the mess and headed toward the door.

"Sorry," Rosemary whispered to his retreating form. Face aflame, she crouched on the ground and began picking up the chunks of glass. The brunette waitress rounded the counter and hurried toward her with a pile of napkins.

"Here. Let me help you." She flashed a ruby smile.

"I–I'm so sorry," Rosemary stammered, frantically piling the shards into the napkins. Sticky chocolate coated her fingers.

"Don't be," came a masculine voice.

Both Rosemary and the waitress looked up. A tall man in a pressed gray suit stood over them.

"What?" Her voice came out choked.

"That bum ran into you. Saw the whole thing from my table by the window." He gestured toward an empty table topped with a plate of food. "The manners around here are getting worse every day. That idiot should have apologized instead of leaving you here covered in chocolate." One side of his mouth angled in a grin. The sudden magnetism of it stole her breath. "Here, miss." He held out his palm. "Allow me. Dottie here will finish cleaning up. Won't you, doll?"

"Of course." The waitress flushed and beamed.

Stunned, Rosemary placed her sticky hand in his and let him help her to her feet. Standing, she came up to his shoulder.

"There. You see." He flashed another grin. "No use crying over a spilled milkshake." He winked.

The waitress laughed. Rosemary just stared at him, caught in the spell of his gaze. Strikingly handsome. Those were the two words that best described him.

"Now, the least I can do to make up for the rudeness of that jerk is to offer you a seat at my table."

His words snapped her back to alertness. "Oh, I couldn't possibly—"

"I insist. Dottie, bring another milkshake for the lady, please. Put it on my tab." Before she knew what was happening, Rosemary found herself seated opposite him at a small table just left of the window. A half-eaten hamburger and fries sat at his place, along with a soda.

A couple of minutes later, Dottie brought over a new milkshake and set it in front of Rosemary.

"Thank you." Rosemary wiped the stickiness from her fingers with a napkin.

"Thanks, Dottie. You're swell." One hand resting on the table, he smiled up at the waitress.

"No trouble at all, Mr. Powell. Anything for a regular like you." The waitress dimpled before hastening away.

Rosemary wrapped both hands around her milkshake and faced him across the table. "You didn't have to do this."

"Nonsense." He picked up his hamburger and took a bite. Wiped his mouth with a napkin. "No trouble at all. I come here most Saturday afternoons. Great hamburgers."

"Oh," was all she could think to say.

"Aren't you going to try your milkshake? After all the trouble you went through to get it, you really should have some."

A little laugh escaped. "I guess I should." She lifted her straw. Cold chocolate goodness slid down her throat.

"Well?" Hands folded on the table, he watched her. He had brown hair, several shades darker than the chocolate. He wore it slicked back and combed away from his forehead.

"It's really good." She dabbed the corners of her mouth with a napkin.

"I should try it sometime. You know, I come here all the time, and I've never had most of the stuff on the menu. A hamburger, fries, and a cherry soda. Every week."

"How dull." The words flew from her mouth before she could think.

"It is dull." He took a drink of soda. "Amazing, isn't it, how easy it is to get into a pattern. The same thing day after day. Even in Hollywood."

"You'd think there'd be no shortage of excitement here," she said.

"But you're wrong." He gestured with a fry. "Things never change. The faces do, maybe, but nothing else. You've done it once, you've done it a million times." She read it in his gaze, heard it in his tone. Disillusionment. How well she recognized the symptoms— from herself. Much as you tried, much as you wished it different, something was missing. It was part of the reason she'd taken a vacation to begin with.

Perhaps that was why she didn't thank him and leave. Perhaps it was why something compelled her to continue sitting there, talking to him. She didn't know this man. He could be a con man or a criminal or worse. But the waitress seemed to know him, although that wasn't really much of a recommendation.

Decisions that weren't perfectly sound had never been her thing. Making the decision to sit here with this stranger was dubious at best. And yet she stayed.

"It sounds like where I come from. Every year the circus comes to town at exactly the same time. The five and dime puts up posters, the kids save pennies for weeks. It's always the same." She took a sip of milkshake.

"Is it us, or is it them? Are we really so jaded, or is life really so dull?" He leaned slightly forward, his green-eyed gaze holding hers. She'd never seen eyes quite like his, green flecked with gold.

"Well, I don't know about where I come from, but here, surely there must be some new experiences. I've waited years to see Hollywood. Dreamed about it."

"You say that now. Try living here. The glitter isn't as long-lasting as people think. It starts to fall off." He finished off the remainder of his hamburger. "Except these. These are still great." He wiped his fingers.

Rosemary swallowed another drink of milkshake. She'd come to Hollywood looking for new experiences. Well, she certainly was having one now. Sitting across the table from a stranger. Only he didn't seem like a stranger. She couldn't possibly have seen him somewhere before, yet it seemed as if she had. But where?

It didn't matter. She had to go. She wasn't stupid. The city might look all glamorous and golden, but she was here as a single woman. Alone. Who knew what kind of slick types lived within its borders? This man could be the personification of trouble. In capital letters.

Leaving her milkshake half-finished, Rosemary stood. He looked up from his soda.

"I really should be going." She placed both hands on the back of her chair.

"What?" He set aside the napkin. "Already?"

She nodded.

"You didn't finish your milkshake."

"It doesn't matter." She gave a self-conscious laugh. "Thank you for the milkshake and for the conversation. It was very nice of you." She turned away and headed for the door. What had she been thinking? It wasn't safe to talk to strangers. She wasn't a naive teenager. She ought to know better.

She let herself out and hurried down the sidewalk, heels clicking. A breeze ran its fingers through her hair. Back to her hotel to pack and spend the evening with her book. Just as she did every night, even at home.

See, even a vacation hadn't really changed her life.

Footsteps sounded behind her. She looked over her shoulder. The man from the drugstore stood a pace away, backdropped by a souvenir shop. "Wait."

She spun to face him. "Why?"

"You said you've dreamed about seeing Hollywood. I can show it to you. Take you wherever you want to go." He sounded eager, his words coming fast.

She shook her head. "I'm sorry, no."

"No?"

"No," she repeated, turning away.

"Why not? You just got done saying how dull life is. If you came here for excitement, why not have some?" His words sounded like a salesman. But his tone, it almost pled with her.

She turned back around. A car motored past, kicking up gravel, leaving behind fumes of exhaust. "Because I don't know you. That should be reason enough."

"I don't know you either, and I'm still willing to take a chance." That grin again, angling one side of his mouth.

In that instant, she was back in the movie theater in Ainsley Falls, a bag of popcorn on her lap, the silver screen stretching in front of her. A man stood on a New York sidewalk, looking at a woman as if she were the whole world.

Let's leave all this behind us, baby. You know we don't belong here.

She shook her head. No, no, no. Her airways constricted. It couldn't be. . .Cliff Powell.

"No trouble at all, Mr. Powell."

Oh no. Impossible. Not *the* Cliff Powell, whom the girls swooned over and called a second Gable. She didn't often make it to the movies. A library clerk's salary didn't permit it. But she'd seen at least one of his pictures. And, of course, she'd read about him in the papers.

He watched her now, head tilted slightly to one side.

"Cliff Powell?" The words emerged high.

"That is my name, yes." He said it like a statement. Not like something he took pride in. Rays of late afternoon sun framed his chiseled features, and she understood afresh why the girls swooned.

Her heart thudded beneath her practical blue, chocolate-splattered suit. "I really have to go."

He nodded. "Sure. You probably have someplace else to be." His voice sounded exactly as it had in the movie. Like deep, rich music.

"Not quite."

Oh no you don't. Walk away, Rosemary. Walk away. Heaven help her, she didn't. Instead, as if by one accord, they started down the sidewalk.

"You said you wanted to see Hollywood. Maybe if I showed it to you, I might remember why I once liked the place. What you say? Ciro's? Seven o'clock?"

"Um. . ."

"Look." He spread his hands. "You can meet me there. Dinner, dancing, and then you go back to wherever you're staying. How about it?"

This wasn't like her. Not at all. She was practical Rosemary, who worked the front desk at the library and read stories to schoolchildren. She didn't dance, not even with Paul.

Yet here she stood, somewhere on Sunset Boulevard, as Cliff Powell asked her to go out with him. It was the kind of thing that happened in one of his movies.

What would Paul think if he knew? Her fiancé.

Stubborn temptation tugged at her. It would just be for a few hours. She'd be going home tomorrow. If she said no, there would never be another chance like this. Ciro's. . .

Their steps slowed. He didn't fill the silence, seemed willing to let her debate with herself. Was he so certain of his charms that he knew he'd get a yes? The ladies' man who owned the silver screen would be. But was that the man beside her?

She stole a glance at him. He had his hands in his pockets and walked, head slightly bent. Despite his handsome profile, in that moment, he looked almost ordinary.

"All right." Once the words left her lips, she couldn't take them back. Nor did she, admittedly, want to.

He looked up at her. Smiled again, the corners of his eyes crinkling.

"Terrific."

She started to turn away, but he called after her.

"Wait. What is your name?"

She glanced over her shoulder. "Rosemary," she answered. "Rosemary James."

That dangerous half-moon of a grin again. "See you tonight, Rosemary."

She'd lived her life making few mistakes. If tonight was to be one, well, maybe she'd earned it.

⚶ *Chapter 2* ⚶

*H*e'd put bets Rosemary James wouldn't show.

Cliff Powell motored down Sunset Strip in his midnight-blue Cadillac convertible, wind riffling his hair. Some stars had chauffeurs. He preferred to drive himself. The city was ablaze with brightly lit nightclubs, sleek cars and limousines carrying the rich and fabled to their evening destinations.

What had possessed him to ask her? For that matter, what had possessed him to look up from his lunch? He ate at Schwab's Drugstore because they had great food, not to talk to some dame he'd never laid eyes on in his life.

Rosemary James emanated two things he knew well—being scared and feeling out of place. It had been sympathy, pure and simple, that made him stand up when that bum practically plowed her over. Sympathy that made him order her a new milkshake and ask her to sit at his table.

And then. . .

Then it became something more. Her innocence intrigued him, the sparkle in her soft brown eyes when she spoke of wanting to experience Hollywood. It wasn't her looks. Good grief, no. By starlet standards, she was passably pretty. He could have asked half a dozen up-and-coming blond bombshells to go out with him, and they'd all have said yes.

So why her? Why now?

Cliff honestly didn't know.

He parked his car, opened the door, and stepped out. Nice evening, balmy, hint of a breeze. Why, in Ohio, he'd have been huddled in front of the woodstove, and Aunt Janet would be pulling out the long underwear from the bottom bureau drawer. "*It's a nippy one*," Uncle Jack would say, and he'd holler to Aunt Janet about the whereabouts of his woolen socks.

Cliff ran a hand down the front of his pressed tux, his Rolex wristwatch catching in the light streaming from the front doors of the club. He didn't often think about life on the farm, conjure Aunt Janet's softly lined face and Uncle Jack's booming voice. But tonight he let himself get lost in a moment of nostalgia for those cold late-autumn nights. Next week was Thanksgiving. Uncle Jack would be talking about turkey and arguing with Aunt Janet that this year she had to put sage in the stuffing. And Aunt Janet would fuss about how she didn't like sage until Uncle Jack harrumphed and gave in, with a peck to her cheek.

He ought to phone them. He'd bought them a telephone a few years back so they wouldn't have to go a mile down the road to the general store to place a call.

A taxi pulled up. Cliff's gaze went to it. The driver got out and went around to open the door. The last traces of sunset bathed the sky.

A woman in a silver evening dress stepped from the back seat and smoothed both hands down her skirt. Rosemary.

Good thing betting wasn't one of his vices. He'd have lost that one.

Cliff strode toward her, footfalls firm on the asphalt.

A shy smile touched her lips. The silvery sheen of her evening dress shimmered in the streetlights. Her auburn hair curled around her heart-shaped face, and lipstick reddened her mouth. She wore no jewelry.

"Good evening." The words rolled from his tongue.

"Hello." Her cheeks turned pink. He couldn't remember the last time he'd seen a woman naturally blush. She'd spent most of their time together doing it, and now again tonight. It was kind of endearing, actually.

Pulling his leather wallet from his pocket, Cliff turned to the taxi driver and handed over some bills. "Be back here for the lady at ten sharp."

"Certainly, sir." The man hastily pocketed the cash. "You can count on it."

"Thanks." Cliff tipped a nod to the driver. He offered Rosemary his arm. "Shall we?"

She placed delicate fingertips on the sleeve of his tuxedo coat. They moved in the direction of the entrance, joining other arriving couples dressed to the nines in suits and silks. Elaborate fur wraps bedecked most of the women's shoulders. Any excuse to show off a mink coat. Rosemary's arms were bare, her evening gown simple.

He leaned close as they approached the doors. "You look very nice."

"Thank you." A smile tugged her lips at the compliment. "So do you," she added.

He chuckled. "Thanks."

Lights and white-jacketed waiters ushered them through the front doors. Ciro's swept them in with a flourish. Cliff tried to look at it through Rosemary's eyes, for the first time, as she would. Walls draped in pale green silk, rich red sofas lining the room's perimeter. Tables set with white linen cloths, silver and crystal were positioned in intimate clusters around the room. Music crooned from behind the bandstand as the musicians played an instrumental rendition of "Cheek to Cheek." Waiters carried trays of drinks while men and women laughed and mingled.

Cliff stopped by the maître d's desk. The middle-aged man looked up from a black binder, round face breaking into a smile.

"Good evening, Mr. Powell. We have your reservation right here. Jarvis." He motioned a waiter over. "Escort Mr. Powell and his guest to their table."

"Certainly. Right this way, please." With a bow, the waiter led them to their table near the back of the room, as Cliff had requested. He sensed eyes look up as they passed, recognized the familiar burn of gazes upon him. Always the same. Hollywood's favorite pastime. Look and be looked at. That and getting a load of the postmortem in tomorrow's papers. He scanned the room, recognizing many familiar faces, though thankfully not those of Hedda Hopper or Louella Parsons. He didn't want his evening with Rosemary picked apart by the press.

The waiter pulled out Rosemary's chair. She sank into it, gaze on the elegant table arrangement. Candles glowed from the center, pristine white menus with scrolling black lettering in front of their places. Cliff took the seat across from her.

A table for two near the back of the room. Just what he'd asked for.

It was what happened when you were a star. What he asked for, he got.

Cliff opened his mouth to say something to Rosemary, but she wasn't looking at him. She'd half-turned in her chair and took in their surroundings with wide eyes.

She turned back to him. "That woman over there. . .?"

He followed her gaze to the sleek woman holding a wine glass in both slim hands, red hair upswept, diamonds sparkling in her ears. "Katharine Hepburn?"

"Why, it really is her." Rosemary gasped. "She's one of my favorites. She was terrific with Cary Grant in *Bringing Up Baby*."

"Yeah, that was a great one. I chatted with her a couple of weeks ago at the Derby." But Rosemary was staring again.

"That isn't. . .Clark Gable?" she whispered, pointing to a dark-haired man laughing with his table companions across the room.

"Sure." Cliff leaned back in his chair.

Another waiter came around. "Something to drink, miss?" He gave Rosemary a look of mild curiosity. Of course he wouldn't recognize her. Almost always, in the past few years, when Cliff had walked into the room with a dame on his arm, it had been Hazel. Or else one of his costars for a publicity event. After Hazel. . .Well, he'd not gone out much in the three months since she'd broken their engagement.

He refused to think of her tonight.

Rosemary hesitated.

He leaned toward her. "Do you like champagne?"

She bit her lip then shook her head. "I. . .well, I don't really drink."

Before he could check it, his brow rose. As did the waiter's. She didn't drink? He couldn't recall a lady ever declining his offer of champagne. "Skip the champagne, Harry." He turned to Rosemary. "Please, order anything you like."

She looked up at the waiter with a smile. "A Coca-Cola, please."

"Very good, miss." The waiter nodded. "And for you, sir?"

He usually went for a scotch on the rocks, or at least champagne.

But somehow, with Rosemary and her Coca-Cola, drinking himself didn't seem appropriate. "I'll have a Coca-Cola too, thanks."

"Very good, Mr. Powell, sir." The waiter turned smartly and wove his way through the room. On the bandstand, a man in a white tuxedo and black bowtie took the microphone. The musicians strummed a slow melody, and the man's honeyed voice filled the room. The laughter and conversation lowered to a ripple as he sang a husky rendition of "One and Only."

Cliff knew the song because it had been written for one of his movies, *The Other Girl*, where he starred opposite Betty Grable. The film had started his career. But after listening to that song over and over on set and at premieres and publicity events, it grated on his nerves.

But Rosemary listened with a rapt expression. She wore her emotions on her face—another rarity in Hollywood—and he leaned back in his chair and watched her for the sheer delight of it, while the crooner behind the microphone sang. *"You're my one and only. Always, my one and only. . ."*

The song ended to mild applause. The waiter brought two glasses of Coca-Cola and placed them on the table.

Cliff picked up the glass of fizzing brown soda. He chuckled softly. "Well, what shall we toast to?" He held the glass loosely in one hand.

"Oh, I don't know." An impulsive smile tipped her lips. "To magical evenings?"

"Magical evenings." He clinked his glass against hers, took a drink, and set his glass atop the tablecloth. It wasn't half bad, at that. "So, Miss Rosemary James, tell me about yourself."

She set down her glass. Soft light made her auburn curls shine. "What is there to tell?"

"About you. Your life, your dreams, what you think about

when you wake up in the morning, when you go to bed at night." He folded his hands together and rested his elbows on the table. She intrigued him. It didn't take ten minutes to see how different she was from the women he'd known over the past five years. He wanted to know more about her for reasons even he himself couldn't fully understand.

She laughed softly. "I'm a simple person who lives a simple life."

"Somehow, I doubt that. Come on. Tell me." He flashed his signature grin. Powell magic, the fans called it. Rarely had it been genuine. Except with Hazel.

Why did her name continue to invade his thoughts? Like a splinter one couldn't get rid of, no matter how much one dug.

He forced the thoughts away and focused on Rosemary, her sweetness an antidote to the bitter taste of betrayal.

She sipped her soda. Set down the glass again. "I grew up in Ainsley Falls. It's farm country, about five hours north of here, the quintessential small town."

He'd never heard of the place. "And what do you do in this 'quintessential small town'?"

"I work at the library as assistant to the head librarian."

He couldn't stop the involuntary laugh. "You work at the library?" She didn't fit the picture of a typical librarian—a spinster with prim hair and an even primmer expression. Not this auburn-haired girl in the silver dress who loved Katharine Hepburn films. She was too. . .too . . .

"Don't laugh. It's not funny, anyway. Libraries are wonderful places. Don't you read?"

"Of course. Every issue of *Variety*," he deadpanned. But the grin tugging at his lips gave him away.

"Figures." She laughed again. "I love books." She drew in a long breath. "In the pages of a story, there are no limitations."

"Obviously you're talking about fiction. Life is one big, long limitation you have to fight to move past. Even I can't have everything."

"Can't you?" Her voice was a bit breathless.

He shook his head slowly. Hazel again. "No one can." He picked up his glass, ran his thumb along the base. Looked up at her once more. "You live in a small town, you're a librarian. What else?"

"I'm engaged," she said softly, almost so softly he couldn't catch her words. But he did.

Engaged. Of course. A girl whose eyes sparkled like that wouldn't be otherwise. Some lucky guy took one look into those soft brown orbs and fell hard.

A pang of envy shot through him and made him almost laugh at himself. Cliff Powell, jealous of some guy he didn't know over some girl he barely knew. Maybe he was crazier than he thought.

"Okay. Engaged. To whom?" He watched her closely for the telltale signs of a woman in love. Flushed cheeks—she blushed about everything else—a gentle smile.

"Paul Cartwright." It was a statement. And there were no flushed cheeks. "He's the son of the. . .our local minister. Paul's going to seminary. He's there right now, actually. He wants to get married over Christmas break."

How nice. Married to the son of a minister. Cliff could picture the fellow now—pale, earnest face behind wire-rimmed spectacles. Dull and prosaic. He studied her hand, resting gently on the edge of her glass. "No ring?"

She shook her head, curls dancing. "Paul couldn't afford an engagement ring. We'll buy wedding rings though. It will be simple—the wedding, that is."

"Simple. Like you."

She nodded, resting her chin in her palm. "Simple. Like me."

The waiter returned. "Are we ready to order?"

He glanced at Rosemary. Neither of them had opened their menus. She shrugged. "What's good? You know better than me."

"Two orders of beef mignonette then." To Rosemary he added, "It's a Ciro's specialty."

"Sounds delicious."

The waiter took their menus, leaving them alone again. Rosemary gave a little grin. "Your turn now."

He spread his hands wide. "No, no, no. You haven't told me what you think about in the morning when you wake up and at night when you go to bed."

Her eyes danced. "It's a secret."

He chuckled. "A secret, huh?"

"Mm-hmm."

"Just one thing then. C'mon. Or my own lips will be forever sealed, m'lady." MGM would fire him if they heard how bad his British accent was.

She tilted her head. A minute passed. "I want to become a nurse," she said quietly.

"A nurse?"

She nodded. "I want to help people. You know, really make a difference. Not just shelving books and watering the geraniums, but saving lives. There's a war going on. It might come here, and then they'll need even more nurses." Her voice had gained confidence. He could see her doing it, wearing white, walking through a hospital ward with a purposeful step, bringing comfort to her patients just by being there.

"You'd make a fine nurse."

A smile unfurled. "You really think so?"

"Yeah."

She fairly glowed, as if this was the first time someone had affirmed her dreams. That kind of affirmation mattered far more than bland compliments.

"Okay. Your turn." She rested her elbows on the table and propped her chin on the backs of her intertwined fingers.

"There's even less to tell about me."

She blinked. "But you're Cliff Powell."

A trace of frustration nudged him. *You're Cliff Powell.* The name, the brand, the glitz.

"Exactly. That's the point. The world already knows it all." Some of the tension bled into his tone.

Her eyes darkened. "Well, I don't. I don't follow movie star gossip. If it wouldn't hurt your pride, I'll even admit to having seen only one of your pictures. It was a couple of years ago. That's why I didn't recognize you. Besides, there's more to all of us than our exteriors."

He shifted in his seat, discomfited. He wasn't used to answering personal questions, really answering them. Sure, you made statements for the press, usually coached by your agent. Smiled for the flashbulbs. That was life in Hollywood. But reaching deep inside another human heart, well, that didn't happen, no matter what the movies liked to make viewers believe.

"Let's start with something simple then. How did you come out here?"

He lifted his drink to his lips. It was a familiar story, one repeated in newspapers and magazines. Farm Boy Finds Tinseltown Stardom. "It was in 1936. My parents died when I was three years old." The last had come out of nowhere. He wasn't even sure if it had been his own voice uttering it.

Moisture filmed her eyes. "I'm sorry. My mother passed when I was eight. I never knew my father."

They were both orphans. Somehow, that strengthened the bond between them, gave him courage to go on. "Growing up, I had it pretty good. My aunt and uncle took me in. They had a farm in Ohio. *Have* a farm. They were great. *Are* great. But always in the back of my mind, there was this wondering about the wider world. Wanderlust, I guess you'd call it."

Elbows on the table, Rosemary held her glass in both hands. "I know the feeling. It's worse than having a headache. Aspirin can't cure discontent."

Cliff gave a dry laugh. "I wish."

"Go on."

"You sure you want to hear this?" He wasn't even sure he wanted to tell it.

A vigorous nod.

"Okay." Where was he? Oh yes. Wanderlust. "A friend told me he was heading to California to work at his cousin's golf course, and I jumped at the chance to go with him. It was a sight easier than baling hay and getting up at four in the morning to milk the cows."

He chuckled. "Of course, the Hollywood bug bit me as soon as I got out here. I started going to auditions, paying for some lessons with my tip money. I wasn't getting any callbacks though. But one afternoon I was mowing the golf course when a guy came up to me. To make a long story short, we chatted about this and that, and he asked if I'd ever wanted to be in pictures. Turns out, he's this high-profile agent, and he invites me to his office the next week to discuss my future. I was twenty, and I only had one suit." How well he remembered trying to clean and press it. "He offered to represent me. Said he was looking for new talent. A few weeks later, I got my first job. This B movie comedy—*The Lady Takes All*. I played the heroine's younger brother. It was a small part, and I didn't expect much to come of it. Then reviews started coming in. Of course, the critics said the movie was lousy. But two little lines near the bottom of this one review said, 'Refreshing performance from newcomer to the screen, Mr. Cliff Powell. We hope to see more of him.'" He ran his finger in a sweeping motion, imitating a line of type. "After that, opportunities started coming in. In 1937 I made that picture with Betty Grable. That was my big break."

"And Hazel Morgan?" The melodic notes of soft music mingled with the couples on the dance floor. Cliff stared absently at their swirling forms, the mingling of black-suited men and resplendent women.

"I thought you said you didn't follow Hollywood gossip." He cracked a smile, but it felt off-kilter.

"You'd have to live under a rock not to hear about that." She echoed his wry smile. "Of course"—she blushed again—"if you don't want to talk about it. . ."

"I don't want to *think* about it, if you want to know the truth." He rubbed a hand across his jaw. "Hazel and I made five pictures together in three years. Separate, neither of us were all that great. But when they put us on screen together. . ." He snapped his fingers. "Dynamite."

"And?" Her voice was gentle.

He stared down at the tablecloth. "And I fell in love with her. Asked her to marry me, thinking she loved me as much as I loved her."

"She didn't?" Rosemary's gaze radiated empathy.

"I thought she did. Even Hazel herself thought so for a while. But a week before the wedding, she eloped with a New York steel magnate."

"Did she say why?"

Cliff shook his head. "Nothing of substance. Nothing that said she was really sorry. Like I said, I try not to think about it." Talking about it had rubbed him raw. He hadn't spoken of it at all in the three months since it happened, save that horrible press interview when he'd forced himself to make a statement. Let bygones be bygones.

"But you have to. To give your heart away again, you have to make peace with the past." Her voice was low. Fierce.

He rubbed a finger across his upper lip, pondering her words. "You don't say."

The waiter returned with steaming plates of food, cutting off their conversation. They thanked him, and he moved on to another table. Cliff pretended fascination with his plate, forking a bite of the tender seasoned beef. In reality he cared far more about Rosemary's reaction to it than the meal itself. Her delicate fingers deftly worked her knife and fork. She took a bite, and her eyes fell half closed as she chewed.

"Good, huh?" he asked.

"Oh yes." She smiled.

As they chatted and dined, something inside Cliff shifted. This girl was the real deal. When she laughed, it was genuine. When she said something, she meant it. No Hollywood simpering for her. She even blushed, for goodness' sake.

Yes, there was something rare about Rosemary James. Something that drew him.

Something he could never attain.

In his arms, anything could happen.

Oh, she was drunk. Not on champagne—he'd looked surprised when she refused that offer, but on him. The way his warm hand encircled her waist as they swayed on the dance floor, the scent of his cologne, his gaze on hers. The bandleader lured the crowd onto the dance floor with soft strains of "Dream a Little Dream of Me." The melody wrapped around her, and she leaned instinctively closer.

His eyes crinkled as he smiled, and a few strands of smoothed-back hair fell slightly over his forehead. Her heart skipped a beat.

This attraction—it was powerful. And dangerous. The latter emotion whispered in her mind, but she pushed it away. Though it was crazy to imagine, if the way he'd watched her during dinner, shared the pain of his past, was any indication, Cliff felt it too.

And was he ever a good dancer. Of course, he had to be, considering how many movies he'd made. He led without overpowering, added an artistic finesse to his movements without looking ridiculous. Even she, who only knew the rudimentary steps, moved with confidence, her steps matching his.

Dream a little dream, sang the bandleader.

She was dreaming all right. With her eyes wide open.

The song ended, the fourth they'd danced. Cliff turned to her, a hand gently resting on the small of her back.

"It's getting late," he said quietly. "I should see you to your taxi."

She nodded, regret tugging sharp. The evening had come to an end. Even fairy tales faded at the stroke of midnight. Cinderella had to leave the ball and return to her stepmother's home. Of course, the prince pursued her, but that was a story. This was real life.

Not fiction and not the Hollywood dream of Cliff Powell's movies.

They left the gilded and perfumed nightclub and stepped into the darkness. Lights glowed from marquees, a different kind of starlight. Stillness encircled them, save for the rumbles of cars and taxis, far-off voices and laughter. She sucked in a breath of chilly air.

Cliff turned to her. "Well, this is goodbye, I guess."

She nodded. His hands settled on her shoulders, heat penetrating through the thin fabric of her dress. He gazed down at her in the meager light, a renegade thatch of hair falling over his forehead. He looked as regretful as she.

Sudden tears stung her eyes. She would never see him again. Of course she could sit in the back of the theater and view his next picture, but it wouldn't be like this. She'd watch his lips form the right words, see his face close-up and larger than life, but it would just be an act. The man who'd paid for her milkshake and swayed with her to the strains of "The Way You Look Tonight" would be lost to her.

How was it possible to miss someone you'd only spent a few hours with? For those same hours to have taken up a place in her heart that made them seem like years?

She pressed her lips together, shaking her head back and forth. She was supposed to return to Ainsley Falls after her vacation and prepare to wed Paul. A decent man who said he loved her. But he'd never looked at her like Cliff did. Never teased her or listened to her. She'd accepted his proposal because it was the expected thing, and for her, an orphaned library clerk, a good match.

"Thank you for everything," she said softly.

He shook his head, hands falling from her shoulders. "It is I who should be thanking you. I haven't spent an evening like this in I don't know how long. Maybe never. There's something about you, Rosemary James." He rubbed a hand along his jaw. "Something real and genuine. Something. . .blast it, I don't know."

The look in his eyes, haggard and world-weary and desperate, was her undoing. Her rationality fled in a haze of blinding longing that eclipsed everything else. All she wanted was him, his mouth on hers, his arms around her.

For tonight. Just one night.

She lifted her face to his, drawing him toward her with her gaze. "Cliff." Her voice was a ragged whisper.

In response, he pulled her toward him, a breath away.

The moment his lips met hers, all else ceased to be. She wrapped her arms around him, standing on tiptoe, his strong arms crushing her against him. He was spicy cologne and breathless abandon, filling her with piercing longing, whelming her body in warmth. Their breaths came fast, frantic. His hands tangled in her hair.

Ask me to stay. Ask me. . .

Blinding headlights cut through the darkness. They pulled away, jerked from the moment. A taxicab stopped a few feet away.

Cliff strode toward it, straightening his tie with one hand. She stared at his retreating form, fingers pressed to her still-warm lips. Her mind swam. Cliff exchanged a few words with the driver then walked back to her. His expression told her everything she needed to know. That was her cab.

And this could be nothing more than goodbye.

Their gazes met, heavy with the tincture of regret. Her throat tightened. She had to say something. Had to walk away, toward the cab and away from him.

Tears burned her eyes. She blinked them back.

"Goodbye." The single word was all she could choke out. She walked past him, skirt trailing the ground, heels making a hollow clicking sound on the pavement. Before the driver could get out, she jerked open the door herself and climbed in the back seat. Her heel snagged on her skirt. Fabric ripped. She didn't care.

"Where to?" The driver's eyes met hers through the rearview mirror.

She stammered the name of her hotel, and they jerked forward. She turned toward the window.

Cliff still stood there. A solitary man in a suit backdropped by the bright lights of a nightclub that represented all that was his life. His shoulders stooped. She'd never seen anyone look more alone.

Then he was gone, the nightclub faded from view, the street a blur of harsh lights and glittering buildings. She leaned back against the leather seat, eyes shut, taking jagged breaths of musty air. Her nails dug into her palm. She welcomed the pain.

Anything to keep from crying. To make her forget.

Cliff's face rose before her mind.

The first she could manage until she reached the solitude of her hotel.

The second she could never do.

That night he drove home fast and reckless, swerving around corners, the lick of wind in his face and the screech of tires two sensations that brought a miserable kind of satisfaction.

The taxi driver had unwittingly saved Rosemary. Cliff wasn't about to play the saint. Kissing her could have all too easily led to more.

Which made him a snake. Perhaps not by Hollywood standards. Here such affairs were as ordinary as street signs. To be honest, he'd rarely gone in for that kind of thing, though he'd had offers aplenty. Women flung themselves at him regularly, gorgeous, desirable women. He always waved them off with a smile and a few trite compliments.

But Rosemary wasn't from here. She was different. Yet he'd acted on his impulses, and had the driver not shown up, she would've paid the price. Because what could he offer her beyond a few hours of pleasure-drugged forgetfulness?

Nothing. He had everything, but in some ways nothing. Not one blasted thing that really mattered.

She wasn't some swooning adolescent girl pining over Cliff Powell. She said she'd only seen one of his pictures. No, the stars in her eyes when she looked at him as they danced. . . Could it be possible that she'd been attracted to him, kissed him, because he was himself and not the silver screen idol beloved by the media?

A vision of her saying goodbye with genuine tears in her eyes stood stark in his memory.

Maybe.

His hands tightened on the steering wheel. He swore under his breath.

She'd gone. Back to her life in her small town. Back to her fiancé.

For yes, the woman he'd danced with and kissed was engaged. *Engaged*, for crying out loud.

"Typical, Powell," he muttered.

Not content with wrecking his own life, he had to go and mess with other people's lives.

He spoke a few terse words into the security intercom. The front gates opened and he pulled into his driveway. The immense stone house with its manicured grounds and gigantic swimming pool in the back—his home. Back when he dated Hazel, it had been his pride and joy. Redecorated with her in mind.

Now she was out of his life, and he couldn't stand the place.

He leaned his head against the steering wheel, eyes shut. Tonight had made him realize that he'd been content with a lie. He wasn't living. *Existing* might be a better word, going through the motions of parties and photo shoots, film premieres and speaking scripted lines in front of cameras. None of it meant anything.

He had to do something. And he didn't mean locking himself inside his house and swilling his way through a case of scotch.

His uncle's weathered face rose before him. What would Uncle Jack think if he could see him now? Likely, that his nephew was pathetic. He'd be right.

Cliff lifted his head, staring up into the inky sky. Stars glimmered from the heavens, a canvas brighter than any conjured in a studio backlot.

He had to do something that mattered, that benefited a cause greater than himself. He'd made himself the man he was today through a lot of hard work and sacrifice.

With that same strength, he could, would, become someone different. Someone better.

Someone worthy of Rosemary James—the woman who would never be his.

Chapter 3

Tanauan Airfield, Island of Leyte, Philippines
Four Years Later, December 11, 1944

They strode through the mud across the airstrip, a bunch of guys in aviator caps, yellow Mae West life preservers, and whatever else they'd managed to put on. By now their marine issue had gotten pretty ratty. Besides, it was as hot and sticky as all get-out in the Philippines, even in December. So Lieutenant Andrew Patterson, or Pat, as the guys called him, wore a T-shirt he'd probably had since his college football days, and Lieutenant W. J. Taylor was dressed in an old marine button-down with half the buttons missing.

Cliff grinned to see them. He was just as sweaty, dirty, and seasoned as the rest. He walked near the head of the line, in step with their commanding officer, Major Jim Walker. But only the new recruits called him that, most of the time. To his guys, he was Glim, named thus on account of his extraordinarily white-blond hair.

Some thought lack of military formality made men slack. For the boys of VMF-219, it only strengthened their ties of brother-hood. Glim was no sidelines commander. He flew all missions, even the dangerous ones.

They'd already been given a thorough briefing on today's second mission, to be flown in collaboration with the Army Air Force. Now the guys made bets and traded insults while Glim had a few words with the line crew chief, Sergeant Bill Brannigan.

"Pat's bird. Is it flyable?" Glim's forehead furrowed. His boots sank into the muddy, rutted strip. During his years in the Marine Corps, Cliff had rarely been tempted to expect favors due to his status as a Hollywood star. But what he wouldn't give right now for a bunch of Seabees to repair the blasted strip.

"I'm no miracle worker." Brannigan's Irish brogue was thick as potato soup. He scratched his balding head, burly arms streaked with grease. "That Zeke sure punched some holes in him. I patched 'im up, but we need a new shipment of supplies somethin' fierce."

Glim turned to Cliff. Pat was Cliff's wingman.

"If the thing flies—" Cliff began.

"It flies, Cap'n Powell," Brannigan interrupted.

"Then let's get it in the air." Tension laced Glim's Brooklyn accent.

"Go lick 'em." Brannigan thumped Glim on the back with a gap-toothed grin. Cliff would lay bets the guy had lost the missing teeth in a bar fight. If so, he doubted the other fella was still walking. Before their very first mission, Brannigan had nearly knocked Glim flat. Now the major barely winced. He turned sharply and faced the assembled men.

"Let's get going."

The men jogged down the line of navy-blue planes, reaching their various F4U Corsairs. Cliff's was near the middle. He'd been through a lot with his lady, and after as many missions as he'd flown in her cockpit, she looked more than a little worse for the wear. Once his biggest accomplishment was his name next to Hazel

Morgan's on a theater marquee. Today he was a triple ace, helping America win the fight for freedom. A fighter pilot, exposed to as much risk as the next guy.

In minutes all of the squadron was in their cockpits, engines idling. The feel of taxiing down the runway and lifting off was like no other in the world. Even tired after this morning's mission, Cliff couldn't fail to appreciate it. He just plain loved to fly. Danger could meet a guy anywhere. If there had to be a reunion, why not in the air?

The goal of this afternoon's strike was the destruction of a convoy of enemy ships off Panay. Thirty P-40s loaded with five hundred instantaneous fuzed bombs and twenty-eight F4U's carrying a thousand four- to five-second-delay bombs between them would be in the air. Carrying this kind of payload made maneuvering the Corsairs more difficult. But they'd done it before.

Glim came on the radio and read off the coordinates. Cliff adjusted his navigation controls. The Army flight was striking first with dive bombing, and VMF-219, along with three other squadrons, would follow.

"Feeling okay, Pat?" Cliff asked. The airwaves crackled as they gained altitude.

"Why, yes, Dr. Powell, I'm just fine and dandy." Cliff could hear the lazy chuckle in Pat's voice. "Slept great last night, ate a filling, if lousy breakfast, emptied my—"

"He means your airplane, you lunkhead." But Glim was joking too. If there had been anything serious, Patterson would've spoken up right away.

"Oh, that," Patterson drawled. "Well, that's just fine too."

"All right, you two. Save the gabfest for quilting circle. We need to maintain radio silence."

The airwaves went dead. Below, as far as the eye could see,

stretched the blue waters of the Pacific. For years fighter pilots had been flying missions across this carpet of blue. When the war first started, the Japanese had better aircraft and better pilots. Now, the scales had tipped. The war would draw to a close this coming year, Cliff reckoned, both in Europe and the Pacific.

It was a fine thought, but not one for today. All that mattered was making it through this mission.

Time ceased to have much meaning in the air. Soon they approached the target. Cliff spotted the destroyer ships in the water far below. His pulse skipped. They maintained formation and altitude while the P-40s peeled off in twos and threes, diving down. Even at eighteen thousand feet, a shuddering sound filled Cliff's ears as bombs exploded. His muscles tightened as he watched.

Pretty soon they wouldn't be up here alone. It was only a matter of minutes before the Zekes—Japanese fighter planes—would show up and want payback for the "present" being unloaded over the destroyers.

Fiery flack shot upward in heavy bursts toward the planes.

I guess we've woken them up.

Glim gave orders over the radio. Cliff pulled his plane into position. He turned his head. Patterson was right beside him.

"All right, guys, let's go," Glim ordered. "Keep it tight."

Cliff turned his plane, coming in fast and low. When he was over the target, he released the payload. His plane jittered. Bombs fell. They hit the destroyer dead-on, exploding in a fireball of orange and smoke. A burst of satisfaction arced through him.

Beautiful. How's that for good aim.

Then. . .Zekes. Upon them, their gray bodies with "meatball" circles filling the sky like a horde of vultures. Adrenaline surged through him.

"I've got one on my tail!" Pat's voice.

"Hang tight, Pat. I'm coming." Sweat slid down Cliff's back. Pulling full flaps and chopping the throttle, his plane pitched and dove toward the Zeke. Within range, he opened fire. Bullets pinged, peppering the plane's side. Cliff kept right on firing. Flames streamed from the Zeke's tail as it dove in a collision course toward the ocean.

Cliff glanced behind him. Two Zekes at the same altitude turned toward him.

In a head-on run, a Zeke will either turn aside or blow up, so said the book.

Cliff turned into them.

The Zeke should be turning aside, right about now. . . .

It didn't. Apparently this Japanese pilot hadn't read the book.

His stomach knotted. He didn't let up, all six .50 caliber guns firing at once. Prop to prop, closing in fast. Pieces flew off the Zeke's cowling. Bullets tore through Cliff's plane. Pain seared his left leg.

Cliff ground his jaw, ignoring the pain, focused on the Zeke.

Come on. Come on.

Too late. He nosed the Corsair violently down. A horrible ripping sound.

He sucked in a sharp breath. The Zeke had sheared off half of his rudder and the left stabilizer.

Boy, did he have his hands full.

Pitching toward the ocean, the plane vibrated as if it would fall to pieces.

"Powell!" Glim called over the radio.

"Oil pressure's zero. My engine's seizing. I'm bailing out." The odor of burnt oil filled his nostrils. "And. . .I've been hit."

"Okay. Patterson, follow him down. Good luck, Powell." Cliff hung on to Glim's steady voice, drawing strength from it, as he struggled to level the plane.

He gritted his teeth, vaguely aware of blood seeping through his torn trousers.

He cracked open the canopy, released his safety harness, grabbed his inflatable raft.

And bailed out.

A whoosh of air stole his breath as his parachute ballooned. In the sky above, the battle raged. He knew Patterson had followed him down, would be watching to make sure he made it.

Falling. Falling.

He hit the water.

If you land in the drink, there's good odds you won't come back.

A buttoned-up flight instructor had told him the exact odds once. He couldn't remember what they were. But they weren't great. Not to mention, he was wounded.

His brain began to fog. Loss of blood. Sharks. Good thing he had repellant. But would it work?

He forced himself to undo the straps of his parachute and get his raft inflated. Water soaked through his clothes. In the distance, he glimpsed the burning destroyer. At least he'd hit right on target. It would be lousy to die knowing he hadn't.

He crawled onto the raft, fighting for every movement. Blood mingled with salt water in a spreading red stain.

No. He refused to die. He'd survived too much, worked too hard. He was a triple ace, a better man than the one who'd frittered away years in Hollywood.

Many who die in war are good men.

Panic clawed his throat. Then a sudden peace descended. What an irony that his time in a squadron filled with men who drank and gambled and cussed had turned him, Cliff Powell, into a praying man. He read the Bible Aunt Janet had given him in boyhood, and he prayed because war had proved a more fearsome thing than he'd reckoned to find.

"Lord." The word gasped from his salt-coated lips. "Help me."

In the skies men battled for freedom. Below, in the waters of the Pacific, alone, waves rocking his raft back and forth, Cliff Powell battled for life.

❧ *Chapter 4* ❧

Palm Springs, California
January 2, 1945

"ay to start the New Year off with a bang. A fresh shipment of men in half an hour. The orthopedic ward is sure going to be busy. Hope you didn't wear your feet out tripping the light fantastic while ringing in '45."

Rosemary turned from her bent-over position, tucking in a sheet on one of the white metal beds lining the airy receiving room. Lieutenant Samantha Baker leaned against one wall, arms folded across her chest. Even in her beige-and-white-striped seersucker nurse's uniform, she still looked the spitting image of Rita Hayworth.

"You know full well I was on duty over New Year's Eve. And I really don't dance." Not since that night at Ciro's with the man who still had the power to steal her breath whenever she thought of him. Thankfully such thoughts found her less and less with each passing year.

"Of course you don't. Although if "Stardust" was playing and Dr. Kendall asked, you might change your mind." Sam arched a sculpted brow with a knowing grin.

Rosemary flushed and returned to her work, plumping pillows and tucking corners, readying the bed for the wounded man soon to occupy it. "Don't you have something better to be doing? There's a pile of sheets on that mattress over there. I'm sure whoever is to rest there would appreciate lying under, not over, the covers."

"Aye, aye, Lieutenant." Sam gave a mock salute.

Rosemary finished the bed and left behind the small receiving room with its six cots. Quiet footsteps sounded on the linoleum as staff hastened to their posts in the admittance ward. Familiar faces filled the large main room—fellow nurses Lieutenants Ann Wilkes and Rebecca Carlson with clipboards, teenage ward aides filling water pitchers and carrying food trays, medical sergeants carrying piles of fresh pajamas and robes.

The doctors came in last, assessing everything with businesslike authority. Dr. Gardner strode toward Lieutenant Ann Wilkes, the head nurse on Orthopedics, and spoke quietly with her. Her eyes widened, and she pressed her hand to her bodice in an uncharacteristic display of astonishment. Rosemary moved to stand near the door, listening for sounds of the arrivals.

"Good afternoon, Lieutenant James." A familiar voice made her turn. Dr. Grant Kendall stood just behind her, wearing his usual pressed white coat, graying black hair parted to the left, tall frame filling the room with an air of authority.

Rosemary gave a quick smile by way of greeting. "It seems we're in for a busy afternoon."

"More than fifty wounded. But with you on duty, I know they'll be in capable hands." A smile softened his usually serious gray gaze.

"That's kind of you to say." In the months she'd worked at Torney General Hospital, she'd seen Dr. Kendall nearly every day, but he rarely gave out compliments. Until recently she'd not known he was aware of her existence beyond being one out of many nurses. The praise warmed her. Dr. Kendall couldn't fail to win the respect of both patients and nurses. She'd rarely met anyone with more dedication to the job.

"It's not kind. It's honest."

The rumble of ambulances cut off any answer Rosemary might have conjured.

"They're here," said one of the ward aides, blue eyes wide. The news circled through the ward, uniformed doctors and nurses and aides watching the doors for the first sign of activity, faces firm with purpose.

In minutes, broad-shouldered corpsmen carried in stretchers bearing the new arrivals.

Rosemary glimpsed the wounded men as the corpsmen trooped past. Always, it struck her how young they were, barely older than high school students. A few turned their heads and gazed at her. A redheaded man with a Purple Heart fastened to his shirt grinned. An ambulatory patient limped by on crutches, a towheaded young man with his arm in a sling following right behind.

Two more corpsmen stepped inside. Afternoon sunlight streamed through the open doors. As they passed, the young man on the stretcher reached out a hand to her.

"Nurse. Please." Circles ringed wide eyes set in a pale face. The corpsmen moved out of the aisle, still holding the stretcher. Rosemary bent and grasped the young man's hand. Beneath the outline of his blanket, there was a noticeable absence. He'd lost both his left arm and leg.

"Yes?" Rosemary gave a warm smile, looking into his scared gaze.

"I don't feel—" He heaved. Rosemary dashed across the room, ducking past a ward aide. She grabbed a bedpan and cloth from a tray of supplies and raced back to the stretcher. By now the corps-men had laid down the stretcher, and only one remained. Rosemary pushed the bedpan in front of the young man, holding his head as he retched. Vomit stained his pajama shirt and blanket, its aroma stinging her nostrils.

"There now. It's all right." She wiped his mouth and called to one of the ward aides to take the bedpan and bring a glass of water. The corpsman shifted, hands behind his back. "Come back in a couple of minutes," she told him then turned back to the patient.

"I'm disgusting." He lay back against the pillow with a groan. "Half gone and useless and stinking worse than a hog trough."

The pretty young ward aide handed the water to Rosemary and took the bedpan. Her nose wrinkled at the wafting stench, and she hurried away. An involuntary reaction, but a good nurse was trained not to show such emotion.

"See. She can't stand to be near me. No normal girl can." His face twisted.

"Have a drink." Rosemary handed him the glass. Holding it for him when he had one perfectly good arm would only validate his feeling of uselessness. He drank, water dribbling down his stubbled chin. She took the empty glass then looked into his eyes.

"Listen here." Her voice was firm. "Spend a couple of hours in this hospital, and you'll find there are lots of men like you. Worse off, even. But we nurses and doctors are here to help each and every one of you. You're in good hands now. I promise. There's no need to be scared." She wasn't a doctor, but she'd seen enough similar instances to know the young man's vomiting was a result of stress and anxiety, rather than something more serious.

The corpsmen returned. Rosemary looked up. The chaos had begun to die down, most of the new arrivals situated in receiving rooms. She needed to get her list from Ann and greet the men assigned to her care.

"Hang tight, big boy, and don't give these guys any trouble." She gave the young man an easy grin, as if she hadn't just watched him puke out the contents of his stomach. Sometimes what these boys needed most was for someone, a pretty girl, to treat them like a normal man, instead of a patient. "You don't want to miss out on all the fun we have around here. And believe you me, do we ever have a good time. Games, picture shows, concerts, all sorts of things. You'll fit right in."

The young man cracked a faint smile. "Thanks."

Rosemary patted his shoulder then stood and hastened through the halls to find Ann. She caught up with her in the corridor outside of the receiving rooms. Ann's cap was crooked atop her brown corkscrew curls, and spots of color stood out on her cheeks.

"Sorry I'm late," Rosemary said. "Do you have my list?"

Ann thumbed through her clipboard. "Here." She pulled a piece of paper free and handed it to Rosemary. "They're in Room Six. One of the corpsmen has been settling them in." She gave Rosemary a strange look.

"Something wrong?"

Ann shook her head. "I don't have time to explain now. I should've been upstairs ten minutes ago."

Rosemary shrugged and hurried down the hall. Dr. Gardner strode past, an intern and a nurse in his wake.

She stopped in front of Room Six and gave a perfunctory knock before breezing in. Six men waited for her. One was the redhead she'd seen earlier. He grinned again, face turned on the pillow toward her. A young man with his left arm in a cast sat on the edge of a cot, a comic book in his lap. He gave a shy smile.

"Welcome." She clasped her hands in front of her skirt. "I'm Lieutenant James. I'll be one of the nurses taking care of you, as well as helping you through the admittance process. You'll all get a checkup and a bath, and then we'll see to your individual needs. I'm sure some of you would like cigarettes or Coca-Colas or chocolate bars—"

"Yes, please, ma'am." The redhead's grin crinkled his freckled face. "To all three."

Rosemary smiled. Whatever his injury, it obviously hadn't stolen his sense of humor. "We'll see what we can do for you. . . ."

"Private Brady, ma'am. Or you can call me Gordon." He winked.

Rosemary continued addressing the room as a whole. "And if you wish, we can arrange for you to make telephone calls to family or friends, letting them know you've arrived safely." She scanned the list as she walked around the room.

Lieutenant Thomas Atherton
Private Gordon Brady
Private Joseph Miller
Captain Clifford Powell

Clifford. Powell. Her heart lurched like a train braking fast. It was a different man with the same name. It couldn't be Cliff, her Cliff.

She reached the cot in the corner. A man lay upon it, eyes closed, blanket tucked to his chin. Until she stood beside his cot, he could've been any other sleeping patient.

But he didn't need to be awake for her to recognize his features—the wavy hair and chiseled jaw that had graced theaters across the country. His lips parted with an intake of breath, those same lips that had once melded to hers.

Her own breath shuddered. "Captain Powell?" Her voice emerged tinny, too bright.

He cracked open one eye. Then the other. A sleepy grin unfurled on his lips. He blinked, eyes focusing on her. She stood by his cot, fingers digging into the list, gazing down at the last person she'd expected to find within the walls of Torney General Hospital.

Rosemary. . .was here? He couldn't wrap his mind around it. Rosemary James, the shy library clerk, the girl he'd taken to Ciro's, the woman he'd never forgotten, worked at this hospital?

He'd have chalked it up to some strange kind of delirium, but the ever-present throb in his stump, the cloying dryness in his mouth, and the voices of the other patients confirmed he wasn't delirious and this was reality.

Throughout his entire military career, he'd been dogged in his insistence that he be treated exactly like every other soldier. No special privileges. So after the operation and a period of stabilization in a rear area hospital in the Pacific, he'd been shipped back to the States and brought to Torney General Hospital. He vaguely remembered one of the guys in the ambulance mentioning the Palm Springs veterans' hospital had once been the El Mirador Hotel. At least he was in familiar territory. He'd spent the night at the luxury hotel multiple times on weekends in Palm Springs. Only it wasn't a luxury hotel anymore, but a hospital with wards and Army personnel and. . .nurses.

He'd been moved with the others to a ward in the orthopedics section of the hospital, and Rosemary had disappeared after checking vital signs. Corpsmen helped the men with baths and into clean pajamas and robes. Cliff barely registered any of it. The ward rang with voices and laughter. Everybody wanted to make phone calls and eat a hot dinner. Cliff thanked the uniformed corpsman who aided him, and he received a quick nod in return. If the young man knew he'd just tended to *the* Cliff Powell, he didn't let on.

Cliff was glad of it. He'd never be that Cliff Powell again.

His gaze slid down to the empty space on the mattress. Where his leg had once been.

He grimaced. It was an act of Providence that he was even alive.

Footsteps squeaked. Cliff looked up. Rosemary stepped into the ward, checking in at the head nurse's desk.

The twist inside him had nothing to do with physical hunger. The passing years had put him through the proverbial wringer, aging and altering him. Those same years had only made her prettier. Even the severe Army nurse's uniform couldn't hide her beauty. Strands of hair escaped her pinned-back curls, and her eyes sparkled. She'd tanned since last he'd seen her, her skin burnished golden. Her smile flashed as she spoke to one of the patients.

Why now? He hated the emotions rising inside of him. In his days of flight training and combat duty, he'd entertained the thought of finding her after it was all over. Telling her that she'd inspired him to be a better man, and he owed to their meeting much of who he was today. He'd played those reunion scenes through his mind like a movie reel. They always ended the same way.

With a kiss as earth-shattering as their last.

He'd never bargained on meeting her again, not like this. A broken man, physically at least. Sure, he was proud to have fought for his country and grateful to be alive—men a million times more deserving would never return to families and loved ones.

But he was no longer whole. Would never be again.

He couldn't deny the gaping loss, the stifling fear. What would his future be now?

"Captain Powell?" Her voice, cadence soft. He didn't even have to look up. But he did anyway. She stood to the right of his bed, her eyes on him. A lemony fragrance teased his senses, and auburn wisps skimmed her cheeks.

Rosemary James wasn't merely pretty. Stirringly, undeniably

beautiful, yes, those were better words to describe her.

He couldn't think that. There was Paul, remember. She'd probably been married for years by now. Only, her last name was James, not Cartwright—for some reason he'd retained that detail. So she wasn't married?

"Yeah?"

She held a clipboard and pen in both hands. "Dinner will be here shortly, and we're arranging for telephones to be sent in after that. Do you want us to set you up with one?"

He rubbed the back of his neck. Of course, his return to the States would make the papers, no doubt partnered with a description of his heroics during the mission and a reiteration of his many air victories. The type of story the press loved best. The wounding of one of America's screen idols would stir the public into even greater fervency for victory. The recruiting offices would have a heyday.

Most of his casual acquaintances would read about it in the paper. And who else honestly cared? His aunt and uncle had both passed while he'd been in flight training, and he'd no other family. No real friends except the guys in his squadron. Boy, he missed them. Patterson, his tent mate and wingman, who snored like a buzz saw and was forever asking for a signed picture of Lana Turner. Brannigan, who could out-cuss any marine in the South Pacific, but who often worked 24/7 without complaint just to keep their airplanes in flyable condition. Glim, who loved nothing better than a rousing sing-along after a long day and led them through every mission with steely determination—

"Is there someone you wish to call? To let them know you're here?" A touch of impatience tinged her gentle tone.

Good grief, he'd kept her standing there while he ruminated. He shook his head. "Nah. Let the other guys use the phones. I've got nobody to call."

"Is there anything else I can get you then?"

He shook his head, considering making some joke about "unless you have a new leg," but it felt stupid, so he didn't.

Her brow crimped. "What are you doing here?" The question fell from her lips like something she'd fought to keep back.

"In the hospital?" His lips quirked. "Isn't that obvious?"

She blew out a breath. "That's not what I meant."

"My plane crashed into the drink. I got shot up, and they couldn't save my leg." He rubbed the back of his neck. "Why are any of these guys here? To get well."

Her throat worked with a swallow. "How is it feeling? Any pain?" She pulled back the blanket. The bottom half of his pajama leg had been pinned up around his stump, the gray fabric concealing the bandages.

He shrugged. "Nothing to kick about." He cracked a wry smile at the terminology. Well, he couldn't kick, and he refused to complain.

Rosemary didn't smile. "Dr. Kendall will be by later this evening to examine you. Then we'll change the dressing."

The *we'll* implied she'd be a participant. He didn't know whether he should look forward to that or dread it.

"Until later then." He wondered if his famous Powell grin was as effective from a hospital bed. His lips stretched, out of practice.

She merely smiled and covered up his leg, moving on to the next bed without another word. He leaned back against the pillows, hands folded atop the blanket, staring at the whitewashed ceiling above. Blank and white.

Like the canvas of his future life.

Chapter 5

So what's he like?"

Rosemary flicked a glance over her shoulder. Sam sat on her twin bed in the narrow double room, filing her nails. The grating sound sent involuntary spiders down Rosemary's spine.

"Who?" Rosemary kept right on twisting her hair into pin curls, fingers moving deftly through the familiar motions.

"Cliff Powell. He's your patient, isn't he?"

Rosemary said nothing. It was after nine o'clock, and the aspirin she'd swallowed had done little to alleviate the ache in her temples. The last person she wanted to discuss was Cliff Powell. Her heart was too riddled and confused to talk about him. She'd barely had a chance to think about him. How he'd sat with clenched jaw during Dr. Kendall's examination and her redressing. The sight of his wounded limb, the ugly scars. He bore little resemblance to the man she remembered, the shameless flirt who looked as if he could conquer the world and every feminine heart with barely a lift of his finger.

"Come on." Sam flung her nail file onto her bedside table and bounded across the room, settling on Rosemary's bed with a bounce. "Spill it."

"Wouldn't that be breaking patient confidentiality?" Rosemary pinned a rolled-up strand of hair in place. Her bedside lamp cast a yellow glow across their beds covered with cherry-red comforters.

"Of course not. I'll be back on Orthopedics tomorrow. Besides, I don't want to know about his case, silly. I want to know about him. C'mon. Tell me just a little bit. I'm your best friend."

Well, that was true. They'd been together since nursing school, sat in shocked silence at their desks when the news of the attack on Pearl Harbor broke. After that, their training took on a greater purpose. No longer were they working to become ordinary nurses, but a kind of soldier in the fight for freedom. Following graduation, they'd been assigned here. Not overseas, but to this stateside hospital. Rosemary had wanted to transfer, to go somewhere dangerous, where the real fighting was, but Sam talked her into staying. After a week nursing broken young men who arrived wondering if they'd ever have a future, Rosemary knew she'd made the right decision.

"There isn't much to tell." She'd told no one about her time with Cliff in Hollywood, not even Sam. Some things were best kept locked inside oneself. And today, well, she'd only spoken with him briefly.

It had been enough though. To glimpse the altered man he had become.

"I can't believe he's really here. I loved all his movies." Actually Sam loved all movies and could spout actor names, picture dates, and film titles from here to Timbuktu. "The ones he made with Hazel Morgan—" She pressed a hand against her pajama-clad chest. "In every scene, he either made you laugh or made you swoon. And then, he and Hazel broke their engagement." She propped her chin in her hand. "They used to show him in the newsreels, after he joined the Marine Corps. Hollywood's Ace, they called him. I can still see him, standing in front of his plane, in his aviator's cap and Mae West, smiling for the cameras. But when the reporters praised him, he said, 'I'm just another guy, doing a job for my country.' I wonder what he'll do now." Sadness tinged Sam's gaze.

Rosemary busied herself with her hair, unable to deny what her friend's words did to her. She rarely went to movies, but on one of the rare times she had, they'd featured Cliff in the newsreel. He'd been exactly as Sam described. The devil-may-care smile on his face had wreaked havoc with her tamped-down emotions for weeks.

He still had that smile.

She sensed Sam's gaze on her, and Rosemary looked directly at her friend. "He's right about one thing. He's just another guy. His stardom didn't keep him from being wounded, and it won't help him face things now. He needs the same care we give every other man. The same hope that they have a future beyond their infirmities. I intend to give him that." Her hands clenched, and her words came low and fierce. Like a vow.

Sam's eyes widened. "He must've made some impression on you. You look as if you'd annihilate anyone who stood in your way. It's the Powell charm, I tell ya. And by the look on your face, wounded or no, he's still got it in spades."

Heat blazed through Rosemary's cheeks. "I care about all of my patients. It's our job."

Sam didn't look convinced.

Rosemary didn't blame her. That night she lay on her side, cheek pressed into the pillow, eyes shut, but unable to sleep.

Cliff Powell had changed her life. Because of him, she'd broken her engagement to Paul. Even now she could still see the pain in the eyes of that good and decent man when she'd told him she didn't love him enough to marry him. He'd said little, his eyes pools of sorrow. Last she heard, he was a chaplain somewhere in Europe.

Because of Cliff, she'd given her notice at the library. Life was more than dusty books, and her trip to Hollywood had shown her that. She wanted to live fully, to help people, to be more than the shy orphan girl she'd pegged herself as. She'd been prepared to work night and day to afford tuition fees to nursing school.

Then the head librarian, Mrs. Edwards, had called her into her office on her last day and handed Rosemary a check for full tuition. To Rosemary's gasps that she couldn't accept it, Mrs. Edwards said that, as a spinster, she'd no one but her ne'er-do-well brother to leave her savings to, and Rosemary would be doing her a favor by taking it off her hands. Rosemary had hugged the woman who'd been, in her own way, a second mother. She then headed off the next day to fill out applications. She'd been accepted at the California Hospital School of Nursing. Three years later, she'd graduated.

Yes, she owed Cliff Powell more than he'd ever know.

But she had a chance to repay that debt by devoting her energies to his recovery. He had stamina and strength. Those traits could be put to good use.

The look on his face when he'd first glimpsed her, well, his injury had not detracted an ounce from his magnetism. His time in the Pacific had bronzed his features, sharpened his lazy handsomeness. His wry grin when he said he'd nothing to kick about. . .

Her eyes flew open. Last time she'd melted under his charm. Given herself to their foolish, reckless kiss.

The remembrance of Dr. Kendall's compliment from this morning, the way his gaze followed her, recalled itself to mind. Sam had repeated hospital gossip that Rosemary James was the first nurse Dr. Grant Kendall ever looked at as more than a lesser-ranking colleague.

She'd already given up one man in her life because of Cliff Powell.

She wouldn't do it a second time.

※

According to the salt-and-pepper-haired doc, Cliff would be ready to start therapy in a few days. He wasn't sure exactly what that entailed, but he couldn't wait.

He'd been hospitalized since the moment Air-Sea Rescue brought him back after picking him up, a half-dead man lying in a mess of blood on his raft, despite his crude attempts to staunch the flow. He didn't remember much of the days following his operation. The world had been a haze of intermittent pain and drugged-up oblivion. Now the pain had subsided enough to be bearable, although he had to admit there were still times he'd have embraced the dulling effects of more medication. It was a sickly horrible sensation to feel pain in a part of one's body that no longer existed. At first it took all his self-control to refrain from shouting, crying like a baby. Phantom pain, they called it. When he asked the doctor at the rear area of the hospital for an explanation, the man gave him some mumbo jumbo that didn't make a lot of sense.

Maybe he could ask Rosemary.

Except he hadn't seen her all morning. After breakfast the nurse on duty and some of the ward aides had set about providing the men with things to occupy themselves. Cliff marveled at one of the inventions, a projector with a storybook printed on microfilm so a man in a body cast could read on the ceiling. The patient, whom Cliff could barely see due to the white plaster cast encasing his body, loudly expressed his delight.

It amazed him how good natured most of the guys were, considering the circumstances. Conversation and laughter filled the sunlit ward. A man on crutches crossed the room to light a cigarette for a man missing his right arm. One man read aloud the funny pages to those in the beds nearest. The nurse on duty, a dead ringer for Rita Hayworth, laughed right along with them.

Except the man in the bed to Cliff's left. He'd been there when Cliff arrived, and from yesterday afternoon until now, he'd heard the guy speak five sentences, if that. He lay on his back, propped up by pillows, totally oblivious to the antics of the other patients. Whenever the Rita Hayworth nurse stopped by, he answered her questions in a toneless voice.

He'd lost both of his legs. Cliff shook his head with a stab of sympathy. War was a brutal beast.

The kid held something in his hands, listlessly turning the pages. Cliff craned his neck to see. Ah, a movie magazine. Claudette Colbert's pixie face peeped at him from the front cover.

Cliff watched him for a few minutes. The boy stared at each page so long he must've memorized them. Across the room, the man in the body cast was still going strong with his on-the-ceiling comic book.

Finally Cliff couldn't take it anymore.

God, show me how to help this guy.

"Hey," he called, shifting his body so he lay as near to the edge as possible.

No answer.

"Hey."

Nothing. A page turned.

Oookay. Well, desperate times called for desperate measures.

"You know, Claudette Colbert is even prettier in person."

A slow head turn, giving Cliff his first glimpse of the man's entire face. Brown hair and green eyes. Young, like somebody's kid brother. And drawn and miserable.

"Huh?" His forehead scrunched.

"Claudette Colbert. A real nice girl. I just saw the cover of your magazine and thought you'd like to know."

"You've met her?" The kid looked at Cliff like he was loony.

Cliff nodded, straight-faced. "Know her pretty well. Had her over to my house one night for a barbecue. Clark was there too. Gable, you know."

"You're nuts." The kid shook his head. But at least he was talking, and in a normal tone of voice.

"No, I'm Cliff Powell."

"Cliff Powell. . ."

He chuckled as recognition dawned in the kid's eyes.

Then his chin jutted. "I don't believe you. Do a scene from one of your pictures and prove it."

Cliff scratched his chin. A scene from one of his pictures. . . Could he? Shucks, why not?

"Hey, Lieutenant." Unfortunately he'd forgotten the nurse's last name. Across the room, she set a thermometer on a tray, jotted something on a chart, then headed over.

"Something I can get you?" The gleam in her eyes revealed *she* hadn't been oblivious to his identity.

"You know, you look just like Rita Hayworth. Anyone ever told you that?" He laid on the charm a bit. After taking samples of his blood for laboratory testing and watching his faltering attempts to navigate the room on crutches, surely she'd be impervious to it.

She flashed a million-watt smile. "Why, thank you, Captain Powell. That's real sweet of you."

He leaned forward. "Help me out with something, will you?

This guy here"—he jerked a finger toward the kid, who sat up and listened with interest—"doesn't believe I really am Cliff Powell. He says he'll believe me if I prove it by doing a scene from one of my movies. I don't suppose—"

"I've seen every one."

Well, okay then.

The nurse chattered on. "*A Hollywood Holiday* was my favorite. I saw it three times."

Her and thousands of other female moviegoers. It had been his and Hazel's most popular picture, their second to last. Critics had dubbed it "a screwball comedy with heart, the funniest thing to hit theaters since *It Happened One Night*."

It hadn't hurt their on-screen chemistry that, at the time of filming, he'd been dreaming of proposing to Hazel, spending the rest of his life beside her. He'd popped the question a week after they'd wrapped the final scene. She'd said yes.

From there it all went downhill.

He'd gone out of his way to avoid thinking about that particular picture. He glanced again at the kid's expectant expression. Just seeing the life in his eyes made Cliff's throat squeeze.

He flashed a grin at Nurse Rita. "Three times? You don't say. How about doing a scene and helping me out then?"

She stole a quick glance toward the front end of the room. The head nurse's desk was vacant. She turned back to him. "I'd love to." She laughed. "Which one?"

"You pick." By now, they had half the ward as an audience. A couple of the ward aides hung around in the center aisle, clutching water pitchers.

The nurse tapped a finger to her chin. "Hmm. How about the scene when Wade and Dora first meet?"

"You sure you know it?"

She gave a vigorous nod.

He gave one hard glance at the kid. "Prepare to be impressed."

He was rewarded with a shrug.

Cliff closed his eyes, scrounging for the lines. Remembering the bright lights and cameras and Hazel's lilac scent. He could do this.

He opened them, and he was film star Cliff Powell again, playing Wade Hammett, a man who'd just gotten out of jail after serving a sentence for a petty theft he didn't commit, and returning to the home of Dora Schaefer, the heiress whose family he used to work for as a gardener.

"Why, if it isn't little Dora Schaefer. Making mud pies again, are we?" It came so easily, the articulation, the look. Like he'd never stopped.

"Why, if it isn't the derelict gardener. I thought you were in jail." The nurse did an almost perfect imitation of Hazel's voice and mannerisms.

"I got out. They didn't want me anymore." Cliff stole a glance at the kid. A little grin crept onto his face.

"If jail didn't want you, what makes you think we do?"

"Because you know the truth about what happened that night." Footsteps sounded. Cliff turned slightly. Rosemary stood beside the ward aides. Watching him.

"What truth?"

"You know what I'm talking about, Miss Schaefer. Don't try to deny it. It's because of you I spent the past six months wearing out my pants sitting in a jail cell. Now I'm out, and it's payback time."

"Are you blackmailing me?" Wow, this girl was good, and he'd seen scores of starlet wannabes. She tossed her head in a perfect imitation of Hazel's mannerisms.

"Call it what you like, sugar. The fact remains I'm back." Giggles sounded from the ward aides. He glanced again at Rosemary. A smile framed her lips.

It was the best sight he'd seen since. . .he couldn't remember how long.

They kept going, bantering their way through the scene. When it ended, the ward erupted in claps and cheers. The nurse bowed and gave air kisses. Cliff grinned and thanked her. He couldn't give two dimes about the applause, but the expression on the kid's face made it the most worthwhile performance he'd ever done.

After the applause died down, the ward returned to business as usual. Rosemary and Nurse Rita—Lieutenant Samantha Baker—exchanged a few words, heads bent over a clipboard. Then Lieutenant Baker disappeared, and Rosemary circled the ward.

He watched as she tended the kid, whom Cliff learned was named Joe Tolliver. They chatted for a couple of minutes about the performance, and she asked him how he was feeling and took vital signs.

Cliff was waiting when she stopped beside his bed. Her slim fingers pressed his wrist as she took a pulse.

A hint of her lemon scent wafted over his senses. He had the sudden urge to bury his face in her hair. Was it as silken as it had been all those years ago?

"Nice show." She smiled. "I felt like I had a front row seat at Grauman's Chinese."

He shrugged. "She's quite the actress."

Rosemary noted his pulse on his chart. "Sam. . .er, Lieutenant Baker, is always going to the movies. I think she considered a career in acting but decided against it."

"Wonder why." He rubbed his thumb along his wrist where her fingers had been.

"Well. . ." Rosemary's smile tipped to the right. "Much as she loves the picture shows, she knows it's all an illusion. Whereas here, helping people, couldn't be more real."

He nodded. "You're right. It wasn't until I got to know the men in my squadron that I realized that very thing."

She looked down at him, face flushed, hair escaping from her beige military cap. Totally sweet and utterly—

A pained voice called out from the opposite side of the room.

She spun, hurrying away from him.

He stared after her, wishing things he couldn't wish. Last time, she'd left an imprint on his heart, the pattern of which still remained. Less than a day into their reacquaintance, and already. . .

It had begun again.

Chapter 6

Rosemary rubbed a tense muscle at the back of her neck. Her shift on the orthopedic ward would be over in half an hour, and the night nurse would come on duty. Much as she loved her work, her protesting feet begged for a soak.

She made final rounds, settling the men in after dinner. The afternoon had been taken up with half of the men heading off to physical therapy, leaving her with the care of the other half. Surprisingly Joe Tolliver gave the faintest hint of a smile as he was wheeled away. He'd been at Torney three weeks and usually approached PT appointments with the sullenness of a six-year-old doing extra math homework. When he'd returned, he and Cliff spent a long time talking. She'd even heard laughter.

Perhaps seeing a movie star like Cliff in a similar situation to his own had awakened something in Joe that none of the doctors or nurses had been able to achieve.

She pulled the covers up around Dave Branson—the man in

the body cast—and set the used toothbrush and rinse cup on a tray. He'd been asking her to find him another comic book to read with the projector. She'd promised to look around.

"Sleep well, Dave."

"Now, you won't forget about the comic book?"

She shook her head. "Scout's honor." She moved on to the next patient. As she worked her way around the room, awareness heightened as she drew nearer and nearer to Cliff's bed.

Seeing him this afternoon, bantering with Sam as they played their scene, had made her heart do flutters that had to be medically dangerous. As had the sparkle in Joe's eyes as he talked about what a great actor and swell guy Cliff Powell was. The kindness of the action, when Cliff had to be undergoing misery and pain of his own, brought swirling warmth and more flutters.

She straightened her shoulders as she approached his bed. He tapped his fingers on the blanket, as if impatient.

"Can I get you—?"

He grabbed her wrist in a grip both gentle and strong. The warmth of his skin against hers brought more irrational sensations. What was wrong with her? She touched men all the time.

"Five minutes. I just want to talk."

"I'm supposed to be doing my rounds—"

"Caring for the sick. Well, I'm sick." His gaze twinkled with a charm that ought to be illegal. "With boredom. I haven't spent so much time sitting around in my whole life. If you don't talk to me for five minutes, I'm afraid I may well go into a decline. And you wouldn't want that on your conscience, would you, Lieutenant?"

She had men flirt with her all the time and usually several requests for dates per week. It was all part of the territory of caring for lonely men who just wanted a pretty girl to make them feel normal. It didn't seem to register with most of them that she also dished out their medicine and emptied their bedpans.

But never had flirtation made her want to respond in kind, to smile because she was flattered instead of amused.

She glanced at her watch and around the ward where most of the men were already dozing off. "Three minutes. But only because I'm scared of what it would do to morale if you went 'into a decline.'"

He leaned forward. A few buttons gaped open at the collar of his pajama shirt, revealing a tanned lean chest. She yanked her gaze away.

"I wanted to tell you I'm sorry." All teasing had left his eyes. He studied her intently in the semidarkness of the ward.

"For what?" Her brow creased.

"For. . .what happened that night. I shouldn't have kissed you. There's no excuse, except I was a dishonorable lout."

She started. He was apologizing? When she was as much at fault as he?

This was a man altogether different. With humility in his gaze, and his voice weighted with shame over what he'd done.

"You don't need to apologize." She twisted her hands at her waist.

"Actually I do. I thought about you a lot after that night. I saw myself through the eyes of someone like you, a woman of genuine trust and honesty." He rubbed a hand across his chin. "Suffice it to say, I didn't much like what I saw."

"You shouldn't think of me like that." Their voices were whispers in the quiet ward. "I wanted to kiss you as much as you wanted to kiss me." Her cheeks blazed at the admission. Yet his honesty deserved hers in return.

"What did Paul say?" She sensed his gaze on her left hand.

She loosed a sigh. "I broke up with Paul."

He shook his head. "Oh Rosemary. I'm sorry."

"Don't be. It was the best thing I could've done. We weren't right for each other." She picked at a stray thread on his blanket.

"Well then, what say we forget the past and start over, shall we?" He glanced down at the empty space beneath the blankets.

She nodded. "I'd like that." A smile edged her lips.

"Me too." He smiled back. Not like Cliff Powell for the flash-bulbs, but with the texture of new beginnings.

"I think our five minutes is up." But she looked at him, not her watch.

He nodded. "One more thing."

"Yes?"

"If you could get me a Bible, I sure would appreciate it."

Her eyebrows went sky high. "A Bible?"

"I don't seem to have too many demands on my time at the moment. I've only read bits and pieces. I'm trying to get better at praying. Figured I might find some tips."

Cliff, a praying man? Well, this was new. Of course, she'd found her own faith in the years of war. Listening to news broadcasts and caring for boys broken beyond recognition did that. It either made weak faith stronger or made you turn away from it altogether. She'd chosen the former. The knowledge that Cliff had also only deepened her respect for him.

"I think I could scrounge one up."

"I can pay you," he hastened.

She shook her head. "We're here to make you as comfortable as we can. It's the least we can do in return for what you've given."

"Thank you, Rosemary." Her name was music on his lips, a song she wished would linger.

She busied herself with going through the motions of taking his vital signs and noting them on the chart, helping him as he used his crutches to walk to the lavatory. Determination tightened his face with the effort, his stump useless and weak. He'd start therapy soon, begin to gain strength. But it was never an easy process.

God, help him. The prayer filled her heart as he waved her away and hobbled back toward his bed on his own, teeth gritted. *Surely, in all of this, somehow, You have a plan.*

January 23, 1945

Cliff was tired, but it was a good kind of tired. A fatigue that came from progress made.

And he'd made progress. The afternoons in physical and occupational therapy were beginning to reap results. He'd graduated from initial exercises done lying on his bed, and today spent time in the occupational therapy room, pumping a knee-high treadle. Its purpose was twofold—it helped regain circulation in his stump, and the press punched holes in belts.

Now he made his way through the halls on crutches, along with others from his ward, accompanied by a ward aide.

"Say, can you bring me a Coke, sweetheart?" Private Brady walked alongside the pretty blond ward aide. Therapy was working for him too, helping him regain the use of his left arm. "I was a good boy and followed doctor's orders all day."

"I don't think you could ever be good." The ward aide laughed.

Their conversation blurred into the background as they stepped inside the now-familiar ward. Cliff's gaze zeroed in and found its target.

Rosemary bent over the bed of a new arrival, helping him shift positions. For a wisp of a woman, she possessed surprising strength.

He went to therapy as much for her as for himself. For the pride in her gaze as he slowly improved. Within these four walls, he'd whittled his world down to her smiles, her glances, the nuance of her gestures. The way a dimple appeared in the corner of her right cheek, her penchant for humming off-key Glenn Miller as she pushed carts and took temperatures.

Knock it off, Powell. You're starting to sound like a sappy record.

He got himself into bed and leaned his crutches against the wall. Beside him, Joe flipped through a new movie magazine. His hospital robe lay across the end of his bed. In here they all dressed the same, just like in the Army. Robes and pajamas instead of military issue.

"How was it today, tough guy?" Cliff asked.

Joe shrugged. "I made it through my routine and they added a few new things. Lieutenant Baker brought me this issue of *Photoplay*." He held up the crisp magazine. Ingrid Bergman smiled coyly from the cover.

"That was swell of her." Cliff's gaze turned toward the sound of footsteps. Rosemary walked toward them, pushing a cart.

"Hi, Joe." Her tone was bright. "Busy afternoon?"

"So-so." Joe returned to the pages of his magazine.

Cliff waited until she'd stopped beside him. "Don't I get a greeting? Or must I feign agony to gain your attention?"

She rolled her eyes. "Not today. Dr. Kendall wants your dressing changed. So you've got me for a few minutes."

The aforementioned Dr. Kendall was currently on the other side of the room with another nurse, behind Dave Branson's screened-in bed. Cliff undid his pinned-up pant leg and pulled it up, revealing white bandages, then sat back against the pillows. Rosemary rolled a screen around his bed, giving them a curtain of privacy, then pulled on a pair of gloves. He kept his eyes on her face, her lowered eyelids, the wrinkle in her brow as she worked to remove his old dressing.

"How long have you been a nurse?"

She placed the old strips of bandage onto a tray using something that probably had a proper medical name but looked to him like a pair of tweezers. "I started school in January 1941. Three years later, I graduated."

"No more Miss Librarian then?" Cool air hit his exposed stump as she removed the bandages.

She shook her head with a faint smile. "Besides, I wasn't a librarian. But no. I figured it was time to get out of the stacks and into real life. Not that there's anything wrong with library work, but I was using it as an excuse to hide." She set a pair of silver scissors on the tray of soiled dressings.

"Hide from what?"

She kept her eyes on her work. "From taking risks. From fear. My vacation. . .you know, the one where we met"—she drew in a breath—"it was the first time I ever voluntarily stepped outside the boundaries of comfort. I had to do it so much at the orphanage, that once I got out, I avoided it is much as possible." She looked up and met his gaze. "Have you given any thought to what you'll do after you leave here?" She flashed a cheeky grin, reminiscent of sitting across the candlelit table at Ciro's. "My turn to ask a question now."

"Well, you sure picked a lulu," he muttered, staring down at the jagged scars, the skin taut over his stump. An ever-present reminder of what would never be again. He blew out a sigh. "Of course I have. I guess I've thought more about my future here than in, well, ever. At the front, you don't think about stuff like that. You just try and make it through every day alive. Living one more was a victory in and of itself."

Rosemary's hands had stilled, her head tilted as he spoke.

"Every so often, after we completed a certain number of missions, we got to go on leave to Sydney. Before we left, we always drew our pay. Some of the guys"—he shook his head at the memory—"especially if they didn't have wives and kids, blew every cent in a couple of days. Dining at nice restaurants, playing cards, getting drunk, wooing girls, because they knew this might be their last chance. For many of them, it was. Seeing guys that were good pilots, I mean really good, go down with their planes. . ." He swallowed hard. He should stop. "It does something to you. And then this." He gestured to his stump. "My life's gotta count for something. I still don't know the answer to *Why me?*, but there's gotta be one. Some reason why I'm alive, even though I can't think of a single one for why they're not."

An expression of tenderness came across Rosemary's face. "God will guide you, Cliff. You wait and see."

"Ah, Lieutenant James." Dr. Kendall's tone was all efficiency. Cliff hadn't even heard the guy step behind the curtain. "I see you have everything in readiness here." He gave Rosemary a smile warmer than professional as he slipped into a pair of gloves. She returned it with one of her own. Cliff's jaw tightened. Why'd she have to smile at him, anyway? Weren't there rules about fraternization?

It was a smile, you lunkhead. The voice in his head sounded like Glim, Brooklyn accent and all. *Get over it. She was being nice.*

Maybe Rosemary was. But he'd seen enough to know Dr. Kendall had more up his sleeve than friendliness.

"How are we today, Captain Powell?" His gloved hands probed Cliff's stump. "A little swelling. Of course, that's normal with increased activity. How are you finding the exercises?"

Cliff answered the doctor's questions in brief, emotionless replies. Kendall seemed to be going out of his way to look at Rosemary, ask her opinion.

Blast it all, why? Rosemary was what, twenty-four or twenty-five? Kendall had to be at least forty-five. Sure, he was a good doctor. Very good, Cliff begrudgingly admitted. Not bad looking either, he guessed, if you liked men thin and graying at the temples.

Did Rosemary and Kendall have an understanding? Of course, someone as sweet and beautiful as Rosemary would have scores of men wanting to date her. The male mind was about as simple as two plus two equals four. Beautiful woman plus sweet woman equals abundant male interest. And Rosemary was more than that. She was smart and funny, genuinely cared about her patients, and loved God. The last two were proven by the Bible she'd handed him a couple of days after he'd asked. In the front, she'd slipped a note inside, saying she'd underlined a few favorite verses.

Cliff shook his head. Rosemary arched a brow at him. Kendall had left her to do the redressing.

Heaven and the Marine Corps help him, he wanted a chance to win her heart.

But did he have one?

Chapter 7

*D*r. Kendall had asked her for a date several times, but their evenings off hadn't coincided. Until tonight. Rosemary had donned her dress uniform, powdered her nose, curled her hair, and swiped on a new shade of lipstick.

Now she sat across from Dr. Kendall at a modest Palm Springs restaurant as a waitress left them with menus. A pianist tickled the ivories with low music, and all around them other couples, many in uniform, were eating or looking over menus. Leaning toward each other and talking.

"Is it ever nice to rest my feet." Rosemary fought a wave of awkwardness. She saw Dr. Kendall every day, but on the wards they'd jobs to do, cases to discuss. Now that there weren't any wounds that needed draining or prescriptions to write up, they had to somehow fill the silence.

"Yes, it is." Dr. Kendall laid aside his menu, leaning slightly forward. He wore a dress uniform too, and his hair looked freshly trimmed.

She caught a waft of something like cologne. He'd never worn any before. "Did I tell you how nice you look?" His earnest gaze studied her, a smile edging his lips.

"No, but thank you for saying so now." Her cheeks went warm.

The waitress set glasses of ice water in front of them and scurried away. Rosemary wasted no time in taking a sip of hers, letting the cool liquid slide down her throat. Pity she couldn't douse her face in it.

Why had Dr. Kendall asked her out? She was no one special. Just one nurse out of many. He could have asked Sam, with her Rita Hayworth looks, or Betty, a war widow in her midthirties, who always had a cheerful word for everyone.

"You're probably wondering why I asked you out."

Rosemary jumped. Could the man read minds as well as diagnose patients?

"A little." She gave a sheepish smile.

"I'll tell you then. We've been working together for months, Rosemary. I find myself drawn to you." He smiled. Somehow, it never reached his eyes or made them crinkle. "I've never made time for a relationship of a romantic nature. My patients always came first. But then I met you. I want to get to know you better. Spend more time together. Someday, maybe even. . . Well, we'll worry about someday later." He folded his hands on the table. Capable hands that gave men without hope a new lease on life. What would those hands feel like holding hers? Cupped around her face as their lips met?

She lifted her water glass and took a gulp. He followed her movements, as if waiting for an answer. Her mind tumbled. Dr. Grant Kendall, one of Torney's finest physicians, wanted to date her with hopes of *someday more*.

Did she want this? He was a good doctor, a man of faith—he'd spoken before about attending church when it didn't conflict with work. They actually attended the same church but had never bumped into each other there.

"Have I upset you?" His brow furrowed. "I'm sorry if I came on too strong."

She shook her head, fingers wrapped around her water glass. She'd been here before, with Paul. But they hadn't been suited. He planned to be a pastor and live in the same small town for the rest of his life. She'd always wanted more, even then, though she never voiced it.

Grant Kendall was a physician. They had something in common. Could she grow to care for him, love him?

She looked into his hopeful face, his kind eyes.

In time, perhaps. She'd never again promise herself to a man she didn't love, but what was the harm in a few dates while they got to know each other?

"I'd like that." She sounded certain. Like a confident woman who knew her own mind. If only she felt like one too.

In return, he reached across the table and squeezed her hand. His fingers were cold, but his grip was strong. She smiled back, but her mind wandered to Cliff's warm grip, his hands around her waist as he kissed her outside of Ciro's.

She had to stop. She couldn't keep comparing every man she met to Cliff Powell. Either the one in memory or the one whose living reality faced her afresh every time she set foot in the orthopedic ward. The former could be explained away as a girlish fixation. An image of him this afternoon, grinning as he joked with Joe, filled her mind. The latter would be much more difficult to erase.

"You have visitors."

Cliff set down his pencil. Rosemary stood at the foot of his bed.

"Visitors?" He laid aside the crossword puzzle he'd been doing with Joe. He wasn't expecting anyone. Of course, the press had asked for interviews. He'd granted them just one, a few days after his arrival. It had, of course, made the next day's papers. Hopefully done some patriotic good. And he'd received telegrams and a couple of fruit baskets from studio acquaintances and a large bouquet from the president of MGM. It had stunk up the ward so badly he'd told Lieutenant Baker to get rid of it stat.

"I think it might be your agent. A woman's with him. They're in a visitor's parlor. I'll walk you down." Rosemary waited while he retrieved his crutches and chucked the puzzle book on Joe's bed.

"A seven-letter word that means 'note.' Figure it out."

Joe said something in reply, but it didn't register. His heart thumped hard. Why did Max want to see him in person? He'd been one of those who sent a basket of fruit and a note.

And who could the woman be? Max's wife?

Rosemary left the ward in the charge of Lieutenant Elliot then led the way into the corridor.

The familiar pale yellow walls and scrubbed linoleum floors blurred as they walked. Cliff's throat went dry. He inhaled the familiar antiseptic scent. The last time he'd seen Max, Cliff had sported a sharp gray suit. Today he wore a maroon robe and gray pajamas identical to every other guy here.

The hospital was a world unto itself. The men here were like him, the doctors and nurses caring and supportive. Here he wasn't Cliff Powell, but a patient who took pride in small achievements. Like trying on his first prosthetic yesterday. It had taken some getting used to, and he could only wear it for short periods of time at first, but he'd walked a few yards with the aid of parallel bars. A couple of guys cheered, just as he cheered for them when they cleared a hurdle on the road to normalcy.

But Max?

He paused, leaning heavily on his crutches. Rosemary met his eyes, chin tipped upward, hair straying from its pins. He wanted nothing more than to take her small frame in his arms and hold her close. A steady constancy in the midst of this storm.

"You can do this, Cliff." She didn't offer to send the visitors away. Just told him he could do it. Her confidence in him touched like a balm. As did his name on her lips.

"Yeah. It's just. . ."

"I know it's hard." She placed a gentle hand on his arm. Oh, to imprint the memory of her slim fingers there for the rest of time. "But it's not all in your own strength. God goes with you."

He carried her words with him as he entered a parlor-like room reserved for patients and visitors, Rosemary's footsteps clipping back to her ward.

Max Redford stood by the window overlooking the hospital grounds where patients sat taking in sun and fresh air, accompanied by nurses and Red Cross Gray Ladies. An ironic smile edged Cliff's lips. He and Max had been here together before, when Torney General Hospital was the luxurious El Mirador Hotel.

War. The king of altering both people and places.

Max turned. A smile broke across his swarthy face. "Hey, Cliff." He bridged the gap between them and clapped a hand to Cliff's shoulder. "Good to see you."

"How are you, Max?" His agent had changed little except to go paunchier around the middle and grayer in the hair. His eyes still held the same foxy look, large frame encased in a navy suit that was a newer cousin of the one Cliff had last seen him in.

"Great, great."

"Cliff." A voice floated from the doorway. He glanced behind him. Judith Haysley stood in the entrance. She glided toward him, a vision of platinum-blond curls, dressed in a cherry-red suit.

"Judith. What a surprise." His throat went dry again.

"It's good to see you, darling." She stood on tiptoe and pressed a kiss against his cheek, leaving the scent of her perfume and a trace of lipstick in her wake. She stepped back, thick lashes blinking fast, gloved hand pressed to her slim midsection.

"What. . .what are you doing here?" He hadn't seen Judith since the week before he left for flight training. They'd had one last evening of dining and dancing. Time with Judith had always been safe, no expectations attached. After Hazel broke their engagement, she'd been the only woman he'd ever willingly gone out with.

Well, Judith. . .and Rosemary.

"I just got back this week. I've been on tour with the USO. Max phoned and told me he was coming to see you." Her plush lips curved upward. "Of course I had to come. You don't mind, do you?"

"Mind?" He probably sounded like a stammering idiot. Control. He needed control. "Of course not. It's great to see you both. Please, sit down." He gestured to a chintz sofa.

Max and Judith both sat. A wing chair rested kitty-corner to the couch. Cliff moved toward it, hobbling on his crutches. He sensed their eyes on him as he sat and leaned his crutches against the chair. Beads of sweat broke out near his hairline. Even something as simple as sitting down took twice as much effort. His stump stuck out awkwardly.

He forced himself to ignore it. Loss of a limb did not define a person. Hadn't he just told Joe that only yesterday?

"So what's new?" He leaned his elbow on the armrest.

"Besides the war?" Max chuckled. Judith smiled slightly. "Not much. Of course many of our best stars are off doing work for the war effort. Gable and Stewart are in the Air Force. And like Judy said, she just got back from a USO tour in the Pacific."

"The guys must've been thrilled to see you." He gave Judith a hopefully genuine smile. She had guts going overseas like that. She was billed as "Our All-American Nightingale" and the star of several MGM musicals, as well as a hit soloist on the radio. He could well imagine the excitement of the GIs when Judith Haysley graced their stage.

"I think so." Judith smiled. She sat poised on the edge of the sofa, skirt skimming her knees, gloved hands in her lap. It looked like a magazine pose. Contrast that with Rosemary who once crashed in a chair beside his bed at the end of her shift, teasing that a nurse never stood when she could sit and never sat when she could lie down. He'd gallantly offered to scoot over, and her cheeks had burned red before she made a hasty departure.

Since when had he started comparing Judith and Rosemary?

"Ah, Judy. You're too modest, sweetheart." Max patted her knee. His long legs stretched in front of him as he managed to look alert and casual at the same time. "So what's the prognosis, Powell?"

What. . .? What kind of a question was that? Max must have spent too much time staring into that Hollywood sun not to take note of his condition.

Cliff's astonishment must have shown on his face, as Max amended, "I mean, when do you expect to be released?"

"Within a month or so, I figure. They've got me in all sorts of therapy, and I'm adjusting to a prosthetic limb." He kept his tone matter-of-fact, his gaze steady. This wasn't some silver screen version of the effects of war. The men in this hospital were the real deal, true heroes. Not a one of them needed the commendation of a type like Max Redford.

"Excellent." Max clapped his hands together. "You'll want a little time to rest up, and then we'll pull together a tour."

"A tour?" Good grief, he sounded like a weak echo.

Max nodded. "You and Judy, raising money for war bonds, doing shows at hospitals like this. Just think, her singing, your comedy. Not to mention. . ." He waved his hand vaguely in the vicinity of Cliff's missing leg. "Think of all the money the folks at home will plunk down after seeing what the Japs did to a star like Cliff Powell. You can do radio broadcasts like Bob Hope. We'll get together a few more stars."

"Whoa." Cliff's chuckle came out forced. "Slow down a bit. I'm not so sure—"

"About what?" Judith blinked. "Just think what you and I can do together, Cliff. Raising money for war bonds, visiting hospitals and training bases. They need us." She pressed her lips together. "We must *all* do our part." If voices could be marketed, hers would sound great on a recruiting poster.

I did my part. Shot down sixteen planes, got a bunch of medals. Lost my leg. What more does Uncle Sam want?

He knew the answer. No one must shirk their duty. All must fight for victory. It was both an honor and necessity.

But what was his duty now? He rubbed the back of his neck.

Max and Judith stared at him. They expected an answer. His country expected an answer.

"Give me time to think about it, okay? I'm still working on stuff here. The doc hasn't even given me a day pass. But we'll talk again."

"Take your time. I know you've been through a lot," Max said.

They made small talk for another fifteen minutes. Cliff itched to go back to the ward, to see Rosemary and help Joe finish the crossword puzzle. Once, he'd been so comfortable with these people, called them friends. He couldn't count the number of pictures snapped with Judith on his arm, or her lips bussing his cheek as she had a few minutes ago.

And now?

The depth of camaraderie he'd experienced in the Marines, and now with the guys in this hospital, was a well compared with the droplets of what he'd once called friendship.

Now he needed to chart his own path. A new one.

⚘ *Chapter 8* ⚘

February 14, 1945

*I*f there was one thing she'd learned working at this hospital, patients took every excuse to break up the routine and plan something special. Valentine's Day was no exception. When Rosemary and Sam arrived on duty in the morning, garlands of cutout hearts were strung across the walls, and they'd been showered with little gifts, many homemade in therapy classes, and paper valentines with both touching and laughable sayings.

How fine these men were—facing their new realities with grins and get-it-done attitudes. How proud she was of all of them.

Rosemary stood in the supply closet refreshing her cart with supplies. Wall-to-wall shelves lined the dim interior. She grabbed a stack of towels and placed it on the cart. Now, where were those kidney dishes?

The supply closet door creaked open.

"I'm almost through, Sam." Sweat trickled down her spine, her backside in the air as she reached to the back of a bottom shelf.

"Happy Valentine's Day."

She stood and whirled around so fast she knocked her head on the edge of the cabinet.

Cliff stood inside, the door closed behind him.

"Same to you, and why are you trying to render me unconscious?" She rubbed her throbbing head, nurse's cap atilt.

"If you were unconscious, you wouldn't be talking." He took a step closer, the space between them narrowed to nothing. "Here. Let me see." His breath smelled of Wrigley's spearmint gum. He gently tunneled his fingers through her hair, the touch exquisitely soothing.

Her breath emerged ragged. "What are you doing?"

"Examining your skull for external injuries." Oh, was that renegade gleam in his gaze ever dangerous. "What does it look like I'm doing, Lieutenant?"

Her heart pounded. His freshly shaven jaw was inches from her face. One move. That's all it would take for her lips to brush his.

"I. . .I'm fine." She swallowed. That is, if you called being approximately five seconds away from fainting over the bliss of his fingers entwined in her hair fine. She ducked away. His hand fell to his side.

She tried to focus on something else, anything, to quiet her mile-a-minute heart. Seeing him working so hard to walk more and more with the aid of his prosthetic limb was definitely not helping her efforts to ignore his attractiveness. He had this little boy smile every time he circled the room and visited the guys without his crutches. Joe was learning how to walk with prosthetics too. Both of them wanted to take dancing lessons from a famous instructor who'd once worked on routines for Fred and Ginger but now devoted his energies to showing men like Cliff and Joe that dancing could still be a part of their lives.

"Brought you something." Cliff drew a small black box from the pocket of his bathrobe.

Their fingers brushed. Hers shook as she stared down at it. "You didn't have to get me anything."

"Didn't get it." He gave a little grin. "Made it."

Gently she opened the lid. A pair of delicate silver earrings lay nestled in a square of midnight velvet.

Her breath caught. "You made these." She lifted one and held it up. Silver wire had been twisted into a rose-shaped pattern and affixed to an earring base.

Cliff nodded. "This kind of stuff is supposed to be for the guys working on their hands, but they let me have a few materials. Do you like them?"

"Do I like them? They're. . .they're beautiful." Her throat tightened inexplicably. "No one has ever given me jewelry before." She placed the earring next to its mate and closed the lid. "Thank you."

He leaned one hand on the edge of her cart. "It's the least I could do. You deserve diamonds for the care you've given each of us."

Blast it, now he really was going to make her start crying. And in the middle of her shift, no less. "Seeing you get well is worth more to me than diamonds."

Silence fell between them as they gazed at each other.

"I got another pass."

"Another one? You must be some prize pupil." She grinned, needing teasing to bring them back to familiar ground.

"Either that or a prize nuisance." The corner of his mouth tipped up. "Lieutenant Baker told me you've got all day off tomorrow. And I was wondering, if you don't have anything to do, if you'd like to spend the day with me."

Spend the day? Not "go out with me"? Not a date then. Should she be relieved at his phrasing? "Where?"

"Somewhere I need to go." His grin turned mysterious. "Anyway, it's really your duty as a nurse to accompany me. It's only my second time out, you know. Something might happen."

Her brow arched. "So you want a babysitter?"

He shook his head, no longer kidding. "I want you to come with me. And I'll think up a list of excuses that'll stretch from here to Detroit just to get you to say yes."

She wanted to shake him and tell him to stop it. Stop being so charming, so sweet. Stop making her. . .

She ought to say no. But somehow she couldn't form the words.

"Okay then. Nine a.m. tomorrow. In front of the hospital." She placed her hands firmly on the cart handles.

He held the door for her. As she walked past, his whisper brushed her ear and wrecked her concentration for the rest of the afternoon. "It's a date then."

⚘

Last night he'd phoned a department store and bought a suit, then rented a car and a driver. Now they cruised toward Beverly Hills, scenery flashing by in a blur. Rosemary sat on the plush leather back seat beside him. She'd surprised him by coming along with few questions. Perhaps she sensed he needed to do this and was fulfilling her duties as a nurse, even on her day off, by coming with him.

She either had a sense of responsibility the size of Mount Rushmore, or she cared for him as much as he cared for her.

The drive from the hospital to Beverly Hills took three hours. They'd stopped once at a gas station along the way. He'd bought bottled sodas for all three of them.

He knew he couldn't overdo it, but what a feeling it had been to walk into that crummy gas station on two legs, the cashier none the wiser, both that he was Cliff Powell and that he'd spent the past months in a hospital bed.

The closer they drew, the more familiar everything got. Rosemary stared out the window as they reached the ritzy neighborhoods often included in bus tours of the area. Then she turned toward him with an expression probably meant to be no-nonsense, but which ended up looking just plain endearing.

"Okay, Captain Powell. I've had just about enough of the mystery. Where are we going?"

"You'll see in a minute." Maybe she'd be disappointed. He was taking her to his house—a place he hadn't seen since leaving for flight training—not to a glitzy theater or to some other entertainment hotspot.

"Is this when you tell me you're not actually Cliff Powell, but a wanted man, and you're about to hold me hostage for a million dollars?"

His eyes widened. "Rosemary, you don't really—"

"Gotcha!" She grinned. "I had you going there, didn't I?"

He shook his head, leaning back against the sun-warmed leather. A chuckle escaped. She giggled. They were still laughing as the driver stopped in front of the gates.

"Roll down your window and press that button." Cliff indicated to the driver. "Let's see if anybody's home."

The driver did as directed. After a few minutes, the line crackled. "Yes?" came a gravelly voice.

Cliff leaned forward, calling out the open window. "Hey, is that you, Jonesy?"

"Yes." His groundskeeper sounded suspicious.

"It's me. Cliff! Open the gate."

"Mr. Cliff! Well, land sakes—" The gate opened, cutting off the rest of his words. They drove through and up a circular drive.

It did something to him, seeing his home after all this time. Sun rained down on the stately butternut stone mansion as if in fanfare for his return. It was an estate like many in the area, with grassy lawn and immaculate landscaping, a swimming pool in the back, a patio where he'd hosted Hollywood's finest for splashy barbecues.

It was also home. His.

Rosemary's eyes looked like golf balls.

Time to fess up.

The driver pulled to a stop, tires against gravel. Cliff turned to Rosemary in the sun-warmed car.

"Is this—?"

He nodded. "This is my house. I haven't seen it in years. You're probably going to think I'm a selfish jerk to take up your day like this, but I wanted you with me when I saw it again. To make up for it though, I can promise fresh-squeezed orange juice from my tree in the back and, if I play my cards right, the best spaghetti and meatballs you'll ever eat."

She laughed and opened the car door. "I wouldn't miss it."

He instructed the driver to wait around until they were ready to return, and that if he went around to the back entrance, he'd find the kitchen and some lunch. Then he climbed out and stood, the lick of wind on his face, staring up at his home.

He could come back tomorrow if he wanted, for keeps. With his finances, he could hire private care to help him through the final stages of recovery.

But if he did that, he'd be leaving Joe and Dave and Rosemary, all the others. He didn't want to fall back on his money because he used to be a big shot, and isolate himself here. He wanted—

"This is a, um. . ." Rosemary glanced up at him, one hand holding her uniform hat. She'd dressed in a different uniform than the one she wore on the ward, a crisp jacket and fitted skirt hugging her trim waist. "Nice coat closet."

He laughed again. It was part of the reason he'd brought her.

Had he come alone, he'd have been tempted to lapse into depressing ruminations best left in the past.

"Come on." They made their way up the wide front steps. Rosemary kept a hand under his arm, steadying him. Had it not gone against his conscience, he'd have pretended to stumble, just so she'd move in closer. Knowing Rosemary though, that would probably get him stuck resting on the couch all afternoon.

He'd have turned the door handle, but as they reached the top step, it opened wide. Mrs. Park and Jonesy beamed.

"Welcome home, Captain Powell." A sheen filmed Mrs. Park's eyes. When the door closed, she clasped both of his hands in her birdlike ones. In the years since he'd seen her, her cloud of gray hair had grown more silver, the network of lines in her face more pronounced.

"Now, Mrs. Park, we'll have none of that handshaking. Who do you think I am? President Roosevelt?" He wrapped her in a hug. She smelled like clean soap and fresh-baked bread.

"It's so good to see you again. When we heard what happened. . ." She swiped beneath her eyes.

"I know," he said quietly. "But it's all okay now."

He turned to Jonesy, clapping him on the shoulder. "How are you, Jonesy?"

"Never better, sir. And delighted to see you." His groundskeeper's baritone voice was as rich and warm as before. His eyes crinkled as he smiled, teeth gleaming white in his coffee-hued face.

These two people had been with him for years. When he'd gotten drunk for a week following his breakup with Hazel, it had been Jonesy who picked him up off the floor and told him to sober up. And from the very day he'd hired her, Mrs. Park had been the grandmother he never had.

Cliff turned to Rosemary, drawing her forward. "I'd like you both to meet Lieutenant James. She's one of my nurses at the hospital and a dear friend besides."

Rosemary smiled warmly. "I'm very glad to meet you both. And please, call me Rosemary."

Mrs. Park and Jonesy echoed greetings.

"I figured I'd drive over and have a look around the place and show Rosemary. I know I didn't give you any advance notice, but I don't suppose you could whip up some of your world-famous spaghetti?" Mrs. Park never fell for his Powell grin, but he flashed it at her anyway, just to get a rise out of her.

"World-famous, my foot. It's just plain old spaghetti and meatballs. Don't believe half of what he says, my girl." Mrs. Park gave Rosemary a conspiratorial smile.

"Oh believe me, I never do." Her laugh rang out like a chime.

They set off, Mrs. Park promising to tell them when lunch was ready. Together they strolled through the main-floor rooms—living room, billiard room with pool and card tables, a library lined with books he'd rarely had time to crack open. French doors offset the dining room. Cliff pushed one open, holding it for Rosemary. They stepped onto the tiled patio overlooking the rolling landscape. A set of steps off the patio led down to the swimming pool, covered with a tarp today. Orange trees laden with fresh fruit stood nearby, making Cliff's mouth water for their sweet taste. Nothing beat eating an orange plucked fresh.

Rosemary stared into the distance, arms folded across her chest, curls fluttering in the breeze. He came up behind her.

"Do you like it?"

She glanced at him. "Yes." A dimple appeared in her cheek. "It's as grand as I imagined."

"You've imagined my house?" He gave her a long, intent look, lips twitching upward.

"Of course not!" Her cheeks reddened. "You know what I mean. It's how I imagined someone like you would live."

He rubbed a hand along his jaw. "I really ought to do some good with it. Turn it into something. A place for soldiers to vacation when the war is over, you know." He was thinking out loud, something he didn't do often. With Rosemary, it was easy.

"It's so peaceful here." She tilted her head back toward the sky, eyes closed. Wind rustled in the trees, the air balmy.

"The opposite of how it is over there. When the war is over, there'll be a lot of healing needing to take place. Not just in those who've been wounded, but in ordinary guys whose scars are not outward. A week here with their families. . ."

"They could go swimming, play games, read books." Rosemary faced him, eyes alight. "With a house this size, you could host—"

"There are eight bedrooms upstairs."

"Four families. I can see them now. The kids playing on the grass, swimming in the pool. The men and their wives sitting on the patio, taking in this beautiful sun. In the dining room, eating Mrs. Park's spaghetti." Rosemary's words tumbled over each other.

"Picking oranges. They could come from all across the States. I could get some stars together, do a show to raise money for more household staff and the upkeep of the place. All the families would have to do is pay their transportation. We could take them through an application process. There'd be a terrific waiting list—"

"But with a week's stay, and four families at a time."

"Sixteen families a month."

"It could be done."

"Just think of it." They looked at each other, excitement contagious.

Rosemary paused, biting her lip. "But would you really do it?" Her brow wrinkled. "Give up your house?"

He shrugged. He'd always been impulsive, but this was a mansion in the heart of Hollywood they were talking about. Katharine Hepburn and Claudette Colbert lived only a few miles away.

An image of Glim here, with his pretty redheaded wife and their three kids, and even of Joe with his parents, rose inside Cliff. Laughing. Relaxing. Moving past the war.

"Why not? I have enough in my savings to buy a cottage somewhere. What do I need with all of this? I could always close it down for a week once a year if I wanted to. I've always rattled around here all alone anyway."

In a blink, Rosemary launched herself at him. Her arms went around him, and his world became lemons and soft curves. His arms came around her for a glorious moment, and then she drew away, flushed.

"What was that for?"

"For you." He ached to kiss her smiling lips, linger on the dimple of her cheek. "Because you're incredible."

No. He was flawed. He'd lived years in pursuit of fame and fortune for no one but himself. His past he could never redeem.

He looked into Rosemary's smiling face.

But perhaps, with God's help, he could reach for a better future.

Chapter 9

*L*ittle changed in the days following the one she'd spent with Cliff. A day like none other. They'd eaten spaghetti in the dining room, a sun-drenched breeze streaming through open windows, Mrs. Park and Jonesy joining them like part of the family. Talking. Laughing. Cliff shared his ideas with his housekeeper and groundskeeper. Both of them looked at him like they saw a new man, but they approved wholeheartedly of the plan. Cliff said his leg was bothering him, and for Cliff to complain, there had to be real discomfort, so they left soon after. Rosemary fell asleep on the ride back to Palm Springs, sated and sun-warmed.

She awoke cuddled against Cliff's shoulder.

When she admitted the last to Sam, her friend practically swooned, comparing them to Clark Gable and Claudette Colbert in *It Happened One Night*.

"She woke up on his shoulder when they were on a bus. . . ."

Rosemary's protestations that *It Happened One Night* was just a movie did no good. Sam had the two of them mentally married off.

Sam needed to get over her romantic delusions. Cliff hadn't hinted at any interest in Rosemary beyond friendship. The Valentine's Day gift? She'd gotten half a dozen from other patients, though none as carefully crafted as the earrings. Asking her to come with him? He'd explained that. He hadn't wanted to go alone.

Friends. Just friends.

She couldn't expect Cliff to care about her in any other way. When she'd met him in Hollywood years ago, he'd been a different man. The Cliff Powell of today was honorable. He wouldn't kiss her again unless he meant something by it.

Rosemary hurried down the corridor, rubber soles noiseless on the linoleum, pushing her supply cart.

"Lieutenant James." Dr. Kendall—Grant—caught up with her. He carried a stack of patient charts beneath one arm.

"Afternoon." She turned the corner toward the orthopedic ward.

"Can we talk?"

"Now?"

He nodded. "Just for a minute. In there." She found herself following him into the supply closet along with her cart, the door closed behind them.

The second time she'd stood in this supply closet with a man. The first had been a week ago, but she still remembered every detail. One brush of her fingertips across the box containing her earrings brought it all to mind.

"What's so important?" She leaned against a cabinet. They'd gone on a few dates since their first. She genuinely admired Grant Kendall, both as a physician and as a person. But as they chalked up more time together, she sensed him beginning to feel more.

"I'm leaving Torney." His gaze met hers in the dimness.

She pressed a hand to her middle. "Leaving? Where?"

"I'm going to Chicago. There's a veteran's hospital there, and I've been transferred. I'm to be lead surgeon. It's what I've been wanting. A chance to put my skills in OR to good use. There's no openings for that here. And I grew up in Chicago. I've already secured an apartment not far from where my mother lives."

"Congratulations." Her smile came easier than she'd reckoned it would. He was saying goodbye. That though they'd gone on a few dates, his career came first. Surgery, not general ward duty, was his true passion. He had much to offer his new position. "I'm happy for you. You'll do well."

"Rosemary, Rosemary." He took one stride toward her, pulling her hands into his. "You don't understand. I don't want you to congratulate me. I want you to go with me."

"Go with you?" She swallowed. "What do you mean?"

"I've already asked. There's a job for you too, as a head nurse." Still holding her hands, he lowered himself to one knee. She gasped. "I want you to marry me."

Her heart pounded crazily in her chest.

"I know I promised we'd take things slow, but this is too important an opportunity to pass by. You must know how I feel about you." His gaze was firm. Much as it was on the ward when a nurse or internee failed to anticipate his need for a certain instrument.

"Must I?" Her brain seemed wrapped in gauze. Dr. Grant Kendall was on his knee proposing. To her.

He chuckled. "You're surprised. I understand. It's all a shock. You don't have to answer right away. Take a couple of days to think about it." His gaze pressed into her.

She nodded. "I. . .I will."

He stood, looking down at her. "Good. You'll be a wonderful wife as well as a nurse. I know it. Don't worry about anything. Just focus on how you feel about me." His smile was tender, as if calculated to banish all her uncertainties.

She nodded again. He opened the closet door and peered out, looked over his shoulder at her. "All clear."

She returned to the ward and focused on her patients, going through the motions of the afternoon, Grant's words an echo in her mind.

Dear God, what am I to do?

Everyone was talking about Tuesday evening—two days away—when Bob Hope and the cast of The Pepsodent Show were set to perform in the hospital auditorium, along with special guest Frank Sinatra. The following morning Cliff was to be discharged. With the help of physical therapy, he'd regained strength in his limb and adjusted to the prosthetic. He'd continue to exercise on his own, along with regular appointments with a physician. There was no reason for him to stay on. New patients, fresh from the front, needed his bed.

Which left the question of what his future would hold heavy on his mind. Should he do as Max suggested and go on tour with Judith? He had to admit, he enjoyed performing, and he and Judith worked well together. Witnessing the excitement of the patients in the orthopedic ward over Hope's appearance reinforced the necessity of giving both active-duty soldiers and convalescing patients something to look forward to.

Yet Cliff still hesitated.

He sat outside, taking in late afternoon sun, watching hospital personnel hurry across the grounds, off to one of the many buildings. Patients sat in wheelchairs or walked about on crutches or with arms in casts, Gray Ladies and nurses attending them all. Cliff had chosen a spot away from the rest, wanting to be alone. An empty chair sat next to his, but so far no one had claimed it. His expression must be scaring everybody away.

The air smelled balmy and fragrant with trees and flowers. Behind him the impressive facade of the former El Mirador Hotel rose proud. Serving a purpose deeper than luxury for the shallow rich. He'd served a deeper purpose too, for a time.

"Hi."

Cliff glanced behind him. Rosemary stood close to his chair, hands clasped in front of her. The sight of her twisted him inside. More than anything or anyone at this hospital, he would miss her. Deeply.

"Why weren't you on duty this afternoon?" *Nice, Powell. You're not her commanding officer.*

"They needed me in OR. One of the nurses who usually works there sprained her knee and is on bed rest. I've been there since seven this morning."

"Shouldn't you be resting now?"

She gave a tentative smile, sunlight golden on her face. "It wasn't so bad. And I wanted to find you."

She did? As if piloted by a daredevil, his heart did a barrel roll.

Rosemary sat beside him, smoothing her skirt. "I'm wondering if I could ask your advice."

His advice? Well, what had he expected her to say? *I love you, Cliff, and never want to leave you.* Not likely.

"Sure. Though I'm not sure I have much of value to offer."

"When one is faced with a decision, how should one make up their mind?"

"Huh?"

She bit her lip, as if fighting for words. "What I mean to say is, should one look to logic or to the heart? When there are two good choices, how should one choose?"

He rubbed the back of his neck. "Funny you should ask. I've been thinking about choices a lot myself lately."

"And?"

He measured his words, choosing carefully, forming his own ruminations into sentences for her benefit. "I think one should never look solely to logic or solely to the heart. Both have their place, but giving over to one and ignoring the other is a recipe for disaster. Above all, I figure we should ask God." He should be flattered she thought enough of him to seek his opinion. Did it mean she shared his feelings? That what had been between the two of them had deepened in these past weeks?

He wanted it to be so with an intensity he couldn't remember feeling about anything before—fame, fortune, even Hazel's affection.

She looked down at her clasped hands. "Someone has asked me to leave the life I've built here to be by his side. And I'm not sure what to do." She met his gaze, her own full of questions.

Someone had asked her *what?*

"What do you think?" the words came automatically as he scrambled to unknot her meaning.

She shook her head. "I don't know. Part of me wants to say yes. But part of me isn't sure." She sucked in a breath, eyes wide. "It's Dr. Kendall. He's leaving the hospital to accept a position somewhere else. He's asked me to go with him, to marry him."

The breath leeched from his body like he'd been punched in the gut. Kendall had asked Rosemary to marry him? Of course he'd noticed the way the doc looked at her, but to offer marriage implied they'd spent more time together than on the ward. She'd been dating him. While she'd dated Kendall, he'd fallen for her.

Idiot. Falling for this twice in one lifetime. First Hazel, now

Rosemary. Rock-headed fool lured by a pretty face couldn't learn a lesson just once.

He fought for control. Rosemary was nothing like Hazel. Hazel played with him as if he were a game put aside when no longer amusing. Rosemary had cared for him tirelessly. Encouraged him, treated him with kindness. Considered him a friend. He'd be a heel if he couldn't put aside his own emotions so as not to fail her.

Focus, Powell.

"If you love him, then by all means say yes." He paused. "But if you don't, then there's your answer. Life is hard enough without bringing a loveless marriage into the mix."

"But aren't respect and admiration just as valuable, if not more so, than love?"

Her words told the truth. She didn't love Kendall. But because she wasn't in love with him didn't mean she loved someone else.

Least of all me.

Bringing his feelings to her attention would only be unfair. Just as unfair as when he'd kissed her, knowing she was engaged to someone else. That had been selfish. A mark of the man he'd once been.

He scrubbed a hand across his jaw. His stump ached. "Maybe it could be. I can't decide for you. Only you can make this decision. I've given you all the advice I have." His words came out clipped.

Her eyes darkened. But before he could discern their expression, she turned them downward. "Thank you," she whispered. "I. . .I should go." She stood and walked away.

He didn't look at her. Couldn't. She wasn't his. Kendall had proposed to her; he had more of a right than Cliff did. Kendall was a respected doctor with a whole body. In comparison, his own life— as an actor who'd scrambled to the top, only to find out the view wasn't much better than down below—was a lame joke. Sure, he'd been a good pilot and intended to do his best to live his new life by a different standard, but was he good enough for someone like Rosemary?

No. He would never be good enough. Never measure up.

And there it was. The reason he'd come to Hollywood in the first place. Growing up as the orphaned nephew on a farm less than prosperous, he'd lived with the realization that there were people better, more privileged than him. So he'd set out to become one of them. When the critics praised him, MGM contracted him, and Hazel said she loved him, the feeling of being less-than had evaporated. The same went for his time with his squadron. He'd become a triple ace, while other pilots were hard-pressed to shoot down even one enemy plane. In doing his duty for his country, he could again imagine himself as worthy, even more easily than in Hollywood. In the hospital he'd done the same thing. Befriended the guys, strived to excel in his therapy, lived for Rosemary's smile. Proving to himself that he was worth something, even here. Cherished the thought that Rosemary would trust him, love him, make him whole through both.

His fingertips pressed into the sides of his skull.

What did it mean to be enough, to be worthy? Was it what others said about you or how you thought of yourself? A compilation of both? Or neither?

God. The cry came from a raw place within. *Help me.*

He sat staring at the blades of grass curling around his shoes, thoughts rolling through his mind.

Maybe worthiness wasn't found on a marquee or in serving one's country, or in being anything special at all. No matter what he did, would it ever be enough? Or would he always want more approval, some new reason to think well of himself, forever feeding an emptiness that would never be sated?

Honestly yes.

God loved him. Not a conditional love, but without boundaries or restrictions. And from what he'd read, the Bible assured him that God had forgiven all of his sins.

So why couldn't that be enough?

Even if he never gained the love or approval of another living person, couldn't God supply the deficiency? Couldn't seeking God's will and resting in the knowledge that he was following His plan fill that void?

Even if Rosemary married Kendall and he never saw her again, couldn't God be enough through that too?

To all of it, yes.

God, if this is true, help me to live like it. Show me that in Your eyes I'm enough. Show me what to do.

Cliff rose from his seat and slowly made his way toward the hospital. He was scarred. He was flawed.

But for the first time, the place of empty questions was filled with wholeness.

He was enough, not because anyone else said so, not because he himself thought so, but because he belonged to God.

❧ *Chapter 10* ❧

February 27, 1945

*E*xcitement sizzled through the hospital. Tonight the auditorium would be filled with patients, staff, and some of the locals, as Bob Hope broadcast his Pepsodent Show and gave the men a dose of morale.

If only she could get her hands on some morale herself. Rosemary had already volunteered to work on one of the postoperative wards during the show, since all the guys in her ward would be attending the program.

Staying busy was best. Then she didn't have to think about anything but helping wounded men get well.

She still hadn't forgiven herself for confiding in Cliff. What did he know about her problems? What did he know about her feelings for him?

Not a thing.

What had she expected? That he'd follow her announcement with *Don't do it, Rosemary. I love you. Marry me?*

And she thought Sam lived too much in the movies.

At least one thing had become clear. She'd rather remain alone than be with someone she didn't love. She needed to tell Grant. It wouldn't be fair to keep him waiting.

An ironic smile curved her lips as she hurried toward the dining hall. They said only stupid people make the same mistake twice. She'd turned down Paul because of Cliff. Now she was about to do the same to Grant.

Because of Cliff, she knew what it meant to love someone. Neither Paul nor Grant deserved to marry a woman who didn't feel like that about them.

Moving like an automaton, she filled a plate at the counter and took her tray to a corner table. The dining hall buzzed with activity as hospital staff grabbed a bite to eat before returning to work. Chatter rippled and laughter rang out in merry peals. Everyone anticipated tonight.

Rosemary picked up her fork and stabbed it into a green bean. Her stomach rebelled.

Against her will and better judgment, she'd given her heart to Cliff, first that long-ago night, and now again. Somehow she had to find a way to take it back.

She was twenty-five years old. Thousands of men had been killed in the war, leaving women widowed and girls without sweethearts. If she turned down Dr. Kendall, she'd most likely live out the rest of her life alone.

Rosemary pressed the tines of her fork into her mound of mashed potatoes, smashing them down.

Once, not long after she'd started at the library, she asked Mrs. Edwards why she'd never married. She envisioned the woman's lined face and clear blue eyes behind a pair of thick, round glasses.

You don't need love to have joy, Rosemary. You can live as full and as good a life alone as you can with a man.

Rosemary, in the throes of a Jane Austen reading craze, had asked how such a thing was possible.

With God, honey, Mrs. Edwards had replied. *He makes the impossible possible. With Him, nothing is too hard to endure, because we don't endure it alone. He's walking right beside us. And with Him, it's less about enduring and more about trusting that His best is our best too, even if we don't see it right then. Like it says in Romans, He works all things for our good.*

By now her potatoes were a cold, demolished mess. Rosemary set down her fork.

His best is our best too.

Could it be? In spite of all the horror they'd witnessed during these years of war?

Something else Mrs. Edwards said filled her mind, her slow voice as clear as if she sat across the table now.

There are only two choices. To trust or not to trust. If we don't trust, we're miserable. If we do, then even if we're disappointed in the outcome, at least we have peace.

Rosemary sighed, leaning her face into her hands.

Lord, I have two choices. To trust or not to trust. Help me trust You with my life. Give me joy, even if my future doesn't include any love but Yours. And please. . .take away my feelings for Cliff. He's leaving tomorrow, and I want to forget about him. Bless him in his new life. I know he loves You.

That afternoon she found Grant and told him she couldn't marry him. He looked more shocked than anything else. But he accepted her best wishes for the future. Then she returned to the ward and kept busy. The men were just coming back from physical therapy. Cliff walked near the end of the line, steps slow but assured. He grinned at Joe, walking haltingly beside him with the aid of crutches and prosthetics.

Cliff Powell smiled like he did everything else. All-in, no holds barred. The same generous way he'd offered his home to returning soldiers. He had faults. But he had strengths. And she, undeniably, loved both. Loved him. Her heart wrenched.

She had to say goodbye. He'd be at the show tonight, and by the time she went on duty the next day, his discharge would be complete. One goodbye. Then she must forget.

She waited until they'd all settled down and she'd done a circuit of the room, checking charts and making sure everyone was comfortable. Lieutenant Elliot had disappeared into the ward kitchen and the head nurse wasn't at her desk, so no one but the patients were around to see that Rosemary saved Cliff's bed for last. She scanned his chart, sensing his gaze on her. Then she rounded the bed until she stood near the head, her skirt brushing the mattress. She'd set Dave up with his projector, and laughter came from the other end of the room. Good. It would muffle their conversation.

She forced a smile. "Looks like you're all set to be discharged tomorrow."

He nodded. He sat on top of the blankets, leaning against the headboard, face turned toward her. So handsome, even in those regulation pajamas, it made her miserable just looking at him.

She'd have asked about his plans, but it wasn't her business. She'd done her job as a nurse. Nothing more was required of her. Still. . .

"I took your advice." Oh, she was doing it again. Trying to make something happen that would never come to pass. But the words rushed out anyway. "I'm not going to marry Dr. Kendall. You're right about a loveless marriage. It wouldn't be worth it."

A strange expression came over his face. She waited for him to speak. Seconds passed, and he said nothing.

Get it over with, Rosemary.

"I didn't come to tell you that though. I came to say goodbye. I won't be seeing you tonight, and tomorrow you'll be gone. I just wanted to say—"

A commotion at the door cut off her words. Two people strode in—a curvy blond woman in a sleek blue suit, and a tall man with slicked-back hair and a face she recognized from Sam's movie magazines.

"Hiya, fellas." Bob Hope flashed a Pepsodent-enhanced grin. He stopped before Dave's bed. "That's okay. Don't bother getting up, kid. I'm nobody important."

The room dissolved in laughter, led loudest of all by Dave.

Rosemary slipped away and settled behind the nurses' desk while Bob and a woman she guessed was Frances Langford toured the room, stopping to talk with each man. She pressed a hand to her cheek, focusing on the open schedule book in front of her.

She'd said her goodbyes to Cliff.

Now it was time to move on.

There were few things worse than an unfinished conversation. The lingering ache of what might have been.

Rosemary had turned down Dr. Kendall. And she'd come to Cliff to say goodbye.

He didn't want goodbye. He wanted forever. The two of them as one, for as long as God pleased for them to dwell on this earth.

The superficial infatuation and desire he'd known with Hazel was nothing compared to what he felt for Rosemary. She encouraged him in his dreams, cherished her faith as he did, teased him yet treated him with honor and respect. He wanted to love her, protect her, wake up beside her. . . .

He needed to tell her and fast. The pain on her face when she'd said goodbye—surely that had to mean she cared for him too.

But even if she rejected him, he wouldn't live with the regret of not knowing. War had shown him life's brevity but also its beauty. When one was given the chance to take another breath, one must use every moment in living for what mattered most.

Cliff sat in the sun-warmed visitor's parlor. Bob Hope was finishing his tour of the wards, and he'd suggested they catch up afterward.

Cliff had used the interim to get dressed, and he stared down at his clothes, the same suit he'd worn when he'd taken Rosemary to his home, boxed up and sent over that not-so-long-ago morning from some Palm Springs department store. He ran his fingers across the light gray fabric. His pants brushed his shoe tops, hiding his prosthetic limb.

The loss of his leg was a death of sorts. One he'd always have to live with.

But loss could give birth to new beginnings. He'd found one in this hospital.

The door opened. Bob breezed in, larger than life and grinning. Cliff rose and shook hands heartily. They exchanged greetings, and Bob sat on the sofa.

"Where's Frances?" Cliff asked.

"I lost her." Bob laughed. "I don't remember which ward. Last I saw, some fella was asking her to hold his hand. They all think she's made of celestial ether. I'm not going to be the one to tell 'em she's as human as the rest of us."

Cliff laughed. They chatted about the rest of the cast for a few minutes.

"So how much longer are you stuck at Torney?"

"Discharged tomorrow, actually."

"What will you do then?" Bob pulled a cigarette case from his pocket.

"I'm not really sure." He and Bob had never been more than casual friends, but he found himself wanting to talk to someone about it. "Max Redford wants me to team up with Judith and do a tour selling war bonds, performing at hospitals and stateside Army bases."

"And?" Bob flicked the lighter and put the cigarette to his lips.

"I know one thing I want to do. Open up my house as a place for servicemen and their families to go for some R&R after the war. After what they've been through, they could use a vacation. I've spent the past couple of years in barracks and tents and a hospital ward. If I moved back in, I'd feel like a die in a cup rattling around."

Bob nodded.

"But the war isn't over yet." Cliff blew out a breath.

"Let me tell you something that might help make up your mind." Bob leaned forward, cigarette between his fingers. "I know I go up there and kid around a lot, but what I've spent the war doing. . .well, it's more than a career for me. Looking out at those kids in the audience, whether they're active soldiers or patients at this hospital, knowing they've been through hell and some of them won't make it home. . .There's purpose to what I'm doing. Even if all I'm giving them is a half hour of laughs and Frances's songs, it's more than that really. It takes them back home, makes them forget the war, even when we're joking about it. I may not have put on a uniform and taken up a gun, but I'd like to think I'm still fighting, in my own way."

Cliff had never seen this side of the famous entertainer. Bob's gaze burned with driving intensity and depth of emotion. Cliff had listened to the radio shows, heard the Christmas broadcasts when

Bob broke away from the usual jokes to speak poignantly.

Could he accept Max's offer and bring something to the comrades he could no longer fight alongside, even if it was as Bob said "just a half hour of laughs and music"?

Ask any of the men and women who listened, and they'd tell him it was so much more. A boost of morale. A connection with family back home who listened to the broadcasts. A moment of recalling the substance of humanity in the midst of brutality.

He could keep fighting, in a way. It would mean long hours of travel and hard work, but everyone was giving those things these days. Could this be God's way of handing him a new purpose?

Bob smoked and sat in silence, as if letting Cliff absorb his words.

"Thanks. You've given me a lot to think about."

"I charge five cents for advice," Bob deadpanned. Cliff chuckled, shaking his head. "But I'll waive the fee if you'll do a favor for me. After the recorded half-hour show, I thought we'd stick around and do a little something more. It'd be great if you joined us."

Cliff nodded without hesitation. "Be glad to." Maybe what he'd brought to his ward, and especially to Joe, he could bring to the audience. A sense that if Cliff Powell could go on with life in spite of being less than whole, they could too.

A crazy idea took hold, a shadow of the old Cliff. Did he dare?

Rosemary had given him so much. She deserved something extra special and grand. Even if it meant putting himself out there for embarrassment and rejection, she was worth it.

She'd already told him she wouldn't be at the show tonight, but if he got Sam to get her there afterward. . .

"On one condition," Cliff added. "You can do the closing number, but I want the one before that."

"Sure." Bob snuffed his cigarette in the ashtray.

"Great." Anticipation worked through him, along with anxiety, as if he were about to jump from ten thousand feet with a parachute that might or might not work.

He'd lay it all out then let her make her choice.

Hoping, praying, for her to choose him.

Chapter 11

Stillness blanketed the ward of resting patients in white iron beds. Having made them as comfortable as she could, Rosemary sat behind the nurses' desk, rolling bandages.

As her fingers worked, her mind drifted to the show taking place in the auditorium building. She'd glimpsed Bob and Frances touring the hospital, admired the way they had with the patients. It would've been fun to see the show.

But heaviness still weighed down her heart. Better the other girls enjoy themselves, since she'd only be able to enter into the entertainment halfheartedly.

Rosemary glanced at her watch. It would be over soon, and she'd be relieved of duty for the night. She'd go back to her room and eat the chocolate she'd been saving for a rainy day, then have a good cry. Both would no doubt put her in a better frame of mind come morning.

She'd never see him again. Early tomorrow Cliff would be gone.

Her heart felt shredded beyond surgical repair.

She pressed her lips together, focusing on the bandage through a blur of tears. That wasn't true. God could heal her. Even if, right now, walking through her ward without thoughts of Cliff and the time they'd shared in it sounded as far out of reach as touching the moon.

Rosemary looked up at a sound near the door. Sam, dressed in her best uniform, lipstick cherry red on her mouth, rushed up to Rosemary like a human cyclone.

"I've got orders to relieve you. You're needed in the auditorium."

"Needed? Why, is something wrong?" Rosemary set down the bandage.

"Just go, will you?" Sam planted her fists on her hips.

"What about the patients?" Rosemary swept her gaze across the ward.

"I'll stay with them. Hurry!" Sam bounced on her toes, a grin tugging the edges of her mouth.

Rosemary stood. "I can't just leave—"

"You're leaving. Orders are orders."

"Whose orders?"

"I'll tell you later." Sam gave her a none-too-gentle shove toward the door.

She rubbed her shoulder and shot Sam an offended look. "That hurt."

Sam grinned from her place at the nurses' desk, looking not at all sorry. "It's what friends are for. Now, scoot. Pronto."

She walked double-time toward the auditorium. What was going on? She shook her head. Probably just Sam wanting her to get in on the fun, hoping to cheer her up.

Rosemary hurried through the familiar hospital corridors, inhaling the scents of antiseptic and purpose. What had ever made her think for a moment about leaving? She belonged here, in these hallways, with these people—men like Dave and Joe, Sam, the other nurses.

Home was not a building. It was a sense of rightness, of knowing one's corner in this vast universe. She'd found it here. Would find it still, wherever there was a need for nurses. A life rich with meaning.

By the time she reached the auditorium doors, breath gasped from her lips, and her face flushed warm. She pushed open the double doors and slipped inside the dimly lit room. Patients, nurses, and soldiers packed the place. Beneath the stage lights, cozied up to a microphone, Frances crooned to the crowd amid whistles and cheers.

Rosemary's forehead creased.

Someone touched her arm. "Lieutenant James?" A lanky young man in a private's uniform stood beside her.

"Yes?"

The man leaned toward her to be heard above Frances's singing. "Your seat is up front. First row. I'll walk you up."

Am I ever going to let you have it, Samantha Baker.

Before she could protest, the private had a hand on her arm and was leading her toward the front. He gestured to her seat and left her there. So much for rank giving her a say-so. She found herself sitting between a uniformed major and a young man wearing a bathrobe and a bandage on his head.

Both applauded loudly when Frances finished her song. Bob took the microphone, the lights bright upon his suit-clad form.

"Ladies and gentlemen, that was Frances Langford singing "It Had to Be You." And I'm sure all you guys will agree. . .it had to be her."

Laughter rippled through the crowd.

"Well, we've got just a little time left here tonight, and it's my privilege to introduce you all to a very special guest. Many of you have seen him in such popular films as *The Other Girl* and *A Hollywood Holiday*."

Rosemary's heart jumped.

"But what some of you may not know is that this well-known actor has spent the past two months as a patient right here at Torney General Hospital. Yes, sir, Captain Cliff Powell has proved himself not only to be a first-rate actor but a first-rate citizen of this country, earning the title of triple ace during his days flying with his squadron in the Pacific. The war took something from him, ladies and gentlemen, but Captain Powell is here tonight as an example of the American spirit. We fight back. And it's my great privilege to let you hear from him tonight. Ladies and gentlemen, Captain Cliff Powell!"

The room burst into applause and cheers. Rosemary clapped along with the rest, but it was as if other hands than hers did the motion. If she hadn't been up front, she'd have fled. Hadn't she already spent all day trying to forget? Seeing him on that stage would devastate her in more ways than one.

But as Cliff strode across the stage, she couldn't look away. He shook hands with Bob, and then Bob moved into the shadows when Cliff took the microphone. He smiled at the crowd from center stage, the lights making his dark hair gleam. To look at him, walking with barely a limp, one would never guess all he'd been through.

She could at least take pride in knowing she'd been a part of that.

"Thank you, Bob, for that fine introduction. Well, it's been a great evening. We've been privileged to listen to Bob Hope, Frances Langford, Frank Sinatra, and the rest of this very talented cast.

But I'm not here tonight to give Bob an even bigger head than he already has."

The audience laughed.

"No, I'm here for another reason. Like Bob said, I've spent the past couple of months at Torney General Hospital, learning to walk again. And tonight I want to publicly thank each and every one of the doctors and nurses and the rest of the staff for the work they've done on behalf of the guys here. You probably already know war isn't limited to the front lines. There's a battle going on here too, a fight for the rehabilitation of those who've been wounded in service to our country. And these brave men and women are on the front lines of that war, along with thousands of other medical professionals at home and overseas. We owe them so much."

Applause thundered through the auditorium, led by Cliff. Rosemary clapped too, tears misting her eyes at his heartfelt words. Why did he have to be so amazing? If he'd been less, maybe her heart wouldn't be in tatters.

The applause faded. "There's a particular person in the audience to whom I owe a special debt of gratitude. I've had several fine nurses care for me, but there's one in particular I want to acknowledge. A woman whose strength and kindness helped me to go on when I wasn't sure I could." From his place on the stage, his gaze met hers. Rosemary swallowed past the lump in her throat.

"And in the past weeks, I've committed one of the biggest clichés in the book. I've fallen in love with her, and it's been anything but cliché." Though hundreds filled the auditorium, the intimacy of his voice reduced the space to only the two of them. Tears slid down her cheeks. "I'd like to dedicate this number to her and to all of our sweethearts. Love is one thing the enemy will never be able to take from us." He gestured offstage, and in seconds, music swelled.

With the magnetism that had earned him accolades, yet with

the genuineness of these past weeks, Cliff began to sing the first stanza of "Dream A Little Dream of Me."

The words transported her back to Ciro's and dancing with him, when he'd stolen her heart in the space of an unforgettable evening.

Not once during the song did his gaze leave hers.

When he finished, the room broke into applause that could have continued for minutes had Cliff not held up his hand.

"Thanks very much, all of you. But I sang that song for one person in this room tonight." He paused, clearing his throat. "And I'm hoping now, if she feels the same way about me, she would join me up on stage so you all can meet her." Tenuous hope and uncertainty filled his eyes. He'd laid his feelings bare for the entire auditorium to see.

Now he stood up there alone, waiting for her without knowing if she'd come.

Her heart swelled with its own music.

She stood and walked toward the steps. Applause shook the room as she stepped onto the stage. But she barely heard it. Her eyes and attention riveted on him only as she crossed beneath the lights and stopped beside him.

He gazed down at her as if he couldn't believe it. "You came," he whispered, voice choked.

"Oh Cliff." She flung herself into his arms. He held her close, swallowing her in strength and warmth, his spicy fragrance.

There, before God and all of Torney General Hospital, they shared a kiss sweeter than any she'd known yet.

Far away, she heard cheers and whistles. But she scarcely heeded them, lost in his touch, the rightness between them. The realization that this was no dream, but reality. A gift greater than she deserved.

He broke the kiss, gaze delving hers.

"You planned this, didn't you?" she whispered through her smile.

He grinned. "Guilty as charged, Lieutenant."

They turned toward the audience. A sea of faces stared back at them, a dark blur beyond bright lights.

Cliff spoke into the microphone. "Ladies and gentlemen, this is Lieutenant Rosemary James. An officer and a nurse and, God and the lady willing, the future Mrs. Cliff Powell."

She looked into his eyes as the room erupted in cheers. "The lady *is* willing. Very willing."

He grinned and kissed her again.

In their kiss lay many things. Joy. Awe.

And the promise that, no matter where the future took them, the substance of their love and the goodness of God would always bind them together.

Author's Note

Dear Readers,

It's been a joy sharing Cliff and Rosemary's journey with you! I pray these pages have drawn you closer to the One who holds all of our futures.

This story is a melding of several historical themes close to my heart. The first is my longtime admiration for heroes of aviation, instilled in me by my dad. Growing up, I spent many winter evenings sitting on the couch beside him watching episodes of *The Black Sheep Squadron* and other aviation-themed films. His passion for aviation introduced me to war heroes such as Gregory "Pappy" Boyington, and the crew of the *Memphis Belle*. So when it came time to choose my hero's contribution to the war effort, I knew I wanted to make him a Marine Corps pilot. Special thanks to Colonel Gene Pfeffer of the National Museum of World War II Aviation for answering my many questions, and to my dad, for being technical adviser for the aviation portions of the story.

The second theme is my unashamed love for classic movies and actors such as Clark Gable, Cary Grant, Jimmy Stewart, and William Powell. During this project, I had a blast watching tons of black-and-white movies and calling it "research." As I read accounts of the many brave men and women who could have continued their safe careers in Hollywood but instead chose to place themselves in dangerous situations to serve their country, I was moved and inspired. It was also a delight to include Bob Hope in this story. I'm a huge fan of his radio shows and chose Torney General Hospital as my setting partly because Hope did indeed do a show there on February 27, 1945. Listening to the broadcast and imagining my characters in that time and place brought this story to life. I've long admired Bob Hope's dedication to bringing laughter to the men and women on the home front and overseas, and loved giving him a cameo appearance in the story.

Last but certainly not least, I'm proud to honor the sacrifice and dedication of the women who served as nurses during the harrowing years of World War II. Their work to bring healing in the midst of destruction inspired me afresh during the writing of this novella. May we never forget their bravery, and the bravery of all who served on behalf of truth and freedom. We owe much to their legacy, and as the years pass, it's imperative we continue to keep their stories alive for generations to come.

Blessings,
Amanda

ECPA best-selling author Amanda Barratt fell in love with writing in grade school when she wrote her first story—a spinoff of *Jane Eyre*. Now, Amanda writes romantic, historical fiction, penning stories of beauty and brokenness set against the backdrop of bygone eras not so very different from our own.

She's the author of several novels and novellas, including *My Dearest Dietrich: A Novel of Dietrich Bonhoeffer's Lost Love*. Two of her novellas have been finalists in the FHL Reader's Choice Awards.

Amanda lives in the woods of Michigan with her fabulous family, where she can be found reading way too many books, plotting her next novel, and jotting down imaginary travel itineraries for her dream vacation to Europe. She loves hearing from readers on Facebook and through her website amandabarratt.net.

More from Barbour...

The Mail-Order Standoff (coming February 2020!)
Marriage plans are put on hold in the Old West when
four mail-order brides have second thoughts.
How will their grooms win their trust?

Right on Time by Angela Breidenbach
Could two people be less suited than an English gentleman and
a western gal who is used to giving the orders? From the wild Montana
Territory to the refined Kentucky horse farms,
can Timothy prove worthy of Tara's heart?

Pistol-Packin' Bride by Margaret Brownley
Attorney Wade Bronson didn't expect to get shot on his
wedding day—and certainly not by his mail order bride...

The Bride Who Declined by Susan Page Davis
Rachel Paxton turns down a mail-order proposal,
but a few months later she learns the man she rejected
has died—and left his ranch to her in his will.

Twice the Trouble by Vickie McDonough
When Connor McLoughlin and his cousin Brian order a pair
of mail-order brides, they think they're getting two sweet Irish lasses.
But what they get is a stage load of shenanigans.

Paperback / 978-1-64352-244-9 / $14.99